# DAYBREAK ZERO

# ACE BOOKS BY JOHN BARNES

*Directive 51*
*Daybreak Zero*

# DAYBREAK ZERO

## JOHN BARNES

ACE BOOKS, NEW YORK

THE BERKLEY PUBLISHING GROUP
Published by the Penguin Group
Penguin Group (USA) Inc.
375 Hudson Street, New York, New York 10014, USA
Penguin Group (Canada), 90 Eglinton Avenue East, Suite 700, Toronto, Ontario M4P 2Y3, Canada
(a division of Pearson Penguin Canada Inc.)
Penguin Books Ltd., 80 Strand, London WC2R 0RL, England
Penguin Group Ireland, 25 St. Stephen's Green, Dublin 2, Ireland (a division of Penguin Books Ltd.)
Penguin Group (Australia), 250 Camberwell Road, Camberwell, Victoria 3124, Australia
(a division of Pearson Australia Group Pty. Ltd.)
Penguin Books India Pvt. Ltd., 11 Community Centre, Panchsheel Park, New Delhi—110 017, India
Penguin Group (NZ), 67 Apollo Drive, Rosedale, North Shore 0632, New Zealand
(a division of Pearson New Zealand Ltd.)
Penguin Books (South Africa) (Pty.) Ltd., 24 Sturdee Avenue, Rosebank, Johannesburg 2196,
South Africa

Penguin Books Ltd., Registered Offices: 80 Strand, London WC2R 0RL, England

This is an original publication of The Berkley Publishing Group.

This is a work of fiction. Names, characters, places, and incidents either are the product of the author's imagination or are used fictitiously, and any resemblance to actual persons, living or dead, business establishments, events, or locales is entirely coincidental. The publisher does not have any control over and does not assume any responsibility for author or third-party websites or their content.

FIRST EDITION: March 2011

Library of Congress Cataloging-in-Publication Data

Barnes, John, 1957–
    Daybreak zero / John Barnes.—1st ed.
        p. cm.—(A novel of Daybreak ; 2)
    ISBN 978-0-441-01975-5 (hardback)
    1. United States—Officials and employees—Fiction. 2. Regression (Civilization)—Fiction.
3. Political fiction. I. Title.
    PS3552.A677D39 2011
    813'.54—dc22

                                                              2010047491

PRINTED IN THE UNITED STATES OF AMERICA

10  9  8  7  6  5  4  3  2  1

*For Stephen and Michael Rodriguez,*
*known troublemakers*
*May the world you will be running*
*be a bigger world than this,*
*with better things to do,*
*and just as many challenges*

# Scyros

*snuffle and sniff and handkerchief*

The doctor punched my vein
The captain called me Cain
Upon my belly sat the sow of fear
With coins on either eye
The President came by
And whispered to the braid what none could hear

High over where the storm
Stood steadfast cruciform
The golden eagle sank in wounded wheels
White Negroes laughing still
Crept fiercely on Brazil
Turning the navies upward on their keels

Now one by one the trees
Stripped to their naked knees
And danced upon the heaps of shrunken dead
The roof of England fell
Great Paris tolled her bell
And China staunched her milk and wept for bread

No island singly lay
But lost its name that day
The Ainu dived across the plunging sands
From dawn to dawn to dawn
King George's birds came on
Strafing the tulips from his children's hands

Thus in the classic sea
Southeast from Thessaly
The dynamited mermen washed ashore
And tritons dressed in steel
Trolled heads with rod and reel
And dredged potatoes from the Aegean floor

Hot is the sky and green
Where Germans have been seen
The moon leaks metal on the Atlantic fields
Pink boys in birthday shrouds
Loop lightly through the clouds
Or coast the peaks of Finland on their shields

That prophet year by year
Lay still but could not hear
Where scholars tapped to find his new remains
Gog and Magog ate pork
In vertical New York
And war began next Wednesday on the Danes.

—KARL SHAPIRO

# DAYBREAK ZERO

# ONE:
# LOOP LIGHTLY THROUGH THE CLOUDS

A black flag, grayed by the blowing desert dust, snapped and yanked at the pole at the Ontario, Oregon, airfield. From the rear cockpit of her Stearman biplane, barely five feet behind the roaring engine, Bambi Castro couldn't hear the cracking and booming of the flag in the wind, but even a quarter mile above, she could see the way the flag bent the pole. It would have been a scary landing, but now she wouldn't be landing.

The black flag meant CONTAMINATED FUEL HERE, DO NOT LAND. The biotes that had spoiled the aviation fuel on the ground at Ontario were as contagious to avgas as refrigerator mold was to cucumbers. The most common strains of biote could turn the fuel in the Stearman's tank to yellow-orange vinegar, lumpy green goo that resembled baby diarrhea, or brown sludge that reeked of cheese, but there were thousands of one-off biote strains that might do something equally bad. If any biote contaminated the Stearman, the whole fuel system and engine would have to be pulled out, boiled, and reinstalled, taking one of the last dozen working airplanes in the United States out of service for weeks.

Bambi banked right and pulled the stick back, putting the Stearman into a circling climb. Coming around to the west, the propeller and engine roared even louder at the hard work against the wind. *Didn't even get a chance to warm up,* she thought; even in July, she needed a couple of sweaters, gloves, helmet, and scarf at cruising altitude, a mile and a half above the high desert and with the plane's propeller and motion putting a hundred-mile-an-hour wind always in her face. Well, nothing to be done for it; she couldn't land here and she needed to get above and upwind as quickly as she could. *I'll need to drain and check at Baker City. Gah. One more thing between me and dinner and bed.*

Holding the stick with her knees to keep the Stearman spiraling upward, Bambi dragged the Ontario mailbag from the front cockpit and rested it on her lap, tearing it out of its paper grocery bag.

*Mostly Athens bureaucrats bashing antlers with Olympia bureaucrats, but the mail must go through.*

She pointed the nose north to cross west, to the windward, of the field. With the stick between her knees and her feet steady on the rudder pedals, she gripped the eyebolt that protruded from the concrete-filled tin can in her right hand, and balanced the mailbag and streamer on her left. She whipped the weight downward in a seated slam dunk and tossed the mailbag and streamer across her body over the side.

The mailbag rig cleared the stabilizer; the weight pulled the rope to the mailbag taut, and the red streamer unfolded behind, fluttering down onto the former golf course by the airfield.

Ontario was *screwed*. All the fuel on the ground would have to be burned, and the tanks, pipes, and hoses scoured with boiling water and disinfectant, and then there would be a three-month quarantine to confirm that exposed fuel was no longer becoming infected. Their mail would have to wait for a train that had a decontamination car—perhaps twice a month, because there just weren't enough steam locomotives.

*Actually, I could give a shit about the nice folks in Ontario. I'm about up to my own ass in trouble.*

Bambi had pushed hard to reach Ontario today—taken off from Pueblo as early as she could get the ground crew to forgive her for, and then flown all the way to Ogden, Utah, on the first hop; on the way she'd dropped mail to Rangely, Vernal, and Provo, but she'd elected not to land because that exposed the Stearman to the dangers of biotes and nanoswarm. She had planned to land only at Ontario, with Baker City as her only Plan B.

*Oh shit. If Ontario's infected, what about Baker City?* Baker was even more exposed to the wind off the desert; from here to the coast there were dozens of gas stations whose abandoned tanks seeped foul-smelling goo, thousands of houses where vinyl siding had decayed into slime, and tens of thousands of abandoned cars and trucks sitting on their rotted tires, their fuel tanks reeking of vinegar, refrigerator mold, or spoiled milk. A single spore from any of those could bring ruin, as one probably had for Ontario.

*Well, I can't fix yesterday's poor planning now.* At eight thousand feet she leveled off and throttled up; the little plane shook with the effort of flying into the wind. Below her, the brown scrub and dirt of midsummer late afternoon sent up unpredictable thermals, and swirled with thin gold and gray dust; to her right, big piles of cumulonimbus roiled above the mountains. Late-summer afternoons out here were a nightmare for a tiny powered kite like the Stearman.

She rechecked instruments. Oil pressure, temp, tach, airspeed all fine, altimeter and compass as they should be. The little tank of lye solution that sprayed the alternator and spark coil, preventing nanoswarm from taking hold, was low.

The fuel gauge said *Make Baker soon.*

Half an hour later, ten miles out of Baker City, she dared go no closer; the storm squatted over the little desert town like a Rottweiler guarding his bowl. She turned ninety degrees right, heading northeast. If some clear sky opened to her left, soon, maybe she could get around the north edge of the storm and follow it in to land behind it.

The little Stearman shuddered and jerked in the gusts; Bambi thought too much, uselessly, about shear and stress on a canvas biplane wing. She climbed as high as she could, opening the throttle wide, burning more fuel but it was a race she had to win.

Half an hour later she had lost. In her fight with the storm, she had been hoping to beat it with a quick right cross; but it turned out the storm packed a mighty left haymaker. Off to her left, more thunderheads sailed toward her like God's own galleons.

She might barely make it back to Ontario, but that would sacrifice the precious plane.

She could land on a road, but to sit through a storm on the ground the Stearman needed shelter—a high school gym or a good-sized auto repair shop—because the wind could slam the little fabric-and-wood biplane around like an empty cardboard box. Besides, even if she had known where there was a suitable building with a landable field or road, everywhere out-side the towns in this country there were biotes and nanos on the ground, wrecks on the highway, bandits and tribals in the burned-out buildings.

Running as fast and high as she could, Bambi followed the road to the Snake River, and the river into Hells Canyon, toward the last friendly sun-light, hoping to see a place to land.

In the depths of the pine-lined canyon, the Snake River was already in darkness; the road beside it occasionally looped up into the light. *Can't land where I am, and dead in a short while is better than dead in a* really *short while.*

Still running from the storm, Bambi turned due east out of the canyon, over even wilder country, crossing the low range of mountains.

*There.*

Where a low saddle in the mountains to the west allowed daylight through, she found a long almost-straight stretch of highway, and a few buildings surrounding a dirt parking lot. She came down quickly in a big semicircle; no wires or poles, either, and the pines weren't moving; the storm winds had not yet come this far.

To give herself as much road as possible, Bambi came in about twenty feet above the treetops, descended into the shadowy tree-surrounded meadow enclosed by a curve in the road, and touched down in the long, straight uphill stretch she was aiming for.

The wood-spoked tail wheel bottomed on its springs, the Stearman slammed down like a brick, and the greased-linen tires made a heavy *whump!* on the road. The tail wheel lifted momentarily, sending her heart into her mouth, but the plane settled onto its wheels, and she rolled smoothly up the hill in the mountain twilight, idling the engine to keep some forward way with the propeller; the tops of the Douglas firs were still in sunlight but the road was dim.

She passed a shield sign for US 95, and mile marker 178 as she taxied over the top of the rise. She throttled back further but the engine gasped like a dying fish and the prop stopped cold; out of fuel. *Well, it got me to the ground.*

With no brakes on the wheels, rolling down the gentle slope, she used the flaps to hold the plane down against the hill and keep it from taking off like a hang-glider. At the open gate in the chain-link fence to her right, she turned in an awkward pivot into the parking lot. *No cars, just a couple jeeps and horse and canoe trailers by the building. Must've been a summer resort only, with almost no one here on Daybreak day.*

She bumped along the central aisle, slowing to a stop as the saggy, soft linen tires dragged on the gravel.

The chain on the door of the big steel storage building yielded to the bolt cutters from her emergency kit. Grinding through rotted plastic fittings and glides, the metal of the tracks and wheels shrieked as the big door rolled up on its counterweights. The last gleams of daylight revealed nothing scary like bears or dangerous like people. The room smelled musty and unpleasant, like a furniture store that had been closed up too long, reeking of rodents and decay.

The wood-and-fabric Stearman was so light that with effort, Bambi could drag it into the big building by its tail. She tied off the wing and tail eyebolts to pillars. She couldn't force the door down manually, but the Stearman was at least secure against the wind; it could stand a little rain. She grabbed her gear from the forward cockpit.

In the last shimmering gray glow of twilight, the sign on the little house said VISITOR CENTER. *Oh, good,* I'm *a visitor.* The door was unlocked.

Her candle lantern revealed racks of brochures, a toilet whose seat had crumbled into dust, a steel shelving unit with piles of paper-covered clay-like goop that had probably once been office work trays. The leather sofa and desk chair must have been well-enough sealed to keep biotes out of their foam lining. Unlike some places she'd slept on some missions, there was no wildlife to chase away or mummified corpses to drag out and bury.

Bambi set the candle lantern on the desk and unpacked her emergency radio. The glass jars had clean, unbroken seals with no trace of nanoswarm's white-gray crusts around the edges, and the transmitter went together easily. She cranked the little magneto to charge the capacitors, pausing every few minutes to wipe all the contacts with a lye-soaked rag; no visible nanoswarm was forming. Inside the little electroscope made from a baby-food jar, the aluminum-foil leaves did not sink perceptibly while she counted off twenty seconds orally; the capacitors were holding charge. *Time for the less-fun part.*

Night and storm had arrived while she worked on her radio; it was full dark and pouring. In flashes of lightning she made out a wooden post at about the right distance. Rather than get her clothes wet, she stripped, put her boots back on, and ran to the post, trailing the modified 100-foot extension cord behind her. She clipped the booster-cable clamp on and dashed back. If she hadn't gotten too turned around in the dark, her antenna probably ran east-west, so the mountainside should reflect it in the right direction easily.

To avoid getting water near the radio transmitter, she toweled off with her dirty shirt, put on her spare, and made sure no drips lurked anywhere. When she checked the radio, the electroscope's leaves hadn't descended discernibly; that was very good.

She'd practiced her Morse religiously, and now she made that key clatter, sending her message three times before the electroscope's leaves collapsed together, indicating the energy in the capacitors was gone. She cranked it up again and sent five times before the charge again dissipated; repeated the process a few more times.

No immediate response clicked in the earphones of her crystal rig. She sent CL (*dah-dit-dah-dit, dit-dah-diddit*, the code for going off the air), and left her phones on while she dug into her pack and fixed herself a cheese and jerky sandwich. When she blew out the candle, her watch showed only 9:30. She put her gun and ax within reach of her sleeping bag on the big leather couch, and positioned the headphones by the chair cushion that was her pillow, so that, in the forest silence, any signal might wake her.

Days like this could make you wish the great majority of the human race hadn't died in the past year, and there was still Internet, cold beer in the summertime, and cybercrime.

*Heather O'Grainne is gonna freak when she hears a plane is down. I sure hope that radio message got through somewhere, or it's gonna be hell for everyone else till they find me.* The thought that Heather would be on top of this, and meanwhile she had food in her stomach and a warm dry place to sleep, put things in perspective. As Bambi drifted off, the last distant lightning flickered, and the rain settled to a soft patter. *The radio will wake me up, and it'll be Heather.*

**ABOUT AN HOUR LATER. MOTA ELLIPTICA, TEXAS (WEST TEXAS RESEARCH CENTER). 11:30 PM CST. WEDNESDAY, JULY 9, 2025.**

The planning room looked like a parlor commandeered by a Civil War general, the night before a battle. Golden light flickered from oil lamps, and the men and women stood around the big tables covered with maps and charts, or traced lines with yardsticks and string on the carefully hand-drawn charts on the walls.

Arnie Yang rested his eyes on the tacked-together sheets of graph paper covering much of the north wall, no longer really seeing the huge graph. He could have drawn it in his sleep; the horizontal axis was *Transmission dates*, the vertical *Events*, both axes marked in six-hour intervals from December 18, 2024, to June 15, 2025. Squares, triangles, circles, and diamonds represented phases of the moon, changes in transmissions, sightings of bright flashes on the moon, and EMPs; yarn linked one point to another.

The scientists and analysts at Mota Elliptica knew, now, that the fourteen EMPs which had struck since Daybreak were caused by helium-3 pure fusion bombs, wrapped in glass made from melted moonrock, exploding at between sixty and thirty miles above the antenna of any powerful radio transmitter. Because the helium-3 fusion reaction produces an ideal mix of relativistic protons and soft gamma to induce an EMP, even though the bombs were not big by nuclear standards, for about a hundred miles around the point directly under the burst the induced electric currents were strong enough to heat wire fences, power lines, and water pipes red-hot, and sometimes weld railroad tracks or cause arcs in the steel frames of skyscrapers. Hundreds of miles beyond that, the induced current was still strong enough to blow every fuse, throw every circuit breaker, make fire-starting sparks, build up electric charge on metal objects, and cook any chips or transistors that nanoswarm had not already destroyed.

Tonight they were going to try to provoke another one.

As usual on a fire-up night, tempers flared. Arnie turned around to see Ruth Odawa, his chief for math and computation, shouting at Malcolm Cornwall, his meteorologist. "Hey—," Arnie began, but then his deputy, Trish Eliot, waded in like a den mother separating two angry Cub Scouts.

"All right," Eliot said. "What's this about?"

Odawa's arms were folded. "He keeps calling the EMP device the enemy weapon, and I know it's because he wants his Army buddies to take over—"

"It's a nuclear bomb exploding over our country—," Malcolm said, in a correcting tone suitable for an unruly puppy or a recalcitrant undergrad.

"Does this have anything to do with doing fire-up in twenty-one minutes?" Trish asked. After a moment Odawa and Cornwall both admitted it didn't, and got back to work.

Once again, Arnie was glad he had promoted Trish to his deputy. Over her strange, goggle-like glasses—her plastic frames had decayed and Trish had made a contraption of coat-hanger wire and leather straps to hold the lenses—she glanced at Arnie and winked.

He winked back. Almost half his scientists were Tempers, loyal to the Temporary National Government at what used to be Athens, Georgia, and the other half were Provis, loyal to the Provisional Constitutional Government at Olympia, Washington. Arnie had played a role in establishing both governments, and so was trusted by neither; but while the country was breaking into Provis and Tempers, Trish had been taking a long, dangerous hike all the way from Riverton, Wyoming, to Pueblo. When she had finally heard about the split, she had simply refused to take a side.

Plus she'd been a Little League coach, which made her perfect for dealing with Arnie's tech people, who sometimes resembled confused and frustrated children, and often resembled entitled parents.

"Checklist?" she asked Arnie.

"Yeah, it's time."

The checklist was an inventory of about three hundred pieces of mail and radiograms that should have been received before running the next experiment. The scribbled notes were pinned to a large bulletin board next to the main analysis chart as they came in. In quick order, Arnie read off the list, and Trish pulled the corresponding note from the board, dropping it into the file. It was how Goddard might have cleared a rocket launch in 1938, but it was the best they could do to ensure that in the still-functioning parts of North America, rails, pipes, and long wires had been grounded; planes would land and drain their tanks within twenty-four hours; precious surviving tech of all kinds would be inside some kind of Faraday cage within seventy-two hours; phones, hams, and telegraphs (in the few places where they still existed) would be unplugged; volunteers would watch the moon; and fire watches were standing by for the inevitable spark-ignited surprises.

They finished the checklist with ten minutes to spare. Meanwhile Cornwall had reviewed weather to make sure the moon observers would mostly have clear skies, Odawa had re-run the predicted outcomes matrix, and Daniels, the Army intelligence officer, had once more reviewed her "unusual activity reports"—the euphemism for "as much as we can find out about where the tribals are and what they are up to."

The control bunker had begun as a storm shelter; sometime in the twentieth century it had become a fallout shelter. It was about two hundred yards from the house, with a broad firebreak between, because the irreplaceable electrical gear did not belong near irreplaceable paper on the biggest EMP bull's-eye on the continent.

Trish fell into step beside him. "Do we have a full set of programming for this run?"

"Yeah, all the regular stuff and more so. We have five hours of documentaries and news, fifteen hours of music, twenty new *Tech Tips* episodes, but those are short, of course, and a thing called *Obso-Leet!* that was Abel Marx's idea."

"Obsolete?"

"'Obso' as in obsolete, 'Leet' as in L-three-three-T. Promoting the coolness of identifying old-time machines and putting them back in service; people don't necessarily recognize a mechanical adding machine, a grain auger, or a cow pump, let alone know what they're good for. We also have President Weisbrod and the Natcon Nguyen-Peters each blathering on about what good things the Provis and the Tempers are doing, and why everyone should come to Olympia or Athens. And we have more than a hundred anti-Daybreak messages scattered all through."

"You know perfectly well," she said, affecting to be frustrated by his obtuseness, "that what I want to know is—"

"There are also two full episodes each of *A Hundred Circling Camps*, *Orphans Preferred*, and *Rosie on the Home Front*."

"No spoilers! Don't tell me what happens in *Orphans Preferred*!"

"Same thing that happens every time. We reinforce national unity and provoke Daybreak hard enough so they decide to hit us."

"You sound like you're sure there's a 'they,' and they think and plan. Have you gone all the way over to the Tempers?"

Arnie kicked at the ground. "Lots of people are asking me that, these days."

"Yeah, but *I'm* the one who has to get other people to do what *you* want. Come on, Arn, as my boss and my friend, what are you thinking? Why are we even putting WTRC on the air, and taking the damage from that, at all anymore? I thought we had established everything we could."

"Not quite everything. Look, we've only got a few minutes till fire-up. Once it's running, we can talk."

"Deal, but I'm holding you to it." She was smiling, and he wasn't sure whether it was his imagination but she seemed to be walking closer to him than usual.

The electric lights in the control center made the arrays of equipment seem too vivid to be real. Pahludin, the chief engineer, looked up as they came in. "Power's up everywhere, all running clean and true, so we're ready to fire up as scheduled."

Arnie glanced at the clock, showing just a couple of minutes to midnight. "All right, let'er rip on time."

Mota Elliptica had become the home of West Texas Research Center by a series of locational accidents. The mota itself, an undistinguished patch of Texas plains two miles across and barely a hundred feet above the surrounding emptiness, would have been Oval Bluff or Egg Butte if Anglos had been there first. It looked like nothing much, but it lay in the middle of a powerful, reliable wind stream and offered tough, solid rock to anchor to, so more than a decade before Daybreak, the Department of Energy had built an experimental wind farm there to test a new blade design.

The new blades were not any better as blades, but their sharp, narrow tips drew frequent lightning strikes, so Mota Elliptica was re-purposed for research into an innovative passive charge-dispersal and conductor system (PCDCS) for surge protection. PCDCS was a real success—it had preserved Mota Elliptica's windmills through countless thunderstorms, and now through five dead-overhead EMPs.

Unfortunately, while the special materials from the surge control project—primarily a fine violet powder that seemed to be a room-temperature superconductor—had worked perfectly, and seemed to be biote-proof, all records had been either electronic or blown up in Washington DC. Chemists using decades-old methods were analyzing the violet powder now, and perhaps in a decade or two they'd be able to make some.

Till then, Mota Elliptica supplied enough power to WTRC to produce freak effects nearby—they broadcast using old-fashioned AM because it was easier for people around the world to make receivers for it, and AM notoriously could be received, if powerful enough and close enough, on drainpipes, lightning rods, and even weathercocks, but at least they knew it was getting through. QSLs had come back to them from Perth, Tierra del Fuego, Diego Garcia, Tashkent, and Kamchatka. WTRC reached the world.

The clock counted down to midnight. The tape whirred to life inside its positive-pressurized argon-and-ammonia chamber, the most nanoswarm- and biote-proof containment they had been able to devise so far. The monitor speaker came alive with the voice of Chris Manckiewicz: "People of Earth, this is WTRC, the radio voice of the Reconstruction Research Center, broadcasting from West Texas Research Center at Mota Elliptica—"

Manckiewicz introduced short messages from Graham Weisbrod, the President of the United States if you thought the Provisional Constitutional Government in Olympia, Washington, was legitimate. Then Cameron Nguyen-Peters, the Natcon of the Temporary National Government in Athens, Georgia, the man in charge of restoring true Constitutional government if you leaned that way, delivered a message exactly as long. The order had been settled by coin flip and would be reversed on the next cycle through the programming.

If everything worked, a flash in Mare Fecunditatis on the moon sometime in the next four days should be followed, 73 to 85 hours later, by an EMP directly over Mota Elliptica. By then the complete loop of programming would have played at least eleven times.

"How's signal strength?" Arnie asked.

Pahludin grinned. "Daybreakers in Panama are picking us up on their dental fillings. Our planet is hearing us, Arnie; if there was anyone to listen on Mars, they'd hear us too." The men fist-bumped, and Arnie and Trish handed out chilled pre-Daybreak beers for a toast before the first-shift running crew took over.

As they walked back to the house, Arnie decided that Trish Eliot was definitely walking close to him. *Have to think what to do about that, but maybe not tonight. Kind of built funny, big butt and small top, a little frog-faced.* Arnie knew that was unfair. It wasn't Trish's fault that his last girl-friend had been Allison Sok Banh, who pretty much defined "head-turner," was far out of his league, and dumped him to become the First Lady in Olympia.

*But if it weren't for Trish, I'd be so lonely here—*

The farmhouse had probably been the spiffiest thing in the county when the newspaper landing on its porch said GARFIELD ASSASSINATED. In the century and a half since then it had been a successful farmhouse, then a failed hotel, then a boarded-up derelict advertised as a "fixer-upper Vic-torian." Probably no previous owner would recognize it now, with its steel shutters, faced with mirrors, covering every window; mirror-covered roof; silver-painted walls; and carefully rounded-off corners and edges. In the gray-blue moonlight it looked like a just-beginning-to-melt tin model of Auntie Em's house.

Trish had begun as his senior electrostatics engineer because she had a mostly completed doctorate in physics and a willingness to try, and he had a desperate need and a minuscule applicant pool. Her great gift for dealing with people—a gift Arnie felt he totally lacked—had proved more impor-tant than her adequate talent for explaining weird electric effects.

The warmth of her body close beside him in the cool summer night was distracting. "Pahludin was a great choice for your radio chief," she said, quietly. "One of the few of them that doesn't resent you."

"Are the techies still saying a real scientist should be in charge?"

"All except Odawa. She says a real mathematician should be." Trish shrugged. "You know, before the next experiment, I wish you'd take three days or so, and spend some blackboard time, and just let the technical people know what you do and why you're in charge. Half of them think it's nepotism because you were Heather's protégé, and the other half think it's because Heather can't tell one guy who works with numbers from another."

"What do *you* think?" Arnie asked.

"I think you're a pretty good boss. And a statistical semiotician is prob-ably the closest thing Heather has to a cryptographer. I'm guessing you're part of Heather trying to keep the PCG and TNG from going to war, by settling one of the big questions between them. The Provis want it all to be a big accident that's over now except for the moon gun, so they can reconstruct after Daybreak. The Tempers want it to be Fu Manchu or Doctor No sitting on a mountain someplace giving orders so they can have a war with Daybreak. The Provis would be more comfortable in a reconstruction, and the Tempers would be more comfortable in a war. Like the guy with a hammer sees a nail, and the guy with the wrench sees a bolt."

"What do *you* see?"

"That you're the only guy who doesn't know what it is and wants to find that out before he reaches into the toolbox." Her hand slipped around his biceps, light as a toilet-paper noose, and he didn't shake it off. "And I want to be on your side. Can you tell me what this experiment is about?"

"Well, kind of. Remember I don't have the tools to do what I used to do. No web to crawl, no bots to crawl it with if there was one, no ESCARR to analyze the data with if I had that, no big blazing fast supercomputers that could run ESCARR if a copy of it survived. So I did what you do when you have no way to analyze the data you don't have. I just took a pretty good stab at setting things up to maximally offend Daybreak."

"And the point of that is—"

"Well, it's putting together several likely guesses into a complete SWAG. The analysis team thinks the moon gun was built by robots or nanos smuggled onto the Iranian-Chinese expedition of 2019. We've confirmed Daybreak existed long ago enough to do that, and we know it infiltrated thousands of organizations and movements well before 2020. The moon gun is less than eighty miles from where the lunar manufacturing experimental module landed, after all.

"We've established experimentally that the moon gun shoots at every big stationary radio source eventually, but if there are symbols for *Daybreak sucks* woven into it with enough frequency, it shoots sooner and uses a more intense EMP. So in the experiment before the last one we sent *Daybreak sucks* as the common interpretant of all the hundreds of different representema—"

"Uh, slow down, Doctor Yang. All I ever got through was quantum physics and relativity. Explain it so my tiny mind can grasp it."

He laughed. "Do you have any idea how good it feels to be talking to someone who *wants* to know? Instead of just demanding 'Have you proven the liberals in Olympia are all sissies yet, and what should we blow up?' or

'Have you proven the nuts in Athens are warmongers yet, and how soon can we start rebuilding the interstates?'"

"Let me see if I do understand, Arnie, without getting into the vocabulary, okay? So two shots ago you broadcast pure news and entertainment, hardly mentioning Daybreak, and the moon gun didn't fire for almost four days, as if it were conserving its resources—whatever those might be. Last shot you had a shitload of little bitty 'Hey Daybreak, eat shit' messages— almost that obvious—and it hit us earlier than it ever had before, like it was scrambling to nail us no matter what the cost. So you've proved that whatever controls the moon gun can tell the difference between one message and another, which means it's either a real smart AI on the moon, or a bunch of smart guys in a cave on Earth with the remote for the moon gun. Right so far?"

"Perfect. So the material we're broadcasting in tonight's experiment will look much *more* anti-Daybreak to a human being, because we aimed much more elaborate versions of *Daybreak sucks* at known human hot buttons. But an AI will interpret it as much *less* hostile, because it contains a tiny fraction of the gross count of keywords and triggers that I used last time."

"For example? If I know you, and I'm starting to, you have an analogy."

He shrugged. "Sort of. Suppose you were trying to find out if it was me or a clever AI reacting to a racist rant, by how much effort we put into killing you for it. The AI would count every time the words 'slant' or 'slope' occurred—even if it was slanted news or a ski slope. I'd react to references to laundry, buck teeth, bad driving, and 'Yankee got five dollars for good time?' even if they were less numerous and didn't use the common vulgar terms. And if you checked to see how fast we punched your bigoted nose, that would be different between a racism-detecting AI and a real-life Asian.

"So these last two experiments were calibrations of Daybreak's response: how does it respond to Daybreak-neutral versus Daybreak-sucks messages? This experiment is to see which response a phrased-for-humans version of *Daybreak sucks* triggers. If it shoots back hard and fast and damn the expense, probably there are people holding the remote on the moon gun. If it shoots back at its convenience, just normal radio suppression, the moon gun is a robot."

"And . . . Heather and the RRC want to know this because . . . ?"

"Well, fighting a smart machine that follows complicated rules, like the Provis think Daybreak is, is different from fighting human leadership, which the Tempers think Daybreak has. Which in turn is different from fighting what I'm afraid Daybreak *really* is." He sighed, hoping she'd pick up the hint.

"Sometime soon, I want you to tell me what you're afraid Daybreak is, and why it frightens a smart, tough guy like you so much. But at least now I know what you're up to."

Several images of the moon danced in the mirrored exterior of the old farmhouse. The gray plains around them, a mixture of scrub and grass waving in the stiff wind, glowed dim gray-green. They stopped short of the porch to finish their conversation, away from the others.

Trish was standing very close now. "So I don't screw things up by accident—how much does Heather know of what you're up to?"

"Well, every time I try to talk to Heather about it, she freaks out and tells me not to waste resources on a question that doesn't matter. So, this time . . . as far as she knows, it's to help settle the Provi/Temper argument."

"So she doesn't know."

"Not really." He felt embarrassed to admit this was all behind the back of his friend, mentor, and leader. "Sooner or later I'll have enough to make her listen and see why this is important. But I won't get the chance if I tell her what I'm doing right now."

"Thanks for trusting me," Trish said quietly. "Let's talk more tomorrow—after I've heard the new *Orphans Preferred*. Don't tell me if Lewis makes it back alive!"

"I haven't listened to the whole thing myself," he admitted. "I gave them text to insert, but I didn't want to know any spoilers. Are we a pair of geeks or what?"

She giggled and fist-bumped him. "Hey, geeks rule. Let's try to have lunch, just us, soon, so you can tell me about the rest." She went inside with a little wave; he stopped briefly to talk to the security guard and make sure everyone was locked in for the night.

His bedroom on the second floor, at the opposite end of the hall from the men's and women's common bunkrooms, didn't seem as lonely tonight. *I really can't keep pretending I don't know Trish likes me. Quite probably That Way. This stuff is always so confusing. Maybe I should call Heather and talk it over—*

He laughed at himself. Whenever something got really scary, whether it was the end of civilization, atom bombs from the moon, or girls that liked him, he wanted to talk to Heather O'Grainne.

**5 HOURS LATER. NEAR PINEHURST, IDAHO, ON US ROUTE 95. 4:15 AM PST. THURSDAY, JULY 10, 2025.**

Bambi woke at dawn, pulled on her pants and boots, and transmitted again. While she listened on the headphones, she ate another cheese and jerky sandwich; she heard nothing. After this meal she had material for about four more sandwiches.

She washed up in a steel bucket of icy water from the pump behind the building, used the toilet, and flushed by pouring her washwater in. *Can't say much else for the place but there's mostly-indoor plumbing.*

A pile of outgoing mail bore the letterhead:

BIG RANGE OUTDOOR ADVENTURE CENTER
CANOE TRIPS * HORSEPACKING * OUTFITTING

She was glad she'd been warned. In her improvised hangar, the Stearman was fine, just damp around the forward edges—an hour of morning sun would fix it.

But last night's mystery odor was mummified horses. They lay with heads propped against the automatic watering troughs, which would have failed whenever the electricity did. The barn had protected them from larger scavengers who might have torn the bodies apart. Rats and mice had tunneled them, and insects had eaten the soft parts of the faces, leaving skull or patches of skin. For the most part hide still covered the bones and the remaining desiccated flesh.

She could smell that with the big door open, water had blown in to moisten the dry flesh and start the rot afresh. Later today the barn would reek.

Bambi had grown up a horse-crazy rich girl with an indulgent father, and the sight of the horses, stretched toward their troughs, mouths open, touched her more than the unburied millions of radiation victims in Los

Angeles, the three-storey-high pile of charred bodies in St. Paul, or the frozen drift of the drowned, an island of protruding hands and feet, in the river downstream from Sioux Falls.

October 28, the day Daybreak hit, would have been in mud season here, when tourist businesses shut down because it was too cold for hikers and riders but there wasn't enough snow yet for skiers. It looked like the caretakers had never come back; the horses had died helplessly penned up.

*I want out of here, soon.* Bambi turned to go back to her radio.

The wide doorway framed a dozen men and women, all armed, dressed in old coats, decorated hats, immense amounts of handmade jewelry—*tribals*. All had weapons drawn, mostly spears and axes, but a couple of them were holding drawn wooden bows, the arrows pointed at Bambi, and one was whirling what could only be a real, honest-to-God little-David style sling.

The stout woman in the center, who wore what had probably been a homecoming tiara before it had been decorated with small machine parts and colored stones, said, "In the name of the Blue Morning People, I declare you our captive. Raise your hands over your head."

Bambi put her hands up. The bows relaxed, the sling stopped spinning up to speed, but the spears stayed leveled. *You guys'll be in so much trouble when Heather hears about this.*

## ABOUT THE SAME TIME. PALE BLUFF, NEW STATE OF WABASH (PCG) OR ILLINOIS (TNG). 6:30 AM CST. THURSDAY, JULY 10, 2025.

Chris Manckiewicz was coming back from putting together a series of articles about life in the Temper capital at Athens, Georgia, and had caught a ride on the Gooney Express with Quattro Larsen; as always, heading back for Pueblo, Quattro had chosen to land in Pale Bluff. The main reason for choosing that route was to visit Carol May Kloster.

Carol May's pancakes with apple butter (supposedly the orchards that surrounded Pale Bluff had been planted by Johnny Appleseed himself) would have been justification enough, even if Carol May hadn't been one of the Reconstruction Research Center's most important agents, and Chris's best stringer. She handed Chris her pieces for the *Pueblo Post-Times*. "Got my pieces for you on the table, Chris. It'll save the telegraph man's finger if you just take them along."

He speed-read as he ate; they were "the usual fine work," he said, amused at how that made her blush.

To most people, Carol May probably looked like any other small, plump lady in a hand-sewn dress, but Chris suspected she was one of those invisible people who drives history—not that she would ever admit it.

As the Secretary of the Pale Bluff Town Meeting, she'd taken down and transcribed Graham Weisbrod's brief speech to the Pale Bluff city council when his plane had been forced down here during his escape from the TNG's prison. Chris had obtained a copy from her a few days later, and immediately seen that if now-Acting President Weisbrod kept his word— and if Cameron Nguyen-Peters, who ran the TNG, could see it—Weisbrod's "Pale Bluff Address" was the basis for reunification. Chris figured it would probably enter American history alongside *The Crisis*, the Gettysburg Address, and "we choose to go to the moon." And now that he had been editing her work for a while, he couldn't help noticing that though the ideas in the Pale Bluff Address were Graham Weisbrod's, the stirring phrases and ringing cadences were pure Carol May Kloster.

Chris turned the last page of her last article and read,

*Chris, don't look up or let Quattro know. Bambi's plane is down in Idaho, she's okay and has radioed in, Larry is on the way, and Heather says don't let Quattro know till you land in Pueblo, so he doesn't freak. CMK.*

"That last piece," he said, "really has an impact, but I can see why they don't want word to get out."

"Exactly," Carol May said.

Quattro, who rarely read anything, kept his attention on his pancakes.

Carol May said, "Excuse me here, but I'm going to have to talk your ears right off, because I think we've got big trouble here, and it's going to take some time to explain it. Lieutenant Marprelate, the representative from the TNG, doesn't say much out in public, but he spends a lot of time with the town militia, and Freddie Pranger says he's always reading the Constable's Log. He scares the hell out of the gun-and-war kind of conservatives, and draws a *lot* of maps. My guess is, the TNG has this place in mind for a fort.

"And the Provi guy here is no better. Congressman Tornwell, our rep for the New State of Wabash in the PCG Congress, at least has to be away at Olympia, but his idiot nephew here treats Marprelate like he's an army of occupation, and I know he's hiring kids to put up anti-Temper graffiti.

"So if anything the Provi-Temper tension is getting worse. Definitely *not* what we had in mind when Heather made them make peace back in April. Tell Heather I said it's serious."

Chris nodded. "We will."

"Okay, second big thing, which might just be personal. My niece Pauline, a few weeks ago, decided to go off with a tribal boy, up to the northeast of here, and there hasn't been a word heard from her, or any of the other kids that went with that band of tribals, in six weeks now, and on their way out of the territory they trashed a little town just north of here, Wynoose."

"Trashed how?"

"Smashed everything, killed some people, took others with them—the survivors, and there weren't many, all moved down here. I don't suppose the Army has any plans to do anything about the tribes?"

"It'll be in the next *Post-Times*," Chris said. "Tribals were threatening to wipe out some of the Old Amish families in Pennsylvania. That Temper general, Grayson, basically fought his way down the Yough Valley and brought the Amish out—with all that farming knowledge we'll need. The Amish told Grayson that the tribals had been talking like Daybreakers, telling them to quit killing Mother Gaia with their plows, ordering them to liberate their poor oppressed horses, that kind of thing, and had been threatening and intimidating them."

"Well, good on Grayson, then. When that tribe camped here, supposedly it was for peaceful trade, but we had a good number of brawls here in town because so many tribals wouldn't shut up about how nice the world is since Daybreak, and our people who lost relatives and friends in Daybreak weren't going to take that. Anyway, I'm worried about Pauline, and more worried that nobody comes over the border anymore, and Freddie Pranger admits he's scared to scout in that direction—he still does, but he's *scared*, and you know Freddie, that's not natural."

Quattro nodded. "We've got some things in the works, and some of our people are pushing to make the tribes a bigger priority. They don't look as much like harmless bad cases of PTSD as they did three months ago."

"Just so Heather knows and she's thinking about doing something; if she's on the job I don't worry. I'm sure right now she's distracted—having a baby will distract you, every time. Can I get more food into you before you go? Flying that plane looks like hard work to me."

"Any excuse for more of the apple butter," Quattro said.

**ABOUT THE SAME TIME. PUEBLO, COLORADO. 6:30 AM MST. THURSDAY, JULY 10, 2025.**

Heather O'Grainne always ignored her alarm; she was too large and heavy, this far into the pregnancy, to go downstairs to her living quarters, the antique wind-up alarm clock would run down in a couple of minutes, there was no one else in the building at this hour, and she had just climbed up here to her office anyway. It had only been this last month when she'd gotten really big, with this great whacking *thing* in front of her; a lifelong athlete and only reluctantly a bureaucrat, she felt as if this were some terrible prank of nature. She rested a hand on her belly and thought, *Get big and healthy before you come out, kid, but don't waste any time.*

She slid out the map table from under the big desk; what was on it was not a map, but her version of a critical path chart, almost three feet by six feet across. No one saw the whole chart except herself, and only half a dozen trusted senior agents and analysts even knew it existed.

At the bottom was the word DONE, dated January 20, 2027; that and a few other Constitutionally fixed dates were the only things written directly on the chart itself. The rest was a tangle of pinned-on index cards, colored with stripes of watercolor and heavily scribbled and rescribbled in India ink, with the stripes linked by strands of cotton yarn of the same color. *The software of 1950 melded with the hardware of 1850,* she thought, *in hopes of getting us to 2050.*

Paths where bad things were developing were in yellow; paths where necessary good things had to happen were in green; the places where they crossed were underlaid with pieces of red construction paper, and the red construction paper sheets were sometimes linked in red thread. The branching paths spread upward from DONE like a messy, branching tree until the tips of the branches—representing today—were a tangle of yarn and cards, a few green, more red, most yellow.

She studied the chart and reminded herself of a few issues for today: whether to promote the tribes from minor to major nuisance (but General Grayson's expedition against them, down the Youghiogheny, seemed to show that they could be overcome with some effort); whether the rapidly expanding Post Raptural Church was a force for stability, a force for chaos, or just a force; whether the peace she'd brokered between the Provisional Constitutional Government in Olympia, Washington, and the Temporary National Government in Athens, Georgia, was deepening and taking root, or tearing and weakening as the Provis and Tempers alike enacted mostly symbolic policies that seemed mainly intended to irritate each other.

The green strip that said EMERGENCE OF A UNIONIST, MODERATE CENTRALIST CANDIDATE FOR PRESIDENT still did not reach back to the present day. Every reasonable candidate was needed elsewhere, like Quattro Larsen, or politically tainted to some important faction, like President Weisbrod of the Provis or Natcon Nguyen-Peters of the Tempers. There were some unknowns she could push her propaganda people to promote, but no very promising ones. Her best-qualified candidate, General Lyndon Phat, had pissed off the Provis almost as much as the Tempers who now held him under house arrest in Athens.

Well. Gloomy picture established, time to see how it changed. She reached for her inbox.

Arnie had fired up the EMP-trap again—new green card for the DEFEAT MOON GUN pathway. That was good, but better still it meant WTRC was back on the air, and she could have something to listen to this morning.

She pulled her headphones down from the peg and flipped on the grounding and antenna switches. Nothing.

The old LED Christmas tree bulb, which acted as the crystal, looked fine through the clear glass of the protecting Coke bottle, but inside the coil enclosure the capacitor contacts were crusted white. The signal from WTRC, twenty times the power of the big old Mexican "outlaw" stations, had induced enough current in the coil to grow nanoswarm overnight. Wrapping her hand in a dry towel, she laid the metal of a wooden-handled barbecue spatula across the contacts, discharging the capacitor with a bang like a pistol shot, then cleaned the poles and contacts with sandpaper and lye.

Back in her chair—*If I get any bigger I'll either need a full-time assistant or a tugboat*—she tuned in WTRC immediately. She smiled to hear Elwood Debourrie, who played easy-on-older-ears coustajam with lyrics that were militantly anti-Daybreak. *If putting that message in their kind of music doesn't provoke them, I guess we'll have to put on a game show called "Who Wants to Electrocute a Bunny?"*

The music so improved her mood that she took the next note off the top of her inbox with near optimism, till she saw:

> *Emergency Channel Listening Post Pueblo/RRC.*
>     *Header. Received At 10:36 PM MST on 7-9-25, CRYP: Clr. SIG: TCAR-NW-9.*

Shit, TCAR—Transcontinental Air Route. Flight NW 9, the one that left Pueblo headed northwest on the 9th of the month.

Bambi Castro.

And pilots only radioed if there was trouble, such as:

forced off rte @ BkC **BRK**

no fuel **BRK**

safe ldng @ US 95 1/2 mi N of ID mi mkr 178 **BRK**

Plane OK **BRK**

Me OK **BRK**

Rqlnst **BRK**

B Castro

EOM

"Request instructions," Heather said aloud. "How about, come home safe with the plane?"

As if to mirror her mood, the radio program changed from Elwood Debourrie to *A Hundred Circling Camps*, a Civil War divided-family drama which Arnie had packed so full of symbols of national unity that sometimes after listening, Heather felt John Wilkes Booth had been unfairly maligned.

At least Bambi said she and the plane were okay. Maybe Larry Mensche was somewhere nearby and could be put on the job? Last she'd known, her most effective and least obedient agent had been near Ontario, Oregon, still looking for his daughter Debbie, who had escaped from the Oregon women's prison at Coffee Creek the day after Daybreak hit, headed into what had quickly become tribal territory. *I wish Larry would check in more often.*

At the Main Street messenger stand, half a dozen teenagers surrounded a pot of hot soup on a hibachi. "Ration coupon, four meals, at the main kitchen, to get this to Outgoing Crypto," Heather told Patrick, her personal bolt of lightning.

He was deep-brown skinned, all bony legs, gangly arms, appetite, and energy—the delight of some high school track coach, pre-Daybreak. His father had been on occupation duty in Tehran when Daybreak hit, and his mother had started out for her job in Colorado Springs on October 29, and never returned; that thirty-five miles of I-25 was now a litter of abandoned cars and decaying bodies.

She handed the teenager the folded message, which he dropped into the pouch around his neck, and the ration coupon, which he tucked into a leather wallet and dropped into his pocket. Whooping "The mail must go through!" (*Orphans Preferred*, Arnie's Pony Express radio drama to make national unity cool for kids, had seemingly taught every kid in the United States that phrase) Patrick shot off, ragged shirt tail flapping over his baggy shorts, hard-soled moccasins slapping pavement.

*Man, I wish I could still run.* Heather's next stop was Dr. MaryBeth Abrams, half a mile away; yet another reminder of how different her body was now. *Oh, well, forward waddle.*

## ABOUT THE SAME TIME. ONTARIO, OREGON. 6:15 AM PST. THURSDAY, JULY 10, 2025.

Larry Mensche got a radiogram at the first real breakfast he'd had in three weeks, which followed the first real hot bath and the first real night sleeping in clean sheets. It canceled his first chance to do laundry and his first full day of meals eaten at a table.

He was grateful that the radio staff in Ontario had not checked to see if he was in the Reconstructed Radisson Ontario, as the place styled itself, last night when the message from Bambi came in; he couldn't have done anything effective till this morning anyway.

He was not displeased. He hadn't been up US 95 yet, so he'd be covering new territory in his private search for his daughter, Debbie, missing since Daybreak day. He knew she was somewhere among the tribes—not good, but at least she hadn't starved in a locked cell at Coffee Creek Women's Penitentiary, where her habitual bad checks, petty theft, and impaired driving had landed her. He'd been lucky to reach Coffee Creek only nine weeks after Daybreak, and picked up her trail from there; he knew now that Debbie and a dozen other women had reached this general area, bent on joining a tribe, though he didn't know which one they'd found.

The hotel owner accepted an RRC purchase order for Larry's bill, conserving his cash and trade goods. "I guess the RRC is more stable than any bank we have. I still don't get it, is the RRC Provi or Temper?"

"Yes." Larry was trying not to fuel gossip. The owner looked annoyed—accepting that p.o. had been a big favor. Larry softened it a little: "The Provis and the Tempers in Athens are both trying to bring the country back together under the Constitution. Mostly they disagree about mechanics and details. We're trying to help them in the areas where they agree. What we're *not* is against either of them."

"I guess that's the answer you have to give."

"Well, that, and it's true."

"For an outfit that calls itself the Reconstruction Research Center, you don't seem to have much information."

"Hey, we're a *research* center. If we knew anything it wouldn't be research, would it?"

The owner shrugged. "I guess government hasn't changed *that* much since Daybreak. It's still hard to see what we get for our taxes."

*If you're paying taxes,* Larry thought, *you're the only one. I guess habits of speech die hard.* "I do need to research one subject. I've got to outfit an expedition up into the wild country north of here in a hurry. Do you know anyone that can rent me some mules, help me handle them, and doesn't mind carrying a gun on the job?"

The owner grinned. "Is it okay if it's my brother-in-law?"

"You're right, things haven't changed *that* much."

Ryan and his son Micah lived on the far side of town, but this wasn't much of a problem; Larry had only what would fit into his backpack, and anyway he needed to check at the biofuel plant to see if they had any avgas they were reasonably sure was sterile.

As he walked he saw that Ontario, Oregon, was in better shape than most towns: Fortifications mostly finished. Militia drilled and ready. Salvage crews working through ruins in an orderly way. Community mess hall reliably open. The blacktop on the streets was falling apart, of course, as the volatiles in the asphalt spoiled, and there were still flooded spots, packs of feral dogs, and abundant cars and electric wires yet to be hauled away, but you could feel the town coming back together.

The biofuel plant had clean avgas, and Ryan and his son Micah were indeed open to the idea of an expedition north into the mountains. "To make good time," Ryan said, "you want to under-load the mules and use more of them. Mile Marker 178 is 108 miles away, a week's trip nowadays. To fill up your friend's tank, I make that three mules hauling four jerry cans each, with not much else, plus two more mules for supplies for the three of us, so's we've got hands free to fight when the tribals turn up."

"You're sure they will?"

"I don't go up there unless the money's awful good. Tribals are why."

"Then I won't haggle about money," Larry said. "So five mules will do it?"

"Unless you want to ride, or pay for me and Micah to ride."

"Nah. People ought to be self-propelled."

Detailing Ryan and Micah to acquire supplies, fill jerry cans, and load mules, Mensche went to the post office to radio Heather and then to the town square to trade for ammunition.

At the biofuel plant, Larry found Ryan and Micah almost ready to go, and paid for the fuel with another RRC p.o. Larry sprang for a quick brunch at a stew-and-bread stand in the square, and they set off at about 10:30 in the morning, not bad for a job he'd been unaware of at 7:00.

Like Larry himself, Ryan and Micah wore a mix of camo, denim, and deer-skin, and carried black-powder guns, crossbows, axes, and big belt knives. Together, they looked like three old-time mountain men who had walked through a time machine for a ten-minute shopping spree at Wal-Mart.

The mules' hooves clopped over the high truss bridge, loud in a town with no automobiles or electricity, but soft and lonesome against the roar of the river below. *One down, and one hundred seven to go.*

## ABOUT THE SAME TIME. PUEBLO, COLORADO. 8 AM MST. THURSDAY, JULY 10, 2025.

"Given that everything I know to do came out of a 1942 Merck Manual," Dr. Abrams said, "I think we're doing *real* well to tell you that you're going to have a baby. Other than that, all I can really say is that nothing I can find is wrong."

Heather sighed. "I understand. Really I do. But I'm having my first kid as a widow right after my fortieth birthday. Look, the main thing I wanted to ask—is it true that a mother's stress can affect her baby?"

Abrams laughed. "The manual here tells me to assure you your kid won't get a birthmark."

"Uh, I guess I was worried about the more modern superstitions."

"Why? You might as well have a quaint old-fashioned superstition to go with our quaint old-fashioned way of life. At least don't add the stress of worrying about the stress. Eat well, sleep as much as you can, stay active as long as you can without overdoing it, and do your best to remember that you're a strong healthy woman and everything about the pregnancy is textbook normal—even if the textbook is eighty years old and came out of a dusty library basement."

"What the hell, that's no worse than half the congressmen I used to work with." Heather left with the same comfortable feeling Dr. MaryBeth Abrams always gave her. *I suppose it's one more way we're back to the old days. Reassure the patient and let nature do its thing. Not unlike what I'm trying to do with the United States.*

She was most of the way back to the old Pueblo County Courthouse when Patrick charged around the corner, holding out a message. "I checked at Room F to see if there was anything for you, Ms. O'Grainne, so you wouldn't have to wait for their regular delivery."

Room F was Incoming Crypto.

"And I bet they gave you one lousy coupon."

"Well, it's a pretty good coupon, actually," he said, smiling. "I hear it's gonna be hamburgers at the Riverwalk Kitchen tonight, a train hit a cow over by Goodnight."

"Well," Heather said, "since it's hamburgers, you and Ntale will both want seconds and one of you might even need thirds." She scribbled out a coupon for five entrees; he pocketed it and handed her the folded message. "Gotta run, Ms. O'Grainne. The mail must go through."

It was a note from Larry Mensche:

arr ontor lst nite **BRK**

bambi down abt 100 mi n of here **BRK**

US 95 1/2 mi N of ID mi mkr 178 **BRK**

located clean fuel **BRK**

located mules & skinners **BRK**

departing now **BRK**

plz authze $3k govt scrip **BRK**

will need on return (est 12 days) **BRK**

no troops/planes/special indic @ present but plz stdXjic **BRK** no worrying & tell Q 2 **BRK**

Mensche

EOM

"Plz stdXjic" was Larry's personal abbreviation for *Please stand by just in case.* Plz stdXjic had turned out to mean he'd needed a troop of cavalry, two doctors, three kegs of beer—not all on the same mission. It took her a moment to realize that "Tell Q 2" meant "tell Quattro too"—in other words, that Quattro wasn't supposed to worry either.

She felt a kick and looked down. "All right," she said. "Larry's in Ontario, Oregon, and he's on the job. *None* of us is supposed to worry."

## ABOUT THE SAME TIME. OLYMPIA, NEW DISTRICT OF COLUMBIA (FORMERLY IN WASHINGTON STATE). 10 AM PST. THURSDAY, JULY 10, 2025.

Allie Sok Banh's first thought was that she'd have to speak sternly to Brianna about who was allowed to make appointments with her, or at least cut Allie in on any bribes. Other than a kickback, there was no possible reason Brianna had given a half-hour in Allie's already-impossible schedule to a delegation from the tribes, and no way that the First Lady/Chief of Staff could properly meet with the tribals at all. *After all,* she thought, *since I run the White House for President Hubbo-baby, that makes me the second most powerful person in the second most functional government in the former number one, currently about number twenty, nation on Earth. I'm at least five steps too important to be talking to . . .* She looked down at the list and winced. From Sunflower Hammerhand of the Sunhawks down through reps for the Sunrisers and Morningstars, on to George Madisonsson of the Blue Morning People, and at the end: COALITION REPRESENTATIVE: MR. DARCAGE.

All of them would be people who used to be named something normal like Bill Smith or Ashley Gonzalez, who had absorbed some goofy

Daybreaker ideas about the end of the world and gone off to be inept tree-worshipping bush hippies and make-believe Indians. The only real issue she should have with them was whether to assign them to the Justice Department for arrest or HHS for mental health evaluation.

But here they were, in her outer office. And the architects of the former Governor's Mansion of Washington State had neglected to provide her office with a back door.

Well. She'd now used up three minutes of the allotted half hour. If she stretched out introductions and small talk, she might run out of time before Crystal Earthmommy, Shining Woowoofeather, and Barks at the Moon could voice their silly demands. *I just pray I won't have to accept any gift with beads or feathers or any other Camp Forest Fruitcake shit.*

They looked like the chorus of a community theatre production of *Hair*: braids, dreads, Stetsons and cloches decorated with machine parts, one hat that appeared to be a mummified turkey. Most were in multiple shirts, baggy pirate pants or granny skirts, and some kind of knee boots or leggings. All of them were white—tribals were New Age hippie wannabes whose mythology derived not-too-remotely from Conan, Xena, Tolkien, heavy-metal Nazism, and *The Da Vinci Code*, and the First Nations very sensibly despised them.

Mr. Darcage was easily the winner of the Best Dressed Fruit Loop award. He had dreads, but neat ones; wore a hat with a feather, but it was a bowler with just one feather; and was dressed in a tuxedo coat over a baggy white shirt with neckerchief, and black pants tucked into knee-high deer-hide boots. He bowed and began the introductions.

As she watched, she realized that *Darcage is the only real one; if there's any deal to be done, it'll be with him.*

When all the handshakes and bows had been exchanged, Darcage said, "The group has chosen George Madisonsson of the Blue Morning People to present their petition."

It began with a long, flowery prelude from the United Tribes of the Et Cetera and the And So Forth, in which each tribe named its founding values and claimed a history that had nothing to do with the events of the last eight months, when they had actually come into being. Darcage was appointed to be their representative to Olympia, and if the Federal government had any problem with any member of any tribe, he would—

Allie shook her head. "You're American citizens. If one of you breaks an American law, you're individually responsible to the city, county, state, or Federal government. If the guy next to you breaks a law, and you try to get between him and the arresting officer, that's assaulting an officer, breach of peace, or obstructing justice, maybe all of those, and you will be arrested and tried for it. The Federal government does not give a shit about your little hippie-Indian or elven-Nazi clubs. The constable of the tiniest township has full authority to bust your silly asses if you break any law."

The long silence was not awkward for Allie.

After looking around, George Madisonsson tried to go on. "Due recognition of the tribes under the new constitution—"

"There's not going to be a new constitution," Allie said. "And you won't be recognized under the existing one, either, unless you put together a lot more votes than I think you have. We have states, counties, municipalities, and some more unusual categories like commonwealths, trust territories, overseas bases, interstate compacts, and Native American reservations. We don't have tribes, autonomous republics, satrapies, or—"

"Or Castles?" Darcage did not raise his voice or look up.

"The so-called Castles are large, fortified private homes. Legally they're no different at all from a big hotel or dude ranch with an extra-large security service."

Darcage gestured for George to go on. "The territorial rights claimed by each tribe in the league are—"

"Irrelevant," Allie said. "Absolutely irrelevant because all of that land is under some combination of the sovereignty of the national government, the jurisdiction of state and local governments, and the control of its legal owners. Daybreak, and the bombs, and the EMPs, did not abolish the Federal government. It sits here. They did not abolish the states—"

Darcage said, "Superior, Wabash, Allegheny, New England, and Chesapeake."

Allie froze.

. . .

The vast area from Champaign-Urbana, Illinois, to the tip of Maine, and from Norfolk, Virginia, to Milwaukee, was a devastated wasteland, the Lost Quarter, far worse off than any other region of the country. Within the Lost Quarter, only about twenty-five struggling settlements here and there along its edge still called in to report famines, disease outbreaks, and tribal marauding. Seventeen contiguous states were functionally gone, with some bordering counties in Minnesota, Wisconsin, Iowa, Tennessee, Kentucky, and North Carolina also in ruins and not communicating. Just weeks before, General Grayson, acting on the orders of the Temporary National Government in Athens, had taken six battalions north along the Youghiogheny Valley in Pennsylvania to evacuate a few hundred Amish families with desperately needed skills. They had been attacked by and fought tribes literally every day, carrying out more than three hundred of their own wounded and taking more than fifty deaths. Everyone said that if it had been anyone other than Grayson, it might have been much worse.

It had forced the Temporary National Government at Athens to admit that there was no hope of restoring a state government quickly in Pennsylvania, let alone in other states in worse straits. The Tempers had declared all those states "suspended" and given the state governments of both Illinois and Michigan "observer status" since neither had any meaningful control over its own territory. There was no provision, of course, for suspending a state, or granting it observer status, in the Constitution.

Here at Olympia, Graham Weisbrod's Provisional Constitutional Government had decreed the existence of five New States, temporary agglomerations of existing counties with portions of the Lost Quarter. Superior, with its state capital in Green Bay, was functioning; Wabash, with a nominal government at Quincy, Illinois, was going through the motions; Allegheny's legislature, if they could manage to hold an election, would meet at Steubenville, Ohio, and about a dozen PCG agents were there, trying to raise a militia and begin pacifying the area. New England and Chesapeake were still completely unorganized.

The five New States had been created because Allie and Graham had believed they'd be able to control the appointment of their senators and representatives, creating a solidly dependable majority in the Provisional Congress; this would allow them to enact the programs Weisbrod had advocated for decades before Daybreak. By sending Grayson and the Army into what was supposed to be Allegheny, Cameron Nguyen-Peters, the Natcon of the Temporary National Government, had made the New States look like a sham, and the Provisional Constitutional Government like a hapless pretender. He had also revealed, by the public admiration for Grayson, that the American public did not want a relief area named Allegheny; they wanted a state named Pennsylvania. And Darcage had just thrown this into her face. More importantly, he had *known* that that was what he was doing.

. . .

As if he had somehow perceived Allie's last thought, Darcage said, "These are the positions that the United Tribes intend to press, which I will be advocating here in every forum. You reject them now, but since they are matters of simple justice, eventually someone, sitting in that chair, will say 'Of course.' In the vicissitudes of politics, it may even be you." He turned to the other tribals and said, "As we discussed, I should like to confer privately with Ms. Sok Banh—"

"My last name is Banh," Allie said, evenly, "and I won't be saying anything privately that I wouldn't say publicly."

"Matters have been tense, I believe, and a short private chat to establish a cordial relationship—"

"Won't have any effect at all," Allie said. "If I want to consult with the tribes as such"—*or, say, get the ski report from hell*—"I know where to find you."

As the delegation filed out, Darcage stopped at the door and closed it, remaining inside with her.

She yanked the cord under her desk to bring in a guard.

Darcage said, "I am in a position to mobilize appropriate activities by the tribes to influence the 2026 special election, and frankly, you and President Weisbrod cannot afford to pass up any possible source of help. The election will very likely turn on the question of whether Provis or Tempers look like the people who can run a good reconstruction, and reconstruction will be impossible without our—"

The door opened and a muscular young sergeant of the President's Own

Rangers pushed in and pinned Darcage to the wall. "Mister Darcage," she said, "I told you to leave."

After Darcage was removed, Allie canceled her next two appointments, pleading a headache. She stood at the window. More than usually, Olympia's mall looked like a dank, dirty miniature of lost and cratered Washington.

*The thing is, Darcage's right. Everything about the 2026 election will be a squeaker, and we need all the help we can get, including his, if he has any to give. Of course, there's no reason to believe he can deliver, but then, I won't know unless we talk, will I?*

Graham would make a hopeless mess of this; President Hubby was sometimes such a big Goody Two-Shoes, and this was a matter for a subtle mind that didn't shock easily. *Such as mine.*

### ABOUT THE SAME TIME. PUEBLO, COLORADO. 11 AM MST. THURSDAY, JULY 10, 2025.

Heather set down the pile of papers, reports on tribal activities in the Lost Quarter, the Rio Grande Valley, the Columbia Basin, and the many smaller tribal areas. *All right,* she thought, *Larry Mensche wins the argument. We can't treat the tribes as a minor problem anymore.*

She spent about twenty minutes changing things around on the chart. Many of her previous bosses might have thought this was busywork; to Heather, it was a way of thinking hard about an issue, because to decide how to represent it, she had to decide what it really was. The more she thought about the tribes, the more she realized that she didn't know, and needed to know—and that they were important.

Her next area was no more comforting: the peculiar tangle of politics in the Temporary National Government, especially the balance of power after Collum Duquesne's death. You could defeat the tribals; you had to win over the TNG, and one of the best voices in the RRC's chorus was now suddenly, terribly still.

*Poor Cam must feel so alone,* she thought. Her old friend had had no gift for making friends even when he hadn't been squarely in the way of so many powerful people.

She found a new report just in from Red Dog, brought in by Quattro and Chris on the Gooney earlier that day, and plunged into it to see if she could form a picture, in her mind, of what was happening in Athens; she was sure that she'd be moving some cards and strings, because she's always had to for every Red Dog report before. Fighting her drowsiness—she was off coffee until Leo or Riley was born—she bent to her best-placed agent's report.

# TWO:
# GOG AND MAGOG ATE PORK

Cameron Nguyen-Peters hadn't cared one way or another at first when the mixture of colonels and ex-business execs who were the Board of the Temporary National Government had asked to begin every meeting with an "inclusive non-denominational" prayer. A third-generation Washington bureaucrat, it hadn't occurred to him that down here "inclusive non-denominational" meant "equal time for nuts and total nuts."

He'd learned to nod without hearing. The Board met in a small amphitheater where presidents of the University of Georgia once panhandled groups of wealthy alums; it had a long heritage of talk with no attention. Reflecting through droning had become Cam's soothing review time before the acrimonious politics.

Not today.

Reverend Abner Peet, head of the Post Raptural Church, had been kept out of the praying rotation for three months by the votes of General Grayson, who was Cam's Deputy Commander in Chief; the colonels who headed up Defense, Intelligence, and Security; and Collum Duquesne, the freeholder of Castle Newberry and Cam's advisor on economic development. Their five votes tied the Board at 5–5, with Cam casting the deciding vote.

But Collum Duquesne, a wily old bastard who had managed to cobble together the manufacturing complex in Newberry, South Carolina, that was supplying black-powder weapons to the Army, rehabbing tons of museum technology, and supplying parts for half of the TNG's tech projects . . . Collum, with his big laugh, warm hug, and sheer charm . . . had flown in for Board meetings, showing off his exclusive use of his rebuilt Piper Cub. On his way home from the last meeting, he had slammed into a mountain in a summer thunderstorm just outside Newberry.

Five Post Raptural Christians on the Board outvoted four military officers. Cam would not be allowed to appoint another advisor on economic development, because "if that's something the private sector should take care of, then let's let them take care of it," as Reverend Whilmire put it.

*I could just dissolve the Board. I created it and recruited it under the rules laid down in Directive 51;* surely if it had been his to create, it could be his to alter or abolish? Cam was the Natcon, the only person in the room whose authority derived directly from the vanished Federal government—

Reverend Peet's cadences were rising and building; he was soaring to the end of the prayer with metaphorical drums banging, cymbals clanging, and horns blazing away. "—guide the Christian men in this room, and bring Christ to the men who are Christian in name only, to see the clear hand of God in the Rapture of so many missing millions, to recognize the Tribulation now under way, and to make the declaration, here and now, to move toward the God-ordained Christian States of America, and to cease the persecution of those of us who try to do Your Will. Hear us for we ask in the name of Jesus Christ, who taught us praying to say, 'Our Father,' . . ."

Everyone except Cam and the colonels leapt into the Lord's Prayer; the rest jumped in later, Cam latest of all, and then he screwed up again by forgetting that it was "sins" and not "trespasses" that were supposed to be forgiven.

At the end, the five Post Rapturals on the Board rose and applauded before rushing down to congratulate Peet at the podium.

*When that clown sprang the Lord's Prayer on me, Grayson was right on it. I'm not sure whether I'm more worried that he was listening, or that I was caught not listening. Next Sunday Peet's going to be trumpeting why-won't-the-Natcon-say-the-Lord's-Prayer, and the* Athens Weekly Insight *will be pushing to make me say it in public.*

He rose from his chair, mechanically thanked Reverend Peet, and watched Peet's exit, as stately as a king leaving the minor business to the lackeys and minions. *And what's with the black robe and a doctoral stole? Up till now every preacher managed to pray in a black shirt with a funny collar.*

When the Board finally took their seats for business, Cam hammered his way through announcements: For issuing new money, engravers were ready, paper wasn't yet. The first Stearman copy with the new no-electric all-diesel engines would test-fly this week. Tribals had attacked a train outside Las Cruces, and Rangers were on their way to lead New Mexico Guard and allies from the California Castles for a punitive raid. Talks between the Springfield and Quincy governments in Illinois/Wabash were stymied. Foreign Relations had asked for military backup for Post Raptural missionaries in the Caribbean; Cam bluntly told them he was not going to use scarce military resources to rescue preachers who were trying to subvert friendly governments. The Post Rapturals used their new majority to record a protest and declare that the Board should have binding powers.

"I have the power to create and appoint a Board, which is then to be self-governing," Cam reminded them. "And the Board is to serve at my pleasure. A Board that is hell-bound to overthrow the Establishment Clause—"

"A strong perspective on the Bible and the Constitution," General Grayson said, "is well within the bounds of real American political thought."

"This strong perspective seems to be that the way the Reverend Peet reads the Bible supersedes the way anyone with eyes reads the Constitution," Cam said. *Ouch. Grayson brings that out in me.*

"The context of the Constitution," Grayson said smoothly, "is that the Framers were Christian—"

Colonel Chin, advisor for Security, asked, "Does this matter?"

*Bless her heart.* "No, and I'm ruling it out of order. Under Directive 51, I am to hand over power only to a competent Constitutional authority. If we don't follow the Constitution here—including the Establishment Clause—then it is we, not those hippie nuts in Olympia, who are outside the Constitution. I might find it necessary to rule that Graham Weisbrod is competent after all, and that you would owe your allegiance to the Olympia government."

"This state has been a home of rebels before." Albertson, the former Louisiana State Secretary of Education, was the staunchest Post Rapturalist on the Board.

"It has, and the answer to your proposal was delivered by General Sherman. This meeting is closed."

On their way out, General Grayson tagged Cam's elbow. "You know Reverend Peet is now urging Post Rapturals to pray for your death?"

"Does that make a difference?" Cam asked the general.

"It might." Cam could never decide whether Grayson's weird smirk was cynicism, contempt, or Grayson kidding God about making the world so silly. "God has been known to find human hands. We have to go over the incoming reports this afternoon, we can talk more then. Take a long lunch with a friend and decompress—it's what I do. Later, my friend."

"Later," Cam said, trying not to visualize Grayson's "long lunch" with Jenny. *Well, I guess it probably does decompress him. My problem is I can't buy lunch at the prison. Guess getting lunch isn't as important as seeing my only friend.*

## 15 MINUTES LATER. ATHENS, TEMPORARY NATIONAL GOVERNMENT (TNG) DISTRICT (FORMERLY IN GEORGIA). 3:25 PM EST. THURSDAY, JULY 10, 2025.

General Lyndon Phat was sitting in the window seat he liked; the security forces kept people off the former golf course it overlooked. A squat, strongly built man with salt-and-pepper gray hair and a baggy face that looked much older than his body, with his reading glasses perched on his nose and his legs stretched across the seat, he looked like a professor reviewing before a lecture. "Don't ask me how I am, Cam, the answer is always going to be 'Just fine except they won't let me go.'"

"Okay, I won't ask that. What are you reading, Lyndon?"

"Reviewing the decisions before the Sicilian invasion."

"General Patton?"

"General Alkibiades." At Cam's blank expression, Phat smiled. "See, this is what happened to ambitious kids like us. The Sicilian invasion in 415 BC was a great example of ignorance compounded by stupidity and turned to complete hell by overconfidence. But it wasn't on the College Boards, so we never learned it."

Cam sat down. "I want to tell you about a mess. Collum Duquesne is dead, and Castle Newberry passed to his son, who is Post Raptural. So we lost our majority on the Board, our alliance with the biggest Castle in the neighborhood, and all of Collum's common sense and drive, all at once. And for that matter I am going to miss the hell out of the big goof and I have no time to mourn."

Phat gestured for Cam to sit next to him, and put an arm around him. "Had you ever had a command job before President Pendano made you the Natcon?"

"I'd run plenty of staffs. It's not the same thing."

"No, it's not." Phat leaned back, but left a hand on Cameron's shoulder. "You feel like every possible decision you can make is wrong and no matter what happens you're bound to lose out, and there are a million important things you won't even get to touch."

"Read my mind."

"We had a lot of wars in the teens and early twenties, Cam. I went to all of them, in command at one level or another every time. I wasn't kidding that I'm glad not to have your job, and I can't tell you how to do it. But I always found if I could think of the one thing I could accomplish, put everything into that, and find the nerve to let the rest go to hell—"

"I can't let the Post Rapturalists have the Board," Cameron said. "If they control that, they'll find a way to get rid of me, proclaim their Christian States of America, and have a war going with Olympia in three weeks flat."

"Then take your Board back," Phat said.

"I guess that's what I needed to hear. I'm not sure how I'll do it and it won't be easy, but now that I've said it out loud, I can feel that it's what I need to do."

"Don't rely on Grayson. There is always some other purpose running through that guy's head," Phat said, "and it's never the mission. Way too much like Alkibiades, actually."

"Well, at the moment his main focus is his new wife—Reverend Whilmire's daughter with the freak-show rack."

"Yeah, you said. And the rack comes with the reverend." Phat glanced at the clock. "Speaking of which, you have a meeting with Grayson, don't you?"

"Yeah." Cam rose. "But I needed to come by here first. You always help me feel more ready for the world. Hey, what finally happened to Alkibiades?"

"Best general of his time, but no one could trust him. Every brilliant success followed by a spectacular act of betrayal. Played for so many sides that we'll probably never know who assassinated him." Phat pulled his glasses back down onto his nose, pointedly looked at his book, and said, "You'll be late."

## ABOUT AN HOUR AND A HALF LATER. ATHENS, TNG DISTRICT. 4:15 PM EST. THURSDAY, JULY 10, 2025.

Sometimes Jenny was so damned beautiful that it seemed to Jeffrey Grayson that she was physically impossible. He stepped into his living room, set down his briefcase, and she rose from the couch where she had been lounging in a perfect little tight white you-will-stare-at-my-body outfit, throwing herself into a flirty, froufy rush into his arms, so that it seemed as if she went from the perfect pose on the couch to the tongue deep in his mouth in a single gracious breath.

*God, half my age, but fifty times my youth and energy.*

Some clergy might object to the *sheer intensity of the sexual relationship,* a phrase he used in his diary at least twice a month—whenever he was even in the same room with Jenny, everybody picked up on it. People objected to all sorts of things that were not their business. But after all, they were married, by Jenny's dad, in fact, and Reverend Whilmire hadn't seemed to have a problem with a son-in-law his own age, and who the hell else's business was it?

Jenny was exactly Grayson's idea of beautiful, and if there had been snotty media people around no doubt they'd have picked on him for marrying a Nazi-pinup-girl fantasy: creamy, almost eggshell white skin, huge blue eyes, very full lips, and a Barbie-doll boobs-on-a-stick body. (*Another good thing about Daybreak,* he reflected. *Barbie dolls are extinct, all rotted away, so there's not a convenient term for mocking the women I'm attracted to.*)

He didn't know if it was nature, or Whilmire's upbringing, but Jenny was one of those rare young women who act as if they like to please men for its own sake. And smart—when he explained things to her she always leapt forward to exactly his point.

And the values. She understood what his country, his Army, his every-thing were really all about.

Sometimes it seemed he'd brought her into the world, fully formed, just by having longed for her his whole life. "Now sit down with me, baby," she said, "and you tell me everything everyone said at the meeting this morning, and then all about your meeting with that weird little man."

*That weird little man* was what she called Cam; sometimes it bothered Grayson, because it didn't seem like any way to talk about the rightful leader of the free world. *But then, when a girl grows up with her father eternally at the right hand of God's number one guy, I suppose she loses her reverence for titles and positions. Maybe that's another one of her strengths.*

"There's one little favor I want you to do for me," she said, and, memories of his long-ago first marriage grabbing him, he tensed. But a moment later he relaxed when she said, "I want you to look something over and see if I did it right. You just never have time to work on your articles about the Yough Valley campaign, baby, I know you don't, but since you have all your notes in order, it's not a problem for me to write from them, and I have nothing to do all day. So I've got the last installment done, and just like the others, I'd like to have you make sure I'm accurate, because—believe this or not, baby—being a minister's daughter is not the best training in the world for being a military memoirist."

Grayson leaned back and laughed. "No, but I guess being a general's wife is. You realize this means the entire article series will be by you?"

"Baby, you did all the fighting and you beat the daylights out of the tribes. I'm just getting you the credit for it. Now read through it, correct the facts and don't you dare inflict any modesty on it, and we'll have it off to Chris at the *Post-Times*, and the rest of our time for ourselves. Which"—she had slipped a foot out of her pump, and was sliding it into his trouser leg—"we will need, because it's time to celebrate our three-month anniversary."

## ABOUT THE SAME TIME. NEAR PINEHURST, IDAHO, ON US ROUTE 95. 1:30 PM PST. THURSDAY, JULY 10, 2025.

If she and the plane had not been on trial for their lives Bambi would have considered this to be the dullest meeting she'd ever attended. The heavyset woman who had led the arresting party, Helen Chelseasdaughter, argued that the solution to the problem of having captured evil technology and an evil Fed was to tie the Fed into the plane and set them both on fire; with luck it would also destroy the steel building, removing more blight from the face of the Earth.

Michael Amandasson, Bambi's court-appointed defender—a tall good-looking guy who might have worked well on the cover of a romance novel, especially since he wore his vest open without a shirt—conceded that the plane was guilty of being a plane, but said Bambi was probably reformable after a few years of slavery with the other recent captive.

The prosecution accused Michael Amandasson of wanting to save Bambi as a slave because he wanted to own her; he vehemently denied it but Helen Chelseasdaughter pointed out he was male.

The apparent judge, Susan Marthasdaughter, reminded everyone that Bambi was a woman of color, so if they did put her to death, they ought to do so quickly and mercifully.

*Geez, if my old pal Dave Carlucci was here, he'd be complaining his ass off about reverse discrimination. Wish he was here, though. With about thirty other Feds.*

Helen Chelseasdaughter demanded that Bambi testify about her actual cultural heritage, purpose in landing here, and any other information she thought relevant.

"Well," Bambi said, "my family are Old Californians; they had a rancho with furniture they'd looted from San Juan Capistrano before the '49ers turned up. So my ancestry is Hispanic but it's not the least bit poor." *(Good going, Bambi, give them another reason to torch you.)* "As for what I was doing, I was flying mail on the Pueblo-to-Olympia northern route when I was forced off the main route by bad weather, ran out of fuel, and had to land. There'd be ransom for me and the plane if you were to contact the Reconstruction Research Center in Pueblo; they'd pay—"

"That's three things that are wrong right there," the prosecutor said, folding her arms. "Reconstruction is what we don't want, research leads to technology and all that bullshit, and we're decentralist."

"How much ransom?" the judge asked.

Michael Amandasson wondered if they could just ransom the mail, destroy the plane, and keep the captive, and was accused of masculinity.

Susan Marthasdaughter said, "Why don't we break for dinner, medita-tion, and rest, and resume in the morning? Also, we'll feed the prisoner and give her a blanket; there's no reason for unnecessary suffering."

*For the first time since I went into law enforcement,* Bambi thought, *I'm kind of liking a liberal judge.*

## 2 DAYS LATER. CASTLE EARTHSTONE, IN THE LOST QUARTER. NEAR THE FORMER VILLAGE OF PALESTINE, KOSCIUSKO COUNTY, INDIANA. 7:44 AM EST. SATURDAY, JULY 12, 2025.

Robert figured, *What the hell, today might as well be the day I ask, Karl must be in a good mood.* The soldiers behind them carried two big strings of bluegill, bass, perch, and walleye. Nine months after Daybreak, a whole spring hatch hadn't been fished except by Karl and Robert; they'd caught all these in the hour around dawn. There'd been plenty of ducks and geese too, but Karl'd said to let them go till fall, give'em a chance to raise one family without interference.

The sun lay blood-red on the treeline; their shadows stretched far ahead. A deep red sunrise no longer meant a storm; sunrises and sunsets were always blood-colored now by the soot in the air. Robert inhaled the cold damp of early summer morning, delicious before the broiling afternoon heat and humidity.

It was a good morning. Did he want to risk spoiling it by maybe setting Karl off? As assistant lord or whatever he was—Karl had never given him a title, he was just "Robert" to all their people—Robert was the only person at Castle Earthstone who could say "Karl" and not "Lord Karl," and the only survivor who knew they'd both been linemen for the electric company, or that their comfortable house in the inner compound of Castle Earthstone had been Karl's hunting cabin last year.

Two soldiers walked at point. Karl followed, with Robert one polite step behind, and the half dozen soldiers of the honor guard (a pretty grand title for fish-gutters, boat-rowers, and hook-baiters) four or five steps behind Robert. The ground, maybe two notches of damp away from being mud, was pleasant on his bare feet; dew from the tall grass brushed his lower legs.

The trail joined the main, dirt road to Castle Earthstone by a burned farmhouse. The skulls on sticks along the driveway were already being obscured by weeds breaking through the macadam; Robert had put that dent in Cindy's himself, when she'd acted like just because they'd been in high school together he couldn't do what he wanted with her and her dumbass stuck-up family.

*I always thought they were stuck up with sticks up their butts, and now here they are. Stuck up with sticks.*

Robert glanced back. The soldiers struggled to keep two big strings of fish from hitting the ground; Robert's string was carefully three fewer fish than Karl's. *Yeah. Good fishing, nice morning, he's ahead of me on every-thing, he's gonna be in a good mood.*

"Uh, Karl?"

The bulky, older man glanced back at him, one bushy white eyebrow up, a grin showing white teeth between his red lips in the middle of the white beard that covered the lower half of his sunburned baldness. *Rings of red and white,* Robert thought, *like a bull's-eye.* "Yeah, Robert, come on up and walk with me."

*Good mood for sure.* "Got some questions. Just wanted some time to talk privately."

"Yeah, we can make some time, and we should do it today. How 'bout over our breakfast beer? If I get snakebit and die, there's a raft of things you need to know, and I've been neglecting that."

"Thanks." Robert dropped back a pace to his usual position.

"No, walk with me the rest of the way. It's good for them to see us talking, it helps remind them that you're not one of them. How d'y'think we'll do for corn? I never grew any before, but that field looks pretty healthy to me; what do you think?"

The barbed wire fence was interrupted by an arch of two-by-fours in a spline-curve pattern. From that, a neatly painted plank sign hung:

CASTLE EARTHSTONE
BLESS DAYBREAK
SAVE MOTHER GAIA

On each side of the arch, four posts held up heads at face height. Inside the barbed wire enclosure, the way bent ninety degrees around the outside of a double wall—two cinderblock walls, four feet apart, the outside about twelve feet high, the inside about eight, filled with trash and dirt between, and with a board floor over the trash.

The only opening in the outer wall was into a double-Z of corrugated-iron-on-plywood walls screwed into posts, to create a narrow, dark passage with two blind corners. The passage had sliding firing windows every few feet and holes for trip sticks at ankle height.

The slaves had worked all day long as soon as the dirt was soft in the spring, every day, as grateful as if the water and canned food doled out by Lord Karl and Master Robert was divine manna, and singing Daybreak songs while they worked.

The inner courtyard of Castle Earthstone was a simple chain-link enclosure with towers at the corners, surrounding Karl's old cabin and an array of canvas-roofed cabins for the soldiers and improvised tents, lean-tos, and crates for the slaves. At the gate to this, Robert told the soldiers, "Take these fish to the kitchen bitches, tell'em clean'em and build a fire in the big barbecue. We'll have'em for lunch."

In the old hunting cabin's living room, Karl and Robert stretched out on old leather sofas facing each other, and opened pre-Daybreak beers chilled in the springhouse. "Nothing like a cold brew before breakfast," Karl said.

Robert laughed and took a chilly swig. He wasn't about to say he missed coffee.

After reviewing the morning's fishing and deciding which field to hunt this afternoon, which slaves to bed this evening, and which creek to fish tomorrow, the two men were quiet, until finally Karl said, "I know you hardly ever talk without being asked, and I know you're thinking, Robert, so what's on your mind?"

One thing Robert liked about Karl: most people thought because you didn't talk, you didn't think, but Karl knew Robert thought all the time. Robert asked, "Who do you talk to late at night over that hidden radio?"

"Daybreak," Karl said. "I am Daybreak, and I talk to the rest of Daybreak."

"And what is Daybreak really?"

"That's like asking who God, or you or I, or anything that took a long, long time to grow is really, or what made it the way it is."

"But it wasn't just a back-to-nature club? And it's not all gone now that the plaztatic world is down?"

"No more than the Catholics are just a wine-and-bread club that folded up after the crucifixion. We knew all along Daybreak couldn't be a one-time thing. Too damn many asshats out there who want their plaztatic TVs and Wal-Marts and cars and stuff back, too many bastards that think they're more important than the Earth so they get to crap all over it, too many shitheads that want to be warm in the winter and fill the world with little shitheads that grow up and want houses too. So Daybreak's not more than half over, even now. Maybe half of what was planned before Daybreak day has not even activated yet."

"That's how a couple thousand slaves turned up in early spring to build all this stuff, and as soon as it was built a battalion of soldiers showed up to move in?"

"That's how. Castle Earthstone was made for a purpose, Robert, and that purpose is still ahead of us. For right now we drill the soldiers, build the castle, and work the slaves."

"I kind of like drilling slaves, too."

"Me too, and I love hunting and fishing and living in a world that's going to be clean and free. But this place has a purpose. That's how I knew to go loot those warehouses the week before the Chicago bomb went off."

"A couple dozen slaves died in the storm coming back, though. I guess even Daybreak doesn't know everything."

"Daybreak knows everything we need to know, Robert. The slaves mostly gave their lives over to Daybreak a long time ago. They're here to help Daybreak root out the last stems and shoots of the Big System. Then they'll die, mostly. The soldiers too. Good, clean, Daybreak people are here to kill the Big System and its servants, then die. We needed supplies for the people coming, because Daybreak needed them to stay alive. After that, when we didn't need as many slaves, they died."

"Is that why we kill the babies?"

"Unhhunh. And that's why we neither of us and none of the soldiers gets a bitch all to himself; nobody can get too worked up about whether any particular little pink monkey is *his* little bundle of Gaia-raping evil. We're going to be the last generation, Robert. But we're going to have a grand time while we do it." He tossed him another cold beer. Spraddled on the couch, in his long red T-shirt, suspenders holding up his baggy pants, Karl looked more like Santa Claus than ever. "Now, cold beer, hot lunch, straightening out the soldiers and the construction, and then more shooting, fucking, and fishing. Daybreak doesn't need us just yet."

"Karl, I don't know enough yet to take over if you die."

"We'll talk more, later today, tomorrow, in a month I'll have you all briefed. No need to rush unless there's something important right now."

Robert thought, taking his time, sipping his beer and watching Karl sip his. "So, Karl, why'd you take me along on Daybreak day?"

"Well, I like to talk and you like to listen. That's a flaw in our whole species, always figuring crap out and sharing it and making more of our stupid selves, just because we're too scared to be really alone and quiet."

"Alone and quiet." Robert held his bottle up in a toast, and Karl beamed and reciprocated.

# THREE:
# THE MOON LEAKS METAL
# ON THE ATLANTIC FIELDS

Tarantina Highbotham had a Ph.D. from Cal Tech, an Annapolis ring, and an honorable retirement from the Navy as a captain—equivalent to a colonel in the other services. Her whole life's experience had been in getting things exactly right.

"That moon is too bright to have so much of it in your scope," she told Henry, the new observer who was just getting his scope positioned. "Just the northeast corner, less if you can. Make sure you can see Fecunditatis, but don't blind yourself with any more light than you have to."

"Yes, ma'am."

She looked around the darkened platform; the rest were right on the money. *All this can't be easy. At least* my *first class in celestial nav involved manual instruments. What must it be like, trying to learn this and do it right, if you grew up filling out a screen to tell the telescope where to point?*

No matter. Wherever they came from, they were doing it.

Henry had been on his honeymoon on St. Croix; on Daybreak day, his new bride had traded her jewelry for a ride to the mainland, leaving him a note. He'd probably never know whether she had gone off with slavers, pirates, coyotes, or just plain idiots. After that he'd worked odd jobs, begged in the street, and drunk, until Highbotham hired him to dig a latrine, and discovered he had been a math major.

Abby, on St. Croix to work for some alternate-energy foundation, had the best paper-and-pencil math skills of all Highbotham's team, and drew well—*better than well*—accurately.

Peggy was a retired high school math teacher who had spent thirty some years with DoDEA. Her husband, a newly retired Marine general, had dropped dead when the Pittsburgh EMP apparently reached just far enough to give him a current surge in the pacemaker. She always showed up in full makeup.

Richard, a beefy old sad sack with a heavy drinker's face, had been an architect; Gilead, dark-skinned and with a prominent Cuban accent, had been a technical analyst for a brokerage.

Now they were Christiansted Naval Observatory, by the authority of Pueblo and the Second Fleet, and when they weren't the Observatory, they were the Caribbean Academy of Mathematics—a brilliant idea Abby had had and Peggy had pushed, feeding about fifty orphaned children in order to lure them in for a heavy dose of math and science. *Those kids might be our most important work—our descendants will still know the world is a planet, the sky is a vacuum, the sun is a star, and the moon's a big rock that doesn't fall down because it falls in a circle.* And *be able to find their way to the other side of the planet, and come back.*

Not for the first time, Captain Highbotham realized she loved her team, and her new work, immoderately. *Truth is, retirement was dull and I hated not mattering.* The moon, just past full, silvered the still figures bent over their telescopes.

Highbotham looked up at the moon, picking out Fecunditatis—the next dark spot over from Tranquility. *Were you trying to tell us something, putting your damned moon gun right next to where the* Eagle *landed?*

They all hit their clocks.

"Where and what?" she asked, quietly.

"Still in the daylight," Henry said. "But a definite flash. A few of the shadows blinked." He was scribbling frantically at his drawing. "I'm marking which ones."

That had been one of his ideas—that as a backup, if the launcher fired while it was still in daylight, and they had pre-drawn the shadows around the suspected launcher location, each observer could check off the briefly vanished shadows. From their checksheets, it might be possible to calculate the location of the launcher.

"Everyone else?" Highbotham asked.

"Confirmed, in the bright area, I'm still marking shadows," Gilead said.

"Confirmed and marking," Abby said.

"Confirmed," Peggy said. "Also marking. I think I saw the flash, marking that too."

"I was blinking, I guess," Richard said, disconsolately.

"You've seen a couple others, and we have multiple observers so someone *can* blink." Highbotham noted times from everyone's clock. "I have 3:04:16.02, 3:04:15.98, 3:04:15.91, and 3:04:16.17 and that is . . . 3:04:16.02. Good work, everyone, and back to the scopes. Henry, I'll want to see how your shadow calculations panned out tomorrow—so take your time, if you need to, to make them good."

Back in the quiet of her house, she copied

*wtrc attn arnie pkg on way 3:04:16.02 fectas agn*

onto the top line of the page, translated all the characters to ASCII, wrote a line of digits from her one-time pad, added, and brought the characters back from ASCII. She ran through the usual annoying precautions to make sure her radio had no nanoswarm, and finally began to tap the key, sending the coded message. *Hand cryptography. Morse. Wonder how soon I'll strap on a cutlass and lead a boarding party.*

## ABOUT THE SAME TIME. MOTA ELLIPTICA, TEXAS (WEST TEXAS RESEARCH CENTER). 3:20 AM CST. MONDAY, JULY 14, 2025.

*So that's it. The EMP will burst over us somewhere between 4 a.m. and 3 p.m. on the 17th.* Arnie scribbled a note and had the desk attendants copy it for every relevant officer, department head, and technician at Mota Elliptica, to get preparations under way at WTRC; gave a short note to the radio room to alert Pueblo, Athens, and Olympia; and dropped a note titled URGENT

INSERT into the basket for the control bunker, so that once an hour they would stop the rolling tapes and warn the planet of the impending EMP.

With nothing more to do, he headed up the stairs for bed.

"So," Trish said, behind him. "Five days of delay before the moon gun went off. Longest ever. Does that mean it's an AI?"

"I hope so," Arnie said. "Because if it is, our job is much easier. And if it's not, it's what I'm scared of. Why are you up so late?"

"Same reason you are. I asked them to wake me if a report of a flash on the moon came in. So was it Christiansted that got the fix?"

"Yeah. As always; best observatory we've got and they're in the right place for a trajectory from the moon that's coming here."

"Did they get an exact fix?"

"Exacter than the last time. We're narrowing in. But the flash happened with Fecunditatis still in daylight, so the launch site is still someplace in a forty-mile circle on our map of the moon. Captain Highbotham will be disappointed."

Trish shrugged. "Highbotham's not thinking about how long it will be before we can go to the moon to deal with it, because that's not her job. Her job was to nail the moon gun's location, and it slipped away again." She peered at him through those strange wire-and-strap goggles; her eyes were an interesting shade of sea-green. "Arnie, you look pretty bummed yourself. Do you just need the sleep, or would you like to get a snack in the kitchen and just hang for a while?"

They made grilled cheese sandwiches and chamomile tea. He was surprised at how good it was; how long had it been since he'd sat down to eat warm food with company?

Trish gave him her puckish, crooked smile. "Is this a secure-enough location for you to share rampant speculation?"

"Not so much rampant speculation as a contagious nightmare," Arnie said, yielding to the warm kitchen and warm food. "Look, it's really a pretty simple thought. Suppose Daybreak really is a system artifact. No central control, no planners, no directors or generals or chairs or presidents or kings, just an emergent property of the communication systems that existed up till a year ago, and now, somehow, is continuing to run in new media and ways, like rock and roll moving from radio to YouTube, or fundamentalism from camp meetings to TV. We're more used to the idea that things move from lower to higher tech, but that's probably just because we had several generations where the tech kept getting higher. So somehow Daybreak is migrating from Internet down to printing press and radio, headed for campfire stories and Gregorian chant, I suppose.

"Now, we know it turns everything it encounters to its own purpose—while it was growing all around us, it took over things like political factions, organized crime gangs, terrorist groups, communes, nonprofits, churches, artistic movements, intelligence services, corporations, maybe even electorates, rather than vice versa. For Daybreak, reproduction and development are one and the same—it makes its ideas by catching on, and it catches on by making new ideas. It can't do things without thinking or think things without doing them.

"It's like how biologists describe a shark—a guidance system for a digestive tract—or what some economists said banks had become, a pile of money with a will to accrete. And that's what scares me. It wants what it wants and goes after it, using whatever it's got, but it doesn't sit back and say '*I want* to reduce humans to the Stone Age,' which would be consciousness, or 'Destroying the world relentlessly is *who I am*,' which would be personality. It gets by without either."

"Drink some of your tea," she said quietly. She was looking at him with the kind of concern he remembered his favorite tutor had, back when life was cookies, *Star Wars*, and test scores. *She's going to be a great mom for someone.*

When he had sipped the warm chamomile and taken a few deep breaths, she said, "You sound like Edgar Allan Poe talking about the beating heart, or the black cat. Now chill for just a sec, remember it's probably not coming for us right this second, and tell me what's so scary about all this."

"Something we're overlooking. People have been the smartest things that people encountered, for at least the last hundred thousand years, right? Individual people have consciousness and personality, and they are smarter than animals, organizations, beliefs, or books. So we've learned that consciousness and personality are the indices of intelligence. *But what if a really big system artifact—still not conscious, still with no personality—can be smarter than any of us?* I mean, Catholicism—the whole system—is smarter than most Popes have been; physics is definitely smarter than any one physicist. Well, suppose Daybreak is smarter than we are. Completely focused in its own purpose, not caring about our suffering, not understanding ninety-nine percent of what it is that makes us worthy of existence—just like a shark eating a human saint or genius—but able to think faster and more deeply using more information than we do?"

She rubbed his hand between hers. "You're tired," she said, "and scared. I wish you would go to bed. We need you rested and well, and we need you to explain this idea coherently so people will listen to you."

"You believe me?"

"I believe *in* you, and I want to give you a chance to persuade me that you're right."

"I just can't help feeling like Daybreak is always a move ahead of me, like every time I ask it a question, it knows what I'm going to ask and its answer is not the truth, but the thing that will do Daybreak the most good. Like it's learning who I am by seeing what I ask, like—

Trish finished her sandwich, and pointed at his. "Eat. It's still warm."

He did. It was good.

"Arnie, if you're afraid that Daybreak really is bigger and smarter than all of us, and that it's just manipulating us into becoming easier to destroy, then if it delayed firing the moon gun to persuade you that it's a dumb AI, *what's the reason?*"

"How would I—"

"You said it's a game or dialogue. Why does an opponent fake anything?"

"Crap," he said. "Once we see the flash, we all know nothing is going to happen for three days, so first we all take a long nap, and then we spend the rest of our three days grounding everything and wrapping it up—"

She held her finger up, eyes widening. In the momentary silence they heard bells, whistles, sirens—all the signals the Army used along the defensive perimeter.

The kitchen door flew open. Lieutenant Quentin, normally the night liaison for the Army forces guarding Mota Elliptica, said, "Doctor Yang, Professor Eliot, we need you to get everyone ready to evacuate, downstairs, *now*. Big tribal raid—"

Arnie and Trish bounded up the stairs; he shoved the door open into the men's bunkroom. "We've got a major tribal raid coming in. Evacuation starts *now*. No arguments." The snoring stopped from a couple of bunks, some men began to mutter; only Harper, the chemist, sat up, groping for his bathrobe. Arnie pushed his glasses up his nose and bellowed. "Everyone, *now!*" The room went dead silent but he could feel that they were all awake. "This is why we ran all those drills. Dress. Put your personal effects in your bug-out bag. Get the books and papers you're responsible for into the marked boxes, and the boxes where they're supposed to go. This is *not* the time to think of better ideas. When everyone is safe, and the records are safe, you may then tell me about all the terrible mistakes we made. Now get moving, do *not* try to figure out a better way, and if you finish early, come to me and I'll give you something else to do. No creativity, just get this done." He turned up the oil lamp, letting it flare, and saw that they were all moving, now.

He ran to his own room, swept his framed photos and treasured books into his pack, thought for an instant, *Wish I was the guy who could just toss the three pictures of Allie into a corner and leave them here,* and shrugged. He'd try *that* kind of courage some other time.

Something heavy slammed against the outside wall, cracking plaster inside. Arnie grabbed his bag and went into the hall; the men's and women's bunkrooms were pouring people into their jobs. Trish and Arnie brought up the rear, urging people down the stairs. She had a moment to turn and whisper to him, "And now I *know* you're right. Soon as we're back in Pueblo we've got to plan what you're going to say to Heather."

Something else hit the outside wall, hard enough to be felt through their feet.

"Trebuchet," Lieutenant Quentin announced loudly. "Like the Mongols used. Just a big lever and fifty tribals yanking a rope to throw a rock the size of a bowling ball."

They all jumped at the loud clang; that one had hit steel shutters on the ground floor. "Keep moving," Arnie said. The snipers in the attic began to fire, and he added, "It's being taken care of. Do your job, and they'll do theirs."

Documents virtually flew into boxes, the boxes seemed almost to close and stack themselves. No more rocks arrived; a sniper called from above that the tribals had abandoned their trebuchet. "Okay, do the optional part of the list," Arnie said.

Engineers and technicians scrambled to put the instruments and other hard-to-replaces into boxes. Trish said, "No response from the control bunker—"

A shutter broke inward through a window, tipping onto the floor inside with a crash; a moment later, an arrow quivered on the floor. The snipers in the attic were firing so fast it sounded like continuous volleys.

Everyone dropped to hands and knees and crawled into the central hallways. *Good, they remembered something else from their drills, and this time without being told.* At another window, the steel shutters rang, but held; this trebuchet crew must be more competent, closer, maybe both.

As Trish and Arnie took quick roll of the scientific staff in the hallway, Quentin rolled in a rack of rifles. "These are pre-loaded—Newberry Standards, same thing the troops are using. Who's qualified on them?"

"Everyone," Arnie said. "I insisted. Some of us don't like it, though."

"Some of us do," Trish said, picking up a Newberry and five four-shot magazines. Arnie stepped forward, and then everyone else was forming a line, the more reluctant taking the rear.

"I'll have other jobs than shooting for some of you," Quentin said, "but it's bad; I think you should all have a gun with you, all right?"

Ruth Odawa sighed. "I hate the things but I hate being clubbed or burned to death even more. I'll carry it but I'll be happy to do almost anything else."

The front door opened and slammed shut in an instant; the sergeant outside said, "In the center hallway."

Carton, a Ranger from Olympia, came in. "Lieutenant Quentin, the colonel says we're going to be surrounded, and he's ordering everyone who can to fall back here. Captain Piersall and Lieutenant Ayache were killed in the first attack. Colonel Streen has direct command of Charlie Company and he's bringing them in here. He's also got both platoons of Rangers. If any of the engineering and scientific party can shoot—"

"We just went over that," Quentin said. "They're armed and ready."

"Armed anyway," Odawa said; Trish shut her up with a glare.

"Where're the TexICs?" Quentin asked.

"Trying to chase the tribals away from the windmills," Carton said. "The tribals swarmed up onto the mota, hundreds of them, with grapnels on big pieces of piano wire that tangle around and wreck the hubs, and rocks on poles to smash up the rotors, and God knows what else. I was on a watchtower up there when it started. We've lost at least four windmills that I know of. A few guys with black-powder repeaters couldn't even slow the bastards down; I don't know how the Texans'll do with lances, pistols, and sabers, but at least they're on horseback." He might have grimaced or laughed; his expression was strange. "Guess we'll all have to stop making fun of our pony soldiers and their cowboy outfits."

"Guess we will," Quentin said. "All right, we don't want to be—"

Bangs, pops, and roars stuttered above. One of the men above shouted something down the stairs; then the front door opened. "Everyone stay down!" Colonel Streen shouted. "Troops coming in!"

Suddenly the house was full of soldiers—over a hundred Temper infantry, in their "Rorschach jammies," the gray wool camo-blotched with India ink that had replaced the rotted-away ACUs; around fifty of the President's Own Rangers, in their black flannel shirts and jeans; a few TexICs, Texas Irregular Cavalry, who looked to Arnie like they'd escaped from a Nashville revue.

Colonel Streen, a tall black man who had never spoken much to Arnie before, came in. "Doctor Yang, if we can all meet in your office, I need to talk quickly with my officers and you."

Arnie's "office" was a walk-in closet, with barely room for the five of them to stand around Arnie's tiny, battered old desk.

"It's the worst." Streen looked a thousand years old. "We're out of touch with at least half the force; the tribal attack overran three blockhouses out on our main line right during rotation, they were inside before the blockhouse crews knew what was happening, and the reliefs coming up were hit out in the open—Captain, thank God your TexICs were on top of that or we'd have lost all those men too—"

"Glad to help," Captain Tranh said, his Texas twang broad and harsh; something about him reminded Arnie of a silly movie he'd seen long ago, John Wayne playing Genghis Khan. "Wish we could've been more use on the windmills, though. I think you have to figure they're all lost; we can run'em off any one windmill but they're right back on it, or after a different one, as soon as we turn our backs. I'm real sorry about that, Doctor Yang."

"It's gear," Arnie said, though his heart was sinking. "People are what matter."

Streen nodded. "Right. All right, now when I was with General Grayson in the Yough, we found out there's no real leadership on the battlefield, even if their plan is sophisticated. Each little tribe has a structured, conditional list of tasks, every single tribal has that list memorized, and they run down their decision tree till they're killed, dispersed, or victorious. So right now out in the dark they're all finding each other, getting the right people on their left and right, and then when they're all in place, there's gonna be one big human wave, like a banzai charge, focused here, coming from all sides."

"That's what the tribals did at Pend Oreille," Goncalves, the Ranger major, agreed; with his chest-length graying beard and all-black uniform, he looked like the wrath of Jehovah. "Fighting them around Grant's Pass we could screw them up with three-man teams intercepting their runners and picking off the guys carrying spirit sticks, because they guide off those. I have six three-man teams out doing that right now; that should buy us a few minutes to prepare."

"Cavalry can probably disrupt even better," Tranh said. "Anyone running between groups of tribals, and anyone carrying a spirit stick—"

"And anyone that either of those are talking to," the major said. "Leave no surviving witnesses—you have to kill the wounded. The tribal is just the medium, you've got to stop the message. If you get a spare second, break the spirit stick or scrape all that holy bric-a-brac off it, so nobody else can use it."

"Do it, Captain," the colonel said. "Cavalry won't be any use pinned against this house, and we don't know how much longer they'll take before they launch their wave."

The Texan saluted and went out, bellowing, "TexICs with me, now!"

"Other than that," Colonel Streen said, "we'll have to open windows—we can't get enough guns on the enemy with those shutters closed. I want the second floor to open all at once, and then the ground floor, each on my command. Any thoughts?"

"Just glad to be here," Goncalves said. "And my sympathies on your losses."

Streen nodded. "Thank you. All right, let's go. If anyone asks, the plan is to fight till we're all dead, they're all dead, or they run away, and the goal is complete victory. Everything else is details. This wave might have three or even four thousand tribals in it, but if all our people are careful about cover, and we don't let the enemy close enough to set fire to the house, we should be all right, because in tribal attacks, the worst is always the first. Can we can stand a siege?"

"There's a month of food for fifty in the pantry," Arnie said, "and we've got an inside pump, so there's water. We rigged up a bucket and pulley in the old dumbwaiter shaft to carry water upstairs; should we wet down the roof and walls?"

"Couldn't hurt," Streen said. "All right, let's go."

On his way out, Arnie grabbed his six least enthusiastic shooters and put them on wetting-down duty, reminding them to keep their rifles with them and ready.

The Temper infantry had three surviving officers, all lieutenants; Streen allocated Quentin to the ground floor, and the other two to the axmen and pikemen on the north and south porches. "Major, if you would assign your two officers for the attic and second-floor commands, and if you and I declare ourselves HQ?"

"Works for me. Nice to have the US Army all back together again."

"Isn't it, though? Makes me feel like Custer."

"I'd rather feel like Anthony Wayne. He won."

A lookout shouted, "Colonel! Drums and singing!"

Arnie and Trish crouched to the right of their assigned window and listened; the melody was instantly recognizable—*All we are saying, is give Gaia her rights.*

Streen squatted beside him. "Any insight into that?"

"All the tribes use it," Arnie said. "It's almost certainly the pump-up before the big wave. Probably they'll go to rhythmic shouting just as they start the charge."

"So when they start to shout in rhythm, they're coming? Is that a semiotics thing?"

Arnie shrugged. "It's probably hardwired in the nervous system. Build up the feelings on long phrases with tones, release them on short atonal grunts."

The singing had grown louder. The front door opened. "Sir." A young soldier leaned in.

"Yes?"

"Flames from the control bunker. Nobody answering our calls there. Too much smoke to see what's happening."

"Thank you," the colonel said. The young soldier slipped back out. "Quentin, double the rifles on the windows that can see the control bunker," the colonel said. "Draw from whatever reserves we have. Don't change anything else. Pass word up to the other floors to do the same. That's where the main shock'll be coming from. Tell them that."

Quentin began giving orders.

Streen turned back to Arnie. "I'm guessing you've lost everyone and everything in that control bunker, but if there's anything important enough we could try a sortie—"

"Colonel," Arnie said, "with the windmills wrecked, it's already the end of WTRC, and the only thing in the bunker we couldn't replace was Pahludin, Bates, Greene, and Portarles. Don't worry about saving anything but lives."

Streen grinned. "One clear objective. Are you sure you're really an administrator, Doctor Yang?"

"I have constant doubts."

The colonel squeezed Arnie's shoulder in friendly encouragement and moved on.

Outside, the singing faded into a chant backed up by drums—

*Mother Earth*
*Gave you birth*
*Give her, give her*
*All you're worth!*

—louder, faster, blending into booming drums and crashing metal.

"I'm going above," Streen said. "Quentin, on my command or one minute after you hear second floor open up, throw the shutters open and give them everything you can from the ground-floor windows. On no account leave a window or door unguarded."

"Yes, sir."

"This'll be it, people." Streen bounded up the stairs, the Provi Ranger major at his heels; the spotted and black uniforms made them look like a Dalmatian and a Lab racing after a Frisbee. *They're enjoying this,* Arnie thought, enviously.

The chant grew louder still, less words than grunts of rage. The shutters above creaked and groaned; volleys of rifle fire roared, a few seconds apart. Quentin clicked his stopwatch.

Streen bellowed, "Lower floor go!"

The men on the porch swung the steel shutters outward in a screech and boom. Arnie rolled to the middle of the window, awkwardly and slower than the soldier and Ranger coming from the other side. The soldier beside him broke out the glass, knocking the shards out with his rifle butt. Trish, Arnie, the soldier, and the Ranger laid their rifles onto the sill and sighted.

The silhouettes in the dingy moonlight became distinct over the barrel of Arnie's rifle—light and dark smears of faces, hats of all kinds, baggy shirts, pantaloons. "Hold, hold, hold," Quentin's voice chopped through the din of the onrushing shouting Daybreakers, as level and even as if advising a taxi to turn right at the next corner. "Choose a target and aim. Fire on my command."

Arnie kept his sight on a tall man with a bushy beard who was waving a hatchet over his head.

"Fire," Quentin said.

Arnie held his breath, tightened his finger, felt the rifle shove his shoulder. As the dense smoke blew away on the night breeze, he saw the man doubled over, probably hit in the guts.

"Choose, aim, and fire at will," Quentin said. "Work fast, people."

As the curtains of smoke opened and closed in front of him, Arnie chose a young woman who was swinging something burning on a rope over her head, aimed, squeezed, saw her fall backwards. *Chamber and the first from the mag.* The next hole in the smoke revealed a man waving a spirit stick—a prime target because every tribal who could see it would be running to follow him. Arnie shot, missed, shot again. As the smoke cleared, he was thinking, *One left, chamber it, fire.* Spirit Stick Man fell almost at the porch; as Arnie reloaded, the pike and axmen were driving back the followers.

Existence settled into counting rounds, searching, aiming, shooting, and reloading.

Feet on the porch.

"Rifles stay down, axes and pikes away from windows, shotguns *now*," Quentin said. Arnie felt feet standing between him and Trish. A great booming roar shook the room. "Rifles, axes, and pikes stay where you are. Shotguns, second barrel, *now*." Another boom.

"Axes and pikes advance. Rifles and shotguns support with fire and *be careful*."

Arnie rolled up into a kneeling position; his back leg brushed Trish's. The porch was an incoherent struggle of flesh, uniformed backs closest to them, hats, plumes, and headdresses beyond. A shaggy man without a shirt, wielding a chain and a small hatchet, rammed between two uniforms; Arnie and Trish beside him shot simultaneously, and the man fell backward, hit in the face and chest.

A tribal rammed through the press, jabbing with a spear. Trish stiffened against Arnie; he felt a gurgle as he planted the muzzle in the tribal's face and pulled the trigger.

The huge, heavy slug folded the man's head inward like a rock dropped onto a pillow, and a mess flew out behind him.

While Arnie's hands chambered another round, he took one instant to look to his right. Trish was pinned backwards by the spear through her neck to the floor, as if she were stretching her knees in yoga. Her goggle/glasses lay in the pooling blood around her head; it was the first time he'd seen her without them.

Back at the window, a space opened between two uniformed backs, revealing a woman wielding two sickles; Arnie shot her squarely in the chest. A pike, swung like a ball bat, swept her body from the porch.

"Rifles, on your feet, advance behind the pikes and axes," Streen ordered. Arnie stood up and stepped through the window, careful of the bodies lying there; a Daybreaker stirred at his feet, and as if it had been a venomous snake, Arnie slammed down his rifle butt on the back of her head.

He moved forward a step behind the soldiers with pikes; stray, unaimed arrows and rocks clattered on the porch roof.

The pikemen danced momentarily backward and forward on the edge of the porch. Streen cried, "Pikes, open for rifles, *now.*" Half the pikemen stepped back and to the side; suddenly it was as if a door had opened for Arnie, and even before Streen bellowed, "Rifles to the front and fire at will," he was there.

The Daybreakers had fallen back just far enough to form a clear space, littered with bodies, between themselves and the pikemen. They were no longer chanting, and the front row was held in place only by the struggling, oscillating, confused mob behind them.

Arnie looked straight into the terrified eyes of a boy holding a machete. He shot him in the face. All around, rifles and shotguns lashed out into the mob. Arnie fired again and again, reloading as fast as he could, as the Daybreakers fell back screaming and begging; when they turned to run, he shot at their backs until his last couple of shots were simply too far to get even the stragglers; by now the roar of fire had faded down to the last few bangs.

Quentin gently pressed down on his forearm. "Point your rifle at the ground, and take the round out of the chamber. The colonel needs to talk to all of us."

## THE NEXT DAY. CASTLE CASTRO (IN THE FORMER SAN DIEGO, CALIFORNIA). 11 AM PST. TUESDAY, JULY 15, 2025.

"I appreciate your coming to see me," Harrison Castro said, as Pat O'Grainne rolled his wheelchair onto the balcony of the big office that over-looked San Diego Harbor. "If you'll join me at the table, let's have a drink and just enjoy the fact that it's a fine day and no one is shooting at us."

Two weeks after the Awakening Dolphin Children's assault, the main keep of Castle Castro looked like what it was: a fortress under a collection of wreckage. The original design had concealed its nature as a system of concrete bunkers by putting stuccoed-plywood and z-brick frouf, fancy stained glass windows with steel veining, and ornate (but heavy) metal gratings in front of the bunker walls, all sunny hallways on the inside, all frivolity on the outside.

During the attacks of the last six months, all that faux decor had been smashed and burned. The charred, broken remains of it now clung in strands and heaps to the reinforced concrete walls between open spots where Castro's own forces had pushed it aside to clear loopholes, observation slits, and sally ports.

"I'm sure glad you built this place," Pat said, "and even gladder that old Heather had a connection to you, to get me in here. It doesn't look like the old neighborhood stayed very nice."

"Well, the people who came out of there sure weren't." Castro poured the sweet red wine that his Steward of the Barracks had assured him was Pat's favorite. To judge by how fast it went into Pat, the steward had been on top of things. *Well, no matter. The old guy took his turns at his loophole, and sober or not, he was a good shot, and how many real fighters aren't hard drinkers anyway?* "One more bit of business I ought to check with you while I have you here and before I forget. Those wheels we came up with for your chair—"

"Working fine. We were lucky to get a wheelwright in here, too."

*Actually luck had nothing to do with it. I put in years developing a big, big list of people with unusual skills I could shelter whenever it finally all fell down. I had so many people on such a diverse list that I was even ready for something as weird as Daybreak turned out to be. But it's better for people to believe in luck; they don't resent it the way they do foresight.* "Sometimes luck is all that matters," Castro said, sipping at the cheap, too-sweet wine and stretching expansively.

Pat was stretching, also, his eyes closed in bliss. "Mister Castro, I'm aware that you have three thousand people here at your Castle, and an old biker wouldn't usually rate a private room in the inner keep. So . . . I kind of think you're hoping to lobby my daughter in Pueblo."

"Why don't we talk business after lunch? I take it you're not offended by my approaching your daughter through you?"

"No, I'm not. *She* might be. She was always ornery; I always thought she became a cop in the hopes of busting me someday. She might throw a hissy fit, but you know, Mister Castro, I've been dealing with Heather's tantrums since she was two years old."

After lunch, Harrison Castro refilled Pat O'Grainne's glass. "Here's the thing. For all its many failings, this has been a good country, hell, a great country, but what it finally died of was what most people thought made it great—it died of democracy. We just plain forget that the first colonies were founded by men who survived all sorts of hardship and danger to do it, and then rose to the top, so you had about four generations of really brutal natural selection, and then afterward all those natural leaders intermarried. So there was a real, genetic superiority about the Founding Fathers, and they wrote a constitution that would keep power where it belonged, in those superior families. And there have been other little pockets of superiority, produced by adversity and breeding, as well—the Louisiana Creoles, the Russian Jews, and if I may say so, the old Californios.

"The Constitution rests on the premise that the only meaningful freedom is the freedom of the alphas to—" Castro heard a sort of wet buzzing.

Pat O'Grainne was sound asleep, his leathery liver-spotted face tipped up to welcome the sun.

Harrison Castro shrugged, called in a servant, and instructed him to quietly return the old guy to his quarters. After O'Grainne was wheeled out, Castro stood a while on his balcony.

In the harbor, the half dozen boats coming out and going in all belonged to him; the second-biggest port on this side of the continent, now, and *it's all mine, if I can keep it.*

## IMMEDIATELY AFTERWARD. CASTLE CASTRO (IN THE FORMER SAN DIEGO, CALIFORNIA). 12:45 PM PST. TUESDAY, JULY 15, 2025.

Pat O'Grainne had always loved crossword puzzles, and always been able to hold his liquor; many nights when Heather was growing up he'd gotten a sixer-buzz on and done a crossword puzzle, flawlessly, in ink, just to show her he could. He sometimes thought that the intellectual stimulation of figuring out "ten-letter word, breathing toward Cleopatra's death," might have had something to do with how well Heather had done in school.

This wasn't very different; first he wrote the letter to her, then he scrawled out his handmade crossword puzzle. 15 across (the day of the month) was "orogeny." He used the definition and the text after it as a key to code the letter he had just written. Sometimes he surprised himself at how fast he could do this drunk; Heather said it was good because he never shortened or simplified messages to make the coding easier.

It pissed him off, though, seriously, that she said he should use the crappy grammar and spelling that he'd have used texting his biker buddies; she said it made the code harder to break, but he thought if some enemy ever did break the code, they'd think he was an idiot.

He returned to his coding:

> . . . *rilly has talk himself n2 this idea tht him n his buddies r tha natch leaders n shud run USA. he wants 2 chg tha constitution n b the fuckin Duke of California. I cud of herd mor but wz gettin 2 mad so faked a snore 2get 2go . . .*

When he had finished, he recopied the code, wrote a mawkish note about how they didn't pay enough attention to him and how Heather was ignoring him, copied the handmade crossword puzzle and the "secret code for you to work out, just like when you were a little girl" below that, and put the finished letter between books on his shelf; he'd give it to Carlucci or Bambi whenever they passed through. Then he put the original into the split log in his fireplace; it was a good thing this summer was so cold and he had an excuse for a fire almost every night.

**THAT EVENING. PUEBLO, COLORADO. 10:15 PM MST. TUESDAY, JULY 15, 2025.**

When Heather couldn't sleep, she'd go upstairs, roll out her chart, and study it. Tonight she felt huge, lonely, and miserable, and bitter experience had taught her that once it reached the point where she couldn't find a comfortable position, she was going to be up for at least another hour. So she padded upstairs, feeling like a grouchy she-bear, lit a lamp, pulled out the chart, and let her eyes just roam.

If there was any consistent pattern in tribal attacks, she thought, it had to be that they were always bigger and sooner than anyone might reasonably have expected. She scrawled a note to Leslie, her librarian for intelligence reports, asking for the action reports on tribal attacks in the last ninety days. *I suppose I'll be able to put Arnie on that one. Poor bastard, Mota Elliptica was such a good project for him, and now . . . well, poop. We had a solid five companies protecting it and we probably needed ten or fifteen. But it's gone now, and God knows how many things we really needed with it.*

She had pinned in more red cards, yarn, and construction paper blocking the DEFEAT MOON GUN path, and she had emphatically moved TRIBAL ACTIVITY way up on the priorities. Looking things over, she thought, *Well, I had been thinking we needed to assert ourselves somewhere; Arnie tells me public opinion won't stay with us if we don't obviously do something to stand up to some bad guys. I was thinking it was time to move against the Castles, but we'd better make it against the tribes.* Her eyes fell on a deep red slash running across the chart. *Now if Larry will just uncharacteristically call in and coordinate, and we get some cooperation from Olympia, I see my next move, plain as day.*

With the choice made, she felt as if some hand had uncorked her head and poured a bucket of sleep into it. She barely made it back to bed before she was out for the night.

# FOUR:
# KING GEORGE'S BIRDS CAME ON

"'Bout eight o'clock behind us," Ryan muttered to Larry. He fiddled with the harness on Mortimer, the most placid mule. "At least two."

They'd been shadowed most of the day. Bambi must still be alive and negotiable-for; if she were already dead and war under way, they'd have shot Larry, Ryan, and Micah from cover and then taken their mules and gear.

The ground was dry, the afternoon was warm, and the little creek running through the meadow ahead of them was inviting. "Let's let'em graze and drink a little," Larry said. "We've got plenty of daylight left." *Give the other side time to decide to show themselves.*

They unburdened the mules, tied them where they could reach the creek, and sat down to a late lunch on a big, comfortable, sun-warmed rock. They had just finished when the woman stepped out of the trees, her hands up.

"I make it three of them covering her," Micah said, softly, looking down at the ground.

"Four," Ryan said, behind his hand. "Bet you missed the one in the tall grass behind that stump. Mister Mensche, what do you want to do?"

Mensche shrugged. "I'm going to walk forward and talk to her. If they start shooting, shoot back and run. Count me dead unless I catch up with you. If any of the hidden ones move suddenly, give me a long whistle. Anyone acts like they're about to use a weapon, shoot, but I think it's going to be all talk for a while." He stood slowly, raising his hands over his head, and walked toward the woman.

*In my FBI days, I was assigned four different hostage negotiations and two ransom turnovers. Carlucci said he gave them to me because I moved slow and looked trustworthy. Hope I haven't lost my touch.*

When he and the woman were a few yards apart, Larry said, "My side won't fire if you lower your hands."

"Neither will mine if you do."

They relaxed. Larry said, "I'm a Federal investigating agent; you can call me Agent Mensche, Mister Mensche, or Larry—any of those is fine. I'm here to inquire into the disappearance of a mailplane and its pilot, Bambi Castro."

"I'm Helen Chelseasdaughter, it's polite among our people always to use both names, and the Blue Morning People sent me to guide you to the place where we will negotiate. We are a people who think long before acting; there will be no quick response."

"Then I won't expect one, Helen Chelseasdaughter. Is it far? Our mules are tired."

"About an hour's walk," Helen Chelseasdaughter said. "May I signal the people with me to come out of cover and join your party, Agent Mensche?"

"That will be fine, Helen Chelseasdaughter."

She raised her arms and waved twice; six tribals broke cover quietly, with hands over their heads. At Larry's signal, Ryan and Micah set their weapons down.

As the Daybreakers and Larry's party continued up the road, no one seemed to have anything to say.

## ABOUT 3 HOURS LATER. NEAR PINEHURST, IDAHO, ON US ROUTE 95. 6 PM PST. WEDNESDAY, JULY 16, 2025.

*Wow, their weed sucks,* Larry thought, taking the required fourth hit off the peace pipe. The council fire had been built in the trail ride center's fire pit; Larry, Helen Chelseasdaughter, and Michael Amandasson were sitting in a row on what must have been the performer's bench, and three hundred or so members of the Blue Morning People were facing them from the bleachers. *I feel the strangest desire to start talking like a crusty old character to the little buckaroos.*

The deal was done; now the tribe was having fun holding ceremonies. Larry was getting good at emphasizing the quality and wonders of the four hundred blankets, two hundred steel hatchets, three hundred pairs of new moccasins, and five hundred sweaters, every time his turn came up—the tribals always applauded. The peace pipes out there must've been being passed along pretty regularly.

When there was only about an hour of daylight left, Larry said he needed to *see* the plane and Bambi. Michael Amandasson led Mensche to the guarded guest cabin.

Bambi said hi and jumped up and hugged him, giving him cover to compose himself from the shock: the other prisoner in the cabin was his own daughter, Debbie.

When they let go of each other, he had his game face on again. He asked Bambi the basics (was she unhurt? could she fly the plane home if they fueled it? was she sure she had room for a takeoff from US 95?) while he rested his hand on her arm, squeezing in Morse:

**2moro eve b ready sunset**

Bambi squeezed back **QSL** (message received).

**QRV 2 run?** (Are you ready to run?)

**C.** (Yes).

**QSO deb.** (Relay this to Debbie).

**C.**

Larry had learned squeeze code back in the '90s when he'd just been starting with the Bureau, and later taught it to Debbie back when she thought that her dad being in the FBI was cool and she'd been preparing to be rescued by her dashing dad from terrorists or a serial killer. Whenever he or Debbie hugged, they'd squeeze and tap didit, didahdidit dididah didididah, dididah—*i luv u.*

After Daybreak, as the most experienced intelligence/law enforcement agent Heather had recruited, Larry had taught it to everyone.

Thirty years and this was the first time he'd ever used it. *Just goes to show there's no such thing as unnecessary training.*

It was lousy tradecraft, but he decided he'd have to be human. "And what are they holding *you* for?" He reached forward, as if brushing the hair from Debbie's eyes.

From the door, Michael Amandasson said, "She's no concern of yours. She's a slave."

Mensche turned, letting his hand fall onto Debbie's. "She is not a slave. She's on American soil and we have the Thirteenth Amendment."

"That doesn't apply to the Blue Morning People. Come with me now, Agent Mensche."

Mensche fixed his gaze on the tribal's face as if contemplating arresting him, and kept holding Debbie's hand, squeezing *i luv u*.

*u 2 dad.*

*CF w bambi*

*C. go now. QMO. luv u.*

*luv u 2. CL.*

*QMO* meant *problem with interference*; *CL* meant *talk later*.

As he walked to the barn to inspect the Stearman (he barely knew enough to identify it as an airplane, but Bambi would have plenty of time tomorrow) and then to the visitor center to use Bambi's radio to call for the ransom, he managed to sound politely interested as Michael Amandasson explained to him, in elaborate detail, that by interfering in a tribal custom like slavery, Mensche and the whole Federal government were being racist, sexist, culturist, and extremely judgmental. He even smiled now and then.

**ABOUT THE SAME TIME. PUEBLO, COLORADO. 9:13 PM MST. WEDNESDAY, JULY 16, 2025.**

"The EMP hit right at noon today," Arnie said. "So, yes, it could have been just a coincidence—maybe forty-five different tribes, everywhere from the Ouachitas to Big Bend and the Sangre de Cristos to Texarkana, *all* started moving at once, because they *all happened* to have working radios and we pissed them off, and then the moon gun *happened* to wait a long time to fire, so the moon gun *just happened* to be a perfect distraction *by pure chance* at the *exact moment* when all the tribes *just happened to wander into* Mota Elliptica simultaneously."

"Why are you throwing all the sarcasm at me, Arnie?" Heather said. "I just asked if it could be a coincidence." She poured him a shot of whiskey and pushed it over to him.

They sat in her office above her living quarters, in the old Pueblo Courthouse. He'd only come in with the rest of the survivors from Mota Elliptica that afternoon. She said, "Streen gave me his action report; no matter how much he blames himself, *no one* could have kept the tribals from wrecking it."

"It was bad," Arnie said, taking the whiskey in one quick gulp.

"Chris tells me the *Post-Times* will call it the Battle of Mota Elliptica. He says that way maybe people will get that we're at war. I don't want a panic—"

"But it might be time for one," Arnie said. "Uh, look. I'm not at my best explaining stuff right now. But I've gotta make you see it, Heather, really, we're sunk if you don't. How many times have I been wrong about anything this big?"

"Arnie, I understand it was rough; Colonel Streen is shaken up and I wouldn't have thought that was possible."

Arnie winced. *Rough. Bad.* And she thinks Streen is just *shaken up? She can't have any idea what it was like. . . . Christ, why am I trying?*

As dawn came up on the morning after the attack, Streen's forces had relieved the three other isolated buildings still holding out, but at the other four working stations, a few bodies lay near the doorways, plumed with arrows and lances, and the rest were burned and smothered inside, curled against walls with hands over their faces. The four radio techs inside the control bunker had apparently been forced back into the flames at spearpoint.

Besides Trish, twenty-two other engineers and technicians were confirmed dead, though a couple might yet find their way in, out of seven missing. Streen's final count on his military forces was sixty-four dead—thirty-eight of his own TNG infantry, eleven of the President's Own Rangers, and thirteen of the Texans (eleven of those, along with one of the Rangers, in a single, too-clever ambush). They were missing three infantrymen, a Ranger, and a TexIC; an actual majority of the survivors were wounded.

"Try to tell me one more time," Heather said. "Slowly, don't yell, don't treat me like an idiot."

"Sorry," Arnie said.

"Quentin told me he thought the scientist that was killed next to you was, uh, important to you." She poured him another shot, his fourth since they'd begun the informal debriefing. "Here," she said, patting her immense belly. "Drink for those who can't."

Arnie took it in one gulp, again, and said, "Yeah. I'm crying. I didn't even notice I was. But I'm crying."

"Well, it's about time."

Arnie looked down, wiping his face and keening. She let him cry, until finally, wiping his face, he said, "Trish Eliot was great . . . my number two on the job, my best friend there, maybe she'd've been more if there'd been time." *And the only person brave enough for me to tell her the whole truth, and to believe me.* "Yeah, she was killed right beside me, and that was pretty awful." *Pretty awful is all the more description I can think of?*

Heather waited for him find his voice again. Usually you could count on Heather to listen.

After a while, she said, "Arnie, there's more evidence than you know about. Captain Highbotham's observatory at Christiansted was attacked this morning—tribals came ashore in small boats from a big sailing yacht, and Highbotham and a party rowed out to the yacht and captured it while the local militia beat the raiders on the beach. Practically a pirate battle, but she won. And yes, it does look like the moon gun and the tribes are either talking to each other, or talking to some common superior. For one thing, we think they might have launched another EMP bomb while Christiansted was tied up in the battle, and Big Island, Cooke Castle, and Oaxaca were all under cloud cover. USS *Bush*, in the Indian Ocean, thinks they detected a flash, but it was daylight and low on the horizon. I guess we'll know in three days. So . . . all right, Arnie, the moon gun isn't just a leftover robot, because there's way too much strategy happening and it understands way too much. And it's not being run by some human overlord somewhere, because like you say, the communications pattern doesn't fit. All right."

*Trish believed me because she was my friend. Heather's my friend too. I just have to find a way to make it real clear.* "So look, here's the thing, put it all together, boss, use that cop brain. How old is Daybreak and how completely integrated? The moon gun and the tribes work together. Encrypted radio all over the Lost Quarter. They're plugged in to each other and they always intended to be that way, and that took preparation way in advance. Well, *how far* in advance? Daybreak themes were there in coustajam music back when that was niche-stuff on YouTube. And if we're right about how the moon gun got there, it must've been designed all the way back in the days of Google-One, Facebook, and Twitter. I can't *prove* more than ten years, but I'm gut-certain Daybreak started before the turn of the century."

"Why do we *care* how old it is? Isn't this just Professor Yang getting caught up in a research project?"

"No," Arnie said. "The whole world keeps pushing me to find the magic bullet, but until we understand how it got here, and how big and complex and sophisticated it is, we don't even know if there *can* be *any* kind of bullet, magic or otherwise. I'm trying to figure out if it's a tornado, a giant shark, a serial killer, or a forest fire, and you're all insisting I tell you what caliber bullet to use."

"You're becoming angry again," she said, softly. "And before Daybreak, you were always 'don't ask me what to do, let me just study.'"

"And if I'd been able to study then, we might know what to do today." His own voice sounded pathetic to him, now. "People want an answer, and they want me to guarantee it's true. They don't want the answer that's true."

"Yeah. All right. You had me with your point that I wish we'd let you research it back then. Tell me the rest of your idea." She leaned forward, hands resting on her knees, listening intently or resting her back or both.

Arnie nodded. "Look how fast the tribes happened. They weren't even in our maybe-trouble file back in March; first we heard of them was right after the war scare and Open Signals Day, at the end of April, when Larry Mensche came in with that report, and then all of a sudden Springfield, Steubenville, Augusta, and Kettle Valley were all trashed between May 10th and May 12th. Maybe a tenth, maybe more, of the surviving population is in tribes, you see? Daybreak had the moon gun ready to go, physically, and it had the tribes ready to go, as a cultural idea with organizers and bards and everything."

"Bards?"

"Something I got out of interrogations. When Daybreak had Jason, for at least three years before 10-28-24, he was fantasizing intensely about being a wandering poet for tribal people and wandering between Castles— and none of that existed then, but in less than half a year, it all did. You see? Daybreak prepared him for a world that Daybreak had designed."

Heather tented her hands and leaned back. "Do we have to decide anything tonight?"

"No, but soon. Look, if I'm right, Daybreak is so far ahead of us—"

"All right, Arn, you've given me the reality." She was nodding, but she looked tired and sick. "Let me give you the politics, and then let's see if we can drag the reality and the politics anywhere near each other, and find a way to accommodate them both. I realize it's true, but you're telling me the worst possible news, because if Daybreak is really everywhere, if we're falling right into its plan, and we don't even know what that plan is, if we have to doubt every move we make . . . oh, man, Arn. Not an easy sell either to Graham or to Cam."

"But if I'm right, and this is true, then we've got to study this thing, understand what it's capable of—"

Heather sighed. "Politically, Arnie, I need a program, some definite number of steps that will definitely defeat Daybreak, so I can get the resources for the study you need to do."

"But you need the study to know what to do, to make sure we're not falling right into Daybreak's plan!"

"I know, I know, I know." She waved her hand at him in the invisible yo-yo gesture that meant *Calm down and shut up.* "Arn, we've got to find a way for you to investigate this, I agree. But right now as far as they're concerned, I'm the dumb bitch that wrecked one of our last big surviving generating stations to prove that the other side didn't like us, and you're my pet head-in-the-clouds Doctor Doofus. Olympia and Athens are looking for an excuse to cut us off and start back down the warpath with each other."

"Do *you* believe me?"

"I believe I can't dismiss you. So find me something somewhere. A few good pieces of evidence that we haven't seen before. A real clear analogy. One good completely counterintuitive thing to try that works. Whatever. Just remember, Arn, the people in Athens and Olympia are much dumber and less patient than I am. It has to be so simple that even an old cop like me can explain it to frightened, imagination-free bureaucrats like them. I know it's probably impossible but you'll have to do it anyway. And soon—because if you're right, we might already be too late. Want another shot before I throw you out and get my motherly sleep?"

"I want ten of them, but I better not." He rose, wiped his face, and said, "Trish was the best, Heather. You don't know what you lost."

"None of us ever do."

He followed her gaze to Lenny's picture; she looked back at him soon enough to see the moment when he realized she was looking at the father of her child, the husband she'd lost in the first month of the Daybreak crisis, and he said, softly, "Sorry. I guess we're all pretty clueless."

"It makes us human, and if you're right, that's what this is all about— staying human. The world will never be able to add up how much we all lost, will it?" She looked at him steadily. "But I am sorry you never had any time together, and that in this new world, we never even have the simple time to grieve."

He nodded his thanks for her sympathy, not trusting himself to speak, because he could hear the rest of the message as clearly as if she'd said it aloud: *But we all know there's nothing anyone can do.*

## ABOUT 20 MINUTES LATER. PUEBLO, COLORADO. 11 PM MST. WEDNESDAY, JULY 16, 2025.

Arnie walked alone; he'd taken an isolated house farther away from downtown, to give himself some privacy and space.

A scraping sound. He spun, cross-drawing his knives from his hip sheaths, hoping all the *sai* katas he'd studied—

"I'll come out if you put away the knives. I mean you no harm." The voice was behind him.

He leapt forward and pivoted. "If you mean me no harm, it won't matter that I keep my knives out. Show yourself."

The tall, thin man emerged from the shadows. The blanket covering the top and sides of his head, his long curly beard, and his large round eyes made him look like a cheap religious painting. Bare feet gripped the warm summer street above pirate-style pants—a big piece of a sheet wrapped at the waist, cut up to the crotch front and back, and sewed up the inside seam.

*Jeez,* Arnie thought. *With a zillion Wal-Marts out there to loot, he couldn't just find some all-cotton basketball shorts?*

"My name is Aaron," the man said. "Last fall, you were looking for me with every weapon and tool that plaztatic civilization still had."

"What are you here for?"

"I'd like to talk to you."

"Well, talk." Arnie's heart was pounding. This guy at least *looked* like Ysabel's description of Aaron, who even now was the single most wanted Daybreaker. "Talk," Arnie repeated. "If that's what you came to do."

"Oh, that's what I came to do, *Doctor* Yang. Doctor, from the Latin *doceo*. Taught, educated, having mastered the documents, learned the doctrine, having been indoctrinated."

"You sound like you used to teach English."

"I do, don't I? After I go, will you look up all the missing English teachers to see if you can find a match?"

"Just an observation." Arnie shifted his weight.

"If people would *confine* themselves to observations, everything would be *fine*. It's their insistence on taking action that condemns the species."

"You're one of us."

"I intend to be among the last of us, actually." Aaron advanced to just out of arms' reach. "So you want to see into the soul of Daybreak. Here I am. What do you want to know?"

"How do you communicate with Daybreak?" Arnie asked.

"That's a rather blunt question."

"I'm blunt, and I don't believe you'll actually tell me the truth about anything. I might as well shoot for the moon."

"Nowadays, the moon shoots for *you*. I don't share my colleagues' optimism that if you understand Daybreak, you'll join it. I think there are plenty of unredeemable people."

"And you don't have any trouble with killing them."

Aaron stared at him, head cocked to the side. "So you are a statistical semiotician, an occupation that could have explained immense amounts about culture and society and all that, but in practice was used to refine methods of selling politicians and soap—not very well because no one could get funding for the basic science to underlie it."

Arnie brought his knives up slightly; he felt like his bowels were trying to pass a frozen cannonball. Aaron's words were—

"You could have told everyone about Daybreak before it happened, but it was the same old thing, wasn't it? Give us the payoff from your research, first, and then we'll pay you to do it. That was where you were last year, eh? You knew Daybreak was coming but they wouldn't let you really study it unless you told them the answers before you studied it." Aaron clicked his tongue. "Very tough on *Doctor* Arnie Yang, they don't want the doctor, the *know*-er, the one who makes *know*-ledge, they want the doctus, the guy who *already knows*. Give us your results, better yet tell us we're already right, and *then* we'll pay you to do the research." Aaron was standing close enough now for Arnie to just step forward and strike, his huge dark eyes holding Arnie's. "And even now, eh?" Aaron said. "Even now, they want you to just tell them what to shoot. They don't want you to understand Daybreak, do they?"

"How old is Daybreak?"

"Everyone I know, before they were in Daybreak, was in something that eventually flowed into Daybreak," Aaron said. "You might say Daybreak is older than itself; whatever parts became the core of Daybreak were there before anyone spoke the word 'Daybreak.' At first it had many different names: the Coming, the Dawn, the Morning Glory, one goofy guy I knew said, 'It's Morning on Earth' constantly. So I surely heard the word 'Daybreak' in that context at least a hundred times before I knew it would be the name of anything, let alone the thing it would be the name of." Aaron cocked his head to the side, peering at Arnie. "Insightful, but *very* academic, *Doctor* Yang. Shouldn't you ask about our troop dispositions? No wonder no one likes that incorrigibly academic Doctor Yang—"

"If you expect me to be ashamed of my education, you've—"

"Oh, but it's not about education. It's about understanding. All thinking beings surely want to be understood, don't they? Consciously or not?" Aaron stepped backward. The shadows closed around him like a slamming door. Arnie was alone in the moonlit street.

Later, at home, he closed and bolted the heavy shutters, checked every bolt and lock multiple times, and stretched out so that his writing pad rested on his stomach and faced the candle. At the top of the page he wrote, *Recent contact with an active long-term Daybreaker has provided evidence of the urgency of a full, in-depth, from-the-ground-up study of Daybreak.* After ten sentences he realized he couldn't remember the conversation nearly as well as the eyes, the rhythm, the too-empty street. The creaking of the old house, and the fantastical candlelight shadows, should have terrified him, he thought, just before he fell asleep.

## THE NEXT DAY. PUEBLO, COLORADO. 9 AM MST. THURSDAY, JULY 17, 2025.

Arnie's "interview room" was a corner second-floor office space over a boarded-up computer store in downtown Pueblo. He had furnished it with wool and cotton blankets thrown over metal folding chairs, facing in a semicircle toward an old writing desk, and a side table with pitchers of water and some bread and cheese for snacks.

He sat down at the writing desk and opened his notepad, just as if he hadn't been gone for more than six weeks. "Well, it's been a while since we've met as a group. I've got some new questions; let's see if they call up any new answers."

Jason Nemarec, his wife Beth, and Izzy Underhill (who was actually Ysabel Roth, but was still at some risk of being assassinated because of her prominence on Daybreak day) were Arnie's only "domesticated" ex-Daybreakers—people who had been fully part of Daybreak and were now reliably working for the RRC. The best estimate now was that on October 28, 2024, at least sixty thousand Daybreakers had participated in some act of sabotage within the United States; perhaps a million sympathizers, posers, and dupes had been involved peripherally during the year before.

Most Daybreakers were now dead, like most of everyone else; most of the living ones were in the tribes, but there must still be covert Daybreaker spies and saboteurs, as well as ex-Daybreakers, afraid to expose themselves to arrest or mob violence, hiding out the way Beth and Jason had for months in the little town of Antonito, far from anyone who might recognize them. It was a legitimate fear; every Daybreaker captured in those first months, despite the pleas of Federal intelligence and law enforcement, had been killed by mobs or summarily executed by local authorities. Trying to protect captured Daybreakers long enough to interrogate them simply got police and soldiers killed with them; shortly, most officials began handing Daybreakers over to mobs, or killing them themselves, as a matter of personal safety.

Izzy was petite, bony, and big-jawed, with long straight brown hair and deep sad eyes. "I'm so sorry to hear about what happened down at Mota Elliptica. It must have been terrible," she said.

Arnie nodded, thinking, *Don't cry.* "We lost good people. We did learn a lot about Daybreak." He looked down at his notes. "Everyone ready?"

They all nodded.

"Then," Arnie said, "do you feel like you joined Daybreak after it already existed, or do you feel like you helped create it?"

"Joined," Beth said, simultaneously with Jason's "Helped create," and they both laughed.

"I'm not seeing the joke," Arnie said.

"We heard about it on the same day from a guy named Terrel," Beth said. "Ysabel was in a long time before we were, so—"

Ysabel screamed and fell from her chair, lying on the floor with her back arched and arms flailing. They had all seen this before; whatever part of Daybreak clung to individual minds, it still protected Daybreak. They cleared the chairs away, and surrounded her with pillows.

Beth said, "Well, Arnie, you sure hit a button that time."

Arnie said, "Yeah, I guess so. How are you two doing?"

"Little bit of a headache," Jason said, "but that could be all the screaming and the exercise."

Beth nodded. "I'm okay. I can feel Daybreak not liking me but . . . I don't know, maybe I just have more natural resistance. It was deep into Ysabel, here. Real deep. So fuckin' much more Daybreak in her than we got in us, you know?"

"Keep telling me, I'm learning."

She shrugged. "We used to kid around and call it Daydar, you know, like gaydar? One Daybreaker tends to know another one real fast and easy, and know how deep in they are and how long they've been. Some of those real long-timers it's like they're all Daybreak, ain't much of them left, it's like you're talking to Daybreak direct without them there at all."

"And we used to laugh at coustajam hippies," Jason added. "People who liked the music, the vegetables, the clothes, and some of the words, but didn't have a clue what it meant. You got so you knew the second you met someone."

"Can someone who wasn't a Daybreaker have Daydar?"

Beth looked thoughtful for a moment. "Well, most straight people have some gaydar, don't they?"

Izzy sighed and turned over on her side. Arnie made sure she was covered with a blanket. "She'll want to sleep it off, and sometimes the easiest time to talk is right when she's just coming out. I can sit here and wait for her, if you both have things to do."

"I think I better stay," Beth said. "She's kind of . . . she gets scared when it's just you there when she wakes up. She told us. Don't get your feelings hurt or nothing, I'm just saying."

Arnie nodded. "Okay." Not sure what else to say, he added, "I'm sorry I'm scary."

Beth shrugged. "Not scary so much . . . just, it's your job, Arnie, you got to push us, hurt us even, to find out about Daybreak—maybe you'll feel real bad after, but you'll hurt us."

"I'm sorry," he said, uselessly, again.

"It's okay," Jason said. "Better that it's you; at least we can tell you don't *like* having to hurt us."

Arnie nodded. *Wow. Daydar. And how Daybreak came into existence or how people get infected is a third-rail question. More stuff to try on Aaron. Get one definite thing out of him, and Heather will be able to go straight to everyone for funds, people, and time—they'll all* have *to listen.*

## THE NEXT DAY. NEAR PINEHURST, IDAHO, ON US ROUTE 95. 3:45 PM PST. FRIDAY, JULY 18, 2025.

The shadows were getting longer, stretching eastward, but sunset was still hours away. Bambi and Debbie had spent the day holding hands or leaning against each other, squeeze-coding, catching up on everything. Bambi found Debbie's enthusiasm for tonight's raid frightening. *But then if I'd been chained for three months between bouts of scutwork and rape—*

The door opened. Debbie slumped like a collapsing sandbag. Michael Amandasson ordered, "Slave, come with me."

Debbie wailed, "Please don't tie me up with the horses again, I'll try to be better!"

"We're not going to do that—"

"Please, not in the kennel with the dogs!"

Michael Amandasson laughed. "You're coming to my private cabin. I have a one-fourth share in the ransom and I'm gonna celebrate."

Debbie stood up, snuffling, wiping her face, catching her balance on Bambi Castro's shoulder. Bambi covered Debbie's hand with her own, gave her a brief consoling hug, and squeezed **QSL QTH**—*I have received your position.*


## ABOUT AN HOUR LATER. PUEBLO, COLORADO. 6:12 PM MST. FRIDAY, JULY 18, 2025.

After they had sparred with fists and feet, taken wooden knives away from each other, slammed each other into the mats, and tried to hit each other with sticks, Mr. Samson ("Call me sensei and I'll kick your butt, call me Master and I'll make you shine my shoes") seemed satisfied. "Well, yeah, you definitely have enough prior training for my advanced class. What do you think, Steve?"

Steve Ecco, a short, muscular man, perhaps thirty years old, with sandy blond hair and a Wyatt Earp mustache, nodded. "Good with me too. Where'd you learn?"

Arnie Yang explained, "Well, Dad pushed me to do all this martial arts stuff, so I did, like I did classical guitar, AP math, Junior Achievement, and all the rest. I was a total GOAT."

Ecco raised an eyebrow. "The only goats we had in Oklahoma were next to the doublewides of the goat-ropers."

Arnie laughed. "Yeah, different cultures. Grossly Overachieving Asian Teenager. One of those Asian kids who was pushed and pushed and pushed. I hated it in high school—if you're an Asian kid who does martial arts, every moron in the world is yelling 'hee-yah!' and jumping at you. But when I got to college, I learned the stress relief value of beating on your fellow human beings, and just kind of stayed with it after college. Nowadays it almost seems easier to practice than not."

Samson nodded. "Good answer. We get too many people here, even now, who want to be either a crime-fighting macho superhero who rips human hearts out with his bare hands, or a Jedi Peacenik Levitation Master who just floats bad people away in harmony with their spiritual nature."

"I've met a few of both kinds, myself. I hope I'm old enough to be over the romanticism of violence. You know, less than a week ago I shot some people, and a good friend was killed beside me. I know I have a Ph.D. and I use big words, but I hope you can overlook those character defects."

"You'll do fine here," Samson said. He was tall, stout but not fat, with thick, straight, iron-gray hair, an eagle-beak of a nose, crooked teeth, and a receding chin, so that he looked like a large muskrat who had borrowed a Senate candidate's toupee.

"Be nice to have another guy in the class who knows something," Ecco added. "The advanced class'll be coming in in a couple minutes, get some water now if you're gonna need it."

. . .

After a brisk workout and some fussing with people's grips in jujitsu, Samson called Jason up for sparring. As they stepped into striking range, Samson sped up and kept coming, swinging slowly and carefully but pushing Jason steadily back until his foot crossed the painted line. "Okay, I ran you out of bounds. In a big room I'd have you cornered, and be beating on you or waiting for my friends to bring around a weapon. What did you do?"

"He didn't get off the line." It sounded more like *lann*, delivered in a flat twang of complete boredom.

"Steve, I didn't ask you," Samson said, not taking his eyes off Jason.

"Just wanted to save time." *Sounded more like* tamm, Arnie thought. Now that was weird. He'd have thought he had as little prejudice as any coastal American could, but something about Steve's flat, hard-edged delivery was like a sanding wheel skipping over a brick wall. *Probably meant to be. He wants to fight—*

"I guess I could've moved to the side," Jason said.

"You guessed right," Samson said.

"Let us show you," Ecco said. "Doctor Yang, you and me are the demo team here." Arnie stood, and Ecco said, "All right, touch is as good as a strike, take it easy, this is a demo, not a match. Now come after me, Doctor Yang—"

"In here I better be Arnie."

"Arnie, then. First time I'll just go back or forward, one straight track, you come at me any way you like."

Ecco was fast and proficient, but since Arnie could just keep alternating flanks, he quickly drove him out of bounds.

"Now," Ecco said, "This time I move off the line. See what you can do."

Arnie had barely kicked once before he was surrounded by a blur of Ecco's hands, feet, elbows, and everything else; he was able to stay in the space, and use his hands and forearms to block most of the fast-but-gently-controlled jabs, crosses, spear-hands, and thrust-kicks, but that was all, and in a real fight he'd have been knocked flat.

"*Ya-me!*" Ecco said, the call to end action. They bowed. "Y'all see, everyone? Arnie's good, but I'm *real* good. But if I stay on that line, he can beat my ass into the ground."

*Hah. Now I get it. Steve Ecco needs to establish a pecking order, when a new guy comes in with skills. Well, no prob. He's definitely a bigger pecker than I am.*

After practice, Samson and Ecco stopped him. "Going to come back?" Ecco asked.

"Wouldn't miss it. That was fun. And I have to get good enough to not look so lame out there."

"Good answer," Ecco said. "I don't suppose that besides being a pretty good fighter and a damned good sport, the Perfessor happens to drink beer?"

"I do. I also listen to country music, and if I had the nerve, I'd chase waitresses."

"Well, then, let's stop by Dell's Brew, pour you some courage, and work on some technique."

"You talked me into it." Arnie had planned to walk home the long way by himself, in hopes that Aaron would reappear, so that he could try out his carefully written, memorized questions. *But the international association of lonely sad guys is obviously holding a chapter meeting, and I wouldn't miss that.* He felt happier and less lonely than he had in a long time.

## ABOUT THE SAME TIME. NEAR PINEHURST, IDAHO, ON US ROUTE 95. 8 PM PST. FRIDAY, JULY 18, 2025.

The sun had already set and the twilight was dimming rapidly; Helen Chelseasdaughter asked, "Will they have light enough to unload all the cargo and still take off again? I don't want children to see technology."

"Their last radio message was that they were delayed but plan to complete on schedule. I'm guessing—there." He'd heard the sputtering, farting roar of the DC-3's motors, running rough due to crappy biofuel and lye-spray getting through the air cleaners. "Here they come. If you don't want the kids to see—"

"Children out of here, now!" Helen Chelseasdaughter shouted. Two young women urged a dozen children to come with them over the hill. One stubborn girl and two boys threw tantrums, insisting on seeing the airplane, and were dragged off.

Bambi said, "It's close to dark. I'd like to take off as soon as the other plane is off the road. Would it be all right for me to taxi over there"—she pointed north of the gate—"out of his way but ready to go as soon as he lands and you see the ransom?"

The gray-haired tribal nodded. "Yes, I want all the machines gone as soon as possible."

Bambi reached out and clasped Larry's hand in a centurion handshake, babbling something meaningless about her gratitude. She squeeze-coded *d still w m in cabin*.

Larry thought, *I would like to know what that son of a bitch is doing—actually no; I'd rather just assume, and deal with it accordingly.*

The engine thunder loudened and deepened. A brilliant, moving star rose above the hill to the south, then dipped below the horizon again; the Gooney was coming around for its approach.

Micah came back from spinning the prop on the Stearman. The biplane made a slow turn across the gravel before it taxied out the gate, Bambi waving from the cockpit. The plane headed north, down the hill, to turn around and be ready for takeoff as soon as the DC-3 was out of its way.

Michael Amandasson had still not emerged from his hut. "Typical," a younger woman behind Larry muttered. "He won't be done with the slave till it's time to claim his share."

Susan Marthasdaughter sent a runner for Michael. The tribals were all staring at the southern sky, at the eerie, blazing glow of an arc spotlight, the first electric light they had seen since November, reaching up into the sky from beyond the crest of the hill as the DC-3 touched down and coasted up.

Micah caught Larry's eye and jerked a thumb toward the path where the runner had gone; Larry nodded. Micah vanished into the dark.

Ryan moved behind Susan Marthasdaughter; Larry stepped quietly to his left, closing distance with Helen Chelseasdaughter.

As the DC-3 crested the hill, the brilliant beam swooped from the purple sky and down US 95 onto Bambi's bright yellow Stearman. She revved up and began her run up the road as the ninety-year-old airliner, painted in Quattro's black and yellow personal colors, wheeled about through the gate.

Bambi roared up the road into her takeoff; the DC-3 in the parking lot thundered and rumbled. No one could hear anything else.

Inside his shirt, Mensche drew the razor-sharp commando knife. His left hand gently drew Helen Chelseasdaughter's elbow down and backwards; as she turned to see what he was doing, his left hand grasped her hair and yanked her head back. His right hand lashed out with the knife in a rising forehand, opening her larynx, and then back through a carotid, cutting to the bone over the collarbone and down the sternum, slipping back upward through her diaphragm into her heart. She tumbled dead at his feet.

Mensche glimpsed people recoiling from where Ryan stood over Susan Marthasdaughter's body. Mensche spun, slashed the young woman behind him across her shocked expression, and swept her feet. He drove an elbow into the face of the man beside her; under the space that opened, he jammed his blade deep into the man's guts, ripping it free as he shoved the tribal backward into the people behind him.

The girl on the ground had her mouth open, screaming, and Mensche stamped on her neck as he turned to slash again, cutting at reaching hands, pivoting, kicking, and slashing to get working room.

Against the plane's lights, Mensche's targets were silhouettes. He struck again and again, flowing from attack to attack in all directions, trying to start and spread panic, whirling to strike blindly, knowing everyone within his reach was an enemy. The fingers of his empty hand formed a tiger claw; wherever it caught, he struck next to it with the knife, kicking and stamping as he turned to clear a big space around himself. His stiff fingers at eye and throat level, and his blade at gut and groin level, swung around with his torso, hurting whoever they found into screams.

A flare burst. Larry dove prone. The slow heavy thudding of a black-powder Gatling gun drowned out even the engines. Some rounds whizzed over his head; others hit the crowd with wet smacks and thuds.

The engines cut and the Gatling died away in an irregular spasm of bangs.

"You are the prisoners of the President's Own Rangers. Lie on the ground, face down, extend your arms in front of you. Don't move."

Larry complied; a few shots indicated that some Blue Morning People hadn't been quick enough. "Now," the voice said, "Agent Larry Mensche, please stand up." Larry stood up carefully; the beam of a reflector lantern swept across his face. "Glad you're okay, Larry," Quattro Larsen said. "Pick your people out of this."

"Ryan, stand up," Mensche said, "and Micah, stay down." The lantern beam picked out Ryan, and Mensche said, "You'd better come over here and join me. Micah, stand up if you're out there."

From the surrounding dark, Micah said, "Still back here. I'm going to walk forward real slow, okay?" He emerged into the glare. All around them, the wounded sobbed and gasped; the Rangers sorted them out in a quick, brutal triage—the dead would be left where they were, for some other tribe to find; the wounded would be asked, once, if they wanted rehabilitation, and killed on the spot if they said no; those able to walk would carry those who could not in a forced march to Ontario, to be sorted into "rehabilita-tion" and "execution" groups.

"Sir? What do we do if we ask and they spaz attack on us?"

"According to the RRC *Field Guide*, that's a yes, but tie them up tight," the captain said. "And if they say yes, and then start shouting Daybreaker shit, shoot 'em."

"Seems pretty rough," Ryan said.

Larry's shrug was a bare twitch of the shoulder. "Orders from Pueblo. Letting the tribes know we mean business, and this Daybreaker shit is not going to be tolerated."

"What do they do in rehab?"

"I don't know, but I hope it hurts. Anyway, we've got one prisoner to lib-erate," Mensche said. "Let's go get her. Also, Quattro, let the Rangers know there are some young kids in a cabin over that way."

On the path, they passed the runner that Micah had killed. "I got her coming back," Micah said, "she just ran neck first onto my knife."

He was trembling, Mensche realized, and said, "Was she the first person you ever killed?"

"Yeah." The young man croaked it out.

"She'd have starved or died of disease before spring; it's gonna be way worse for the tribals this winter."

"Yeah, but I still killed her."

"Yeah," Mensche said. "I'd never even fired my weapon at a human being, before Daybreak. Like Stalin said, one is murder, and there's some number where it's just a statistic."

The cabin door stood open; the reflector lamp's flickering yellow-orange beam revealed Michael Amandasson, hanged naked in a bedsheet from a rafter. His leg was still warm to the touch, his ankle supple, blood was only beginning to pool in his feet; *she must have done it* after *the runner told them the plane was coming in—*

Mensche borrowed the lantern and swept the beam around the cabin, then out on the narrow, railed porch. Off one end, he found a bare footprint in the mud; five feet farther on was a black patch of turned-over leaf mold. Not far beyond that, on the narrow trail leading uphill out of the camp, a branch was freshly broken on a fir.

"She's my daughter," he said. "I think I'm entitled to ask her, Debbie, what the fuck? You know?"

Quattro Larsen said, "Yeah, I understand." He clasped his friend's hand and squeeze-coded *WTF?*

Larry's hand moved to Quattro's arm as he squeeze-coded:
*no idea*
*d marked trail on purpose*
*must want me 2 follow*
*tell h 2 impt not 2 follow*

Larry sighed, not entirely acting, and added aloud, "This might take a few weeks, I imagine."

"You have to do what you have to do," Quattro said. "Thanks for rescuing Bambi, and if you need a ride, the Gooney Express always has a free seat for an old buddy."

"'Preciate it. Give my regards and apologies to Heather."

## 20 MINUTES LATER. BETWEEN US ROUTE 95 AND HELLS CANYON NATIONAL PARK, IN IDAHO. 8:38 PM PST. FRIDAY, JULY 18, 2025.

Mensche had hunted and photographed wildlife as his main hobbies for decades before Daybreak, had good night vision, and had a career FBI agent's knack for following people; he could have followed a trail marked half as prominently. In a saddle of the ridge, Debbie had laid a seven-foot arrow in dead sticks on an old recreation trail.

He laughed out loud. "Deb, I'm the one that taught *you* woodcraft."

Just behind him, she said, "Yeah, but I'm in a silly mood."

He turned and hugged her. They could still hear occasional gunshots, far behind them. She asked, "Are the Rangers shooting all of them?"

"Just the ones who refuse rehab, or try to escape."

"You smell like blood."

"It's from Helen what's-her-face."

"Good, Dad. I'm glad. She had it coming if any of them did. But actually I'm sorry they aren't just shooting them all. There's not going to be any rehab that works. There's a place up the trail where we can sit if you want."

"Sure."

At the base of a low rock cliff, she guided him to a bench by one of the old raised metal firebox grills. He said, "There's something you want me to do or see."

"There is," she said. "It's important and I realized this was the way to do it."

"Good enough," he said, "I'm sure you're right."

"You're not my same old dad."

"It's not your same old world."

"Yeah." She reached out and threaded her hand into the crook of his elbow, the way she had when she'd been little and he'd been her hero. He just waited. *Being here, in the starlight, with just Debbie, is about as good as life has been in a long time.*

"So the runner came to let Michael know the plane was landing. I knew *you* wouldn't be in an outfit that paid ransoms, and besides Bambi had squeeze-coded me that you were gonna beat the shit out of the Blue Morning People. So at first I thought, *I want a special moment here for just Michael and me.*"

"No one would have begrudged you that. We wouldn't even have filed an incident report."

She leaned back in a stretch, extending her feet and wriggling them. "I knew that. But the whole reason I became a frontier scout for the People of Gaia's Dawn was that I needed to escape in a way that would make a difference. I mean I knew right away I didn't want to be a tribal—it's dirty, nasty, and ugly enough now. Eating bark and twigs all winter, once the canned and dry food are gone—gah."

"How'd you end up there in the first place?"

"A couple of nutty witch-wannabes in the group I broke out of Coffee Creek with ran into some would-be bush hippies, and I was hoping to find the guys with the good drugs. So I was one of the Seventy-Nine Founders of the People of Gaia's Dawn. I hope you guys clean out all the tribes; I wish you'd just *shot* all the Blue Mornings."

"Some of us favor that."

"See, I knew I could count on my dad! And that brings me to the thing that I don't think you'll believe till I show you."

"How about if I just believe you?"

She hugged him, very hard, and he felt hot tears on his cheeks.

After a minute, she whispered, "There's still a reason why we need to do things my way, check me out and see if you agree, 'kay?"

"I'm listening."

She sat still. Larry heard only the wind in the pines, and the soft scurry of something small moving through pine needle duff.

Finally she said, "I volunteered as a scout so it'd be easy to escape when the time came, once I figured out what I could take along as proof of what was really going on. And then of all the stupid things the lame-weenie Blue Mornings ambushed me. I must've been the only slave they ever took, which is why they were so hard to escape from—it was like being a miser's last dollar."

"Bad luck happens to the best."

" 'Along with everybody else.' I used to hate it when you'd say that to me about my driving and my partying. But here's the thing. If the tribes were just a bunch of thieving-ass bush hippies with their heads full of prison-paganism and dumbass crystal-worship, I'd figure, hey, they're just plain old social scum like I used to be. But they're something a whole lot worse, and if we just went back to Pueblo, and I told my story, nobody'd believe me without investigating, and there's no time to put an expedition together, let alone find a way for them to see what they need to see. But if you come along and I show *you*, they'll take *your* word for it without any 'further investigation' or 'more research needed' or any of that bullshit which there ain't time for. I just don't want our side to lose three months we don't have. That's what it is."

"It's that bad?"

"Whatever 'that bad' means to you, it's worse." She stood. "We can make it to a Gaia's Dawn scout post by midmorning tomorrow if we walk through the night."

"All right. Lead me."

Shortly after moonrise, she said, "Dad?"

"Yeah?"

"Thanks for taking my word."

The moon rose higher. With more light, they made better time, half-sprinting over rises that were almost as bright as day, then plunging into hollows that, from above, brimmed with darkness, but down in them, the stars seemed to shine especially bright.

**ABOUT AN HOUR LATER. PUEBLO, COLORADO. 12:30 AM MST. SATURDAY, JULY 19, 2025.**

Arnie felt slightly silly about feeling as good as he did. He'd had a few beers. Samson and Ecco had accepted and welcomed him into the beer-and-hanging-out circle of, as they dubbed themselves, Jedi Rednecks, and introduced him to the few other serious martial artists in the circle. It was so friendly and comfortable. Nobody asked him to judiciously frame an exact thought; it was warm and fun and there hadn't been much just-let-your-hair-down in his life lately, or at all, ever, really.

Arnie had always liked country music (initially because it annoyed the crap out of his sophisticated parents). And it was so flattering that they wanted him to help teach the beginner classes.

The dark, empty street seemed so much friendlier, till Aaron fell silently into step beside him.

"I just came from martial arts practice and the bar. Maybe I'm not real controlled; startling me might be a good way to get stabbed."

"Oh, Doctor Yang. Going slumming with the working class, I see. Looking for some bovine blonde in a cowboy hat—a cowgirl, or some might say a cow-girl—to fill the wide open spaces of your heart?"

"That's none of your damned business." Arnie was stalling as he tried to bring his list of questions to the forefront through the beery fog.

"Well, I can hardly fault you for enjoying respect, friendship—and who knows, maybe love—where you can find it, considering how things have been going with your friends and supporters." Their feet beat out a soft rhythm for a block before Aaron spoke again. "So you are interested in how long Daybreak has existed, Doctor Yang? How long has God existed?"

"For those who believe in him, I suppose forever."

"Do you believe in God?"

"Do your questions just keep getting more personal?"

Aaron tugged the blanket tighter around himself, and muttered, "Poor Tom's a-cold, eh? The king and the fool. It's the fool's job to ask hard questions, that's all. Not really personal at all, you know. At all. But if you don't believe God exists, you do believe the concept or the image or the idea of God exists, don't you?"

"I see where you're going," Arnie said. Gah. Sophomore solipsism. "So for believers, their idea of God is the creator of the universe, so there has always been God, whereas unbelievers would just say God came into being sometime after people came into existence. What the fuck's it got to do with Daybreak?"

"You know, better than anyone, Doctor Yang, Doctus of the Doctrine and the Doxology where all Documents are Docked into the Docket, Doctor, that worrying about whether information is relevant is the surest way to prevent learning anything. Aren't all your troubles caused by everyone wanting something relevant right now instead of waiting for you to look into something interesting? How can you start complaining that something is interesting but—"

The voice had become softer and softer, and after a moment Arnie said, "Not relevant?" and turned to find he had said it to the empty street. *And that means I wasn't watching him, either, for at least a full minute. Oh, man, no more walking by myself when I've been drinking, and I need to get Heather in on this.*

That thought seemed to bring back the happiness from the evening at Dell's Brew. *Once I tell Heather what we have, we're going to be able to move so fast. I'm going to* crack *this Daybreak thing.*

The last couple of blocks to his house, he walked with his hands in his pockets, hugging himself with his elbows, surprised by how well things were going and how many friends he had. The world after Daybreak was really, honestly, not so bad at all, at least not for Arnie. *Interesting how it's not relevant.*

## THE FOLLOWING DAWN. HELLS CANYON. 5:20 AM PST. SATURDAY, JULY 19, 2025.

The cliff fell almost vertically away from their feet. It was still night below but the river reflected the indigo of the dawn sky. Before them, a great fan of mighty razor-edged ridges rose directly up from the water into a high palisade veined with dark rock and darker crevices, sawing into the dark cloudless sky.

"There's a path on both sides that connects to a bunch of rocks that you can cross on, if you're lucky and the water's low," Debbie explained.

"Cold as hell down there, I bet."

"Yeah. And dark. But if we start climbing down now, when we get there it'll be light enough and warm enough."

"Is that what you want to do, Deb?"

"Naw, I *want* to spend three weeks in pre-Daybreak Vegas with a no-limit credit card."

He laughed. "Damn straight. I'd join you, just for the casino hot dogs."

Debbie grinned. "On the other hand, I think what we *ought* to do is very carefully climb down to this place I know: a nice sheltered spot under a rock overhang, about half a mile and three hundred feet down from here, right by that hidden trail. Since we haven't heard a trace of pursuit, I think we could chance a fire. On my way out of camp I liberated some beef jerky and a box of Jiffy, so if you've got a mess kit—"

"Happens I do."

"Cornbread and soggy warm jerky for breakfast, get all the way warm, maybe a nap, how's that sound? You bearing up okay?"

"Better than okay, I think. Let's go." He stretched. "If I'm too old for this stuff, I'm still too young to admit it."

Descending a steep spot wet with spray from the spring, he slid for an instant. She caught his arm, he found his balance, and he smiled his thanks. Her surprised smile in response felt like warm lotion on his heart.

# FIVE:
# SCHOLARS TAPPED TO FIND
# HIS NEW REMAINS

It wasn't Arnie's regular hangover: he hadn't had very much beer last night, he'd been up for hours this morning, and he'd had breakfast. Nonetheless he had a headache, queasy stomach, and painful clarity about the world's failings.

What failings?

He was lonely but he had friends; he was frustrated but Heather was listening, and once he told her about Aaron, she'd really listen. And a cool July morning in Pueblo beat the hell out of what he was used to in DC. Clear, bright, high-altitude sunlight made everything pop out of its background. Midmorning was pleasantly warm, not the searing dry heat of late afternoon.

And the world was healing. In March a clear sky had looked like a few drops of blue food coloring in a barrel of old dishwater. Now it was slate-blue again, on its way to real blue. Spring rains had washed a lot of soot out of the air and extinguished most of the fires in the old big cities, though snow might have to smother the last smolders.

*Next summer or the one after, the sky will be bluer than it's been in centuries.* The world was rewildernizing—silly Daybreaker word, but still, from the train coming up from Mota Elliptica, he'd seen buffalo and wild cattle. In thirty years something big with horns would rule the plains again.

*Hunh.* Another note to feed to James Hendrix, over in research. Flying over the Gunnison Valley, Bambi had sighted a herd of yaks. Paul Ferrier had reported flocks of emu in Oklahoma. At Castle Castro down in San Diego someone had found a dead baby kangaroo in a bean field. What had happened to all the imported animals? Were there lions or baboons breeding on the Great Plains, tigers in Louisiana, cobras in Florida?

How would the Daybreakers feel about that? Evolution taking its course, the blasphemous mistreatment of Gaia redeemed into a new kind of wilderness? Or a gigantic replay of dogs on the Pacific islands and kudzu in North America? He could build either narrative, using Daybreaker core signs—that was an intriguing idea. *If I were in Daybreak, and I wanted to embrace the hybrid wilderness—*

*We'll embrace it,* he realized. They'll definitely embrace anything that makes it tougher for human beings.

. . .

Heather waddled in, less than a month to go, over six feet tall, carrying low and all in one place, and Arnie blocked a smile at her exasperated expression—the lifelong athlete having lost control of her body.

She began with the obligatory platitudes, welcoming Arnie back, sorry for the losses at Mota Elliptica, shall not have died in vain, blah blah. Everyone else on the RRC Board looked at Arnie, faking polite concern.

Heather switched to the good news: Bambi Castro had flown her Stearman to Baker City last night, and after extensive checkout and decontamination, it appeared that the plane was fine. "So is Bambi," Heather added.

*Too bad Trish isn't,* Arnie thought.

Larry Mensche had found his daughter. She'd been living as a tribal, and she wanted to come in to the RRC, and apparently the tribe she belonged to had been heavily Daybreaker. "So you'll be getting another cooperative interview subject, Arnie, and she's had a real different encounter with Daybreak."

Well, that *was* good news; he couldn't help grinning. "How soon does she get here?"

Heather's scowl of frustration deepened. "She and Larry didn't fly out

with Quattro Larsen on the Gooney Express and they didn't walk out with
the President's Own Rangers. They're off doing one of those peculiar missions Larry defines for himself."

Arnie said, "Admittedly he doesn't accept direction much, but I think
what he's doing is valuable."

Heather's face flashed brief annoyance. "I didn't say what Larry is doing
is not valuable. I just don't understand it. If you can tell me what Larry is
doing up there in the woods, I'd be grateful. I thought he was looking for
his daughter and cut him slack for that, but apparently that was only part
of it."

Arnie nodded. "Well, I haven't spoken with him in two months, but I've
read his reports. You want my guess?"

"Sure, what the hell. It's got to be better than my paranoid suspicions."

"I think it will be. The tribes are an astonishing phenomenon, Heather.
Think about it. A year ago we were cruising toward a routine election in a
dull, prosperous USA; the worst we had to think about was maybe a fresh
terrorist strike like 9/11, the *Roosevelt*, or the Fed bombing. All the people
who are in the tribes now were mostly ordinary citizens; they were younger
than average, and they listened to a couple musicians and bands more than
other people did, but they weren't *significantly* different from the people you
saw at work or in the house next door. Sometime after October 28th—eight
months, Heather, that's all—they turned into the murdering crazy barbarians we all know and love today.

"Everything else that's originated since Daybreak had deep roots in pre-
Daybreak society—I mean, how could it be otherwise, in just eight months?
The Provisional Constitutional Government is really just the liberal-
Democrat think tanks running a rump government in the old Democratic
Party bastion of the Northwest. The fundamentalist churches and the Army
had been drawing on the same demographics for so long that the Temporary National Government is just those two wings of the old Republicans,
in *their* most reliable area. The Post Raptural Church is the fundamentalists
who've been preparing for the End Times for four generations, playing them
out. The Castles were there from the first Obama Administration on; they
were just eccentric right-wingers in fortified houses, harboring romantic
notions, until society collapsed around them and they started turning into
feudal lords—which was another idea that was already around. Even we,

the RRC itself, are just a bunch of intelligence, law enforcement, research, and PR bureaucrats trying to do our jobs after Daybreak. Our technical centers grew up from pre-Daybreak hobbyists who wanted to preserve disappearing arts like steam railroads, blacksmithing, and celestial navigation. You see? Everything we see around us grew out of something that was there for decades before Daybreak.

"But the tribes are—well? What are they? What were they before Daybreak?"

Heather's head was cocked to the side. "You sound like you don't know."

"I don't. But I *want* to know, because I think they are a major clue to Daybreak. Where they came from, how they cropped up so fast, who they really are, everything—I think that's one of the places where we might be able to understand Daybreak. So I want to know all about them—and so does Larry Mensche. That's what he's doing out there—pursuing the most important issue he knows about, with you or without you."

"Hunh. Well, Larry's reports do read more like ethnography or anthropology than like military intel or law enforcement reports. And every time I'm forced to look at the tribal problem, it turns out to be much bigger than I'd thought." She yawned and stretched. "We have a bunch of routine Board business to clear here, quickly, unless everyone would like to spend hours discussing budget points and policies?" She beamed at how hard all of them shook their heads. "Knew I could count on you all. Arnie, you and I are having lunch, on the government's nickel, this afternoon, and you are going to do your damnedest to make me see things the way you and Larry do, and I'll help."


**40 MINUTES LATER. PUEBLO, COLORADO. 12:30 PM MST. SATURDAY, JULY 19, 2025.**

Since Sumer, the smart and the powerful have always met over food, somewhere discreet, where they can stretch out comfortably and decide what the rest of the world ought to do. Elizabeth I's ministers traded barbs at the Mermaid; the Founding Fathers argued more freely in the City Tavern than in Independence Hall; atom bomb scientists drank at the Owl. When Washington DC still existed, the too-late decision to expand the

Daybreak investigation had been taken in a hole-in-the-wall Cambodian diner belonging to Allie Sok Banh's uncle.

Nowadays, in Pueblo, Johanna's What There Is was the place to be well-fed and not overheard.

Johanna charged by the seat and served family style. She didn't attempt a menu—she couldn't depend on having any particular ingredient, and the big wood stove and barbecue grill in her improvised backyard cookshed were really only adequate for preparing one large common meal.

Heather and Arnie had barely taken their seats in the Mountain View Room—the most isolated room on the third floor of Johanna's—when Johanna herself brought in a crisp field-green salad surrounding a chilled trout loaf, and a side of elk ragout over polenta.

It would have been blasphemy to talk business over such a lunch. When they had eaten all of it, Heather said, "Arnie, my problem is when I listen to you, I'm always saying, *Yes, sure, the way to get good, balanced, accurate knowledge of anything is to pursue it for its own sake*, but when I'm on the radio for any length of time with Cam in Athens, or with Graham in Olympia, I find myself thinking, *Right, we're losing a war here and Arnie's doing pure science instead of figuring out what to hit and how*. And I don't like being a creature of whatever I heard last. I *think* you are right. Can you help me settle firmly into your side?"

"I can try. I wish I knew if it even *is* a war. Originally I thought it wasn't—I thought Daybreak was more like a storm than an invasion—and then I thought that it was, because a storm doesn't pick its targets—and now I think Daybreak is just really hard on analogies; it doesn't behave like anything else, it's just Daybreak. We won't understand anything about it till we admit there's never been anything like it before. But I do understand that we won't get it, either, if Daybreak takes the world down into a dark age while we're still trying to understand. We need to know enough to win, soon enough to use it, and right now we don't even know what it would mean to know that."

"You could be more reassuring."

"Yeah, but you wanted the truth, as I see it."

"I did." Heather brought her feet up onto the couch where she'd half-sat during the meal. "Oh, man, Johanna knows how to make a room comfortable." She groaned. "I really wish I could wait to think about this till after

I get my body back, but that's way too long to wait. So, you think the tribes are the key to . . . well, what *are* they the key to?"

Arnie spread his hands. "Maybe just to finding the right question. But as for your situation with Larry—look, Heather, this is a gift, not a problem. You've got a shrewd investigator who knows the territory, and who wants to look into it. And I can't show you graphs—"

"I don't need'em, Arn, I believe in your intuition much more than you do. If you say we have to know about the tribes, then we have to know about the tribes, and I'll declare that to be Larry's main mission. The biggest problem I see is that whenever he gets back with Debbie, he might want to spend some time getting reacquainted, I would think, and frankly, as much time as he's spent in the woods since December, he's got to be *tired*. And I don't think I have anyone more entitled to a vacation if he asks for one."

Arnie leaned back, thinking. "Well, we need way more than one investigator on the job, anyway, if we want results in time to use them. And though we've learned so much from Larry's exploring the Inland Northwest, that's kind of like looking under the streetlight for the quarter you dropped in the alley, because the light is better. I think we could learn more from penetrating the Lost Quarter, ideally from a traverse of it."

"If anybody ever came back after going in," Heather said.

"Oh yeah," Arnie said. "Oh yeah, it would definitely depend on that."

"Apart from some Army scouts who never get ten miles north of the boundary rivers, has anyone come back yet?"

"Not really." Arnie was looking down at the table. "Two bodies have floated downstream on the Wabash, and one on the James." He dragged some of the water from around his glass into a long thin line. "Heather, it's got to be done, it's dangerous, and it needs to be soon."

"Yeah." She sighed. "All right. I've got an agent that was going to go out to Pale Bluff, just to see how he did on a milk run. He was going to leave late next week anyway. He'll be about twenty miles from where the Lost Quarter starts, by the nearest approach. Ex–Army ranger, did mountain man re-creation, martial artist—"

"Is it Steve Ecco or Dan Samson?"

"Ecco. Is there a difference?"

"Not really. They're both my friends. And I just lost a friend to Daybreak, trying to find out how it works and what it thinks, and I don't know if I'm ready to lose another one."

Heather nodded slowly and sadly. "Someday, I hope, RRC will be big enough so that I don't know and like everyone who works for us. Till then, though, I'm always sending my friends into danger. One more time, Arn, is this the best way to find out what we need to know?"

He seemed to be looking at something a million miles away. "I don't know. I can't know. But it's our best guess, and if we don't take it, we might still be guessing when Daybreak burns the last book. Steve Ecco will be glad to get the assignment. I think he's afraid that he'll never get his chance to prove himself. And I like giving him the chance to do what he wants to do, but I don't want to lose another friend. I know you make harder decisions than that all the time, and I'm being selfish and silly."

"I'd say, just human."

"I just wish being human didn't have to be quite . . . so . . . human."

They talked about how life hurried on, and the friends that they had made and lost, for another hour.

He had walked all the way home in the glaring Colorado summer afternoon, and was checking the temperature of his solar hot water tank with the idea of a long hot shower, before he remembered that he still hadn't told Heather about Aaron.

*But I guess now I don't need to. The conversations with Aaron will give me insights I couldn't get any other way—in fact, yeah. What I extract from Aaron, I can use to plan Steve's mission, make sure he's safe and his mission's productive, and it will be much more believable coming from a guy like Ecco, and from first-hand observation, than it will be coming from my talking to a hippie in a blanket in the middle of the night. RRC will get independently verified information, and my friend will have a much better chance at succeeding at this mission, which is going to mean so much to him.*

*Besides, what the hell could I tell Heather now? That I just forgot?*

**THE NEXT DAY. PUEBLO, COLORADO. 3:20 PM MST.
SUNDAY, JULY 20, 2025.**

James Hendrix was lost in *Great Expectations*; Miss Havisham had just gone up in flames, and he was considering whether it might be worth opening the ice box for some cold roast chicken, and contemplating his tight waistband, trying not to let the idea prey on his mind. *Can't stay under fifty years old, much as I'd like to, but I'd sure like to stay under a hundred kilograms.*

He was far ahead of his students in the literacy class that he taught most nights of the week. But conditions were perfect for reading: on this bright, sunny day, opening one set of drapes and laying a mirror on the floor to reflect up to his white ceiling made lovely indirect reading light where he lay sprawled on his comfortable couch. Besides, he would rather be doing this than anything else in the world. Perhaps some cold water would help him ignore his stomach? He could—

The knock at the door was followed at once by scratching, so he knew it had to be Leslie Antonowicz and Wonder. He pretended to sigh at the interruption, but three seconds later as he opened the door, he was grinning.

"Come on, old man," Leslie said. "It's beautiful outside but I had radio room crypto duty all morning, so I couldn't get out to the fun part of the woods." By "fun part," he knew the tall, slim blonde woman meant some mixture of "scary" and "exhausting." She was beaming at him. "I saw that one window open and knew you were lying here in the dark turning into a library fossil. Now come on, you and Wonder both need a walk." Wonder, hearing his name, woofed once; he was a shepherd-husky cross—James always said, *crossed with a moose.*

"Just so you don't expect us to use the same trees," James said, pulling his boots on.

The morning's rain had left the air damp and cool, and the sunlight since hadn't warmed things much; down by the rain-swollen Arkansas River, they followed the trail away from town, watching Wonder run back and forth and smell everything. Friends from long before Daybreak, they didn't have to talk; James knew that Leslie usually didn't want to spend her weekends in his indolent company, so there must be something on her mind, and she knew she could take as long as she wanted about getting around to it.

He wanted to watch for the moment when she'd say something, but that was too much like watching her all the time, and he didn't feel free to do that: years ago he'd let himself get fascinated by her grace, by the big eyes and high cheekbones, and by her lithe, muscular body, until awkwardly, angrily, she'd told him it was creepy. So he looked at the sky and the river and enjoyed her nearness.

After a while, she said, "Last night, when I was walking home from Dell's Brew, something just slightly weird happened." After a few more steps she said, "Arnie Yang asked me to walk him home."

He fought down the twinge of jealousy; Arnie was their boss and close to Leslie's age. Word had it that the girl he was courting at Mota Elliptica had died in the tribal raid there. He'd long suspected Leslie told him more about her love life than she really wanted to, just to keep him from developing hopes again, and was sorry she had to do that.

She still hadn't spoken, and he was calm now. *Keep it light.* "It's not *that* unusual for a man to ask you to go home with him."

"No, it's not, you dirty old man, but what was really unusual was, he just wanted me to *walk* with him. Expressed no interest in having me come inside. Really didn't talk much, either. Now, since I always take Wonder when I go to Dell's, it wasn't unreasonably dangerous—after we dropped Arnie off we went on home, me and the mutt, no problems on the way and for part of it we walked along with the watch, anyway. But . . . well, everyone's heard how brave Arnie was in the battle at Mota Elliptica, and everyone knows he's pretty good with those double knives he carries. If anything, I should've been asking him to walk *me* home."

"Maybe he's just shy or got cold feet."

"No, I'm sure he wasn't trying to hit on me, James, because I have a pretty good sense of that, and because he didn't hang around me at the bar before, and he didn't ask like a guy who was trying to find company for the night."

"Hunh. What did he ask like?"

"Well, that's the weird part I wanted to talk to you about. He asked like a guy who was really scared. At least that was my first impression. But if you're bringing along backup because you're afraid of something, don't you tell the backup what it is?"

"Well, I would. Maybe Arnie is weird."

"Definitely Arnie is weird. I've just never seen him weird this way before—really, he was terrified. But he didn't tell me what of. Do you know anything about him?"

"Just what I know from working with him. I archived his report on the Battle of Mota Elliptica yesterday afternoon, but it was more or less a normal action report. It's a mystery to me, too."

They walked for another hour and a half, and then James fixed them a light supper before Leslie went home, well before sundown because she had early morning duties. He watched the tall, strong girl and the big dog till they went out of sight around a building, then adjusted his mirror to catch the last hour of sunlight, and returned to *Great Expectations*.


## 2 DAYS LATER. PUEBLO, COLORADO. 10:15 PM MST. MONDAY, JULY 21, 2025.

Tonight was starting out like Stephen Ecco's favorite books and daydreams did. Heather O'Grainne's note, delivered in a neat pocket-drop by Patrick, had asked for a night meeting and specified "tell no one you are coming." Even if it was Heather, not M or Wild Bill Donovan, and the organization was the Reconstruction Research Center, not MI6 or Mosby's Raiders, still, it was a secret night meeting straight out of his fifteen-year-old self's fantasies.

Central Pueblo was inhabited, but it was already dark; candles and lamp oil were expensive, and nowadays people rose early. He saw the watch only once, from more than a mile away.

Knowing himself too well, he tried to fight down his excitement, not wanting the sheer romance to affect the mission. *Sure hope it* is *a mission or I'm gonna feel like a total fool with a headful of dreams. Which ain't exactly unfamiliar.*

Something moved.

He turned, center low, body neutral—and laughed. A gigantic possum scuttled across the road. *You could be a little more romantic, dude. But then I bet you're thinkin', "You could be droppin' a little more food, dude."*

The guard nodded and let Ecco pass. He ascended the dark stairs in the old courthouse; the only open doorway glowed with candlelight.

"Steve, thanks for coming." Heather sat in an armchair with her feet propped up on a desk. "I'm claiming pregnant lady privilege and not getting up; Arnie will show you what's up and then we'll talk about what we need you to do.

Arnie Yang had laid out maps on an old picnic table; standing over it with a pointer, he looked like he was running some weird casino game. On the tabletop, sheets of drafting vellum covered topo maps of southern Illinois and Indiana. Pale Bluff was near the lower left corner of the map, and the upper right just reached to Fort Wayne. A swarm of different marks gathered on the left of the Wabash; penciled lines intersected in the Palestine/Warsaw area and just east of Bloomington. Bridges on the Wabash and the Tippecanoe were tagged with bits of construction paper.

"It looks like you want me to go some beyond Pale Bluff?"

"We sure do," Heather said.

"And come back alive," Arnie said. "*That's* the tough part. There is something real bad happening east of the Wabash and the Tippecanoe, and north of the Ohio; that lobe of the Lost Quarter is much more lost than it was even two months ago, and we can't find out what's happening." His strong, thin fingers walked like dividers down the line of the Wabash, tapping black arrows that pointed across the river. "Stations across the Wabash stopped reporting around mid-May. The flow of refugees dried up by early June. Since then, five different local governments have tried to send someone over onto the left bank of the Wabash, plus these two attempts to cross the Tippecanoe. Every mission disappeared completely, and those were all local guys that knew the territory and had some background. One was a force of four guys.

"But this one—we're not supposed to know about it, but we have a source in the TNG's Defense Department down in Athens. Three weeks ago the TNG's Department of Intelligence sent a team of six Rangers across here"—he tapped a black arrow south of Terre Haute—"and they disappeared with no trace. One of them, too decayed for the pathologist to determine how he died, was found floating dead in the Wabash three days ago."

Ecco tried to look imperturbable while his heart thumped. "And things are so bad over there, they think, that they'll lose that many men trying to find out?"

Arnie's finger traced out the arc of red crosses that paralleled the Wabash.

"Assassinations since April: twenty-two. Town constables, militia officers, sheriffs, mayors, one very diligent postmaster—anybody who was making things work on our side of the Wabash. The seven black circles are the four towns—villages really, none of them had more than two hundred people— that were burned out, and the three Castles. Nineteen black squares mark farms where the family was killed and the house burned. All that's since April first. A few of them might have been Provi or Temper partisans burning each other out, or plain old bandits. But this looks much more to me like we have an enemy on the other side of the Wabash, and it doesn't plan to stay there. Right now the thing we need most is *information*. We need you to see things, figure out what's going on, understand it all—and most of all, *bring it back*."

Ecco nodded, made serious by Arnie's evident passion. "I understand the mission."

Heather said, "Well, we can't define what you should look for, exactly, or where you should look for it. We know *nothing* once you get any distance north or east of Pale Bluff. If it's too hot south of Terre Haute, head north, maybe try crossing the Tippecanoe. And bring back what you see. That's the most important thing on this mission. Don't be a brave lion; what we need is a perceptive weasel."

"Got it."

Arnie said, "Now, this might or might not come up. We're making a guess that the Lost Quarter is nearly hollow—most of the tribes are right up near the edge, where they can live by looting civilization. We're basing that partly on the photos from the surviving Navy reconnaissance planes, which we can't fly nearly often enough now, and partly just on the fact that so much of the Lost Quarter was a radioactive dead zone for months, so it doesn't seem like there could be enough there to keep any sizable number of people alive. So our guess is there's a tough outside and an empty inside. If it turns out we're right, then just a few miles past the border you might find it much easier and safer to travel than it was getting in. So here's something I'd like you to look into *if*—and *only* if—it looks like we're right about that." His fingers traced many pencil lines on the vellum. "Our direction-finding operation has gotten fixes on two stations broadcasting in a code that's not ours, or either Federal government, or any Castle's; all these bearing lines crisscross in these two small areas. We think this one near Bloomington is just a relay or a subHQ: it only broadcasts occasionally, usually after the other one does but not every time. When it does broadcast, it broadcasts for about as long as the first station did.

"The really active transmitter, the one that seems to start conversations, both with Bloomington and with other stations in the Lost Quarter, is this one, between Warsaw and Palestine, Indiana." He laid down a few photographs. "These air photos from February show nothing in Warsaw or Palestine, but this one from April looks like dirt ramparts and walls under construction. So if by any chance, once you're over the Wabash and you've evaded whatever has already cost twenty lives, if you need something to go take a look at, this might be something to look at."

"But you're really figuring I should just get in far enough to see what stopped the others, and then come back?" Ecco tried for a laconic drawl, but the more he looked at that map, the more his heart hammered and his stomach sank.

"Yeah," Heather said. "Arnie is just making sure that if you get a really lucky break it won't go to waste. You remember your Rogers' Rangers rules, the bastard version?"

" 'Don't take no chances you don't have to'? You bet. Just by going on this trip, I've about used up my luck."

"Right answer." Heather nodded to Arnie. "I see why you said to send this guy."

"I want him back," Arnie said. "We've got beer to drink and waitresses to hustle." The two men shook hands; Arnie added, "No kidding. I recommended sending you for a whole long list of good reasons. Make sure you come back!"

"Got it," Ecco said. "And thanks for giving me the break; I wanted a mission like this."

After he left, Heather said, "Is he crazy or what, to want this kind of mission?"

Arnie shrugged. "He wants to be the kind of man who can do it. Men all have dreams about what kind of guy they'd like to be—usually the kind of guy that can do something. It keeps you going when nothing else will, sometimes." He rolled up the maps. "I myself want to be the kind of guy who hangs around with tough manly types. Why do you think I always come right over when *you* call, boss?"

Heather stuck her tongue out and made the raspberry noise.

. . .

On his way home, Ecco kept to the centers of the dark streets. The high, dark haze, the floating ashes of burned civilization, dimmed the waning moonlight more than usual. That was fine with Ecco. Nowadays, the moon was enemy territory; he couldn't shake the feeling that if he could see it, it could see him.

## ABOUT AN HOUR LATER. PUEBLO, COLORADO. 12:15 AM MST. TUESDAY, JULY 22, 2025.

The moon was still low in the sky and dim. Darkness wrapped the old, empty tract houses in monochrome shadow; not just a ghost town, but the ghost of a town.

Arnie wished he'd asked Ecco to walk with him. *We could have gone over mission details, and I could've had somebody to eat late supper with.*

Or he could have just taken a house close to the center of the city in the first place. *I'd already be home. Why did I act like a guy who wanted to be lonely?*

He could see the watch's lantern glinting half a mile away. *I could run and join them and just stay with them till they passed my house. Lots of people do that.* But the time to have done that would have been to catch them on Main, in front of the courthouse; now, they'd wonder what had frightened him. They might ask. What could he say?

Deep breath. Walk and breathe like you're going to fight; if it turns out you are, it's one less thing to worry about, and if not, it calms and clears the—

"Doctor Yang. Doctor Yang, doctus in the doctrine, the indoctrinated doctor."

Arnie spun one step backward into the space he'd been about to walk into, cross-drew his knives and held them at ready. "I've been expecting you."

Teeth gleamed in the dark under the blanket; the eyes were black blobs around the greasy promontory of the nose. "Expecting to stab me?"

"If necessary." Arnie shifted his weight for a better stance.

"Now, whatever happened to that civilized old academic world where everyone took the time to express mutual respect, and dallied a while in chat, and listened patiently to each other before entering into the actual business at hand, Doctor? Shouldn't we be sipping sherry and considering—"

"Manners and respect are products of enough people having enough time and comfort; you are the ones who put an end to that."

Aaron slowly, loudly applauded him. He was the only thing moving or making a sound in the oblong shadows of the houses and the splintered and sliced patterns of dingy moonlight. "You are thinking of holding me and shouting for the watch."

Arnie shrugged. "Why not?"

"Because if you don't, you might get three more questions answered. Whereas if you do capture me, you have to hope my nervous system is no more programmed than Ysabel's was, so I have seizures only about as bad, and that my heart and arteries are in no worse shape than hers, so that I don't have a fatal stroke or heart attack."

"I don't have to hope that hard. I'm thinking about stabbing you." Arnie shifted his weight and let his rear foot rise, extending it in front of him and setting it down. About four more steps would close the gap. "But I would like your answers to some questions."

"What is your first question?"

"What do you do, now, when you have doubts about Daybreak?"

"Daybreak forgives me because I am so powerless, and I let Daybreak fill my mind, so that I can go on and do the work."

Arnie advanced a step; he wondered if weapons were trained on him in the dark. An arrow or a spear out of nowhere . . . but one lunge, tackle him, hold him down, capture a Daybreaker, think how people would look up to him, just one leap—

Teeth showed under the blanket again, and the spots of the eyes narrowed. "Exchange, Doctor Yang. Have you told your owners that you're talking to me yet?"

Arnie swallowed hard; the question was shrewder than it looked, for either he'd have to say "yes," and be led along; or "no," and admit that he was conspiring with Aaron. *Or I might* . . . "I've told them exactly as much as I think they should know; does that make them my owners, or me theirs?"

"Ownership is always an error. Now your question."

Another step brought Arnie close enough to spring, but Aaron was cooperating . . . but, dammit. He couldn't think of what he intended to ask Aaron. He stalled with, "What is the purpose of Daybreak?"

"Purpose is so human, and therefore useless, of no value, a shame. Gophers dig; they don't calculate angles of repose around their burrows. Geese fly; they don't do celestial navigation. We do not need to know the relative marginal propensities to consume of the grasshopper and the ant. Daybreak will free them from human imputation, which makes all things dirty; to the pure, all things are purposeless. No thinky-thinks, no wordy-words, no math, no meaning, no purpose." When had he closed the distance? How did his hands now press down on Arnie's wrists, lowering the knives? "Exchange. My question. Mister Ecco's mission has changed and he is going to the Northwest."

*Right, that's the wrong direction, I can just say yes*—Arnie's head was turning slowly, indicating no.

"Going northeast."

Arnie tried to keep his head still, but he had an eerie sense that Aaron was reading his thought: *don't nod, don't nod, for God's sake don't nod.*

"Going farther east, crossing the Wabash?"

*Don't nod.* "Exchange," Arnie croaked. His hands were down by his sides where Aaron had pressed them. They were face-to-face; Arnie could smell the dirty blanket and the foul breath.

"Ask."

"What are you doing?"

"Daybreak only *does* till day is broken. After that Daybreak does not *do*. Daybreak *is*. I won't take my final turn of exchange now; you will owe it to me."

Arnie was alone on the street. In the distance, dogs and coyotes howled, the sharp yips mixing with the deep bellow of some hound; closer, he could hear the clatter of the watch, with all the gear hanging from their belts and harnesses; closest of all, the sound of the last breath of night wind rustling the leaves of a cottonwood.

Miserably tired, he headed home, resheathing his knives, his mind all on bed, reminding himself to record this in his journal, fighting off the question *Record what?*

## 2 DAYS LATER. CAMP OF THE PEOPLE OF GAIA'S DAWN, IN THE FORMER HELLS CANYON NATIONAL RECREATIONAL PARK. 9:30 PM PST. THURSDAY, JULY 24, 2025.

It had been impossible to conceal that Larry was a Fed—"Dad, you'd have better luck trying to pass yourself off as Sasquatch"—so their story was that Debbie had converted him to Gaia's Dawn while they were both being held by the Blue Morning People, and then the two of them had escaped during the Federal raid.

Tonight he would see *The Play of Daybreak*, the last part of what she wanted him to witness. The tribe performed it every Thursday; this was to be the 483rd performance by the People of Gaia's Dawn.

"But—," he started to say, and shut his mouth, angry with himself for that microbreak in cover.

"Yeah, I know, it's a lot of work, but it's really important," Debbie said, giving him cover. The fast-calculation part of his brain had been about to object that that would have had the first performance on April 28, 2016—more than eight years before Daybreak day, and of course the People of Gaia's Dawn were much newer than that. *So even though they've only been here since mid-February, when Debbie was a Founder, they're already claiming a much longer pedigree.*

Debbie's hand found his under the table and squeezed,

**u wil c**

**smile n stay very cool**

while she explained, "*The Play of Daybreak* is set up so the whole tribe have parts in it—you'll have a part next week—but there's only a few on stage at a time, and while we're not in it, we watch. Since I've only been back for one day, my part has three simple lines, and they'll steer me through it. Otherwise you and I can watch together."

The communal evening meal was a small chunk of unidentified meat and a fist-sized pile of wild greens with some roots and berries. With their current level of survival skills, he guessed around a third of the tribe might make it through the winter, and they'd lose all the kids under five.

At full dark, two big fires burned brightly on each end of the playing area, a flat grassless space backed by a low, crumbling rock cliff. The tribe's dozen slaves carried out full-length mirrors and set them up on lashed-stick frames to mask the fires and reflect the light into the sandy playing area. The reflected firelight did not quite reach the cliffs except when a fire flared up; players spoke before a dark space where rocks or bushes occasionally swam briefly into being, like a world striving to be created out of chaos.

Larry expected something like a small-town Founder's Pageant or a high-school production of *Our Town*. In the first few minutes, he realized he'd underestimated the power of conviction.

The story began with the Seven Misters: Mister Clock, Mister Gun, Mister Electron, Mister Atom, Mister Chemical, Mister Medicine, and the dark god who ruled them all, Mister Smart. Each of the actors, his face and chest painted to represent the power he spoke for, boasted that he feasted on the innocent creatures of the forest, the beautiful body of Mother Gaia, and human flesh, and finished by declaring, "But Mister Smart is smarter than all of us!"

Mister Medicine finished roaring that he would cut off everyone's body parts and poison all their blood, and finally Mister Smart moved into the light.

Mister Smart's head was a gigantic papier-mâché skull which extended a foot above his real head and reached down onto his chest. It was nearly all brain case with a tiny bespectacled and goateed face underneath. The body was naked except for a four-foot-long pink penis, probably a cardboard shipping tube, from which dangled two deflated basketballs. Mister Smart chanted on and on about his plan to rape Mother Gaia to death.

*Jesus, that's parodized from an old 50 Cent hip-hop piece I must've heard back when W was president,* Larry thought. *Too bad 50 Cent can't sue him for plagiarism or defamation or something.*

In the next scene, Gaia despaired and the six Mizzes vowed to die defending her. Larry thought Miz Ocean was pretty cute but Miz Desert had the best voice. The six Mizzes plotted to seduce the human, temporal servants of the Misters. Each Mister apparently had a human being who was his Number One Guy; the Mizzes were going to take them all out for "fun in the bushes," as Miz Prairie declared, "before the Misters exterminate all vegetation." That must have been the comic relief because people laughed.

The next dance and song was, in Larry's lowbrow opinion, the fun part of the evening. *I'm sure that movie critic I used to date would use words like* primal, erotic, transgressive, *and* body-positive, *but I'm just a lowly Fed so I would say this is one great dirty show. If I had to live out in the woods pretending to be an Indian or a hippie,* this *would definitely be the high point of* my *week.*

Each of the six human servants awoke the morning after the seduction to the weeping of the Miz, who then took the man or woman to meet Mother Gaia, before whom the servant fell down in adoration. When all six were in full adoration, Mother Gaia raised them up to form Daybreak, and her lover, Brother Sun, came to teach them how to make weapons for the Daybreak to come.

The servants of Mister Chemical, Mister Clock, Mister Gun, and Mister Electron danced with each other and copulated with various Mizzes to bring forth the Nanoswarm, a chorus of men costumed in lumpy gray and white rags. Mister Chemical's servant teamed up with Mister Medicine's servant to bring forth the thousand-headed Biotes, a chorus of women sharing one vast blanket-garment, with just their green-painted faces poking out. Debbie was one, and Larry thought it was her best work since *The Three Billy Goats Gruff* in second grade.

The Biotes vowed to kill the petroleum and all that came from it, the Whole Plaztatic World, by revealing its true nature and making it rot away into filth, and change it to nourishing food for all of Mother Gaia's children.

*Hunh. Well, I guess if you're planning that your grandchildren will be cavemen, that'll explain biotes to them.*

Finally, Mister Atom's servant came forward and proclaimed himself the protector of all. He would hurl eight mighty nuclear blows against the centers of the Plaztatic World. The first two would go amiss and leave California, the heart and center of Plaztatic World, as a broken and wounded place, but not destroy it to its utmost atoms, because so many good people lived there.

*Holy crap,* Larry thought. *That's why they backdated the tribe's origins and claimed performances started so much earlier; in a few years this'll be a successful prophecy.*

Then, Mister Atom's servant proclaimed, the next five nuclear weapons would be overwhelming and would smash down the Plaztatic World, but then in her compassion, Mother Gaia would choose to spare people of color in the Southern Hemisphere, so the fizzling of the Buenos Aires bomb would be a sign that she would never wholly sweep the face of the Earth again. *The rainbow in the Noah story,* Larry thought. *"I love you so much that you really better not piss me off."*

The actors and the crowd went into a frenzied chant of *so it was foretold, so it was to be, so it was, so we shall tell it,* over and over, as the drums built up to a mighty crescendo and the dancers formed a circle around the Servant of Mister Atom.

*If they win, soon no one will know that they made the "prophecy" up after the event. Anyone can clearly see California isn't in great shape but it wasn't completely destroyed; five huge bombs did go off; and the one in Buenos Aires fizzled, leaving Argentina basically okay. Just because Mother Gaia was such a sweet chick. Or maybe she just loved to tango.*

The dance finished. The servant of Mister Atom proclaimed that he would fly to the moon, and from there, when he saw the Plaztatic World trying to come back into Mother Gaia's sacred sphere, he would hurl his bolts against it. He would depend upon the People of Gaia's Dawn to help him to watch, and sometimes to fight and die for Mother Gaia when he told them it was necessary.

*Hunh.*

No mistaking it. It claimed that they talked and worked with the Daybreak robot, or base, or whatever it was, on the moon. *Thunderbolts from the moon* wasn't even a bad description for the caveman-grandchildren.

The rest of the play was a lengthy singing-and-dancing-and-fighting number. The servants and the Mizzes defeated the Misters with the help of Nanoswarm and Biotes. Mister Smart's dick-and-balls prop was removed and ceremoniously paraded around while he cried out at the loss. Gaia buried him alive (because he could not be killed) and all the servants vowed to sit eternal vigils at Mister Smart's tomb against his rising.

In a big erotic dance number, the Mizzes rewarded the servants by making children with them—Larry thought that the former servant of Mister Chemical, who got Miz Ocean, got one hell of a good deal. The unfortunate servant of Mister Atom had to be childless, so he said farewell, charging the People of Gaia's Dawn with reducing the remaining population of the Earth to about ten million before ascending the ladder into the sky. *I suspect that's some cousin of the Indian Rope Trick, but it sure works well at a distance, by firelight.*

This was the cue for the last big number, a dancing demonstration about how there were tens, and tens of tens, and tens of tens of tens, up finally to $8 \times 10^9$, the population before Daybreak, which had been cut down to $2 \times 10^9$, which now must be reduced to $10^7$.

*Jesus god. They've killed three-quarters of the people who were alive this time last year and the Servant of Mister Atom just told them to kill 199 out of every 200 that are left.*

In all the celebratory cheering and whooping, Larry grasped Debbie's arm and squeezed:

*u right*

She squeezed back:

*we go now*

He squeezed *C*.

Drifting through the crowd, agreeing with everyone who stopped them to say that it gave you so much to think about, they passed into the darkness outside the camp, and jogged away as quickly and quietly as they could. They were less than halfway up the ridge when they heard the angry cries behind them, and ran as if all hell were at their heels.

# SIX:
# THE PRESIDENT CAME BY

General Jeffrey Grayson leaned across Cameron Nguyen-Peters's desk and forced himself not to shout; the sound that emerged from Grayson's clamped throat was a strained, half-voiced whisper. "You have apparently forgotten that you are not a king. You can't just dissolve the legislature—"

"This is not a dissolution because I'm neither calling a new election nor appointing replacements. And the Board of Advisors to the NCCC of the Temporary National Government is not a legislature. It makes no laws and its votes are binding only on its internal organization. So the man who is not a king is not dissolving the body that is not a legislature. What are you so upset about, General Grayson?"

"Some people will say this looks like the start of a dictatorship."

"That's the safest prediction in American politics, whenever any part of the government does anything. Look, if it hasn't occurred to you, General, in 2026 there will be full national elections, in at least our territory, Provi territory, and the states that haven't committed firmly to either side. If we are shrewd, diplomatic, and lucky, we might be able to get California and Manbrookstat, and maybe even Hawaii, to come in too. Do you remember your oath, General?"

"I take my oath very seriously."

"But do you remember it? Because in 2026, if we don't screw things up—

and the PCG doesn't—we are going to put the Constitution back into force. That's what your oath said, preserve, protect, and defend—"

Grayson glowered at him. "I don't need a review—"

"I disagree, but I'll refrain from further lecture. Meanwhile, go home early for the weekend, along with the other officers."

"Along with the—"

"Naturally we have to keep the frontier with the tribes on alert, but otherwise, General, being realistic, the Provis are not going to attack us, at least not soon; the Jamaicans or the Cubans or whoever are not going to land in the Gulf and the Mexican government barely has one functional regiment, which spends all its time and effort guarding their alleged government at Veracruz. So there's a low risk of attack, and because it's been a long time since people had time off, I issued a large number of leaves for the weekend, particularly to commanding officers in safe areas. Some of them went on leave early this morning and will be back Sunday night; some will go on leave this evening for a Monday night return."

The general's face was slack at the realization. "You've neutered the Army."

"Nonsense. Every facility is functional and has proper command— admittedly they are junior officers, aware they lack authority to jump into anything big on their own hook, but in a sudden attack or emergency, they'd show the required initiative. Excellent status for an army on standby. Why, General, were you expecting an invasion? a rebellion? a coup?"

Grayson opened his mouth but nothing came out.

Cam sat forward, folding his hands over each other, and said softly, "Now, listen closely. I am giving *you* a leave from now till noon Tuesday. Out of my own pocket, in fact, I've set you up in a nice bed-and-breakfast in Savannah, and I've taken the liberty of securing train tickets for you and Jenny. She's already packing; just go home, get into your civvies, and go spend a few days. It's on me, it's a bribe, and I want you to take it like a sensible fellow—even if you decide later you can't go anywhere with me politically. We all might as well cool off, and we can be unpleasant later if you wish."

Grayson stood stock-still and said, "And you already set it up with Jenny?"

"Yes I did. You wouldn't want to disappoint her."

Grayson's face showed how potent that threat actually was. Beaten for the moment, he shrugged. "We'll talk more next week."

"Or sometime soon," Cameron said. "You are still my deputy and I still want you to keep that position. Now quit thinking about politics, take your pretty girl away for the weekend, and relax as much as you can. I don't want to have to make that an order."

**40 MINUTES LATER. ATHENS, TNG DISTRICT. 1:35 PM EST. FRIDAY, JULY 25, 2025.**

Grayson hadn't yet made up his mind about what he wanted to do, but when Jenny opened the door and she was wearing one of her "show me off" dresses, her hair brushed, and some of the precious cosmetics applied, he laughed and said, "I guess it's the decision of the household executive that we ought to accept the Natcon's bribe?"

"It is," she said, letting him in and standing on tiptoe to be kissed. "The men are harnessing the buggy and they'll bring it back for us—*and* give Thunder and Fireball full and proper care afterward—as you know perfectly well. So you get to drive me to the station, accompanied by two burly types who will move our luggage. I've packed your civilian clothes so that you will not be striding around Savannah in uniform, scaring people and starting rumors. And Daddy's at work on our response to Cameron's coup."

"Our?"

"You always tell me that a general is political but the Army is not, baby. So, our. You've got a political side, and it's the one Daddy's on."

He kissed her lightly. "What if we're ever on opposite sides?"

"Unthinkable, baby, but fortunately you have a whole weekend off from thinking, courtesy of the Natcon. I'm looking forward to this so much I'm almost grateful to the little turd."

## ABOUT THE SAME TIME. ATHENS, TNG DISTRICT. 2:15 PM EST. FRIDAY, JULY 25, 2025.

"Everyone else is celebrating," Cam said, coming in with a picnic basket, "and I need someone to celebrate with, so you're it. I know you don't drink so I brought along an amazing find: pre-Daybreak Perrier."

"Last for a long time," Phat said. "The spring is around on the Mediterranean side of France. Does anyone have any contact there at all?"

"*Discovery*'s first mission, next year, is to explore the north shore of the Med. But there hasn't been any radio contact since March and all the Argentine expedition is finding around the Med are tribes, and a few dug-in fortified settlements just barely hanging on. Somehow I doubt restoring the trade in Perrier will be a priority for a while." Cam set out the fresh sliced ham, bread, and sliced vegetables. "I also brought red wine. We are going to celebrate *avec des baguettes et du jambon et des crudités, l'eau gasseuse,* and of course *le vin tres ordinaire.* In honor of a place the world doesn't have anymore."

"Wow, you sure know how to throw a cheerful event, Cam." Nonetheless, Lyndon Phat held up his glass of Perrier, and clinked it with Cameron's glass of red wine. "To our billions of absent friends."

"Yeah." They dedicated themselves to the good food, and Cameron said, "I am having a thought that you will not approve of. I think I would like to let you out of jail."

"Like hell. If you let me go, I'm going to have to flee for my life—and the only place to flee to will be Olympia. And if they give me asylum, you'll have Civil War Two on your hands for sure."

"Would you be willing to reassume command of the Army and jail *me*? On grounds that I exceeded my authority by not putting Graham Weisbrod in as Acting President?"

"Well, it's a nice prison, as prisons go, Cam, but it's still a prison. Why are you so eager to move into it?"

"Because I've just slapped down the Post Rapturals and their allies in the Army, and given Grayson a political wedgie along the way. I'm guessing I've got a couple weeks before they hit back hard. And after due consideration, as a serious constitutionalist—and sometimes I feel like the last one in America—right now the God-Army-flag team here is proclaiming their loyalty to the Constitution like a rooster crowing that he's the best hen-impregnator in the county, but they're violating half or more of it. The Provis at least try to go through the forms; they're also doing things that were never envisioned in the Constitution, but my feeling is they're closer to the original intent. At least *they're* not trying to set up an established church, abolish the rights of defendants, or carve out huge exceptions to freedom of speech, press, and assembly. I wish the Provis weren't so loaded up with university types and career Civil Service, and that they had a keener sense of the possible, but their hearts are in a better place.

"So my thinking is this. You and I made a huge mistake. Me by not putting Graham in, and you by not kicking my ass out and putting Graham in. If we'd just stuck to our oaths, swallowed our doubts, and followed the rules, we'd have lived through our disagreements with Graham. He's a smart, persuasible guy, and we'd have brought him around to our side on anything crucial that we *were* right about. So . . . we broke it. Can we fix it?"

Phat leaned back, swishing the Perrier in his mouth, and swallowed, relishing it. "I guess we owe it to the absent friends. I think you've got reach out via Pueblo; you surely don't want Grayson and Whilmire to catch you talking to Olympia on a back channel, but they can't object to your working more closely with the RRC. Do you have a channel for contacting Heather O'Grainne?"

"Not yet, but I'm expecting an opportunity soon. Or maybe I should say my opportunity is expecting soon."

"Boo. We'll talk again, Cameron, but if you don't mind, since we can't accomplish much else just now, let's declare business concluded. I think we should just enjoy the food you've brought, especially since either of us might soon be strictly on jail food."

**THE NEXT DAY. PUEBLO, COLORADO. 12:15 PM MST. SATURDAY, JULY 26, 2025.**

"Remember how much business in DC used to turn around getting somewhere in time for reservations?" Heather asked Arnie, cheerfully, as she dragged herself over to her main worktable. "Well, we have'em at Johanna's, so we need to finish this quick. Wow, all those stairs are a *climb* in the heat."

"Enjoy heat while you can—the weather forecasters are saying this couple of weeks might be our only real summer, and what's coming is going to be like a volcano winter, cold, wet, and early. All the soot."

"Yeah, I know, and I intend to bitch about that when that happens, too. Right here—this is eyes-only stuff for me and my top analyst, and no matter how secure Johanna tries to keep her upper room, it can't be secure enough for *this* conversation."

Intrigued, Arnie joined her at the worktable. She laid out three single sheets of paper from a black folder. "Critical facts. Agents in TNG territory confirm that Cam handed weekend passes out like candy to base and fort commanders, and sent General Grayson out of town, just after dissolving the Board. Looks like he was afraid of a coup. Two, Cam communicated a request to Graham Weisbrod to discuss an earlier merger of the two governments, last night. So it looks like Cam is moving toward resolving the two-government problem by dissolving his own, and it also looks like he's scared that he won't be able to."

Arnie felt strangely numb and confused, as if he'd been told that nothing he was doing mattered, but he made himself say the expected thing: "That might be good news if he pulls it off."

"It might. But this morning, our highest placed agent in Athens—Red Dog—reported that the Post Raptural Church is gearing up for massive protests, and Red Dog thinks Cam might be in danger of being overthrown by a religious revolution, at least as much as he might be by a coup. Red Dog's super-deep source"—*as close as I will ever get to breathing the fact that Shorty Phat is reporting his conversations with Cam to us through Red Dog*—"and Red Dog himself recommend we move strongly to support Cameron. What's your take, Arnie?"

Arnie Yang froze in thought; there was nothing unusual about that, and given how complex the problem was, Heather preferred that he take his time. But when he finally spoke he said, "I guess you have to pay attention to Athens but I'm still really worried about the tribes, and I want to keep focusing on investigating Daybreak."

"Lobby me all through lunch about that and I'll not only listen, I might be persuaded, Arnie. But I really want your take on this. Should Red Dog approach Cam, try to set up a back channel alliance? There's a lot to gain, but if Red Dog is blown, the whole network could be rolled up. Come on, you are the best analyst I've got and my right hand. Analyze."

He looked down at the papers and said, "For some reason, I just can't seem to form a conclusion."

She gave him a full minute before she said, "Well, if that's really your answer—"

"Yeah, I guess it is."

At lunch, he talked of absolutely nothing but Daybreak, the tribes, and the need for further, deeper research.

That evening, as Heather played with her big chart, she wanted to concentrate on the tribal pathway, as Arnie had so emphasized, but her eyes kept drifting back to the tangled knot of yellow and red labeled TNG PARTICIPATES IN RESTORATION. Eight lines crossed and knotted there, and at each report from Red Dog, the number of possible bad outcomes seemed to double and the number of her options seemed to halve. *Could be worse,* she thought. *I could be where Cam is.* But the Natcon had been a friend for many years before, and she couldn't help thinking how much she'd rather have him here, safe, than there, in that bunched knot that looked to her, more and more, like a pit of snakes.

With a sigh, she moved and repinned the few things affected by her small amount of new information, looked at the rest, and could not think of anything to do but wait. *It's the other side's move, hon,* she remembered Dad saying, when he was teaching her checkers. *That's one thing you can never do anything about; they get a turn.*

**THE NEXT DAY. WAYNE CITY, WABASH (PCG) OR ILLINOIS (TNG). 10 AM CST. SUNDAY, JULY 27, 2025.**

Steve Ecco hadn't slept well on the train. He'd awakened every few minutes when something bumped or shuddered. After a quick breakfast of leftover Cold Fried Don't Ask, he splurged on some hot water and soap for a shave and a sponge bath, and put on the clean clothes he'd been saving. *I guess that's about as spruced up as I'm getting. At least I combed my hair.*

The platform at Wayne City was just a big slab of concrete with a frame and fabric roof, and Ecco was the only one who got off there. He didn't quite have time to look around before a tall, thin man, maybe thirty years old, stepped up onto the platform. He was dressed in the mix of deerskin, camo, and denim that tended to be popular among serious wilderness scouts like Larry Mensche; unlike Larry, he wore a large coonskin cap and the seams of his deerskin shirt were fringed. His shoes were low moccasins rather than Larry's heavy snake-highs. "Mister Ecco?" the man said, extending a hand that felt like rocks under rawhide.

"That's me."

"I'm Freddie Pranger. I'm s'pose to take you on over to Pale Bluff. It's a nice day and there hasn't been much bandit or tribal trouble lately, we'll walk it in maybe three hours, but you might want to visit the plumbing first."

Ecco hurried into the public restroom by the station. *Freddie Pranger, Jesus, they sent* Freddie Pranger *to pick me up.* Sure, part of Pranger's reputation was just because he was buddies with Carol May Kloster, the star reporter around here, but still . . . this was like going into San Antonio and being met by Travis, Bowie, or Crockett.

*And why should it matter how Freddie Pranger got to be famous, as long as he really is as good as they say?* He refastened his fly. *Buffalo Bill was nobody without Ned Buntline to report him.* Ecco breathed deeply once, feeling the hand of his inner, smarter, braver self resting on his shoulder, and to himself he said, with far more confidence than he felt, *Wanna be a legend, Steve Ecco, just like you've always dreamed? Here's where we start.*

### 2 DAYS LATER. ATHENS, TNG DISTRICT. 11:10 EST. TUESDAY, JULY 29, 2025.

As the train pulled into the station at Athens, Jeffrey Grayson rose from his seat, gaping at the crowded platform. "My God, there must be three hundred people out there."

"More than that," Jenny said. "Daddy promised me at least five hundred."

Grayson sat down with a thump; he was forever discovering, one more time, the rigorously practical mind that was part of the package with Jenny's pale blonde hair, big breasts, and constant adoring support. "He what? Were you—"

"Well, the family does have a house in Savannah, and Daddy went down there in another car on the same train we did. And then the next morning, you were getting a real good sleep for the first time in months, baby, and Daddy came by the hotel, and we went down to some early breakfast, and talked a little bit. That's all." She snuggled against him. "Just another enhancement to your career, baby."

"Did it have anything to do with the Post Raptural riots—"

"Those were *not* riots. *Daddy* would not have anything to *do* with a *riot*. Those were the people exercising their 'right peaceably to assemble for redress of grievances,' just like it says in the Constitution, honey."

"Quite a few local commanders would disagree. Especially the ones who were shot at."

"You see, that's the kind of media exaggeration—"

"That's from the *Weekly Insight*, honey, which is the Post Raptural paper, and the only legal one in Athens." He slipped his arm around her and said, "Jenny, I know your father is a politician with a backwards collar, and I know this is all part of ordinary life to you. And I'm doing my damnedest to learn to be a good politician besides being a good general. But every now and then you get way past me. I thought it was just some Post Raptural congregations throwing rocks and tantrums about Cam's coup—which unfortunately, under the rules, he had every right to pull—"

"There are rights and there are rights, baby. Haven't you thought about what I said about Tribulation? That even if Daybreak wasn't really the Rapture, so this isn't really Tribulation, this whole change is still doing the Lord's work? And you can't have more rights than you do when you're doing God's work. Now, the things you have to say to them are only that you understand their concerns, they should go home, and you'll be meeting with Cam. All those things are true. Just say them."

Before Grayson could emerge from his railroad car, militia troops had to clear a space on the platform; they helped him up onto an inverted crate, and that was the moment when he realized that like it or not, he would be giving a speech.

The crowd looked expectant, confused, afraid, angry—everything he could imagine. There weren't many signs—paint of any kind was still scarce and difficult to make—but there was one bedsheet banner painted with II SAMUEL 17:3.

"What's that verse?" he murmured to Jenny, who was standing next to him and holding his hand.

"Tell you later, baby, you have to talk to them now."

The way they were looking at him convinced him she was right. Remembering what she'd outlined, he said, "Look, everyone, this is really a surprise, I thought I was just coming back from vacation. But I'm glad to see all of you here, and I'm honored that you turned out for me. I share many of your concerns and I understand what you are worried about." (*Now* there *is a lie,* he thought.) "For right now, I'm going to ask you all to return to your homes, and to your daily lives, and wait patiently for news and developments. All of us love our country, all of us love our God, and all of us will work together to bring about the right course of action. I'll be meeting with Natcon Nguyen-Peters later this afternoon, and of course there are matters we'll have to discuss. For the moment, rest assured that your concerns have been heard."

The wild cheers mystified him even further, but Jenny said, "Baby, that was perfect, especially for spontaneous. Now just give'em a short prayer, be sure you end with Jesus, and send'em all home."

## 10 HOURS LATER. PULLMAN, WASHINGTON. 7:30 PM PST. TUESDAY, JULY 29, 2025.

Neville Jawarah was on the south wall, the dullest sector for a sentry in Pullman. The southeast gate took in at least a few refugees burned out by the tribals, fleeing along the old Lewis and Clark route, and some looters from Moscow. The west gate, at this time of day, would be almost busy, with the last few respectable traders coming in off the road; scammers and outlaws trying to pursue their prey; the inevitable, ubiquitous refugees looking for lost relatives; and a mix of spies pretending to be traders, crooks, or refugees. Most spies the sentries caught were from the tribes; a few were from Castles. There must also be some spies from the TNG, in far-off Athens, since Pullman was loyal to the PCG at Olympia, but presumably a Temper spy would be too competent and professional for an ordinary sentry to detect.

This lousy south wall looked out across the former Jackson Street, and beyond it, a two-block-wide swath of deliberately burned and leveled houses. A simple, gateless, eight-foot palisade with a catwalk four feet above the ground on the back side was adequate against opponents with rocks, spears, and bows. Their bows weren't accurate enough at the distance, so Jawarah stood up, mostly thinking about the poker game tonight and the bets he had down with Jimmy for—

A man and a woman ran headlong into the cleared space from the narrow slot between a wrecked ranch house and its garage, straight for Jawarah.

The gray-bearded man wore a slouch hat, camo pants, deerskin shirt, and knee-high moc-boots. The younger woman was in baggy knee-length dirty red homemade pants, a belted gray tunic that hung to mid-thigh, and a baseball cap. They were running away from something—and nothing out there was friendly.

Jawarah yanked the alarm bell's rope, clanging three times, moved five yards east, and pushed the flip-step over the side of the palisade. Clutching his over-and-under .45 black-powder rifle, he descended, shouting, "This way!"

They turned toward him. As Jawarah ran out to meet them, the man shouted, "Federal Agent Larry Mensche, they're right behind us."

"Follow me!" Jawarah ran back toward his flip-step; the girl, who was running barefoot, saw it, put on a burst of speed, and got there first.

An arrow passed over Jawarah's head. "Over the wall!" he yelled at Mensche. He turned and knelt for a better firing position.

At least forty men and women dressed in a mixture of thrift-store gypsy, low-budget pirate, old hippie, and fake Indian were charging across the cleared space with spears, clubs, knives, and axes. The nearest waved a spirit wand, a stick with a bunch of sacred crap glued to it. Per orders, Jawarah aimed at the man's chest and fired the top barrel.

The tribal pitched forward. Jawarah shot the woman who lunged to pick the spirit wand up. *I don't think she even looked at her buddy,* he thought, *she wanted to save that damned stick.*

An arrow sailed by him; he needed to reload and this was no place for it. He rolled backward and stretched out prone, pulling out his coil-spring crossbow and sending a piece of old welding rod into the oncoming crowd.

Then he heard the most wonderful sound—the slow thudding of one of the black-powder machine guns on the wall, followed by the resonant claps of black-powder rifles firing from the palisade behind him. Staying low, he crawled backwards.

One screaming woman, red hair trailing behind her, wildly swinging a hatchet two-handed, fixed her gaze on him. He threw his small ax awkwardly from his prone position. It cut her shin, and as she bent to grab at the wound, someone above shot her in her exposed back; she sprawled, struggling.

Jawarah's back foot touched the palisade. A voice from above—his buddy, Jimmy: "Wait . . ." Two quick shots, then Jimmy shouted, "Now."

Jawarah scrambled up the flip-step, careful of the sharp glass pieces on top of the palisade, and down onto the catwalk.

"Thanks."

"Had to, you owe me $3.86 from last night's game."

"Yeah, right. Are those Feds okay?"

"Yeah, the cap sent'em straight to the post office—something urgent for the radio. Looks like it's a big deal."

Another arrow sailed over the wall.

"Those guys think so too." Jawarah reloaded. A spear bounced off the palisade between him and Jimmy. He leaned out and pointed down to shoot a tribal who was boarding the flip-step. Jimmy yanked the flip-step in; Jawarah shot at, but missed, another tribal who looked like she was rallying the others.

Normally the tribals broke and ran as soon as they were driven back from the wall, but this particular bunch of hippies from hell weren't retreating; if anything they seemed to be forming up a more organized assault in the wrecked houses across the no-man's-land. But for the moment the open space was clear, and Jawarah rolled over and reloaded. He had dropped that awkward, silly crossbow out there, so at least he wouldn't be responsible for it until the battle was over.

A figure sprinted between two wrecked cars. Jawarah fired, and the body fell and lay motionless.

"You're hot tonight," Jimmy said.

"Yeah, I was just thinking how dull it was. Be careful what you wish for."

Trails of smoke from the houses beyond the cleared area suggested that these tribals were putting together a fire rush, a banzai-style charge with thrown torches and slung balls of burning fabric carried by the less-skilled fighters. The cap had been tough about keeping flammable stuff away from the palisade, so fire rushes had never worked here; no tribals had tried one in the last month. *Must be a tribe that doesn't know us.*

Looked like a long night, but he'd been about to go off shift, so it would all be overtime at the militia rate—more fun and more lucrative than poker, and if it went long enough, he'd get comp time and escape from putting out the second planting of potatoes tomorrow.

They'd be bringing free meals out to the wall, too. Life could be a lot worse.

Jawarah peered over the wall, looking for another good shot, muttering like a crapshooter who has bet ten the hard way:

*Come on out in the park,*
*don't wait for the dark,*
*I'm hot, I'm hot,*
*and it's time to get shot,*
*come on out in the park!*

**THE NEXT MORNING. PUEBLO, COLORADO. 6:15 AM MST.**
**WEDNESDAY, JULY 30, 2025.**

"What do you mean, I need my sleep!" Heather was looking around at her office staff as if she had never seen them prior to turning over this singularly ugly rock. "Larry Mensche comes *running* out of the woods, with a *whole tribe* at his back and radios that he's carrying information too sensitive to send by any code. Followed by a battalion-strength *battle*, and tribals laying siege to Pullman—and you 'decided I needed my sleep'!"

She'd been aware of doors opening and closing around the office while she'd been delivering her tirade, but she hadn't seen MaryBeth Abrams come in. MaryBeth was a big lady—she'd played field hockey for Howard—and the only other woman in Pueblo tall enough to look Heather in the eye. She did, now, and strode up to her. "Your staff," she said, "is trying to protect you and your child. You are two weeks from due."

Heather looked down at her immense belly. "Wow, thanks, I needed to be reminded."

"Well, you are acting like you *need* to be reminded. Heather, *your people are good and they are handling it.* They were *trying* to tell you that a relief force is already on the train from Fort Lewis, with two squadrons of cavalry and half the President's Own Rangers. Your people are taking care of things, and you cannot put yourself in charge of every little thing right now, and that goes double when you're in the delivery room!"

Rocked back by MaryBeth's vehemence, Heather said, "I'm sorry, I worry about my agents. Larry's been missing a while."

Elyse, the youngest member of the staff, said, "To finish out the report, Ms. O'Grainne, he still had his daughter Debbie with him, she's fine, and he said that if you don't swear her in right away, he quits."

"Well, if he's blackmailing me, it's definitely Larry, not an imposter. And Pullman is okay?"

"The local commander says they could lift the siege themselves but they're trying to keep the tribes hanging around long enough for the cavalry and Rangers to catch them," Elyse said.

"You see? You have good people," Dr. Abrams said. "That would be plain as an ax in the head to anyone who wasn't pigheaded, impossible, and you."

Heather sighed, apologized, and soothed everyone's feelings as best she could. When most of them had gone and she had settled down to her uncomfortable breakfast, she thought, *Kid, get here soon. You're missing all the excitement.*

### 3 DAYS LATER. PUEBLO, COLORADO. 11:42 AM MST. SATURDAY, AUGUST 2, 2025.

As Debbie Mensche told of her months with the Northwest tribes, Arnie Yang's pencil raced through his notebook. When Debbie finished, Arnie said, "So at least four months ago, the inner circle of the Gaia's Dawn tribe was taking orders from someone on the radio." He looked around the room. "That would explain how the tribals from the Sangre de Cristos, Ouachitas, and Rio Grande all managed a coordinated attack on Mota Elliptica. Jeez. Orders from the moon." He looked at his three "tame Daybreakers" and asked, "Beth, Jason, Izzy, any thoughts?"

Jason said, "Well, now I know why Daybreak encouraged me to write so much, uh, really bad poetry, and to dream about being a bard and traveling from tribe to tribe; *The Play of Daybreak* and other stuff like it must be part of how Daybreak keeps itself going without an Internet. And the parts Debbie could remember sound a whole lot like the Daybreak poetry I used to write—some of it might even be taken from my poems, I suppose. The tribe idea was definitely there in Daybreak for years before the big day; 'million-ers' like me were totally all about it."

Arnie said, "You'll need to explain that for some people here."

Jason shrugged. "It's embarrassing. But I guess mass murder *should* embarrass people. Within Daybreak, there was a split over whether to go back to horse-drawn plows and organic wheat and like that, you know, simple and natural like in the old TV commercials. We called those guys *billioners* because they wanted the world to have about a billion people. The ones like me that wanted to go back to skin tents, caves, stone knives, were called millioners, because our vision of Daybreak was a planet with fewer than ten million people."

Izzy said, "Or being blunt about it, which is the main way I keep Day-break from taking my mind over again, the big internal debate was whether we ought to kill 7 out of every 8 people on Earth, or 7,999 out of every 8,000."

Heather said, "Arnie, this sounds like one of those times when you try to work me gradually toward a conclusion I'm not going to like. Since you're usually right, let's skip to the part where you tell me that you're now dead certain that the rise of the tribes wasn't an accident, and we have to stop fretting about whether Daybreak really is still there and just say, it is, and we have to fight it."

Colonel Streen said, "I thought that would have been obvious after Day-break started bombing us from the moon."

Arnie balanced a hand. "The analysis certainly leaned that way before, but to my mind this new material about *The Play of Daybreak* clinches it. The tribes are talking with the moon, which is referencing their quasi-religious rituals. I don't want to reopen anything—three months ago, we almost had a civil war because the Provis thought Daybreak had been purely a system artifact, a great big self-generated meme on the Internet, and therefore it was useless to try to find and destroy Daybreak, because it had no single physical location, it was gone with the Internet; and the Tem-pers thought there must be a malicious, intentional command structure someplace, marshaling resources and planning to attack us, and therefore finding and destroying Daybreak had to be our top priority. Well, it turns out, folks, we've got the worst of both worlds: we have a malicious, intentional enemy that has no single physical location. It can and will think of new ways to destroy us, but as for either negotiating with it or fighting it—we might as well try to propose a treaty with, or declare war on, a fashion trend or a pop song."

# S E V E N :
# UPON MY BELLY SAT THE SOW OF FEAR

Steve Ecco felt reluctant to put his pack together before going for his last meal at Carol May Kloster's. He'd come to like Pale Bluff. The neat frame houses and little brick shops, surrounded by dense, wet apple orchards were easy on the eye. Kids here didn't have that haunted, lost expression so many did back home. If you didn't notice the lack of electricity and powered vehicles, you could almost imagine you were back in normal America.

This part of the mission was supposed to be a milk run, anyway. Now all he'd have to do was the part he'd been dreaming about all his life.

*Shit, I'm scared.*

One more time, he inventoried his pack, shuffled through the folder of coded transmissions for Carol May, and made sure he'd left nothing important in the big duffle that he would pick up here when he returned.

On his way to early dinner at Carol May's, he had to stop twice to take info from people who had finally decided to subscribe to the *Pueblo Post-Gazette*, and some other people waved as he walked up Chapman Avenue.

*Technically,* he thought, *Heather was right, that this is lousy tradecraft; you shouldn't have a guy who has operated more or less openly under his own name do a covert op in the same area. But now that I know them, I kind of like the feeling that these are the people I'm really working for, and that what I'm doing is for all of them. And I'll be careful. Jesus God, I'll be careful.* He wished he didn't feel quite so concerned about losing bowel control.

Carol May had baked fresh apple sourdough bread, and stuffed and roasted a good big rabbit. "The neighbor kid knocked Mister Bunny off with a rock," she said. "And saved at least one deserving cabbage in the process. Pegged him on the first throw, *straight to the head and dead as dead,* as the kids like to say. The skills the kids pick up now that there aren't video games!"

Toward the end of that wonderful meal, Carol May said, "I know you'll be up early, so I'll let you get away quick to get as much sleep as you can. But I wanted to ask a favor of you. My niece Pauline went off with a tribal boy when one of the tribes came over here for about a month early in the spring."

"With a *tribal?*"

"He had two good qualities: he looked good with his shirt hanging open, and he wasn't local."

"She wanted to leave?"

"Like water wants to run downhill. She was only back here on Daybreak day because she'd been expelled from IU and she'd come back here to lick her wounds. Her mom died a few years back, and my brother wasn't the kind of guy you go to when you've really taken a fall. I'm as much family as she's got, but she was about due to have another run at the world, and then she got trapped here, and that bunch of bush hippies was her first ticket out of town. Anyway, it was a damn stupid choice, and I told her so. I thought she'd come back after the tribals burned and looted Wynoose on their way back across the Wabash, but maybe by the time she knew the score, they wouldn't let her go. Or I suppose maybe she always wanted to smash up a small town. Live in one all your life and the thought occurs to you now and then.

"Anyway I wish I knew what happened to her. So—don't take one step out of your way or one chance you don't have to, but if you happen to hear anything about a Pauline Kloster—"

"Of course," Ecco said. "When I get back, I'll drop you a short note—even if it's just to say I didn't find anything." *Good, one more promise means one more reason I can't funk the whole damn thing.*

Carol May told him everything she could remember about Pauline, the boy, and the band of tribals. "Stenography?"

"Well, it's what I do and I'm proud of it, but I have to admit, it's a trade like being a blacksmith—"

"Say no more. I've spent all my life trying to be a mountain man or a cowboy or something. And think about all the obsolete occupations people did for a hobby, before Daybreak, that are now the most in-demand skills we have. Steam trains, sailing ships, blacksmiths for that matter. I guess if the tribe keeps any written records over there—I kind of think they don't— she's probably useful and conspicuous. Anyway, you're right, I should go. And thanks for everything."

He was embarrassed by how good it felt that she hugged him and told him to be careful, so much like the way his mother used to send him off to the first day of school.

**5 HOURS LATER. PALE BLUFF, NEW STATE OF WABASH (PCG) OR ILLINOIS (TNG). 11:15 PM CST. MONDAY, AUGUST 4, 2025.**

"'Fraid I can't let you have any more time to sleep than this." The soft voice was like the touch of a dream departing; Ecco opened his eyes to the shadowy shape of Freddie Pranger.

Having slept fully dressed on top of the covers, he sat up and reached for his pack. "Hope I don't sleep like that where I'm going."

"You won't. The body knows when it's somewhere safe and when it's not; you slept deep because you could. Need to use the chamber pot before we go?"

"Yeah."

"I'll be in the hallway."

Ecco made himself comfortable, rinsed his face in the washbasin, and swallowed the cup of lukewarm strong tea with extra sugar and powdered milk he'd left out for himself. He slung up his pack and slipped into the dark hallway.

They took the northwest road out of town; after a couple of miles they turned onto an abandoned farm road, following it to a creek that flowed into the Little Wabash.

They made no sound. The dirty old moon, rising later, smaller, and dimmer every night, almost gone now, seemed only to deepen the shadows. Ecco's attention constricted to the dim, shadowy path beside the creek.

At last they stood beside an old highway truss bridge. "Cross this bridge," Freddie Pranger said, "and follow the river road east." He stuck his hand out, and they shook. "Stay scared so you come back."

"No problem staying scared," Ecco managed. "Thanks for everything." He looked back after he had crossed the bridge; Pranger, of course, had evaporated. At the turn onto the road, Ecco began a slow jog, one he could easily maintain for the scant few hours until the treacherous dawn came crawling into his face over the eastern horizon.


## THE NEXT DAY. PUEBLO, COLORADO. 6:15 PM MST. TUESDAY, AUGUST 5, 2025.

Beth had been waiting since she'd gone to see MaryBeth Abrams at lunchtime, and had told herself that she needed to be patient and nobody should be hit with really surprising news first thing when he came in the door. *And I don't suppose we should call it surprising, either, should we? I mean, it's actually kind of natural.*

In the interim, she tidied things up, and since there was a fresh cabbage, and some nice jerked grouse, she invented a kind of nice little soup and made up some soda bread to serve with it. *Hunh, that smells good if I do say so myself. I'll have to remember that.*

She hoped this wouldn't be one of the days when Jason stopped for a beer at Dell's Brew with his workmates.

He was actually a few minutes early, but by that time their little place was tidier than it had ever been, the soup had been reseasoned to perfection, and she'd thought of four clever ways and two gentle ways to break the news to him. Nonetheless, the moment he closed the door, she blurted, "I'm gonna have a baby."

**8 DAYS LATER. ON THE WABASH, ABOUT A MILE AND A HALF NORTHEAST OF THE FORMER DARWIN, ILLINOIS. 11:42 PM CST. WEDNESDAY, AUGUST 13, 2025.**

Ecco constantly told himself that the five days he'd spent so far on the Illinois side of the Wabash wasn't cowardice or procrastination. Arnie Yang had worked out pathways around the known areas where others had died or been lost, away from the farms and little towns that had been attacked, which Ecco had memorized; the map was as clear in his head now as it had been back in Pueblo.

He'd made it to the Wabash in two days, and started by observing the big bridge at Mount Carmel from a safe vantage point in the ruins. Three hours of steady, patient watching had revealed at least four watchers on the other side, all focused on the bridge. They'd all been relieved at regular intervals. Whatever was over there, it was *organized*.

Between sunset and moonrise he'd departed the charred wreckage of Mount Carmel and headed north. The next morning, from the east-facing upper window of an apartment over an old carriage house in Patton, his binoculars had revealed two different five-person patrols, one in the early morning and one in the afternoon, on the far side of the river. They were dressed like thrift store barbarians or Conan the Hippie, with spears, hatchets, and clubs. He'd slept through most of the day and departed, again, in the dark.

He'd moved farther north and east, staying close to the river except for a long trip around the burned-out area opposite Vincennes. Moving only when it seemed safe, watching the east bank constantly, he'd found every standing bridge watched, every dock and landing burned and blocked, and patrols no more than a few miles apart. He had to hope Heather was right that this was a tight barrier but not a thick one, so that a few miles on the other side of the river the land would be mostly empty, because if it was like this for any distance inland, he didn't think he had a prayer.

Under the trees in a wooded bend of the river, just upstream from the ruins of Darwin, Illinois, he'd spent the day establishing the key facts with binoculars. The landing directly opposite him, a little cut-out docking pool, had been blocked with logs and the dock itself burned, but seemed unguarded. No bridges spanned the swift current for several miles downstream, so if need be he could float for miles while he looked for a safe, inconspicuous place to come inshore. Cover was abundant, with at least a few hundred feet of trees on each side of the river. About a half mile downstream a narrow, slow side channel, well-wooded on both sides, sliced the other side. If he missed that side channel in the dark, he had miles more distance and hours more time to land among trees.

Tonight the moon would rise almost two hours after the end of twilight, more than time enough to float to the other side, with extra time to try to move far enough east to be beyond the Daybreaker patrols. He'd crept down in the dusk and verified that there was a hole maybe twenty feet across by a dozen feet deep where he'd be able to slip in quietly.

Faint stars glowed above the trees on the opposite bank. Time. He descended to the hole. *Too bad there's no way to take a boat over; I hope the jars keep my powder dry and I don't need the gun too quick.* He made sure that his gear was roped to his waist, and then swiftly whipped five old pillowcases, one at a time, through the air, over his head, and into the water, and tied them off. He pushed off, floating on his back, head held up by his pillowcase float, and his bag of supplies resting on his belly.

*I look just like floating debris,* he thought. *Please, God, I look like old junk that washed into the river. Anyone who sees me will see I'm just a pile of floating crap.* He'd lined up three stars and two trees with distinctive shapes downstream; if he could manage to kick his way into the current between them, he'd be in the side channel he was aiming for.

The warmth of the water was pleasant; he'd grown up in the Rockies where running water is freezing cold all year. In the humid night, low fogs, some only a foot deep, drifted along the surface, cloaking him.

He kicked hard but kept his legs well under the water. Fogs rolled across him, darkening the river to a void except for the stars directly overhead; then a clear patch would roll by and he'd catch sight of his stars and his target trees.

When trees were on both sides of him, he turned over. His feet found the muck at the bottom of the shallow channel. His foot caught in something and pulled his head under for an instant, but he shook loose, waded a few more steps, and found a pebbly, rapidly rising surface. Trying not to splash, he waded with his pack held above his head until he was waist deep. At last he stepped from a patch of sloppy muck between the tangled roots of a cottonwood, and put both feet on a muddy bank. Checking the stars, he walked due east.

Something slammed the back of his head. As he stumbled, his head was pushed down and a rope wrapped in three quick turns around his neck.

There were so many of them.

He tried to lie down and make them kill him, but they just shoved a spar between his elbows and back, and pulled him to his feet.

"Stephen Ecco," a voice said, behind him. "We were wondering if you'd ever find the courage to come over the river."

Four big men lifted him by the spar on his back; the pain was bad enough if he went the way they pushed him, and agonizing when he didn't cooperate. They ran him that way, hour after hour, as more tribals joined the group and took turns holding up the spar. At dawn, his feet felt like a bloody mess, but thrown onto his face in the dirt, he couldn't really inspect them.

As his cheek pressed the damp dirt and he lay where he had been thrown, one thought drove him to keep testing his bonds, looking for any direction in which they might loosen: Someone had betrayed the mission. He had to escape and tell Heather.

**THE NEXT DAY. IN AND AROUND THE FORMER TERRE HAUTE, INDIANA. 5:30 AM EST. THURSDAY, AUGUST 14, 2025.**

They were trying to confuse him, but they couldn't hide the Wabash or the sun; Steve Ecco knew he was going upstream near the river. Either they didn't realize how many clues they'd let slip, or they didn't care that much.

Now it was a party of at least twenty people; three of them, he'd pegged as "officers," though he heard no titles used—a woman and two men who took turns deciding things and giving orders. Another seven he'd designated as "guards," who followed the orders of the officers and gave orders to all of the rest. The numerous remainder must be slaves; they only received orders and spoke only when told to.

*Well, if I do escape, I can report that much, anyway.*

At dawn of the first day of his captivity, as gray light began to leak in around his blindfold, he was in a stretch where the road or trail was jammed with obstacles. He tried running headlong, hoping to hit something and get a concussion or a broken neck, or perhaps fall into water and drown. After he'd lost count of his collisions with trees and was staggering, hoping that the next tree or the one after might put him out, they unblindfolded him, braced him up, and forced the bar between his elbows and back again. For the next hour or more they left the blindfold off but again used the spar to push him onward, until the road was clear of felled trees and broken automobiles.

During that brief period of vision, in the brightening gray light, he saw a WELCOME TO PRAIRIETON sign, and another sign for Indiana 63. So he was just south of Terre Haute, close to the east side of the river; they were running him across the bend where the Illinois-Indiana state line begins to follow the Wabash.

Later, when the sun was full up, but still to his right, the road was mostly clear again, and shamefully, he agreed not to make them use the spar, so they re-blindfolded him. A while after that, they ran him down to the river and gave him a cup of water.

Lukewarm river water was wonderful. The next cup of water had been thoroughly dosed with whiskey; they followed that up with some lukewarm soup, probably beef vegetable out of a can, mixed with more whiskey, and then another draft of unspiked water.

When they shoved him into the bottom of the boat, lying on his back in the puddled water was only uncomfortable for a moment before exhaustion, whiskey, and the relief of the food and water sent him off to sleep. Twice he half-awakened when guards screamed at the slaves.

They dragged him out of the boat at about noon, to judge by the feel of the sun. As they pushed him to run again, he noted they were still going upstream, still on their side of the Wabash.

*At that mountain man convention I went to they said a keelboat was lucky to make fifteen miles a day upstream, so since that was maybe a third of a day, they probably just hauled me through Terre Haute. Does that mean there are good guys in the wreckage, for me to look for if I escape? Or was it just too hard to run a blindfolded guy through a smashed ruin that size?*

He ran for much of the afternoon, still north along the Wabash, very close to the border. This forced run had shredded his feet and ankles, and burned up his reserves; he'd need a *long* head start to get away from them, now.

With the sun still high in the sky, they stopped so a fresh party of officers, guards, and slaves could take over. It was a longer stop; the replacement party, while waiting for them, had built a fire, and heated food from cans. They gave him a big bowl of oatmeal laced with rum, more water, and some soup/whiskey mix as well. He fell asleep again, dimly aware that they were carrying him down to another boat.

**ABOUT THE SAME TIME. ATHENS, TNG DISTRICT. 3 PM EST. THURSDAY, AUGUST 14, 2025.**

Cameron Nguyen-Peters had chosen Terrell Hall on the former University of Georgia campus for his executive office building for what seemed like good, sensible administrative reasons: it was an administrative building with a few big and many small offices, old enough so that it had plenty of windows for natural light. If he had thought about the front entrance at all, it was only that the protruding, windowed bay over the covered stairs might be a good place for the eventual President of the United States to give a speech.

He had not thought at the time that the chapel, across the quad, faced it directly, so that the two buildings could also be seen as rival positions—let alone in enmity. But back then, the Post Raptural Church hadn't existed yet, let alone demanded recognition as the First National Church of the United States.

"The best guess we've got," Grayson said, his face tired and strained, "is that there are about seven thousand people in the quad at any one time. Most of them are from outside Athens and some of them walked three days to get here. There's probably twelve thousand overall, but some of them are always off getting food or catching a nap. There are probably two thousand watchers around the other side of the building, so slipping out quietly is not an option."

The chanting rose and fell in long, slow waves of a minute or more. "At least in the daytime they don't need torches for light," Cam observed, "so they don't have them right there, to give them ideas."

"If they want to burn the building in the daytime, they'll find something." Grayson shrugged. "And sir, I don't agree with you about anything, but I don't think you're a coward. If you do what I'm suggesting, I know it won't be because you're giving in or because you're afraid." His small smile was almost a wince. "Though I seriously doubt that you care what I think of you."

"Well, you might be wrong about *that*," Cam said. "All right, the country is already torn in half; we can't have a civil war in the strongest remaining part." He handed Grayson a short, bulleted list and said, "Here's what I'm going to promise to do. Is it enough? Will it get the mobs out of the streets and the people back to work? And will it get the Post Raptural preachers to stop enflaming their followers?"

Grayson scanned it and said, "Yes. I think it will. I can sell this to Peet and Whilmire. And sir, again, I don't think you're selling out. Changes had to come. It's a new time in a new country."

"Yeah, but our oath is to the Constitution of the old country," Cam said. "Whatever happens to me, General, don't forget that."

"I don't think I ever could, sir. "

The techs had cobbled together a crude PA system and kept it wiped clean of nanoswarm, though they pointed out that how long it would last was anyone's guess, and therefore it would be better to speak sooner rather than later. "No reason to delay any further, then." Cameron moved forward to the mike; there was a squeal of feedback that quieted the crowd, and he began. "My fellow Americans, I have—"

A shot caromed off the windowsill above his head. Cam froze, his mind blank, but Grayson moved forward, stepping between him and the mike. "If you're going to shoot anybody today," he said, firmly, "let me request that you shoot me first, so that I will not have failed in my duty to my civilian superiors."

Silence descended on the crowd. Grayson stepped aside, and Cam advanced to the mike. Forcing himself not to hurry, he read off the points: he would reconstitute the Board, naming enough reverends to it to give it a Post Raptural majority; Army and other federal institutions could, if the local commander preferred, fly the Cross and Eagle banner; the First National Church of the United States was hereby proclaimed the official church, but all other non-subversive, non-seditious religions would be tolerated; the Temporary National Government would seek a restored

American sovereignty over the whole territory of the United States, under a restored fully Constitutional authority.

"And finally, please join me in this very short prayer." He let them fall silent and bow their heads; then he said, "God bless the United States of America, and restore our country to us, in Jesus' name we pray, Amen," as Grayson had told him to do. The crowd cheered madly; it was several minutes before, to Cam's relief, they began to drift out of the quad.

As Cam trudged upstairs to his personal apartment, he felt as if he dragged a huge, invisible cross. A late lunch and a nap might be in order. *What do you do when you've lost completely but you can't just slink under the porch?*

At the door to his private apartment, Colonel Salazar was waiting for him. Cam knew the man slightly, as one of the perpetual staffers who inhabit the mid-ranges of any bureaucracy. He was slim, well-muscled, of average height, deeply tanned and black-haired, and other than an immense Saddam Hussein mustache, he had no distinguishing feature anyone could have named. "Sir? There are a couple of things you should sign off on—it'll just take a moment."

"Sure, come in," Cam said. Another minute of delay for the lunch and the nap wouldn't matter. Probably he'd forgotten to sign some of the pile of executive orders he'd hammered out with Whilmire and Grayson earlier that day.

As soon as Salazar closed the door, he said, "Something you need to know, sir. General Grayson knew that shot was going to hit up above the window. The incident was staged."

Cam blinked. "Well, that's consistent with Grayson, and the people around him. Thank you for telling me."

"Information with the compliments of Heather O'Grainne, sir. If you ever need to communicate with her in a secure channel—"

"I won't hesitate to contact you," Cam said. "And my thanks to Heather—"

Salazar saluted and was gone.

As Cam put together a sandwich, and watched the demonstrators pouring out into the streets, celebrating the victory of God and the Constitution (at least as they understood either), he thought, *Well, it's still total defeat, but it's not so bad when you don't feel all alone.*

## THE NEXT DAY. NEAR THE FORMER TECUMSEH, INDIANA. 3:45 PM EST. FRIDAY, AUGUST 15, 2025.

They'd kept Ecco running for most of two days, usually blindfolded, getting him drunk and dumping him into boats from time to time. He deduced they were cutting off long bends by running him across them, but only when they could keep him on this side of the border, and for some reason it was important to keep him close to the Wabash.

At mid-afternoon, Ecco vomited on one of the officers, which was the high point of his day. They let him have a whole wonderful sweet quart or so of unlaced water, and sit and rest while a runner went for a boat. He sat, breathed, and took stock; pressing his feet against his bare calves, he could feel even through the soles of his moccasins that his numb feet were swollen and wet; maybe he'd broken some bones under his instep.

If he got free, he wouldn't be able to run far or fast; at best he might only be able to force them to kill him. His arms had been bound behind his back for most of the time; even with them free, he doubted he'd manage to roll out of a boat to drown, let alone try to swim for it.

As they waited he felt that the slope was steep in front of him, and the smell of water was strong. He went limp and tried rolling down the bank. *Drowning's gonna feel like shit but—*

Rough hands stopped him; he stayed limp, feigning a faint. A slave woman was beaten for not having kept a grip on him.

"That bank's pretty steep." It was the woman officer they called Sunshine. "We're not supposed to let him see where he is, but it'll be a lot easier to move him into the boat if he can see."

Jacob, who seemed to be the CO, grunted. "Let him go down without the blindfold, but put it right back on him."

They unblindfolded him and walked him down the slope; he saw the water tower for Tecumseh, across the stream. Ecco remembered that the town constable had been assassinated there, and a series of fires had been set; what was left of the population had evacuated westward, with stories about rocks and arrows from nowhere and drumming and singing in the night.

They tied him into the boat, but since they left him sober, he was able to rest and think. Who could have betrayed his mission? Some of the people who had known *couldn't* be suspects. Not Carol May Kloster or Freddie Pranger, let alone Heather O'Grainne.

Had one of the ex-Daybreakers that they studied at Pueblo reverted to Daybreak, and learned about his mission?

Some spy in Pueblo who just put things together? Their main communication system was having hungry teenagers run notes between desks; what messages might have been intercepted with some smooth talk and a fresh hot pie?

Dr. Yang? Please, not a guy who'd always treated him with the friendly deference that a man of action wants to see from a smart guy . . . *especially if it's a fake man of action like me,* Ecco thought, bitterly, for the ten thousandth time.

He kept composing the message, with no idea how he could send it:

*Going N on L bank Wabash with 3 officers, 5-10 enlisted, many slaves. Need help urgent. Traitor in Pueblo.*

He fell asleep in the gently rocking boat, and when he woke again, no light was leaking around his blindfold. Sunshine ordered him to climb out and to run; she had to have three slaves lift him, but after some kicking and slapping, he ran, despite the scalding pain in the balls and heels of his feet, and the wracking ache of breathing through sobs.

**THE NEXT DAY. PUEBLO, COLORADO. 8:30 PM MST. SATURDAY, AUGUST 16, 2025.**

Heather was exhausted and she felt like someone had been beating on her guts with a flat shovel for a few hours, so it was almost a relief when Mary-Beth switched over from "Come on, push" and "Breathe, Heather, breathe" to "One last push!"

The next sensation was like uncontrollably having the mother of all bowel movements three seconds after making it to the toilet. She watched the lamplight flicker on the ceiling and thought, *Kid, you're not ever going to hear from me that you felt like a giant turd.*

Everything—the pain, the exhaustion, the sheer sense of *force*—became too intense for her to focus; then suddenly, it was merely painful and she was just exhausted and needed to sleep.

"Hey, sweetie. You passed out and missed the first yodel." MaryBeth Abrams stood beside her, stroking her face with one hand, holding a little wailing bundle in her other arm. "Say hi to Leonardo."

"Leo," Heather corrected her. "He's Leonardo Plekhanov Jr., but he'll be Leo at home. I just hope his friends don't give him any horrible nicknames."

"Well, right now he's working on being called 'Noisy.' Let's set him up to feed and see if that's what the matter is."

He promptly stopped yowling and went to work, contentedly nursing. *Well, Leo, now you've done it,* she thought, looking over his tiny, perfect body. *Mom's going to* have *to fix the world; it just isn't fit for a boy like you.*

## 30 MINUTES LATER. OLYMPIA, NEW DISTRICT OF COLUMBIA (FORMERLY IN WASHINGTON STATE) AND PUEBLO, COLORADO. 8:15 PM PST/9:15 PM MST. SATURDAY, AUGUST 16, 2025.

Ever since high school, at the beginning of each month, Allie had written out a list that began *a year from now,* copying, crossing out, recopying, and changing as the world and her goals changed. *In August 2024, I don't think I'd've typed out "a year from now I will be the First Lady," or "I'll be waiting up to hear about Heather's baby," let alone "and it's Lenny Plekhanov's."*

Graham Weisbrod (*my husband the president, okay, I couldn't have guessed at* anything *last year*) asked the technician, "So do—"

The technician held up a hand. "QSL, Pueblo, loud and clear, go to encryption as previously selected in five, four, three, two, one . . ." She tripped off the pendulum-clock contraption that turned three eccentric plywood cams at different speeds, adding noise to encrypt the signal; in Pueblo, an identical cam set would take it out. The tech talked to her opposite number to ensure that voice was intelligible, handed headsets to Graham and Allie, and said, "About an hour, and you've got a nice clear channel right now."

A very tired, weak-sounding Heather O'Grainne said hello. Graham seemed to settle into his chair in the radio room as if he'd suddenly dropped thirty years and was back in his office, falling back into the old close friendship with Heather instantly. Allie felt childish for feeling left out, as if she were a little girl kicking the ground with a plastic sandal and complaining to Papa that, *Well, but Heather is my friend too* and *Graham is my mentor too*. And she could practically hear her father saying to be a patient child, a wise child, one who others would want to have around. *Which was your subtle Khmer way, Papa, of telling me that people didn't really want me around.*

She tuned out most of the discussion of the sentimental wonders of perfect little ears and toes; she'd seen babies turn grown people into idiots before. This was no more interminable than any other baby, any other time. As Graham and Heather ran out of things to say, Allie realized that, lost in her own irritations, she really hadn't heard much of the conversation. She sincerely wished Heather a quick recovery and welcomed little Leo to the world, sat patiently while Graham did the same in much more time and with many cutesier words, and fought down sighs of relief and impatience.

Arnie came back on the line. "I've dropped the patch through to Heather's room, but we've got a good clear channel up and running on crypto, and about forty minutes left on it, so is there anything you all would like to talk about? We've got most of the section heads for RRC someplace in the building, and it would only take a minute to get one of them in here."

Graham said, "Heather keeps us very up-to-date, so thanks, but I guess we'll just say good night."

He lifted the phones off his head without bothering to get Arnie's acknowledgment. *Or to consult me.* Allie said, "Arnie, if you don't mind just talking, just to talk, we never get time for it on the regularly scheduled crypto radio."

"Sure," Arnie said.

*Oh, good, he sounds happy.* She nodded at Graham, keeping a straight face at his irritated expression. *Looking forward to a Saturday night game of Bang the Pretty Girl, were we?*

. . .

Outside the courthouse, Pueblo would be dark, buzzing with the threat of Aaron, and besides, Arnie was lonely.

Before he could even wonder what to talk about, Allie said, "Geez, Arnie, it's August, remember how last year the big issue was whether to go to Maine or to the Virginia beaches for our vacation?"

"Oh yeah. And we thought it was such a nuisance to have to take the train to Boston and then rent a car—"

"And then we had so much fun," she said. He'd forgotten how musical her voice became when it was soft and low, *across a table in a café, or with her head on my shoulder sitting on the beach and watching the waves, or in bed.*

The conversation ranged through a dozen shared experiences, nearly all of them things that had been routine before Daybreak. They both agreed that it felt good to talk about it, and that they shouldn't do it too often.

"I try not to think about the old days too much," he said. "Phoning for a pizza at midnight, flying to Paris, my old Porsche . . . tonight I put all my time into thinking about typhus among the tribal population this winter."

"Bad?" Allie asked, suddenly alert.

"Bad. Very bad. It's spread by lice, and bathing is plaztatic, not to mention hard to do out in the woods, especially since with all the soot in the air, this is gonna be the coldest winter since 1816. One case of typhus anywhere will spread through that whole population this winter."

"Won't that solve some of our problem for us?"

"Well, sort of. It'll hit the tribes harder than it hits civilization, and if our brewers can make enough tetracycline—"

"If *who* can *what?*"

"Tetracycline stops typhus cold, and you can make it with a yeast, kind of like brewing beer. We've got a pilot plant running here, and if it works, you and Athens both get a crash course in brewing the stuff. Once we have it, some of the tribals might even surrender to get treatment, especially mothers with young kids. But even if it's mostly on their side of the line, I don't like all that unnecessary suffering and dying. Hey—there's only about five minutes left on the encrypting cogs. Gee," Arnie said, "it was great to bat ideas around. Like old times."

"You romantic devil. Reminding me of all the good times in the relationship and using it to segue into typhus, antibiotics, and mass death. You haven't lost your touch. I remember how you rubbed lotion into my legs while talking about the shifting attitude matrix on tax policy," Allie said.

"Funny thing, I remember the legs more than the policy. God, things in the old days were nice," he said.

"Yeah. Oh, crap, Arnie, we don't have much time and I've enjoyed this so much. Listen, if you're not doing too much on Saturday nights, can I call you? Just to talk, old friend to old friend? Sometimes I just need to blow off some steam. I'll send you a message to set it up, regular channels, but save me next Saturday night."

"Sure, I'd like to have someone to talk to, too. We'll talk next week." The cams came to a halt as he was speaking; he wasn't sure whether she'd heard the last of it.

. . .

Darcage was waiting for her, and grabbed her on the back stairs from the radio room to the suite she shared with Graham, pressing a hand over her mouth gently for a moment. "Just so you don't scream from being startled. I wanted to discuss something. We very much approve of your idea of a back-channel contact with Doctor Yang in Pueblo, and we'd be happy to coordinate."

"Coordinate what?" she asked.

"We don't have to be enemies, you know. You must realize that once the Tempers are done with the tribes, they will turn on you, and we are better fighters—"

"About three thousand of yours couldn't take Pullman against five hundred of ours. You die bravely. As for winning, not so much."

"Wait until all the cowardly gunpowder and artillery are gone." The man's face was contorted with rage, but his hand stayed at his side.

"They'll never be gone. We make them and we're going to keep making them. I'll talk to anyone, that's what my job—"

He was gone.

*Why didn't I shout for help?*

. . .

Arnie was almost home when Aaron said, "She's very unhappy, you know."

"Who?" Arnie asked, turning to face the shadowed figure.

Aaron's face was completely lost in the dark void under the blanket. "She's very unhappy. She will dream all week about talking to you again." He vanished backward into the shadows.

Arnie heard the watch nearby. They'd want to know why he was standing here in the middle of the street and the middle of the night. He ran, silently, to his front door.

### ABOUT THE SAME TIME. CASTLE CASTRO (SAN DIEGO).
### 9:20 PM PST. SATURDAY, AUGUST 16, 2025.

Harrison Castro was proud that they'd managed to build a radio voice encryptor to hack into high-level communications between Athens, Pueblo, and Olympia and the various ships and substations. He knew that objectively he would be better off listening to everyone and not letting them know he could, but it was also high time to make sure they couldn't ignore him.

With a perfect excuse, he had brought Pat O'Grainne in here, and was now enjoying showing off the machine.

"We doped out all hundred or so of their eccentric cams, and then we just set up our mechanical scanner." He pointed to the three ten-foot-long rotors, each with a hundred disks. "Every time we get a rotor right, the signal audibly becomes easier to understand. So we tune along one rotor to find the closest to intelligible, then along the next, then along the third, then back to the first, until it leaps out clearly. Do that long enough with enough messages, and eventually you can recognize the code they're using right away, and read all their traffic."

"You do know I never learned enough math to balance a checkbook, right? To me it looks like three giant camshafts and a bunch of guys with Walkman headphones hooked to an old phone plugboard," Pat said.

Castro chuckled. "Pat, I like you. Okay, here's the actual story: I don't really give a damn about most of their secrets—we're practically our own country down here nowadays—but I want them to know they don't have a chance in hell of pushing me around. Now let's call Pueblo, so you can say hi to your grandson."

Harrison Castro himself spent only half a minute congratulating Heather and welcoming Leo to the world, and then he put Pat on and let the sentimental babble flow until Heather admitted to being tired.

Later, in his room, Pat told Heather what he really thought—not about Leo, because they had both agreed he was the most marvelous thing that ever happened, but about Harrison Castro. He made extra sure to destroy the original.

Heather understood perfectly well that Harrison Castro, in the guise of letting her father talk to her, had directly challenged her by letting her know he was listening to Federal encrypted radio, and also established that the freeholder of an important Castle could get access that an ordinary citizen couldn't. Sure, before Daybreak, the CEO of Microsoft would have been put right through to any Cabinet secretary, probably to the President. But a Castle freeholder cracking Federal high-security communications and just coming on line—*as a precedent, it blows.*

Dad no doubt understood that too. Certainly his next covert, encrypted letter would give her a better picture of what was going on at Castle Castro. She'd never found much of a way to tell him that though he'd been kind of a loser at having a career and a fraud as a biker, he'd been great at loving his daughter and being a spy.

Besides, she loved talking to her father, because besides celebrating Leo, he understood how much she needed to talk, and cry, about missing Lenny, and about Leo never knowing his dad. That had really helped.

So, she thought, drifting off, Castro's asshole gesture could wait for later. Then, as so often happened when she told herself a problem was for later, she had an idea. If she could—

The nurse came in. "If you don't expect anyone else to call, it's about time for everyone to rest."

"I didn't expect the *last* call." Heather brushed at Leo's little face and said, "Looks like he's already starting on that rest thing."

"We'll put him right here—see, if you sit up, you can see right into the cradle—and we've got people in the hallway; just call or ring that little bell beside the bed if you need help or if anything worries you. You try to get some sleep." She quenched the oil lamp; dim moonlight still filtered in.

Heather leaned up. Leo's breathing seemed to be strong and steady. As she watched her son sleep, she was already formulating her note to Dave Carlucci, who ran the FBI West Headquarters a few miles from Castle Castro; although she had not quite formulated it, she had a smile as she fell asleep that would have frightened anyone who knew her well.

# E I G H T:
# THE DOCTOR PUNCHED MY VEIN

They unblindfolded Steve Ecco to walk him through the pileup of wrecked cars at one end of Reeder Park. He knew where he was because the memorial statue for the Second Iran War was so distinctive that Ecco had memorized it as a landmark, since it was less than a mile and a half from the still-intact US 36 bridge.

He smelled the river and the trees. *Oh, crap, crap, crap if I could just get loose and run at my old pace, if they didn't have any guards on that bridge, I could be on my way home; plenty of woods on the other side, all I'd have to do is follow the highway and turn south of the burned-out zone—*

The stylized cross on this big, new, glass-and-steel building meant it was a church. Big hands pushed him through the doorway, then toppled him from the top of the stairs down into the basement. He wasn't able to swing his head into harm's way this time either; all he got was a couple more bruises on his chest and shoulder.

The guard at the bottom kicked him on the tailbone, hard enough to hurt, not hard enough to do much damage. His legs were already numb, and they didn't bother asking him to stand; they just jerked him to his feet and threw him onto an old mattress.

Two men came in. The older, heavyset one had a huge bushy white beard;

the younger, slimmer one was the sort of nondescript guy that used to work at some store you went to now and then, whose appearance you couldn't remember by the time you were back in the parking lot.

Bushy White Beard was addressed as "Lord Karl." Apparently Steve was important enough for the lord and his number one henchman to deal with personally. He did his best to collect his thoughts while the two men had a late supper brought in, and ate it, leaving him tied, facedown, and hungry. He was also desperate to urinate, and the diarrhea from the bad food and tainted water of the last couple of days was worsening.

He was startled to realize he'd fallen asleep, and at first he couldn't recognize what he was feeling; then he realized someone was cutting away the bonds on his wrists and elbows.

They flung his arms out to the sides, and flipped him over. Karl and his man stood over him, and Karl said, "Show him, Robert."

The man bent, grabbed Ecco's hand, and laid it on the floor, pinning it with his foot, grinding with agonizing force on flesh just beginning to revive from numbness. He grasped Ecco's thumb with a pair of pliers, raised a hammer, and smashed the thumb with it, again and again; Ecco screamed at the first blow, struggling to pull his hand back, and a strong guard pinned his head to the floor, holding his face toward where Robert was smashing at his thumb, pulling his eyelids open, forcing Ecco to watch.

The battering went on until Robert said, "It's about all fell off now."

"Now," Lord Karl said, as Ecco gasped and sobbed, "that was just to explain to you what kinds of things we do if people don't answer questions. So you probably will want to establish a basis of trust, by telling us everything you can, as quickly as you can."

He'd been ordered to spill everything, anyway, if he was tortured; Heather had specifically said, *You don't know a thing that could really be of any use to the enemy. Trade everything about us to save your ass, Steve—no heroics if you're captured. Spill your guts, right away.*

They hadn't even asked first.

"I understand," he said. "I'll tell you everything."

Karl said, "Tell us the name of everyone who works for the RRC, what they do, and describe everything about them you know. Everything. Start with that big fat O'Grainne bitch."

He described Heather head to foot, told them what her office looked like, gave them directions for finding her window and door in the Pueblo Courthouse, dragged out everything he could remember about her. Every so often Karl would say, "Got that?" and a young woman's voice would read back everything he had said, strangely verbatim, including the places where he stammered and babbled frantically. Her voice was flat, occasionally noting *prisoner gasped for breath*, *prisoner sobbed*, and, one time, reading back a passage when Karl had impatiently stamped on his ruined hand, *prisoner screamed here*.

After her last little reading, Lord Karl said, "I'm sleepy. Got the solder?"

They poured the hot, silvery liquid over the stump of his thumb, and let his hand go; he hurt his other hand and chest trying to clutch the burned, shredded flesh to himself, as if he could comfort it.

Lord Karl said, "Robert, let's sleep in tomorrow; we'll start again after breakfast. Ecco, you have nine more fingers, ten more toes, two more eyes and two more lips, and of course your dick and balls. Poor you. Poor poor poor you."

## THE SECOND NIGHT AFTER. THE FORMER RIVERSIDE BAPTIST CHURCH, IN THE FORMER MONTEZUMA, INDIANA. 6:30 AM EST. SUNDAY, AUGUST 17, 2025.

Steve Ecco was awakened by the girl who had been recording his words and repeating them verbatim. "Please, I know you're in pain," she said, "but they told me I can give you a drink of water for every two pages of shorthand I take." She lifted his head, gently, and poured some into his mouth from a narrow-spouted garden watering can. "I can always say I misunderstood," she said, "but you gotta help me average this out, they'll want a lot of pages if I give you a lot of water."

He looked around. By the light through the dirty windows it must still be early morning. On the other side of the solder, his phantom thumb was still screaming with pain. Before he could stop himself, he glanced sideways. Pieces of his thumb still lay beside the mattress.

"I'll tell you anything you want," he said, hating the way his voice felt in his throat.

He told her everything about everyone at Pueblo, knowing they would use the information, somehow, hating himself, but doing it, every throb of his thumb telling him he had no resistance left. Every so often she paused and gave him a drink of water; the clean, welcome taste brought him to tears.

Ecco had always hoped and dreamed of being the kind of man who would assess the situation and prepare to make a break for it. He forced himself to try; his hands were no longer tied and though his left hand could not bear the slightest pressure, and was probably infected—burns are dirty, crushing wounds are dirtier—his right was at least partly recovered. He sat up while he continued to talk, and felt at his feet; they'd pulled off—no, *cut* off, there was a dank, slimy band of leather around each ankle—what was left of his moccasins, and wound a short piece of chain through the remaining loops of leather. He could probably work free with just his right hand, but it might take time, and he was afraid; what if she yelled and brought in more guards? What if they came before he had escaped, but when he had undone enough so they noticed?

He stroked a finger over the chain and the leather band, willing himself to have the kind of nerve that the heroes in his favorite books did, and while he did that, he described Izzy Underhill in minute detail, knowing perfectly well that he might be helping them, if they took Pueblo, to find her and put her severed head on a stick so they could dance around it.

He tried to be inconspicuous about squeezing his feet together to give himself slack; then he felt a tug and saw that the shorthand girl's left hand was holding the chain to help him slip one loop of it. He pushed through and kept talking, telling them about where Chris Manckiewicz hung out with his printer Abel and his reporter Cassie, and probably helping them figure out how to assassinate all of them if they wanted to. *(Crap, Manckiewicz is a big guy and brave as a lion, Abel Marx is a giant with a bad temper, but little Cassie Cartland is a five-foot-one seventeen-year-old; way to go, Ecco.)*

He worked another loop free, again with the shorthand girl supplying the spare hand he needed, and earned more sips of water. Toward the end, Robert came in and sat watching him; he made himself not look down at the loosened but not yet untied chain by his feet. Robert moved closer and listened harder; *he's just trying to make me afraid*, Ecco thought. *And I don't know if he can make me any more afraid than—*

A slave woman came in, carrying a hibachi of glowing charcoal. At Robert's direction, she set it near enough Ecco's feet so that he could feel its warmth. Robert dropped a handful of old screwdrivers blade-down into the charcoal.

Ecco babbled faster, terrified and weeping. The screwdrivers were glowing when Robert said, "Now tell us about your ex-wife and your three children. I know they're in Santa Fe and your ex-wife is named Kyla, and you have two boys, Travis and Cooper, and a girl, Willow. Tell us what they look like. Tell us what would make them sure a message was from you. Tell us everything about them."

Ecco felt a great surge of relief in his chest; he had just found out there was something he would not do. "No," he said, and then repeated, "No."

"We already know everything you are going to tell us. You won't hurt them by telling. All you'll do is show us that you cooperate one hundred percent."

He dug his index finger against the ball of solder where his thumb had been, and relished the pain. "I won't."

"Last chance. I won't ask you again. Tell us about your family." Robert's hand stroked up his thigh, as if they were lovers. "Can you feel how warm them screwdriver's getting? Think about that here." The squeeze was surprisingly light.

"I won't tell you that," Ecco said. Courage and strength seemed to surge into him. He knew now he would end horribly, but not badly.

Robert said, "I'll do as much as I want whether you talk or not. Then you'll talk, Mister Ecco, but only when I decide you should, after I'm done."

*Here we go. Just like the dentist's office except I gotta hope for a chance to kick the dentist in the balls.*

By the time Robert said, "Time for lunch," Ecco said, "No. No. No," because now it was all he would say.

**ABOUT AN HOUR LATER. ATHENS, TNG DISTRICT.
1 PM EST. SUNDAY, AUGUST 17, 2025.**

The radio tech gave Cameron Nguyen-Peters the thumbs-up and tapped the windup timer, which showed the standard hour. "Hey, Heather, it's me. Okay to talk now?"

"More than okay!" Heather's voice hissed and crackled; the encryption gadget didn't work as well in daylight as it did at night. "So you know it's a boy, Leonardo Plekhanov Junior, who I'm calling Leo, and he's healthy as a moose, and the best baby ever born?"

"Absolutely. Arnie told us all last night, of course, when he sent it out on the secure channels. I didn't call then because I thought you'd want to sleep."

"I did," Heather said. "But to tell the truth, now I'm bored. Tired, but bored. And Leo's amazing and wonderful but not a great conversationalist just yet."

"Well, he will be, if he takes after either parent. Tell me everything about him." Cam leaned back and listened; Leo sounded like every other baby, but Heather sounded great.

In the secure radio room, the big, slowly rotating spindles of plywood cams, the beer-bottle capacitors, and the big spark coils looked like a 1920s mad-scientist's lab. *A hundred years of progress to be back where we started.*

Heather finally wound down and said, "All right, have I put you to sleep yet?"

"Not a bit. This is great."

"Since when is a lifelong bachelor interested in babies?"

"Since I started taking an interest in the future, because that's who's going to live there."

"Yeah, but even the best baby in the world only has so many little toes and eyes to describe."

"Twelve, I believe—"

"*Twelve?* Oh, ten toes and two eyes. For one moment I was hoping I hadn't miscounted. But yes, you're right."

"I'm an ex-baby myself." He had been trying to think of a smooth transition to what he most wanted to say, but there wasn't any, so he said, "Sorry to bring in business, but I wanted to thank you for the help from our mutual friend."

"Business is a great thing to bring in, and I take it our friend let you know we're secure here?"

"Yes, but I'm afraid they'll notice if we talk too often. So I'm afraid I'm taking advantage of your big occasion—"

"Hey, like I said, I'm bored stiff here. And you just gave me an idea. I'll send you a personal letter in the next mailbag—for sure they'll open that—and start off about how much more we need to talk. Since they probably know we dated years ago, I think I'll pretend I've got a crush on you, Cam. You play back. Talk about me enough to bore the people around you. That should give us an excuse to chat more often."

"All right, great idea, as long as I'm not expected to be convincingly romantic."

"I'll just be so besotted I won't notice your sheer ineptitude. Now what's on your mind, Cam?"

"Bottom line, I'm losing out to Grayson and the reverends. He's taking directions from his father-in-law, pulling competent officers out of posts near here, replacing them with people with the right religion, and rotating them out to our frontier with the Lost Quarter. Which I can't really object to because we sure as hell need them out there, but it also means my coup insurance is disappearing. There's forced prayer, strictly Post Raptural, at parades and reserve exercises now. The last editor at the *Weekly Insight* who wasn't Post Raptural is not only gone, but was explicitly fired for being the wrong religion. And guys who've been Republican since Reagan are being thrown out of their party for not praying right. And I object, and object, and object, and—nothing. They just keep doing it." Cam wasn't just embarrassed, as he'd expected to be; he felt as humiliated as if he were admitting he'd spent his inheritance on whiskey and whores and had to ask his best friend to make his rent for him.

"Cam, I know all that. Besides our mutual friend I have plenty of other sources, open and not. Look, we're completely on the same side here. We've got to find a way to either knock Grayson out of the game, if we can't get a deal with him that will put America back together, or bring him back into it and playing under the same rules as the rest of you. So we'd be in this together, even if you weren't a friend."

Cam felt funny in his chest; it had been a long time since someone had just said they were his friend. *Fine dictator I make,* he thought sadly. *Worrying all the time about whether people like me.*

There was still more to admit. "The truth is, I don't know what will happen while I'm out of Athens."

"Well, then bring Grayson along; he's your deputy, he should be with you anyway. And if his followers pull a coup while you're here, just stay. I've got ten jobs that you'd be perfect for."

"Such as?"

"Well, babysitter for the world's best baby comes to mind. He just made the most amazing face."

## THE FOLLOWING NIGHT. THE FORMER RIVERSIDE BAPTIST CHURCH, IN THE FORMER MONTEZUMA, INDIANA. 12:35 AM EST. TUESDAY, AUGUST 19, 2025.

"You're not going to live much longer," the shorthand girl told Ecco. "Do you think water would be okay for you?"

His face hurt terribly. "Don't know, but I'm thirsty."

"Let's try, but let's be careful. I'd hate to hurt you any more." She gave him a sip from the watering can; it felt good, and his guts at least did not rebel immediately. "More?"

He nodded. He wished he could see her, but the last thing he had seen—or ever would see—was Robert bringing the hot screwdriver down into first his left, and then his right, eye. They had broken his ankles and knees with sledgehammers, and branded the soles of his feet, before their rampage across his body was done; his last fantasy of escape was done with.

She gave him more water. He made his mouth shape the words, "Do I need to answer more questions or tell you stuff?"

"I'm here on my own," she said. "I just wanted to ask you something."

"Better ask soon," he said. He was so tired and fading so fast, but he didn't want her to leave him alone.

"Have you been anywhere near Pale Bluff, Illinois?"

It clicked. "You're Pauline Kloster," he said, very softly, barely breathing. "Carol May asked me to look for you."

"Is she okay? Where is she?"

"Back in Pale Bluff."

"It's still there? They told me it was all burned."

"It's still there. And it's nice," he said. "Pretty. It's summer; the orchards are so green, it smells so good." He started to cry. "I was there two weeks ago. It's like you remember. Get moving, now. Get home, Pauline, leave now." He fought down the impossible words that formed in his heart—*and take me with you.*

"I don't even know where I am," she said.

"You're in Indiana, northeast of Pale Bluff, not far north of Terre Haute, on the Wabash. Go home now. They're worried about you, they want to see you."

He felt desperate—she wasn't understanding; she was unbound, unhurt, all she had to do was slip out and run.

"They told us it's all tribes all the way to the Mississippi."

"No, no . . . the Wabash is the line, sorta, and that's the river we're on now. There's a bridge . . . about a mile north . . . it's US 36. Get across it. It's all trees and hills on the other side, lots of woods to hide in, keep running, they might chase you for a day or more, but keep moving. Do you know your way to Pale Bluff from 36?"

"Yeah, I do."

"Go now."

"Can't I do something for you first?"

"What's the name of the boy that tricked you into coming over here?" he asked. "What's his name?"

"Eric, but I haven't—"

"Okay, I'm gonna say you got a message from him and ran off to meet him. Maybe we'll get lucky and they'll look in the wrong direction. Now *go*, Pauline, *go.*"

He was so afraid she'd delay further, and he might break down and ask her to kill him, but he felt her lips brush his forehead and then she was gone. He rolled, found the watering can, bit down on the spout, and drank the last of it.


## 5 HOURS LATER. THE FORMER RIVERSIDE BAPTIST CHURCH, IN THE FORMER MONTEZUMA, INDIANA. 5:30 AM EST. TUESDAY, AUGUST 19, 2025.

When Robert came in to slap Ecco awake, he had slept only fitfully; he tried to sleep on his back with his head tilted back, so that maybe he could choke on blood or a loose tooth, but no luck.

They didn't ask him about Eric, or Pauline, or anything about Pueblo; he wasn't sure what they did ask him about. He just tried to say "no" five thousand times, telling himself he'd surely be dead before he got to five thousand, but he kept losing count and having to start over.

. . .

Eventually they gave up and just finished things.

"Paint him with hot pitch," Karl ordered. "So he'll last. Put him on a post in the middle of the road, on our side of the US 36 bridge, facing the other side. Have a light hand with the tar on his face and do what you can to keep that expression; it fucking makes *me* jump, you know."

"They gonna be able to tell who it was?" Robert asked. "With that tar, he won't look white."

"They don't need to know who it was, as long as they know it was a man and we didn't like him." Karl was in an expansive, jolly mood. "Any word on the steno slave?"

"I've put trackers after her; bet your ass that Mister Asshole In Pine Tar here told her where she was and that she wasn't far from home."

"I figured as much," Karl said, pulling at his beard the way he did whenever he wanted to make sure that everyone understood that any good ideas Robert had, and carried out, were still to Karl's credit for having chosen Robert.

Robert nodded. "Hey, I had an idea for going home. Let's let the crew work our boat upstream each day, and you and me hunt and then meet the boat upstream; that way we don't have to hang around for all that hard work, and we can make a real vacation out of it, hunting and fishing the whole way, but we have the cooks, the bitches, and fresh game every night."

Karl laughed in pure delight. "Damn, Robert, that's why I keep you around, you're my idea man."

## 2 HOURS LATER. NORTH OF SUMMIT GROVE, INDIANA. 9:30 AM EST. TUESDAY, AUGUST 19, 2025.

Pauline woke to the sounds of dogs and men. She rolled off the cot and crept across the floor of the cabin; in the daylight she could see it was an ordinary fishing and hunting shack like her grandfather's, with outdoor junk lying in heaps where the plastic holding it had rotted. In the dark, last night, she'd just followed a trail, looking for somewhere to rest.

She crawled to the window, staying low, and peered out cautiously. The sun was well up.

She heard the men shouting to the dogs. She knew them; two of Castle Earthstone's scouts—she'd taken dictation for their reports. They were not close yet, but they would be.

Pauline felt like punching herself in the head; the night before she had gone just a few miles before holing up to rest and savor the feeling of safety and freedom.

*Well, nothing for it now, but try,* as Aunt Carol May used to annoy her by saying. She looked around; nothing useful right out in the open and no time to pick through the cabinets. She went out the back door, running downhill away from the trackers.

*Fishing shacks are located near water, and water runs downhill,* she told herself. Sure enough, at the bottom the owners had piled logs and rocks into a creek to make a pond. She waded across and upstream; it sounded like they were getting closer, and wading was slow, so she only went up the creek far enough to be out of sight of the pond, and then a few more yards to a pipe-and-board bridge, where she climbed out and followed the one-car track that ran through it, heading south because that was the way back to 36, and from 36 she could get home.

### 9 HOURS LATER. CASTLE LARSEN (JENNER, CALIFORNIA). 4 PM PST. TUESDAY, AUGUST 19, 2025.

Bambi Castro had always thought the area around the mouth of the Russian River pegged the meter for gorgeous: the deepest green on the California coast, the wide rushing river, the beaches and hills, like a movie image of Eden unspoiled. Flying at the Stearman's low cruising ceiling, she could just see a few columns of smoke still rising from the ruins around the Golden Gate, far to the south. *Someday soon, some poor bastards will have to go in there to take a look, and I don't envy them.*

She swept wide over the ocean and came back in across the beach, touching down about as well as anyone could on underfilled greased-linen tires.

She tried to pretend that she was irritated about being called off her regular route, but the chance to fly into one of her favorite parts of the country and stay with one of her best friends rendered her irredeemably cheerful.

In his office, though, one glance showed that Quattro had been worried sick about something. Little bits of torn paper littered the desk; four half-filled water glasses sat among the paper snowstorm; and he lurched more than stood when she came in.

"Is there something wrong?" Bambi asked.

"I've never been this scared before in my life," he admitted. "Bambi, will you marry me?"


## ABOUT THE SAME TIME. ON ILLINOIS HIGHWAY 1, JUST SOUTH OF THE RUINS OF MARSHALL, ILLINOIS. 6 PM CST. TUESDAY, AUGUST 19, 2025.

Pauline Kloster felt like she was jogging through icy fog, and the cool damp as the road passed through shadowy woods threatened that as the sun sank, the night would turn cold. *I'd prolly suck at this anyway, even if I'd had food and sleep.*

She had been running or walking constantly since leaving the fishing cabin, afraid to take time to forage. Besides, the abandoned stores and homes in this country had been thoroughly picked over. At least she'd had plenty of water from creeks and ponds on the way; a few months as a Daybreaker slave had given her trot-proof guts.

She'd wasted the lead time Ecco gave her; she hated herself for that. As soon as she crossed that bridge she should have run all night, as far and fast as she could, right down the middle of the paved roads, so that the afternoon thunderstorm would have erased most of her scent, and maybe waded up and down some streams, anything to put the dogs off.

Three times this afternoon she'd waded from one bridge to another she could see along the stream; each time put the dogs off, but only long enough to let her walk instead of run for an hour or so, because the slow process of working along a streambed cost precious distance and time.

Around the next bend in the road, she found Harry's Chop House, a ruined roadhouse. She hadn't heard the dogs or men in about an hour; perhaps there would be some unlooted food, or something she could use. She staggered up to where the door hung off its hinges.

The kitchen, pantry, and bar were looted down to the last bite; a big pile of empty potato-chip bags lay in the dust in one corner, testifying to how thorough everyone had been.

But there was a two-pound box of cayenne pepper. She tore the top off, dumped it on the soles of her moccasins, threw handfuls across the floor, and went out the back door and along the frontage road, scattering cayenne behind her for a mile or so. *At least the damned dogs will be sneezing their heads off.*

Just at dusk, she found a dead fawn in the ditch, and dragged that behind her till dark, finally towing the deer's remains into a borrow pond, swimming across to come out on a storm culvert. The dim blue moon was coming up as she regained the road and resumed her travel; perhaps she'd just wasted time, but maybe she'd slowed them down.

But long before the moon was overhead, she heard the distant baying; *prolly I* can't *put'em off, ever, totally, 'cause they know where I'm going and there ain't really no other way to get there.* Though her body from the waist down was one big streak of pain, she had picked up her pace. *All I can do is get there first.*

## 2 DAYS LATER. BRIDGE ON THE LITTLE WABASH NEAR WYNOOSE, NEW STATE OF WABASH (PCG) OR ILLINOIS (TNG). 5:12 AM CST. THURSDAY, AUGUST 21, 2025.

By morning twilight, Pauline thought she'd gained some ground, after the dogs and men had flushed her in the middle of the night; she'd started out almost in bowshot of them, diving out the broken window of the abandoned Subway when she heard them, but she'd doubled around and lost them, zagged over to another road, and probably put a solid mile between herself and them.

The gray light let her see the sign: ENTERING WYNOOSE IL.

Her heart sank.

When she had gone off with the tribe, on their way out they'd sacked and burned Wynoose. *That was when they chained me, after I tried to run away.*

*If I had known, one mile before we came here, back then . . .*

*If I had realized where I was the first day we were at Montezuma . . .*

*If I had just kept moving after getting away . . .*

She'd rather have gone around Wynoose, but she needed that bridge. The Little Wabash is much smaller than the Wabash, but in this hill and ridge country, the Little Wabash's channel was often narrow and its current swift, and if she got in trouble trying to swim it, she didn't have any energy or strength left to recover.

Twilight brightened. Many charred buildings gaped, their insides gone, but with concealment for fifty men behind those black, ruined walls.

She passed among the dreary black shells of Wynoose at as much of a run as she could manage. Thick, leafy trees closed in around the road, dense and still black as if some of the night had stuck to them, but a pale red light was reaching down to the road.

She was hurrying down the slope to the bridge when the arrow struck her calf. She cried out and staggered; another arrow flew through the space where she had been.

She broke the arrow's shaft off with both hands (*oh God no oh God don't shoot me in the ass*), leaving its point in her calf, and tried to run on, despite the searing pain shooting up her leg. Another arrow passed an inch from her head, but she was going to cross this bridge, cross it, *one more river to cross*—

She heard them running behind her, and the click of the dogs' toenails on the pavement. She was going to take at least one fucker with her—*make them kill me now, not what they did to Steve Ecco.*

The bridge deck was under her feet now, the other bank just a sprint away, if she could only sprint instead of hobble. She heard the man's breathing behind her—

A flash from the opposite bank, a thud and moan behind her. She gained a step on her pursuer; another flash. The other man behind her screamed.

She heard a clatter of dog claws on the bridge behind her, and then a yelp as something sailed past her; more yelps, and she realized *someone over there is throwing rocks at the dogs.* She hobbled forward, and a man burst out of the brush by the opposite bridgehead and ran toward her, still chucking rocks, his slow-to-load gun slung over his shoulder.

The dogs yipped at each other, broke, and ran; *prolly dog-ese for "I didn't sign up for this."*

The man raced past her, but she knew by the coonskin cap who it was. She looked back and that tripped her. Sitting up, she watched with satisfaction as Freddie Pranger finished off the first, unconscious Daybreaker with a hatchet blow to the forehead. Pranger walked up to the other one, who was still clutching his torn belly, planted his boot on the man's neck, and as the man shrieked "Please!" Pranger whipped his hatchet over his head and brought it down in a deep chop into the back of the man's skull.

Pranger wiped the ax on the dead man's pants and hurried back to Pauline. "Was'at all'at was chasing you?"

"Yeah."

"Well, then, let's fix you up and get you home."

Poor old Freddie looked so bewildered when she started to cry, but she couldn't seem to stop to tell him it was okay.


### 3 DAYS LATER. PUEBLO, COLORADO. 11 AM MST. SUNDAY, AUGUST 24, 2025.

It had been a colder, wetter summer than anyone in Pueblo could remember, so the old Pueblo Courthouse's lawn was still green even in August, and volunteers with weedwhips had been needed to make it presentable, but the dense green was pretty; the blue sky and crisp air, more like October than August, was delicious; and it could hardly have been more perfect for Bambi and Quattro's wedding.

Heather was easily the most comfortable person there; they'd given her a chair, with a pitcher of water and a glass beside her. Leo was continuing to show promise as an extra-quiet baby, occasionally squirming just enough so she had an excuse to look down and gently touch his face; otherwise, she had about fifteen words to say at the appointed time and could just sit and watch the crowd. *Gee, other than the watch and militia on duty, I think the whole town must be here.*

Colonel Streen performed the ceremony; they were going to miss him, as the TNG was sending him over to the former Cedar City to head up a joint punitive expedition against tribals who had set forest fires, smashed irrigation systems, and burned out some isolated homes.

To maximize the political benefits, Arnie had written a short speech playing up hope for the future, union between people and among peoples— not heavy-handed, relying more on the context of the scenery, because, as Arnie said, you didn't have to look far in Colorado to realize it was the state where "America the Beautiful" was written.

Larry Mensche stood proud and tall beside Quattro. *He's such a changed man ever since he brought his daughter back; he was already our best, but now he's sort of . . . magnificent. Weird. Larry seemed like kind of an average FBI agent, dead-ended, had his last promotion, serving his time out . . . and now his name's going to live with Kit Carson and Daniel Boone. . . .*

Bambi looked great in an antique wedding dress, and Quattro was splendid in his tuxedo; at least the fashion for all-natural materials across the last fifty years or so had left some good clothes in good shape.

Heather rose and said the brief sentences Arnie had created for the matron-of-honor speech; there were more speeches than was normal at a wedding because this was a major news event and news went out via the *Post-Times*, so the more words to report, the better. To her relief, Heather got the words out without stumbling, sat back down, and was done with her active part. *This might be the longest break I've taken without being asleep since we came to Pueblo.*

At last the ceremony ended with three volleys from the honor guard. (*Love, honor, and shoot the right people* . . . , Heather thought.)

For the reception, Quattro had brought over a boxcar load from each coast—jars of pickled and dried fish from Washington, coffee from Lisa Fanchion's fleet, dried and canned vegetables from California, molasses from Florida, sweet potatoes from Alabama, oysters from the Gulf, and beer and wine from everywhere. Quattro had contrived to give the whole town one big unrationed meal, sharing about as much happiness as he could. "That's Patrick and Ntale's fourth trip through the chow line, by my count," Heather observed.

"I counted six," Jason said. "But I might've missed one. Patrick said that when Ntale's wedding comes up, he's going to be as rich as Quattro and throw a feast like this—but *bigger, and with chocolate.*"

Arnie grinned. "It's what I told you, Heather. Heroes. It's a rough world nowadays, and kids can't get by anymore on mere role models—they need *heroes*."

"Maybe Quattro could adopt a characteristic slogan," Heather said.

Arnie laid a finger on one cheek. "Let me guess. Anything as long as it's not *the mail must go through*."

# NINE:
# THE DYNAMITED MERMEN
# WASHED ASHORE

"Mid-day from Crypto Incoming, Ms. O'Grainne. Hey there, Leo," Patrick said.

Heather looked up from her lunch. "Hey, you have to stop bringing me more work than I can do before the next batch comes in."

"Oh, sure, you say that, but if I stopped bringing it, you'd be extra mad. Wouldn't she, Leo? Your mom is a tough lady."

"Don't try to enlist my son in this, he's too young to encounter bad influences." Heather gave Patrick the usual allotment of meal tickets, and a hug. He hugged back, hard, collected her outgoing crypto, and was gone, *The mail must go through!* echoing as his moccasined feet slapped down the steps.

She pulled out her big yarn and card chart and began sorting through the implications of the messages. Dave Carlucci, FBI in San Diego, reported that Harrison Castro was making more blustery noises about his right to have vassals; Carlucci thought he'd finally found a Federal judge who would issue the order Heather had asked him to seek. The message ended with PS SAW YR DAD. STILL HAPPY, HEALTH GOOD, WANTS 2 HEAR EVTHING RE LEO ASAP. Heather decided to leave CASTLE CHALLENGES as an area to watch but didn't move its priority up or down.

Sally Osterhaus, overflying a tribal area in Central Oregon, reported what looked like a performance area for a Daybreak play; her sketch would be run by Debbie or Larry ASAP. TRIBAL/DAYBREAK LINK, no change.

From Athens, Red Dog reported that General Phat, being held incommunicado, was healthy, in good spirits, and willing to discuss the issues she'd asked him to; that advanced the FIND PRESIDENTIAL CANDIDATE path substantially. Nice to see some green spreading down a board dominated by red and yellow.

After the first five lines of the message from Carol May Kloster, Heather spoke aloud, and immediately added, "Leo, honey, do *not* make any of those your first word."

She scribbled five notes, and leaned out the window; sure enough, Patrick was sitting on the park bench, reading *Great Expectations* for James Hendrix's class. "Patrick!"

Heather would have sworn that somehow, from three storeys below, that kid managed to get to her desk before she did.

"Deliver as addressed—while they're alone if you can, but don't delay if you can't. Make sure they see my OPEN ALONE IMMEDIATELY note. They won't need to send a reply. Come right back; I'll have another batch." She handed him his coupons. *He and Ntale'll eat for weeks on this.* Her feelings must have leaked through, because he went silently—but if anything, faster than ever before.

**6 MINUTES LATER. PUEBLO, COLORADO. 1:35 PM MST. MONDAY, AUGUST 25, 2025.**

Patrick appeared beside Chris as if he'd blinked into existence, and handed Chris the note from Heather. Chris nodded, set down the page proof he'd been going over, handed Patrick three meal coupons as a tip, and carried the message into the bathroom.

*Immediately prepare anyone who needs to know for your disappearance for an indefinite period of weeks. Grab any hand-carryable items vital to your comfort or security; otherwise plan to live out of one of our standard pre-packed field packs. Come to my office at once. You will be leaving from there. Explanations on arrival. Sorry for any inconvenience but do it. Heather.*

"Yow," Chris said, emerging. "Extra special executive meeting. We need the chiefs of production, advertising, editorial, and subscriptions in the conference room now."

The *Post-Times* actually had only three full-time Pueblo employees, one of whom was Chris, who handled all those areas, and their production room was one big former auto garage.

Abel Marx looked up from his battle with the old press and laughed, a huge white grin splitting his dark face. "Man, that joke never gets old for me, either, Chris."

"Middle-aged men are all brain damaged," Cassie Cartland said, from behind her desk. "That's why they'll keep making the same tired joke over and over. Let me finish one thought . . ." Her fingers clattered over the keys like hail on a tin roof. With her freckles, bowl-cut brown hair, and nose and chin too prominent from sheer skinniness, Cassie looked like a kid on Take Your Daughter to Work Day. She was almost seventeen, the daughter of the printer Chris had used for the *Olympia Observer* and for his first try at book publishing, and possibly had the best instinct he'd ever seen for what went into a news story. "Done. Just thought of a perfect closer and didn't want to lose it. Do we want to use the big conference room since it's the whole staff?"

"Wouldn't that be *another* same tired joke, over and over?" Chris asked.

"Oh, my God, being a middle-aged old poop is *catching*," Cassie said. "By the time I'm your age I'll be as old as you are now." In her ancient wooden swivel chair, she looked like a sixth-grader playing in Dad's office. Abel set his compositor's stool into the open space at the center of the room; he looked like a rhinoceros roosting on a mushroom. Chris sat on the only corner of his desk that was not buried in papers, and avoided thinking about what he might look like.

"Here's the deal," Chris said. "Over in that other job that you guys never talk about, there's something I need to do, *now*, and I might be gone for months. Cassie, open my mail, take over correspondence for the paper, what you say or decide is good with me. Any messages relating to my other job'll be sealed in separate envelopes; take those over to Heather that second, or send them via Patrick, but no other messenger. Drastically overpay Patrick or Heather will have your guts on a stick. For any personal correspondence, remember to respond with 'Baby' or 'Dearest darlingest' followed by their name, tell them I feel just the same way, and sign it 'Your rampaging love-rhino.'"

"Yeah, right. If I see one like that I'll suggest psychiatric help."

"Abel, I wouldn't begin to tell you how to do your job, because you'd stomp me into a grease spot."

"And you don't need to tell Cassie how to do hers, or I will stomp you into a grease spot."

"Exactly," Cassie said. "Headlines for the next issue are: World—Indian and Australian delegations arrive for Big Three summit in Buenos Aires. Nation One—Provi Congress passes Civil Discourse Act, President Weisbrod threatens veto. Nation Two—Post Raptural Church declares Natcon's proposals 'Satanic.' Local—Larsen Weds Castro. Soon as you're gone I'll replace it all with celebrity gossip and beauty hints."

"Glad to know you understand the business."

"One thought, though. Should I write a few stories to sign your name to, so it's at least less obvious that you're gone? Everyone in Pueblo will know, of course, but would it be worth anything to cover for you away from here?"

"It might be. Be sure to put my name on anything about holiday decorating or fashion trends."

"Of course." She grinned at him and said, "Seriously, Chris, I'm scared shitless—without Daybreak I'd be hoping to edit my high school's student news site right now, and you're handing me the most important newspaper in America."

Chris shrugged. "If anybody needs to look threatening, you've got Abel. If there's a need for mature judgment, he's got you."

"I meant I was scared about how much I think I'm going to enjoy this."

"Now *I'm* scared," Abel said.


**20 MINUTES LATER. PUEBLO, COLORADO. 2:10 PM MST. MONDAY, AUGUST 25, 2025.**

Chris Manckiewicz arrived and took his place beside Quattro, Bambi, Larry, and Jason. "Sorry I was so slow, I needed to arrange cover."

"You're well within bounds," Heather said. "All right. Let me begin with the awful news." She detailed it quickly, sparing nothing: Ecco had been intercepted and murdered by people who were clearly waiting for him; Pauline Kloster had escaped and Carol May was recording everything Pauline could remember about Castle Earthstone. "It looks like Pale Bluff is now our last secure settlement on that frontier, which means we've quietly lost a whole tier of counties on our side of the Wabash in the last ten weeks. There are obviously far more people than we'd thought in the Lost Quarter, tightly organized into tribes and apparently into Castles as well, controlled by Daybreak. The best news, and it's not that good, is that I'm now sure I can get the Temper government to mount military expeditions against the tribes next spring—but we'll need ten times what we would have thought."

Manckiewicz saw it first, as she'd expected. "That isn't the worst. We must have a traitor in the ranks, fairly high up to have known what Ecco's real mission was."

"Pauline Kloster said Ecco was caught within five minutes of crossing the Wabash. And that he walked almost up to Terre Haute, seeing patrols all the way. They can't possibly have the resources to patrol their border that thoroughly; they *had* to have known everything. That means high-level traitor."

"That's right. They knew everything," Larry said quietly.

She looked around the room. "I'm not going to tell you who's suspected, though I'm sure the absence of some people is a dead giveaway as to who's suspected, but please don't discuss that. Were you all able to secure complete cover so that you can just go straight from here to the airport? Anybody absolutely have to go get a piece of personal gear or send a note to someone so they won't talk?"

"Covered it," Jason said.

"That's what I was late for," Chris added.

"We keep most of our stuff in the Gooney," Quattro said, "and *we* won't be gone long, will we?"

"No, not you. Good, then. Quattro and Bambi, you're going to take the DC-3 and haul these three guys to wherever they think they can do the best penetration from the northwest, moving toward Castle Earthstone— it's in the Palestine-Warsaw area in Indiana. Work out mechanics of it all in flight, including figuring out where you can refuel in the middle of the night without being conspicuous. Leave *now*, before anything can leak. By dawn tomorrow, Larry, Chris, and Jason need to have landed somewhere north and west of Lafayette. Cross the Tippecanoe, go at least as far as Castle Earthstone, report on what you find."

"What about the traitor?" Jason asked.

"I know none of you are it," she said. "You all have solid verifiable alibis for the whole time when Ecco's mission could have been betrayed. I'll be doing things here to find the traitor, but in the light of what we've just learned about the Lost Quarter, I've got to know what's going on, right now. I can't wait to establish perfect security."

"Why us?" Jason asked quietly. "I mean—well, I have a wife with a child coming, Chris is a very public figure, Larry just found his lost daughter—"

Heather grimaced. "Everyone will have some reason not to go. Out of the ones I can clear right away, Quattro and Bambi, you're in because this mission has to move as far as it can by air. Larry, you've got the woodcraft; Jason, there has to be an ex-Daybreaker along to make sense out of whatever you find, you'll be more use in a fight than Ysabel, and she still has seizures around Daybreak stuff. I'm assuming you don't want me to send your pregnant wife."

Jason nodded, satisfied.

"What am I along for?" Chris asked.

"So you can publish articles and maybe a book that will infuriate the absolute living piss out of all the civilized people and motivate them to rise up and slay and slay and slay till there's *nothing* left of Daybreak. It's war. The public has to want to win it. In less than three weeks we have a summit conference here to get the ball rolling for the restart election, and in fourteen months we're going to elect a new batch of politicians. God love 'em, politicians are all *about* deals, so the way I see it is, the only way to ensure no deals with the devil is to ensure there's no devil. Now, go."

## ABOUT AN HOUR LATER. PUEBLO, COLORADO. 4 PM MST. MONDAY, AUGUST 25, 2025.

Deb Mensche arrived first, right at four. The directions had said not to come early. She slipped in and closed the door so quietly that Heather did not notice her before she looked up from breastfeeding Leo. She didn't exactly jump, but Leo felt the difference and wailed. She helped him find his way back to the nipple. "That was spooky. You might as well be invisible."

"Leo caught me."

"Leo's only been around a week. He's harder to fool because he makes fewer assumptions." Heather smiled at her. "Glad you're here first. Come over here, there's something I want to say softly in case the next people in might hear through the door."

Deb put her ear to Heather's mouth and Heather said, "Your mission will be a decoy, but you're not supposed to know that. One of the two people I'm going to put in charge of briefing you might betray you to the other side. I don't know which. Be super careful and—"

Deb squeezed QRT—stop sending—on Heather's elbow, and went to the door, opening it an instant after Arnie knocked. As he was coming in, Leslie Antonowicz joined them, carrying a large load of books and papers.

"Well," Heather said. "Thank you for being prompt." In a few swift, brutal sentences, she sketched what had happened to Ecco and added that the encrypted station somewhere near Bloomington had been active not long after. That much was true—it had been Arnie's direction-finding stations that had spotted it. "You'll be going in another way," she told Deb, "around Uniontown, Kentucky, a nice little town just above where the Wabash joins the Ohio." She launched into a far more detailed than necessary description of Uniontown, all the while listening intently while she talked.

When she heard the first telltale cough-and-thud of the Gooney's engine starting, she raised her voice, rising from her desk. "Now, listen closely, I can't stress enough—"

She had put her lunch tray as close to the edge of the desk as possible, for just this moment, and now a little turn of one finger flipped it over. The crash of dishes was abrupt; Heather swore loudly, and from his crib, Leo woke screaming. It covered the DC-3 starting its run-up for takeoff; Leo, bless his sound little lungs, could easily have drowned out a missile launch and two rock concerts.

By the time Leo was calmed, the dishes retrieved, and the briefing resumed, Quattro, the DC-3, and the mission were far out of earshot. Heather slipped the note into Leslie's hand as she went, telling her to come back for a different conference in ninety minutes.

"Well," Heather said, as the door closed behind Debbie Mensche, leaving just Arnie for the next session, "my little man here seems to be back to sleep." She kissed Leo and settled him back into the crib. *Sorry about that, kid. Probably not the last time you'll lose some sleep because your country needs you.*

"As long as I've got you alone, Arnie, let me explain that I'm partly compartmentalizing the missions this time. You've got to be in both compartments because you've got the radio direction-finding info our agents need to plan their approach to Bloomington, but I'd like you to pretend you're two people and don't let them talk to each other."

"I figured as much. Who's next?"

"Do you know Roger Jackson?"

"Barely."

"Young guy. Everything I know about him is that he has an abundance of woodcraft and fighting experience and a lack of permanent assignments and family. We're going to send him in along old I-64, a long way from where Deb's going in. James Hendrix did some work on remaining resources in that area, so he'll be the other briefer. I wish we had more than one briefer who knew the direction-finding data; nothing personal, Arn, but we could be much better compartmentalized."

"I've been wanting to beef up our DF operations. If Tarantina Highbotham starts doing those for us, down in the Virgin Islands, the long baseline would let us zero in much more closely on the intermittent stations inside the Lost Quarter."

"Ask her to start on that ASAP."

A knock at the door announced James Hendrix. Because he was so quiet and self-possessed, Heather didn't feel as attached to James, and if one of them had to be the traitor, she preferred him to Arnie, her friend from long before Daybreak, or to warm, funny, adventurous Leslie.

Roger came in while Arnie and James were still looking for something to make small talk about. To keep things consistent with the way she'd behaved in briefing Deb, Heather put an enormous amount of detail into a very simple mission: Roger was to cross the Wabash on the I-64 bridge, just south of Grayville, scout thoroughly before going over, return at the first sign that he was being watched, and otherwise hurry to Bloomington overland, where he would find out as much as he could about that transmitter.

At the end, she told James she had more material to go over with him about possibly re-opening some old coal mines on the Western Slope; since he was, among other things, their paper maps wizard, with a phenomenal memory for anything he had seen once, it was a logical reason for him to stick around. She had been afraid Arnie wouldn't go, but instead, he seemed eager, if anything, to leave.

*Arnie didn't ask one question. When did that ever happen before? But he and Ecco were friends. I don't want him to have sent Steve to his doom.*

Ten minutes after Arnie left, Leslie returned, her backpack loaded with papers and books; Dan Samson was almost at her heels, unclipping his stringy gray hair and wiping his face with a rag. "We raced," Samson explained. "This psychotic child not only runs like a bunny, she's rough with the elbows when you try to pass."

Neither sweating nor breathing hard, Leslie shrugged. "Part of any game is using your fouls—especially when there's no ref."

Once again Heather laid it out: Ecco's death, the need to penetrate the Lost Quarter and find out what was going on, and the too-elaborate discussion of everything, in the hope that if either Leslie or James were the traitor, a telltale detail might make it into an intercepted enemy message. For a long time after Leslie and James departed, she stood by the window, holding Leo, trying to think.

*I don't want it to be Arnie, but I don't want it to be Leslie, either. I keep hoping for time to go fishing, hiking, or climbing with her; I bet before Daybreak she was one of those Rocky Mountain woman athletes that barely ever slept under a roof.*

Heather drew and re-drew the diagram in her head; each of the three agents had been set up with two of her potential traitors. One agent should get through without being intercepted; the two people who had briefed that agent would be cleared, the one who had not condemned.

The sun was already low in the sky. Leo woke and announced mealtime, and Heather did her best to stop thinking, but after Leo went back to sleep, and she stretched out on her bed, she lay awake for a long time. Her thoughts were cold, dark, and sad.

## ABOUT THE SAME TIME. PUEBLO, COLORADO. 9:25 PM MST. MONDAY, AUGUST 25, 2025.

"Hey, I know I'm being a big sissy and all, but are you heading up to the 18th and Blake area?"

"We wish *more* people would be big sissies; it's more fun to have company than to pick up bodies and run for medics when we find them in alleys." Mandy, the watch sergeant, wore a not-quite-fitting steel-pot helmet. *Wonder if she had that in the attic or picked it up from a museum?* "Yeah, we're headed that way, Doctor Yang, we'll take you right to your door. Have they decided whether your place is going to be inside the walls yet?"

"Not yet," Arnie said. "They really ought to settle on where the walls are going to be."

"What I hear, arguments from all the retired officers here's what holds it up. God knows why but a lotta ex-servicemen settled in Pueblo." She pronounced it *Pee Yeb Low*, the way old natives were said to do; it was actually the first time Arnie had heard it that way. "So at every meeting there's fifty guys who think they know the best way to lay out a defense."

"Same at the national level," Arnie said. "Everybody's qualified to plan the train route and nobody'll shovel coal." He hadn't actually found that to be the truth but he knew from past experience that ordinary people liked to hear it.

The lantern created a small pool of cheery light as they left the occupied streets.

Chatting with Mandy, he learned she'd been a kayaking guide, liked militia duty better than salvage work, approved of the new Pope's move to Buenos Aires, and wanted to vote for General Phat. The warm chatter of the healthy young optimist distracted him, but not enough; most of his mind listened for a scrape or thud where there shouldn't be one, told him he needed to strike at Aaron the moment he saw him, and knew he couldn't or wouldn't.

*Oh, God. Ecco was my friend.*

For tonight, he would not meet Aaron. From now on he would always walk with the watch—till he moved in closer to town, and he would, soon. He could . . .

*Pauline said they blinded him with a hot screwdriver.*

The empty city was so still. The watch would keep Aaron away for tonight. But Daybreak was there, always, in the dark voids of the windows, where nothing looked or saw.

## THE NEXT DAY. I-57, JUST WEST OF THE FORMER GILLMAN, ILLINOIS. 5:35 AM CST. TUESDAY, AUGUST 26, 2025.

"You wouldn't think those guys would be able to sleep at all," Bambi said quietly to Quattro. "Another shot of coffee?"

"Yeah, rank hath its privilege—but make sure we save enough to jump-start the team."

"We're on our own thermos, Quatz. I've got a gallon of hot coffee in a thermos and a box of leftover wedding chow for them. They can have breakfast as soon as we dump them out."

"So we're going to deposit our friends there and run like bunnies." Quattro sounded grumpy; probably the idea sat uneasy with his romantic view of himself.

"Yeah. Well, we all volunteered. How come you and I don't just settle in to become the Duke and Duchess of California?"

"Because we'd have to fight a war with your crazy dad. Because we're loyal Americans and we have a neurotic sense of duty. Because it's more fun to fly."

Sometimes Bambi thought she'd married him for that smile.

Morning twilight revealed the bare, dusty fields, wind-drifts of burned cars, burned-out buildings, and knocked-over water towers. On December 3 last year, one of the five biggest bombs in all of history had created a new, artificial bay in Lake Michigan, sending tornado-and-more force winds across the prairie.

"Gillman," Quattro said. The place they were supposed to drop the team. "Highway looks totally clear—should we just land?"

"I think that's all we can do." She unstrapped, went back, and shook them awake.

I-57 ran straight north and south for more than two miles between two overpasses choked with dust dunes; Quattro touched down easily, taxied to lose speed, and came around to be ready to take off into the wind again.

"All right, everybody out, and please remember that if you leave anything behind, you can reclaim it in Pueblo."

Bambi opened the door and the three men shuffled off the plane. Larry looked like he was going fishing; Chris humped his pack with something between a sigh and a shrug; Jason looked around in all directions like a coked-up bush baby. They hurried away to be well clear of the stabilizers and the idling props.

While they checked to make sure they had everything, Bambi took a last look around for anything forgotten. She exchanged thumbs-ups with Larry, brought in the steps, closed the door, and buckled back into the copilot's seat.

The engines roared; they raced along the empty highway and into the sky. Sunlight suddenly flared to their left. Quattro turned west. For the next hundred miles over the blown-flat, burned-black prairie, neither of them said anything.

## THE NEXT DAY. ATHENS, TNG DISTRICT. 10:20 AM EST. WEDNESDAY, AUGUST 27, 2025.

Grayson laid the documents down carefully as he went through them. "Expedition from Pueblo." He jammed his finger down on the long memo from Heather. "Direct espionage into the Lost Quarter, launched from an area we claim." He pointed to Marprelate's report from Pale Bluff. "Without our permission. They couldn't have given us a more perfect reason to cancel the summit."

"Except we're not going to cancel it," Cameron said, coolly.

"We have a chance to preserve everything we've worked for," Reverend Whilmire said. "An almost providential chance, if you see what—"

"Oh, I understand you, Reverend." Cam waved a hand as if trying to shake off a booger. "But I don't care what *you've* worked for; what I am working for is the restoration of the Constitution. Full stop, period, that's that. If you think Providence is doing this, then Providence can damned well be my enemy." The Natcon looked from one face to the other. "The RRC in Pueblo is an agency of our government, charged among other things with researching conditions in the areas that have not yet called in. This mission is as legitimate as if I had ordered it. And it's a tragedy that this man Ecco was killed, but among other things, we're getting the fullest report yet, from Pauline Kloster, about what actual conditions are in the Lost Quarter—and General, you should note that it's clear we need military expeditions up that way, soon, because what's building up in the Lost Quarter can't be allowed to build any longer. So my first order on this subject is that you begin preparations for one or more punitive raids across the Wabash or the Ohio; at the least, we need to trash this Castle Earthstone. The successes you had in the Youghiogheny make you my first choice for the job."

He let that sink in for a moment; he was frustrating Whilmire, but this was a potential enhancement for Grayson's political career. *That's right, Grayson, think about being able to run for president of the whole United States as a military victor, eh?* Then, more softly, he said, "We will attend the summit in Pueblo and we will attend it in good faith. We will reach an agreement with the Weisbrod government and in 2026 there will be a restoration election in every part of the country that we control; in 2027 a fully Constitutional government will take power. That is what I'm sworn to achieve, and that is what I will achieve." *Listen close, Grayson, listen close, do you hear the chance to be president of the whole thing, instead of the reverend's cat's-paw?*

"Subject to the Board's approval and—"

"I reconstituted the Board, Reverend, I didn't give it any legislative power this time around either, and the final decision is mine. Which you have heard."

"Reverend Peet will hear about this."

"No doubt. He not only reads the paper, he owns it. Nonetheless, I am still the NCCC, until General Grayson acquires the nerve to do anything about it, anyway." *If that's really ambition and understanding dawning on that male-model face, they always said in interrogation class that the way to set the hook is to pull it away.*

Grayson's face went flat. "That isn't funny."

"It's not a joke, General. You don't want me as NCCC; you've made that clear enough. But you swore an oath to uphold the Constitution, and I'm a presidential appointee of the last universally acknowledged, fully recognized President of the United States, and your civilian superior. You can take your chance that if you help me put the country together, the people will follow you. I think that's a smart bet. But perhaps you judge the road of Caesar, or Cromwell, or Napoleon to be less of a gamble."

Grayson looked straight back at him, and Cameron thought, *Now say it, now say yes, that's the deal I want. Just inside yourself, for now.*

Whilmire, perhaps afraid of what Grayson would say, jumped in again. "This is all beside the issue of attending the summit. We must not do anything to make the Olympia government appear legitimate."

"And what does the Bible have to say about peacemakers?"

"Your constant sarcasm is—"

"One of the few pleasures I still have. The decision is made, gentlemen. General, if we walk into the Defense Planning Bureau and tell them we need to do raids in force into the Lost Quarter, especially into the Warsaw/Palestine area, can they spec some list of options out for us in the next day or so?"

"It'll make more of an impression if we go there ourselves," Grayson said, with a half-suppressed grin. "Those guys could use a wake-up and shake-up anyway."

"Good, let's go." Though Cameron was a slight, short man, set against Whilmire's beefy lineman-type and Grayson's tall, rangy, physique, when Cam walked between them, they parted like old-time supermarket doors, and then hurried after him, trailing their dignity behind them.

He was out in the corridor before they caught up with him. He was careful not to walk fast, because that might look as if he ran away from them, but by surprising them with that first step, and forcing them onto their back legs, he had gained enough of a head start to force them to conspicuously hurry after him. *My ancestors were Confederate diplomats and the bodyguards of emperors,* Cam thought. *Back when yours were learning to wear shoes and not* publicly *lust after sheep.*

After they caught up, Cam spoke softly. "I think Graham is sincerely trying to bring us together. We might yet manage real peace, maybe even reconciliation, if we're smart enough. We won't throw that out over a snit over authority."

"But if we sacrifice—"

"I was including the other side in 'we,' Reverend. And if you were referring to sacrificing the un-Constitutional expedients that have been forced on me by circumstances, good riddance. We're getting our Constitution back. I know that the general, at least, understands the words 'uphold' and 'defend.'"

Grayson's tone was polite, even deferential—a good sign. "Sir, I think you are unnecessarily antagonistic—"

"I'll accept that I'm antagonistic. I'm not sure I'm as antagonistic as necessary, but I'm doing my best." *Nice fishie, swallow that hook hard.* He hoped it wasn't only in his imagination that Grayson had seen the advantages.

*Of course he could also just shoot me, frame a PCG agent, declare war, and rule by decree. Petty harassment and pranking of guys who are already thinking of shooting me*—Cameron emphatically finished the thought with—*keeps them off balance, makes them look silly, reminds them of all the times they've chickened out before, and gives me some badly needed amusement. Funny how free you are once you just do the right thing; after that all they can do is kill you.*


**5 DAYS LATER. PUEBLO, COLORADO. 6:15 PM MST. MONDAY, SEPTEMBER 1, 2025.**

"Steve Ecco," James said, holding the glass of blood-red wine up.

"Steve," Leslie agreed, and clinked glasses with him. "And all the others going in after him. That's what's hard for me to imagine. Ecco going in was brave, but going in after what happened to him . . ." She extended her glass again.

James clinked it, and they drank deeply, more a passionate communion than a toast. "You know, I'm not used to being around brave people or adventurous people, even now after all we've been through here." He broke off a piece of bread, warm from his oven, and handed it to her; they chewed slowly. "At these Monday night dinners, what did we talk about back before all our friends were going off to risk death?"

Leslie smiled and brushed a strand of hair out of her face. "The Heart of Leslie Antonowicz, also known as The Love Of My Life Of The Week. Ways I tried to get myself killed out in the boons, skiing and climbing and all that. Of course, nowadays the boons are much more dangerous—and given that condoms are extinct, so is catting around."

James sat back, blinking, and said, "I hadn't thought of that."

"Old man, you need to get out more. I know this widow—"

"No, I didn't mean on the personal level. I meant we've got an AIDS epidemic coming. The drugs are gone and it'll be a long generation before we can put the things that make them back together, and we've got famine, epidemics of other diseases, mass grief that we're only starting to wake up and feel—very likely most of the HIV-positive people are going to convert to full-blown AIDS in the next few years. Then on top of that, condoms were plastic themselves, often wrapped in plastic, and anyway we're not making any more of them—I mean, holy crap, we've got to make sure the next generation is careful, you know?"

"Sounds like an oncoming Jamesgram." That was her nickname for his frequent one-page memos to Heather, about every possibility from lions on the Great Plains to cholera in Morgan City.

He made a face. "It was my memo about the situation east of the Wabash that gave her the idea of sending poor Ecco out to Pale Bluff, and I don't know if it was decisive, but I sent a note about the implications of Debbie's report and why we needed to get someone inside the Lost Quarter soon. Jamesgrams have consequences."

"Are you feeling guilty?"

He thought for a moment. "No, I guess not. We had to try. I just feel sorry for Steve Ecco; what an awful way to go."

The corner of her mouth twitched. "One drunken night he tried to pick me up, and I heard the story and philosophy of his life. He died the way he *thought* he wanted to. Bet he didn't like it as much as he thought he would, though. No background music. That's the trouble with an adventurous life, sooner or later it really hurts, and there's no pizza afterwards."

"That seems kind of cold about a guy who's dead."

"Yeah. I'm not sure I wanted to say that, myself. Let's get into that steak salad you said was going to curl my toes."

"Only way I ever get to hear you make noises like that."

"Dirty old man."

The banter was forced, awkward, sounded silly to them both, but it was better than what they had been talking about, and almost ten years of Monday dinners together had at least given them a reliable script for avoiding awkward, emotionally difficult moments. Still, as James sliced the steak into thin strips, he seemed to feel his thumb pressing the handle more than usual, and looked at it with a strange fond tenderness. Seeing that, Leslie began a long, pointless story about someone trying to pick her up in Dell's Brew, and James supplied ten times the commentary that seemed necessary.

## 2 DAYS LATER. UNIONTOWN, KENTUCKY CROSSING. 2:50 AM CST. WEDNESDAY, SEPTEMBER 3, 2025.

In the wee hours in Uniontown, the whoosh of the dark black river drowned out any other sound. The narrow streets—bent, tangled, and truncated by the town's being pinned between the river and the mountains—showed no light; Uniontowners had learned to assume there were watchers across the river.

Debbie Mensche followed her guide for an hour along the trail downstream, until, at one bend, he stopped, let her catch up, and touched her elbow.

The shore-side edge of the triangular rock was about chest high to them; they climbed up onto it and crept a few feet forward on their bellies to look over the edge. Beyond the fast, noisy riffles in the river, the end of the dam reached toward them. Her guide yipped like a coyote; on the other side, at the tip of the dam, a man stood and waved his arms, twice, once, then three times, and finally once again.

With steps nailed and tied on to form a ladder, climbing into the big oak wasn't difficult, even in the dark. The guide tugged on the line that led away across the river, and received an answering tug. He fitted the metal logging helmet over her head and fastened the chin strap; helped her into the harness; and rigged her to the overhead pulley. "Just let your legs trail, and keep them close together. They'll catch you by the legs and guide you in. But even if you lose your grip and come in upside down and flailing, the guys on the other end know what to do, so try to remember you're safe, okay?"

"'Kay."

"Anything at all before you go?"

"No, nothing. Thanks."

"You're welcome. Come back sometime when we can show you our little town. Pack on good?"

"Yeah."

"Harness is good," he said, rechecking. "All right. Grab the handles, walk to the edge, and lift your feet up high. Stretch out again as soon as you clear the platform."

Debbie walked forward to the platform edge; she could see a path had been cut through the branches, and beyond she could see the river, the dam, and the opposite shore. She took a good grip on the handles and bent her knees; at first she was pulling the line down, then pulling it tight, and finally her feet came up, leaving the edge. The forward lurch startled her, but she remembered to extend her legs and then she was . . .

*Flying,* she thought. Like a dream of being a bird. She swooped out through the opening in the tree, and the slope fell away below her; she was gliding down toward the riffles below, looking around at the vast dark river spanning the horizons, the thundering pale confusion where the Wabash poured into the Ohio, and the tree-covered hills.

The dam swooped up under her feet. A man ran with his arms around her calves for about twenty yards, soaking up her momentum, letting her weight settle onto him until he had brought her feet down to the dam. She felt a twinge of regret that the ride had not been longer.

She shook the man's hand; talking seemed like an unnecessary risk, but she wanted him to know she was grateful.

The concrete of the path along the top of the dam gave way to the soft, damp dirt of the trail; she settled into the business of covering distance before sunrise.

## THE SECOND NIGHT AFTER. OLYMPIA, NEW DISTRICT OF COLUMBIA. 11:30 PM PST. THURSDAY, SEPTEMBER 4, 2025.

*Allie, what were you thinking?* Allison Sok Banh wished she'd had one good friend to ask her that sometime in the last few months, before she'd decided that running the Provisional Constitutional Government by combining the Chief of Staff and First Lady duties would be a good move. *God, third straight night I'll be up past midnight. And then I can pretend to sleep on a steam train all the way to Pueblo for the next few days.* Graham, her husband and the president—*God I wish those were three people instead of one*—was safely in bed, leaving the detail work to her. *And didn't I always want the detail work, anyway? Wasn't that where I got my success?*

Also, traditionally, where the devil lives.

"You look tired." Darcage stood before her, impeccably groomed as always.

"I am tired. How the hell did you get past security this time?"

"That would be telling." He did have a warm smile; *probably sold shitloads of used cars, multilevel marketing vitamins, or Jesus before Daybreak.* "You look like you can barely keep your eyelids up; you must feel your whole body is made out of warm, soft lead." His hands were so nice on her neck. "You're just a tired staffer, just a tired bureaucrat, just a tired ambitious person, just a tired wife, that's all. Or is it all of those and more? Look at you, your face looks like it's running down your skull into your neck."

"You have a way with a compliment," she said, leaning forward to let him work the knots out.

"'What is man, that thou art mindful of him?'" Darcage said. "Man in general, man in particular, why so much stress? Couldn't you at least find a species that would accept your hard work and your gift of yourself, and enjoy it, and not complain that it wasn't what they wanted or that you still haven't done enough? Consider how much Daybreak does for those of us in the tribes; I don't think we could exist without it. Imagine how useful the tribes could be—"

She sat back. "Good try!" Angrily, she pushed his hands away from her neck, and shook her head to clear it. Maybe tonight she'd just call security and let them have Darcage; this wasn't working out as she'd hoped it would.

She felt his hands back on her neck again, gripped them to stop him. If she screamed now he'd never get away, but did she want to? She was so—

"Tired, aren't you? We don't want you to do one bit more of work. Wouldn't it be so much easier if we could work together? After all, we want to work with you, and you want to work with us, and we can do each other so much good."

. . .

An hour later, she woke in the guttering light of the oil lamp, head on her desk, strangely refreshed from such a short nap; she was surprised at how much work she had finished; in fact, all that remained was to sign all the typewritten orders, initial all the annotated reports, drop them in the out basket, and go to bed. Funny how she'd fallen asleep just when she was almost done, but the rest had done her so much good.


**LATE THE FOLLOWING DAY. FORT NORCROSS (JUST DOWNSTREAM ON THE OHIO OF WARSAW, KENTUCKY). ABOUT 10 PM EST. FRIDAY, SEPTEMBER 5, 2025.**

"*Officially*," Lieutenant Seacrist told Dan Samson, "we're just a monitoring station. *Obviously* we're here because when they get that train running over the mountains to Lexington, Warsaw is going to be a major port on the Ohio."

The palisade wall of Fort Norcross would have been easily recognizable to Daniel Boone except for the black-powder Gatling guns, the sewer-pipe mortars, and the currently retracted chain-net radio antenna that waited to be hoisted on its mast, which doubled as the flagpole. During the day, Samson had seen the flag that flew from it—the Cross and Eagle.

"In my experience," Samson said, "an introduction about what you do officially and what you do obviously is a segue to the part about what you really do."

"At any given time," Seacrist said, "I have anywhere from five to thirty men patrolling and scouting on the other side. We need to stay deniable, but our business is intercepting their scouts, removing their food caches, burning the little patches of corn and beans they plant everywhere for supplies. You might say the war has already started here."

"Where are your orders coming from?"

"Athens." If Seacrist had stopped there, Samson would have had no opening to inquire further, but after a moment the lieutenant continued. "Program being run by a guy named Grayson, who I hope to vote for when we elect a president again. One-star general before Daybreak and now he's the reason why we're all Tempers here." In the dark it was hard to see his facial features, and his voice was flat as he added, "I know you'll tell them that in Pueblo. It's part of your job."

"Yep. Thanks for the loan of the kayak, and extra thanks for letting me know that I'm going into a war zone. And thanks for what you're doing."

"You can thank Grayson," Seacrist said. "Your kayak's tied up in the shadow of those willows."

"I'm gone already." He slung up his pack, slipped through the side gate of the fort with a handshake from the sentry, and pushed off in the kayak. Following the dim shadows of the trees out onto the river, he angled for the little cove downstream that pierced deep into an overgrown golf course. *I like what you're doing but I really like the old flag,* he thought, and then, because all that was behind him, he put his back into his paddling.

**13 HOURS LATER. PUEBLO, COLORADO. 2 PM MST. SUNDAY, SEPTEMBER 7, 2025.**

Dr. MaryBeth Abrams was good company for the last three hours of freedom Heather expected this month: the ball game between the Pueblo Angels and the Fort Carson Rangers. Heather and MaryBeth were there because everyone was, because the club owner gave Heather free seats along the first base line, and because it was a fine early fall day.

"Besides," MaryBeth said, "this way I can see that Leo is healthy as a moose, and sound confident the next time you imagine something and send Patrick after me."

"I just don't know very much about babies. Nobody gave me a manual, and when something's new to me, I'd rather ask than guess."

They watched the Angels work a double play. "Up to the level of college ball in the old days, do you think?" Heather asked.

"*Small* college. Still it's a nice day for a game. Getting cold fast, though, this year, hope they get to finish the season; they're saying there could be snow on the ground before October."

Fort Carson brought in its strong reliever, and the game settled into a pitcher's duel.

Heather said. "I was kind of having a thought."

"I don't cure those, I'm not that kind of doctor."

"Just curious. Seems to me we've got gazillions of babies lately. Besides those kids that work for me, Jason and Beth, I know four other pregnancies are happening—"

"Oh yeah. Want to know when there's a baby boom on, ask a small town doctor. And I can tell you, there is one *on*. All the common methods of birth control are gone, and people love to boink too much to give it up. But my guess is we ain't seen nothin' yet."

An Angel almost stole third; Heather and MaryBeth enjoyed agreeing that the ump had robbed him.

"You think we're in for even *more* of a baby boom?" Heather asked. "Why?"

"Remember all the uproar about estrogen-mimicking compounds in plastics? Lots of doctors were convinced that was what was behind the 'infertility epidemic,' that it wasn't just late childbearing and prevalent chlamydia. I think maybe the Daybreak biotes have been purging the planet of the mock estrogens, along with tires, gasoline, condoms, and Barbies. I mean, in the last decade 1:20 was a normal babies-to-boinks ratio—"

"I don't think Arnie has shown me that statistic yet."

"Okay, in med school they call it the conception ratio, but then I would have had to explain what it is. Anyway, 1:20 means on the average, last ten years, boink twenty times, make one baby. But back in the 1930s, before they started making estrogen-mimicking stuff, 1:11 was normal. Estrogen-mimicking compounds seem to me like something the biotes would scarf right down, so what's in the environment is being destroyed really fast, and since the plastic factories aren't running, we've stopped making more. So sperm counts ought to be rebounding in all species, and fertility of eggs increasing, and sterility rates dropping, and so on. All that adds up to a real crowd of babies."

"Wow," Heather said. "More revolutions coming."

"To everything there is a season, turn, turn, turn," MaryBeth said, "and the world didn't stop turning just because America decided to break apart, or you fell in love and ended up a mom. It's amazing, the number of things the world keeps right on turning through."

The last inning was quick and dull. MaryBeth asked, "Want to get a beer at Dell's Brew?"

Heather checked the time. "I don't have time before meeting the trains. We're going to make the Provis and Tempers sit down and listen to sense, so that by the time all those babies you're promising show up, we'll have a country for them."

**40 MINUTES LATER. PUEBLO, COLORADO. 3:15 PM MST. SUNDAY, SEPTEMBER 7, 2025.**

"At least it's a nice day to watch them come in," Heather remarked. The two steam trains each flew American flags from the locomotive and the caboose; between, there were two big steam locomotives, coal car, a sleeper for the VIPs, a passenger car outfitted as an office, and the "fort car," a boxcar armored with steel plates bolted to its inner walls, loopholed for the guns of the guards. "But with fifty-eight working full-gauge locomotives on the continent, should two of them be hauling politicians? We really need coal. They're pretty well certain this is going to be a cold, early winter."

"Maybe we could burn politicians," Leslie suggested.

"Too wet to burn well."

"Let's burn them anyway," Leslie said, taking a step forward. She turned to the officer beside her and said, "May I borrow your field glasses?" Leslie gazed at the distant locomotives; for Heather, they were just two tiny three-car trains in the sea of sagebrush, crawling along the track that shone in the afternoon sun, trailing their big plumes of gray-blue smoke.

"What are you seeing, Leslie?"

"Oh, man. You're going to want to burn them both, Heather. Remember how much time we put into making sure they'd fly the real American flag from their locomotives?"

"Yeah, you mean they're not?"

"Oh, they are. That's what I was trying to make out. It's what they're flying from their cabooses."

"Damn. I better look for myself."

Heather peered through the antique field glasses, thinking, oddly, that when these were made, they might have been tested on that locomotive—both were well over a hundred years old.

The lead train, from Athens, flew the fifty-star, thirteen-stripe flag from the locomotive, but from the caboose, it flew the same design with a blotch on the stripes—the Army eagle, superimposed on a cross. The train behind it, from Olympia, flew the correct American flag from its locomotive—but the nineteen-star, double circle flag waved from its caboose.

"You know, if you'd put one's stripes with the other's stars, it would all be fine," Leslie said.

"Do you suppose they both decided to be offensive, independently, or that one of them started it?" Heather asked.

Positioning both the office-cars directly behind equally placed podiums took a long time. Leo began fussing, so Leslie held him and soothed him, since Heather needed a hand free to shake with. Peering at Heather over Leslie's shoulder, he looked immensely weary and irritated. "Yeah, I know, kid," Heather whispered. "I'm not thrilled with either of my old friends, either."

But when Cameron Nguyen-Peters and Graham Weisbrod emerged from their trains, they appeared not to see each other's offensive flags at all; rather, they shook hands cordially enough, introduced their grimacing, stone-faced staffs, and then both insisted on visiting with Leo and looking Heather over to tell her she was doing well. For a few minutes, she let herself remember that the Temper Natcon and the Provi President had both been pretty good guys, and even friends with each other.

*I just hope they remember, because I think their staffs are here to make them forget.*

Afterward, walking back, Leslie said, "I did a little mixing with their staffs. Learned some things. It was General Grayson's wife, and her loony father the reverend, that broke out the Temper flag and had them put it on the caboose; I don't know if Cam even knew they'd done it, it was just the last few miles. Allie Sok Banh was the one who decided to retaliate with the Provi flag. Everyone's mad at their own people, but they all keep saying it's their own affair and they're not about to apologize to the other side."

Leo, back in Heather's papoose pack, belched and fussed; Heather ran a finger down his soft little cheek. "You were right, Leslie. We ought to be testing whether they're really too wet to burn."

# TEN:
# WITH COINS ON EITHER EYE

Heather had deliberately been the last to enter; letting the Provi and Temper delegations settle in first, with just her staff to guide them to their chairs and the coffee, might give them a chance to mix informally. No such thing had happened.

Well, thanks to paranoia and a good staff, Heather had plans out to Z and beyond; time for B. "Just to remind everyone," she said, "this is the first session of the first day and the real purpose is to make sure your chairs are comfy and that we take some photographs of Graham and Cam smiling at each other. Anything beyond that is gravy." *Hunh. No smiles. Allie is making a point of not looking at me, the generals are looking at each other like gunfighters waiting to draw, and Reverend Whilmire could be a mannequin if he had enough expression.* "But in the interests of saving time, and not creating barriers, let's just see if we can agree on this: We will hold a national election on the first Tuesday in November of 2026, to put the United States entirely back in the hands of a regularly elected, fully Constitutional government. In January 2027, we'll swear in the new government, no matter who or what it is, at some location that is not Olympia and not Athens, and both sides will turn over all authority to it."

"I'll need to confer with staff," Weisbrod said, and Cam added, "So will I."

*Not only no smiles. Anger, too, I think, from the staffs; and Graham and Cam looked—embarrassed. That's it. Embarrassed.*

## 20 MINUTES LATER. PUEBLO, COLORADO. 11 AM MST. MONDAY, SEPTEMBER 8, 2025.

Leslie Antonowicz had asked, "Won't they be careful about security in this setting?"

"Some will, some won't. Cam will be tight as a drum. Both generals will be security-conscious. They've all spent their lives in national security and it's engrained. Allison will be careful when she remembers to, but she's an old public policy hack and expects to leak things. Graham is a professor, he blabs without thinking; Whilmire's a preacher, ditto but more so. And the main thing is that we got them to come without staff of their own—except for Grayson's little Barbie-for-Jesus—on this idea of James's that if they both agreed to use the same independent research staff, they wouldn't get into paralysis from only having their own talking points. Very useful bullshit."

"Thank you," James had said. "I try."

Every so often, and she never told him so, James did something to make Leslie wish she was attracted to old, fussy, stodgy fat guys. By carefully stepping out each time that the Temper team started something confidential, and then having to be asked back in to run into the research room and dig up reports, she'd worn them out; they were tired of thinking about her, and now she was furniture when they talked in front of her.

Now General Grayson was on one of his rhetorical rolls. "The whole country could still slide back into the secular swamp, and we can't afford that. This war could last centuries. We are a Christian nation by origin and long custom, and we need to fight as one."

Jenny Grayson was the only person who appeared even to be listening, and her expression of adoration for her general was more fixed than would have been ideal.

Reverend Whilmire broke in. "The important thing is that the Constitution is the instrument of God's will, not the other way around, and to save the true Constitution of this country, when we lost so many good people in the Rapture, God focused the Tribulation to remove the most anti-Constitutional elements—"

"Shall I inform everyone," Cam had asked, staring at his staffers, "that it is the TNG's position that the death, in a period of months, of more than three-quarters of our population, was the decision of a just and loving God?"

Whilmire winced. "That's so unnecessarily harsh."

"Reverend Peet preaches it every Sunday—"

"To Christians, who understand it in context," Grayson said. "The point is that in this struggle the cross is as important a weapon as the rifle—"

As she laid out maps of the Lost Quarter on the side table, Leslie struggled for balance. The repetition bored her, so it was hard to listen, but the content infuriated her, so it was harder still to appear indifferent. She wished Cameron Nguyen-Peters would talk more, and less deferentially.


**20 MINUTES LATER. PUEBLO, COLORADO. 11:30 AM MST. MONDAY, SEPTEMBER 8, 2025.**

"So the assessments from our other sources"—so close physically to the delegations, Heather did not dare even to speak the code name *Red Dog*—"seem to be right on target. Grayson plays up to Whilmire to keep the Post Rapturalists in his corner, and Whilmire just recites Post Raptural talking points. Cam doesn't really have a staff, just a double veto team."

"The general and the reverend aren't much of a team," Leslie said. "Grayson keeps reminding them both about the military expeditions against the tribes he has led. He definitely wants the Post Raptural Church to understand that they are a useful auxiliary to the Army—not the other way round. Whilmire is the exact opposite. And Nguyen-Peters just sits there and asks them if they can agree on anything, when the obvious answer is, they can't."

Heather nodded. "How is it over on your side, James?"

"Like our sources said. Allie wants to just call the shots but Graham Weisbrod is old, tired, and passive-aggressive; he won't do anything *she* doesn't like but he won't take active steps to do anything that might require him to do some work. Norm McIntyre acts less like a three-star general and more like a ten-term Congressman all the time; he thinks about the politics of everything, and all in terms of quid pro quo and deal-making. They're not going to let Weisbrod move, and he doesn't want to."

"So neither of them is just going to overrule the handlers and do the deal," Heather said. "So much for Plan B."

James shrugged. "You had to try. If they could do what they did back in April, we'd have the business settled, the country moving ahead, and everything on track. But it was never likely. Back then they had one big overriding danger, of sliding into Civil War Two, to motivate them, and they had the power because they were essentially dictators. Now they're both losing ground in their own regimes; Allison's bureaucrats run the PCG, and Grayson's church-and-army coalition is tightening its grip on the TNG. Graham and Cam are both answering to invisible elephants in the room, and the elephants want the *legitimacy* of being Constitutional much more than they want the reality of returning to the Constitution." He shrugged and held up his hands. "I'm not judging, I don't think. But it seems to me that part of the problem is that nobody in either staff was anybody of real national consequence before Daybreak, and before the new governments formed. They *like* being important. I understand this. I was an archival librarian in an obscure—"

A tap at the door. "Ms. O'Grainne, the TNG delegation has sent word they're ready."

**10 MINUTES LATER. PUEBLO, COLORADO. 11:55 AM MST. MONDAY, SEPTEMBER 8, 2025.**

Heather listened while Graham read aloud, and then while Cam did. The brief written statements said only that the idea was interesting and the principle was good, and proposed more dialogue. *Not outright rejection. Could be worse.*

"Well," Graham said, "I know that this hasn't been cleared with my people, but I propose that we break for lunch."

Cam rarely smiled, but this was almost a grin. "I propose to accept that idea with a friendly modification: a long lunch."

"Accepted," Graham said.

The two of them stood, smiled, and shook hands. Heather popped a photo; she'd promised Cary at the *Post-Times*, in exchange for a no-leaks-printed policy, that she'd take a few candids every day. *Smiling and shaking hands like they like each other. Score! Try to erase that one from the history books.*

**ABOUT THE SAME TIME. CASTLE EARTHSTONE. 3:40 PM EST. MONDAY, SEPTEMBER 8, 2025.**

Finally, after all Robert's nagging, Karl had shown him how to work the encrypted radio setup, and now because the message wasn't to Karl's liking, it would probably be another two weeks before Robert could get any more information out of him. "It's about time Aaron sent something useful!" the old fat man shouted. "And now it's still nothing useful, just that his contact is dodging him! He had to get help from Darcage just to get his contact to talk to him! And just look at what he's telling us! We should have known about this weeks ago; that fat O'Grainne bitch must've sent the mission out the day after she heard about Steve Ecco. Why the hell wasn't Aaron on the job?"

Robert shrugged. "Making a guess, Karl, Yang might've been freaked out that Ecco got killed, and if a guy freaks and won't talk to him, there's not much Aaron can do."

"So just tell me what the fuck we're going to do now?"

"One, let this Roger Jackson kid through; Yang's still useful and we have to protect him, and you might not've noticed, Karl, but Aaron doped out the two-contact decoy system they're using, there, and basically we can point the finger at either this James guy or this Leslie bitch. All we know about him is he's an older guy; he might be smart or sneaky or something, so I say, throw the shit on the one with the tits, there's a better chance she won't be able to handle it.

"Then we need to trap that deep-secret operation here at Castle Earthstone, where it can look like an unlucky accident. Do it right, and at the end of the day the Pueblo bitch'll've lost six agents and arrested the wrong one from her staff.

"Besides, it's time to get rid of Bloomington; we were only using it to relay to agents in Kentucky and those have all been rolled up, and the techie people at Bloomington are all too close to the border and know too much. If you say go, soldiers can leave at dawn—"

"Go." Karl beamed at him. "That was easy. Robert, you are probably the smartest decision I ever made."

"Love you too, boss. Let me start things rolling; I'll be back later for a drink and some hanging out."

Once Robert had learned that Karl was afraid of being alone, he had lost his fear of him. *I am going to run this place so much better than you.* Robert caught a whiff of broiling deer liver, and contemplated which bitch he'd bed that night. *From assistant lineman to about-to-be-lord in ten months. How could anybody not* love *Daybreak?*

## 20 MINUTES LATER. THE BRIDGE ON COUNTY ROAD 250 BETWEEN THE FORMER WINAMAC, INDIANA, AND TIPPECANOE RIVER STATE PARK. 8:20 PM EST. MONDAY, SEPTEMBER 8, 2025.

"All right," Larry said. "Time. Jason, ready?"

"Ready."

Jason crouched to spring up onto the bridge; he'd rechecked his gear a dozen times and knew nothing was loose. He looked at deck level along the bridge to where a Budweiser truck sat crosswise in the black puddles of its rotted tires, a bulky, dark shadow in the twilight.

Gaze locked on that truck, he felt but didn't see Larry moving into a comfortable firing position on the bank beside him. He heard Chris roll up onto the road and plunge across to the far ditch.

"Chris, ready?" Mensche's voice seemed too soft to carry.

Chris's voice came back soft and clear as one of Jason's own thoughts. "Ready."

"Jason. Go."

The run to the beer truck was not quite as far as the hundred meters Jason had regularly run in high school track, but he had not run it wearing a full pack, or in heavy rawhide moccasins—or worrying about catching an arrow. He seemed to run forever until he bounded up into the truck bed, dropped to his belly against the steel plates and board floor, rolled over once to place his shoulder gently against the truck wall, and swung his black-powder rifle around. He whistled the bobwhite sound, the signal to Larry.

With the hummocks covered, Larry raced across the bridge, his steps soft slaps and scrapes, till a faint thud indicated he was in position behind the concrete abutment. He chirruped like a squirrel with a nut.

Chris rushed across the bridge, surprisingly quiet for a big man, and continued beyond them to the place they'd picked out, a U-haul trailer tipped on its side; Jason rushed to an overturned bread truck as soon as Chris was in place.

The alternation continued until finally they were all at a shed deep in the trees, with the Tippecanoe just a whispering splash and gurgle behind them. After the moon rose, by its dirty blue light, they moved on. Jason thought, *Back when I believed I was a poet, I'd have made such a deal about the soot in the stratosphere and the bomb launcher on the moon. Now . . . meh.*

Concentrating on the roads, trails, woods, and prairie, if Jason had another poetic thought before they camped at dawn, he didn't notice.

**ABOUT THE SAME TIME. PUEBLO. 10 PM MST. MONDAY, SEPTEMBER 8, 2025.**

Arnie Yang had mostly decided that Allie wouldn't be coming. He'd only casually mentioned that he sometimes grabbed a beer. Probably she hadn't picked up the hint.

She appeared at Dell's front door like a vision of pre-Daybreak—linen dress, high-heeled pumps so pricey that there were no synthetic materials to fall apart, and she was even wearing some lipstick and eye shadow—*how'd she get that? I guess if anyone could . . .*

She squinted in the dim lamplight till she spotted Arnie, then strode between the old picnic tables and wooden office chairs; the mostly male crowd fell silent as she passed, more startled by the vision than anything else. Glenda, the waitress, followed her, carrying a mug and pitcher.

When Allie slid into the seat across from Arnie, Glenda set the mug in front of her and poured. "Thank you," Allie said.

Arnie reached for his scrip pad and Glenda shook her head. "Dell's gonna name this the First Lady's Table; you drink free tonight, Ms. Sok Banh, and feel free to bring the president by any time you like."

"That's so nice, thank you, and it's just Ms. Banh." When she had gone, Allie cautiously tried a sip. "Oh, thank God, it's good."

*Same old Allie.* "You don't want to be grateful for anything that you don't actually like."

She did the old shrug and head toss that used to disarm him completely. "Exactly. I hate to waste graciousness." She took a deeper drink of the dark brown brew. "Definitely not wasted here. Well, so here we are a year later, and it's really a different world, isn't it? I mean we used to say that all the time, that it was going to be a different world, but now . . . well, look at us." She held her glass up in a toast; reflexively, he clinked with her.

*She's got a hell of an act going, but I don't seem to fall for it the way I used to.* Disconcerted by the thought, Arnie blurted out, "Well, more of what we do matters more."

"Oh, I always treated any job I had like it mattered. That's how you keep good jobs and get better ones."

"Me too, I hope, but nowadays the job matters to other people, not just to me."

"Arnie, that was always true too. If you'd had better luck or seen what was coming sooner, maybe we could have done something about Daybreak before it happened—and if you had, I'd have been the one who had to carry out whatever the plan was. Nothing's changed, Arn, lives still depend on us, and so do our ambitions."

"I guess in the old days lives did depend on us, but it didn't feel like it, it was all kind of removed. Nowadays, when I need data, I don't tell an intern to look it up and email it to me, I send a man out with a pack and a gun, and he goes because he trusts me that it's important, even though he and I know he might not come back. I really have to count the cost."

"Things got more expensive," Allie said, "but that still doesn't really matter if you can pay the price." She drained the glass; before it touched the table, Glenda was back to refill it. "Or if someone else does."

**THE NEXT DAY. ON THE I-64 BRIDGE ON THE WABASH, JUST SOUTH OF GRAYVILLE, ILLINOIS. 7:15 AM CST. TUESDAY, SEPTEMBER 9, 2025.**

The Wabash is immense—the French explorers originally thought of the Wabash as the main stream and the upper Ohio as a tributary—and the twin bridge over I-64 was more than half a mile long; both bridges were choked with wrecked cars and trucks. Roger had started to cross with an hour of darkness remaining, but the sun had been full up for a while and he was still working his way forward from hiding place to hiding place, trying to stay away from the visible edges of the bridge.

Now that he could see the rest of his way, he hated to come out from cover, but there were just a few more rows of cars to go to the jackknifed semi that, on the morning of October 29, 2024, had blocked two lanes of traffic when its tires all burst, leaving hundreds of cars stuck on the bridge to wait for a state trooper who never came, their tires rotting and bursting, gasoline fermenting into unburnable vinegar, electrical systems encrusted with nanoswarm.

There was a crunching sound under his feet, and splashes in the river below; he darted away from the place where the sealant between the steel web deck and the crumbled and dried blacktop had decayed and broken away, sending a mass of gravel into the Wabash below.

He crouched beside an old rusted Honda Citiscoot; a half dozen bumper stickers, their glue rotted, lay by its rear bumper.

When nothing moved or made a sound after fifteen minutes, Roger rose to take a look around.

Pressed against the passenger-side window, inches from his face, a mummified child looked back at him. The lips had pulled back from the teeth as it had dried, and the eyes had fallen in, but the Spider-Man T-shirt still hung from the bony shoulders, and the hand stuck in the rotting plastic of the door sill seemed about to reach for Roger.

The driver-side window had a bullet hole in it. The long-haired mummy slumped on the wheel was draped in a partly decayed sweatsuit. A tiny shriveled body lay in a puddle of pudding-like slime, which must once have been a baby carrier, in the back seat.

Roger charged down the highway at a dead run; terrible tradecraft, and he wasn't sure what he was running from, but nothing pursued him, and in a minute or so, he was among the trees, beside a ditch full of water, watching minnows and listening to the birds. He ate some jerky, drank from his canteen, and lay back to look at the sky.

Had someone been shooting at the bridge at random? Crazy guy walking through the traffic jam with a pistol? Her ex-husband seeing his chance? Stray round from a gunfight between two stranded drug dealers over a briefcase of money?

With Daybreak remains, you could break your brain, and your heart, trying to understand how someone had happened to die *that* way.

He slept for an hour or so, woke feeling better, and cautiously advanced along the ditch, still headed east.

## ABOUT 2 HOURS LATER. PUEBLO, COLORADO. 9 AM MST. TUESDAY, SEPTEMBER 9, 2025.

As James was laying out the copies of all the available Castle charters, at the request of the Olympia delegation, his knack for invisibility seemed to be holding: they weren't waiting for him to leave to start the argument.

"Graham," Allie said, "this has to be your dumbest ever. You should have said no when Cameron proposed it. Didn't it even occur to you that the TNG is militarily far superior to us, and if we ally with the California Castles, maybe even support some Castles in Temper territory, we can balance—"

Norm McIntyre shook his head. "No, no, *no*. Too high a price. The TNG is right on this one, and it's more important for us than it is for them. The only thing we've got over the Tempers is a better claim on the Constitution, and the Constitution says the United States has no hereditary nobility, period. *No* recognition for the Castles."

"But in six months when we need the help of the Castles—," Allie began.

"If that's ever the case, it will be time for us to go out of business," McIntyre said. "If we cut a deal with the Castles . . . what's next, recognizing the tribes?"

"That was just brainstorming an idea!"

"Okay, we're settled," Graham said. "Allie, I note your objections, I'm just overriding them." He picked up the paper. "Read fast. If there's some trap in here, we need to see it in within two minutes."

"Maybe I can propose a compromise?" Allie said. "Let's say we need another day or two to go over our exact response. That way if we need something to trade, we have it. Then instead of just agreeing, we can make giving them what they want a big favor. I mean, isn't that more practical, doing the same thing we were going to do anyway, but getting something for doing it?"

Reluctantly, Graham nodded. "All right, we'll do it your way."

As they filed out, James was still laying down papers. He waited till they closed the door before shaking his head. Not that it mattered, but this was the third straight time they'd asked for research on a subject, and then argued it out and decided without ever consulting the materials he'd brought them. James smirked at himself; it had actually hurt his feelings that the invisible man was being treated like he wasn't there.


**THE NEXT DAY. CASTLE EARTHSTONE. 6:20 AM EST. WEDNESDAY, SEPTEMBER 10, 2025.**

The long, deep sunrise shadows reached out from the blood-red sun. Jason, watching from thirty feet up in a tree, had been seeing the first torches, lamps, and cookfires inside the main compound of Castle Earthstone for about an hour and a half.

More than forty skulls decorated the gates and walls. The just-rising sun revealed a person tied face-on to a post in front of the main gate; more light revealed a welted back.

A guard came out and threw water over the prisoner, untied the wrists, and let the body fall to the ground. He kicked the body to turn it over—turn *her* over, they saw—and she cried out and moved; he yanked her to her feet by her hair and pushed her toward the gate.

For the next few hours, they circled Castle Earthstone, slowly working their way from one vantage to another. Patrols were slow, apathetic, and rare; workers in the fields were few, far between, and seemingly dazed. The corn and bean fields were tended but not well-tended.

In a clearing in the creek bottom, they found the burial ground. Bodies were half-out of shallow graves; animals had been at them. One large heap of dirt, tunneled by foxes or raccoons, was littered with tiny bones. "Where they put the newborns," Larry said.

Jason said, "That's what the plan always was, all the Daybreak poets worried about how to keep people from breeding back. Did you notice how many women are pregnant and how few kids there are? We used to say that our goal was not just to be the best generation but the last. So . . . Mother Earth needs our help. Babies are the enemy."

"It explains why a place this big doesn't have more crops growing," Chris said. "They're not planning to keep all their slaves alive through the winter."

When they took a break, creeping back to share some venison jerky and dried apricots, Chris asked Jason, "Doesn't it seem weird that the slaves they're killing off are mostly women? Weren't these guys supposed to be goddess-worshipping feminists?"

"That was the warm-up in the Daybreak sales pitch to women," Jason said, thinking how much that sounded like his father or brother. "Some women love the idea of being all Earth-mothery, *I am woman, I give birth to the world, I am the mother the world needs*—I used to riff on phrases like that all the time for my Daybreak poems. But if human beings are a blight on the face of Mother Gaia, and getting rid of them is the paramount goal, you've got to get rid of women.

"Men breed too," Chris pointed out.

"A hundred men and one woman can turn out about *one* baby per year. A hundred women and one man can turn out about a *hundred* babies per year. If you want to get rid of people, you get rid of mothers," Jason said. "But that wasn't what we said to them, not at first. Our first message was, 'You are Woman and the world depends on you.'" He wasn't looking up from his food, lost in thinking about home and his pregnant wife. "That's what got Beth into it; she was from a dirty-ass pack of urban white trash scum that was trying to pretend they were ghetto gangstas because for them it was an upgrade. Daybreak was the first time anyone said they wanted her for something besides her boobs. A lot of women didn't see where it was going till too late. A lot of men, too." He seemed to be a thousand miles inside himself.

"Why don't they rebel?" Chris asked.

"Some do. Beth and I walked into Pueblo and volunteered. I don't know why more ex-Daybreakers don't."

"But why don't they rebel *here?*"

Jason shrugged. "Why do you think there's a whipping post and a boneyard?"

# ELEVEN:
# DANCED UPON THE HEAPS
# OF SHRUNKEN DEAD

Larry, Chris, and Jason waited for sunset in a cluster of trees, near a ditch to give them a covered retreat. Slaves and soldiers emerged from the main gate, followed by the technicians and the favored slaves, and then the lord and his "palace staff."

"If we'd known they were going to do this," Chris said, "we could've spared all that effort counting them."

"At least they're confirming our count," Larry pointed out. They had spent much of the afternoon observing and counting, figuring out that there were quarters for about four hundred soldiers, though less than fifty seemed to be present; fifteen or so in the lord's entourage; about twenty pump-and-windmill mechanics, overseers, and attractive women, in the hut Larry had dubbed the tech-and-trollop shack; and between eight and nine hundred emaciated, sickly slaves.

The whole population seemed to be gathering in a semicircle between the main wall and the outer gateway. Slaves ran to set up front-row chairs for the lord and his staff. Everyone else sat on the ground.

The bass drum beat faster, and other drums joined in. Slaves danced into the center area. This uncostumed daylight version was danced more than acted, but it was very recognizably *The Play of Daybreak*. Whenever the coincidence of wind and volume enabled them to hear a phrase, Larry or Jason or both would nod at the familiar words.

"Look at the way the audience is swaying to the drum," Chris breathed. "Like a rock concert with hypnosis."

Jason said, "Most of them spent years being hypnotized via the screen every night, sinking deeper and deeper into Daybreak, and now they—"

Jason didn't know what moved beside him, but weeks of nerves and months of Samson's training made him draw his short hatchet and chop sideways across the motion, splitting the hand holding the knife between the wrist bones before he knew what it was. He snatched back the hatchet, slapped the knife away with the flat of the blade, and backhanded up the arm and shoulder, using the handle running along the arm to guide him till the blade found the neck and bit deep into the carotid and windpipe. *One out.*

Jason kept his hatchet high behind his head, clearing into his turn with a cloud-hand.

Larry was yanking his commando knife back from a man's throat. Two women had jumped onto Chris, one with arms wrapped around his throat in a half-nelson strangle, the other tangling his arms. They were pulling him over backward as he struggled to his feet.

Jason swung as Chris bucked forward, and struck the upper woman on the crown of her head, sinking his hatchet deep. Chris's freed hands clawed back for the eyes of the woman tackling him.

She shrieked as Larry's knife slashed into her thigh and cut upward, bringing a gush of arterial blood. She fell dying, but the entire crowd was now staring toward them. Jason and Chris whirled to plunge into the ditch.

Larry grabbed them by their collars. "No! This way!"

They ran for a clump of trees and bushes about sixty yards off. Behind them, Jason heard thrashing sounds—*they must've been set to ambush us in the ditch, glad Larry spotted them, run, run, come on, run.*

Larry dove headfirst among the bushes in a tsugari roll, and Jason followed; Chris plunged forward and prone, covering his face with his outturned hands. Things hissed and thudded among the low branches. Something spun and clattered down to the ground, hissing like a furious goose. Larry grabbed it, rose to his knees to throw it, and fell back prone.

Jason felt the boom in the ground, through his chest. Leaves and twigs showered his back. *Beth, babe, if it's a boy we're naming him Larry.*

"Up, run." Larry jumped to his feet and they ran up a slope, across an open field, and around behind a lean-to shed. "Chris, right side, prone firing. Jason, same thing, left side." Larry rolled away from the shed and took cover behind a low hummock.

Back toward Castle Earthstone, horns blew and people shouted. Jason sighted around the side of the lean-to. The soldiers from the ditch were running back to join the main group by Castle Earthstone.

"They're organizing pursuit," Larry said, softly. "Now, see the lord there?"

"Looks like Santa Claus throwing a tantrum," Chris observed.

"He does. It's a long shot, but these big heavy bullets tend to fly straight and hit hard even far away. On three we're all taking a shot at Lord Santa there. If you see him react to the shots but he's not hit, take another shot at him as quick as you can. If you see him hit, look over the crowd and shoot anyone you see giving orders and being listened to. Keep shooting till your magazine's empty and your last round is chambered. There's a long line of trees along an old railroad embankment about a hundred and twenty yards behind me. As soon as your magazine is empty with your last round chambered, get back behind the embankment. Switch magazines there. If you're the only one that gets there, make something up; otherwise wait till we're all there. Got all that?"

"Yeah," Jason said, sighting about five feet above Lord Santa's head, and hoping his guess was right for the long shot.

"Yep," Chris said.

"On three. One, two, thr—" *Crack.*

Black-powder forms a gray, dirty cloud that obscures the shooter's sight and gives away his position. In the long breath while the white blur with its burnt-sulfur stench cleared away, Jason considered the importance of the project at Pueblo trying to make a biote-immune smokeless powder.

The smoke cleared. The big, white-bearded man was on his back on the ground with a dozen people bent over him. *Hit.*

Larry's rifle cracked, and Chris was working his lever; belatedly Jason worked his own and looked around. A young man with a yellow beard and dreads had jumped up on one of the seats in the elite section of the audience and was pointing toward Jason. *Should've kept your mouth shut, dude.* Jason pulled the trigger, worked the lever.

One of the soldiers was facing away from Jason and shouting to a group of people; Jason fired again, and this time the wind carried the smoke away quickly enough for him to see the man diving for the ground.

His sights found a woman leading a group with hoes and axes out of the crowd; he shot lower so that if he missed her he might hit someone behind. That was his four shots: one from the chamber and three from his four-shot magazine. One left. He worked the lever, rolled up, and dashed for the embankment.

Jason caught up with Chris as the older, big man was just clearing the rusty tracks.

Larry was there waiting. "Change magazines. They're acting pretty confused down there. We need to get some distance before they think about using dogs. Best hope we have is to wade in that creek for a mile or two."

Staying low, they ran down the hill. The sun was just setting, and there was plenty of light for them as they waded and splashed along the winding creek between the willows. Every hundred yards or so, Larry stopped them and they stood silently, listening; they had gone about a mile when they first heard the baying of the hounds.

"I used to like dogs," Chris said. "I always put 'dog-lover' in my personal ads and dating-site profiles."

"Well, if you can love 'em after tonight, you are *really* a dog lover," Larry said.

As the first stars came out, they moved along the grassy trace of a dirt farm road running east, surrounded by dense bushes, and slowed to a brisk walk; the sounds of the dogs and shouting had faded into the background. The grimy moon rose, revealing big dense bundles of berries on the bushes around them; Chris reached out, grabbed a handful, tasted one, and said, "Elderberry. This must have been a jam farm. They're ripe."

"Try not to get your hands sticky," Larry said, "but that's dinner. Put a few handfuls in your knapsacks and we'll just eat as we go."

The berries were tart and strong-tasting, with gritty little seeds that got between your teeth. They tramped on in the hazy moonlight, through the thick dew-soaked grass, headed east, deeper into the Lost Quarter.

## ABOUT THE SAME TIME. CASTLE EARTHSTONE. 6 PM EST. WEDNESDAY, SEPTEMBER 10, 2025.

Robert knew that Karl was dead before the old bastard hit the ground; half his face had been torn off and a spray of blood from his back soaked the grass around him. Robert felt for a pulse on the bloody neck just to be sure.

Major Carter, the garrison commander, jumped up on a chair, and yelled that he was in charge now. Robert was about to say, "The fuck you are," and Carter had made eye contact, when Carter's head suddenly went all lopsided and bloody and he fell down.

*It looks like they are shooting everyone who acts like he's in charge,* Robert thought. He moved into the center of a crowd of frightened, weeping slaves, and said, softly, "Now everyone just stay back and let the fighters fight. You all come with me but stay all bunched up, and we're just going to walk into the fort. Get everyone else to come with us if you can."

Most of the slaves were inside or headed there when the soldiers from the failed ambush came back shouting that they needed the dogs. Robert was waiting for them at the main entrance, with the crowd of slaves between himself and the enemy guns. "All right, form up here, out of sight of their position. They're shooting at anyone they see giving orders. Lord Karl is dead. Who's the highest ranking of you left alive?"

Captain Nathanson apparently was—he'd been about fifth in command of the whole force, and Carter's XO for the garrison here while the main force was away, so Robert said, "All right, then. Form your men up for the pursuit, Major Nathanson; you have my permission to take as many dogs as you need, and just leave me eight guards back here. Don't keep going too long if you lose the trail, because we don't know how many other attackers there might be, and this could be a trick. Good luck, Major."

Nathanson saluted and started yelling orders; Robert turned to the nearest overseer. "Bernstein. Have the slaves put things in order for a normal day tomorrow, make it dead clear that that is what there will be, and lock down for the night. Tell the others you're now my chief steward."

Nathanson came back to him and snapped a crisp salute. "The Castle is secured, we've got the dogs, and the men are ready to start pursuit."

"Good. Use your judgment from here on; just don't be away too long, Major."

"It's captain, sir."

"Carter is dead and you are in command."

"Yes, Lord Robert." Nathanson turned back to his men; Robert figured that deal was locked down. *Double locked down if Bernstein figures out that chief steward isn't a bad job either.*

## THE NEXT DAY. WARSAW, INDIANA. 6 PM EST. THURSDAY, SEPTEMBER 11, 2025.

Warsaw, Indiana, was "the kind of pretty little town that sooner or later is used in a nostalgic movie," Chris Manckiewicz said.

"Not anymore," Larry said. "Wonder how long before someone figures out a way to reinvent movies? And I bet there are still paper copies of some of the old scripts around, especially the classics; you think anyone will make *The Wizard of Oz, Saving Private Ryan*, or *Wish on an Emerald* again? But when they do, they're going to have way more than enough places to shoot historicals, for a long time."

The three men were sharing the last of the venison jerky and the elderberries in the corner of a wrecked hardware store. "Isn't it weird how many little towns are named after the great cities of Europe?" Jason asked. "Like every state around here has to have a London, a Paris, a Berlin, a Warsaw, and so on? I wonder if there's anywhere named Pinetree Junction in Europe."

"There's not really much Europe," Chris pointed out. "The North Sea bomb took care of everything between Stockholm and Naples, and Edinburgh and Moscow. There's northwest Scotland and some of Wales and Cornwall, most of Ireland, some northern Scandinavia, and Spain and Portugal. I'm not sure that counts as Europe. It's sort of the Lost Quarter of the Old World."

"I wonder if that's exactly what it is," Jason said. "I don't know how Daybreak *could* move people into it, but I bet it's crawling with tribes, like the Lost Quarter here."

The other two were staring at him; he shrugged, a little defensively. "Look, this is what Heather sent me along for, to have someone with some idea about the way Daybreak works. I mean, it isn't just about breaking human civilization, it's about making sure it never comes back. And to do that they keep hitting us with another wallop from another angle, so we never really adapt to what they've done before they're doing something else. They took away most of electricity, plastics, and petroleum, and while we were still figuring out how we'd rebuild the tech, they knocked us down again with the huge bombs. Then while we were figuring out a decentralized way to reorganize civilization, the moon gun started knocking out radio. And we know they had their fingers deep in the whole Castle movement to break up the authority of the Federal government, and now we're realizing the tribes are there to wipe out any civilization rebuilding—"

"You think the tribes were always part of the plan? They didn't just happen?"

Jason nodded. "Remember the plan was always to be the last generation. The tribes were recruited from low-level Daybreakers, plus disoriented people, while the country was in chaos. They turned them into slaves and armies, and now they're killing the slaves to build up the armies, and then hurling the armies at civilization—like that huge attack at Mota Elliptica. Take down the tech and kill as many people as you can doing it.

"That's what Castle Earthstone is about. They're gearing up for one big drive out of the Lost Quarter—and a pile of bodies and no civilization after. That's why they don't care if most of the slaves don't make it to spring; now that they've served their purpose, it's better if they die."

"That implies," Chris said, squirming for a better position, "that Castle Earthstone was always planned, probably years before October 28th, 2024. Is that too crazy?"

Larry sat still for the space of a breath, looking up into the air, as he did when he thought hard. "Just suppose Arnie Yang is right and Daybreak is one giant, malign intelligence, a mind much larger than our own, one that uses human beings in the way we use the cells in our body, bent on human self-annihilation and nothing else. You'd see things like Daybreak creating the Daybreak poets to infiltrate coustajam music so younger refugees would be already prepared to join the tribes, and to write the *Play of Daybreak*, and a hundred other things."

"Now I know what's been bothering me." Chris looked stunned. "If we could hop on a plane back to Pueblo this second—"

"A big juicy steak, a long hot bath, and sleeping next to Beth," Jason said.

"Yeah, but . . . what would we tell Heather about Castle Earthstone? That it's roughly a battalion-strength fort equipped to fight at about a Roman or medieval level. Nothing behind it, really, just this one big fort in what used to be north central Indiana. But wouldn't that be what Daybreak wanted us to say? While it prepared for something really big?"

"Like how big?" Jason asked.

"That's its pattern. Big blows from unexpected directions. In the past six weeks there've been massive attacks at Castle Castro, Mota Elliptica, and Pullman; *and* Grayson's Youghiogheny campaign won, but it took a fifth of the existing army to go a hundred miles into the Lost Quarter, and they took a beating going in and out. Apparently even in sparse, resource-poor areas, Daybreak can put together regiment- or even brigade-sized attacks. And the Lost Quarter has far more resources, and probably people, than any area we've been attacked from so far."

Larry's head bobbed emphatically. "That's got to be it. Oh, shit, you're right. We aren't the brilliant scouts we thought. We sure as hell didn't walk up the Tippecanoe Valley without being spotted; they stayed hidden from us, not vice versa. We have been *fed*, gentlemen."

"Fed?" Jason asked.

"Intel slang. Sometimes when you identify a spy, you leave him in place and use him to feed disinformation to the enemy," Chris said. "Yeah. If we got away, we were supposed to report that the Lost Quarter is empty, to help hide whatever they're brewing for next spring."

Larry leaned back, chewed on his jerky, thought some more, took a sip of water, and finally said, "Well, hunh."

"Larry, from you 'well, hunh' means what other people mean when they scream, 'We're all gonna die!' " Chris observed. "Could you maybe share a thought or two with us?"

"Sorry, yeah, look, check me out on this. Suppose we do what they'll expect and go south or west. We see nothing that we haven't already seen, and go home and tell people there's nothing big here. Or since Daybreak knows we're coming, we get caught. Daybreak wins either way.

"So I'm thinking, *not* back the way we came. Head east, then north, right *through* the Lost Quarter, then out through the Provi bases on Lake Erie. Daybreak won't know where to look for us, and whatever we're not supposed to see is going to be up that way."

"And we'll run into way more trouble and walk a couple hundred extra miles," Chris observed.

"Yep," Larry said. "And we can put at least three miles, maybe five, into it before dark."

## ABOUT THE SAME TIME. PUEBLO, COLORADO. 6 PM MST. THURSDAY, SEPTEMBER 12, 2025.

*Still someone else's turn,* Heather thought. She looked over her big chart and thought, *Four days of talking and I've added about two cards to this, and haven't moved a line. Abundant noise and heat and not one trace of light or motion.*

Well, maybe that would change tomorrow. Maybe both sides would realize that Harrison Castro's little theft of their thunder was a way to show them all how irrelevant they were—*and irrelevant is the one thing that none of them can stand to be. I hope.*

She saw Graham Weisbrod coming across the courthouse lawn; good, it looked like Allie wouldn't be along tonight, either. The big chart, still unchanged, slid back into place, and she picked up Leo, locked the office door behind herself, and went downstairs to meet Graham at her living quarters. A night of old times' conversation, baby-inspecting, and nostalgic laughter was probably what was really needed, right now, anyway.

## THE NEXT DAY. SAN DIEGO, CALIFORNIA. 3:30 PM PST. FRIDAY, SEPTEMBER 12, 2025.

Pat O'Grainne had lived a long time, and it kept feeling longer, especially with this silly ceremony to get through. *The one thing you can say for being in a wheelchair, it's easy on your feet and the small of your back. All I have to do is not fall asleep. Though I wish I could. Heather is so gonna not like this, and I ain't wild about it myself.*

The crowd stirred down below. A horn group that sounded like an underrehearsed high school band played something or other. Guys in capes and plumed hats (*what's he doing, swearing in the Castle Castro Muske-*

*teers?*) went clumping down the aisle to the silly music, followed by Harrison Castro and a bunch of his officers.

At least their uniforms were plain black, with red berets; they merely looked like ninja Boy Scouts.

*Please, God, let this be short.*

No such luck. A bunch of guys stood up and talked about how Harrison Castro was the cat's pajamas, the bee's knees, the man, and the shit; how historic this, that, and the other was; and the long and short of it was that everyone thought Castro was a good guy and this was a big fucking day.

*Oh, for a tall glass of cold beer. This is only the introduction.*

The main event was four more drummy, stompy, horn-infested parades to bring the freeholders of Irvine, Laguna, Newport, and Castle Rand down the aisle. They lined them up in front of the dais where Castro stood, dressed up like he was going to a science fiction convention as a space mercenary.

Finally the four freeholders were sworn in as Knights Deputies, which was what Castro was calling his feudal branch office managers. He was also declaring himself the Earl of San Diego and Leader of the League of Southern California Castles.

The first time Pat had heard the term, he'd thought, *Leading the League in what, balls or errors?* No matter how many funny suits Castro put on, what he was, was a cross between an old-fashioned asshat contractor and a high-income biker. The old-style contractors Pat had worked for too often in his younger days had shouted constantly about how nobody was going to tell them what to do and that they were free and independent men, while mostly living off government contracts and lecturing actual shovel-jockeys about hard work. The alpha bikers had been dentists, lawyers, or accountants with enough money to buy the really awesome toys; they had been generous with drinks and advice, the gist of which was that if you were as smart as they were, you'd be them, so obviously what you needed was a stiff drink and some bracing advice.

Heather had asked Pat to send her everything he could remember about this ceremony, so he did his best to concentrate on Harrison Castro's speech, the longest explanation Pat had ever heard for why smart rich people deserved to be rich because they were so smart, and were obviously smart because they were so rich. That night in his room, he used up half his candle ration for the week, and there were nine handwritten coded pages. It was cold, so he burned his scratchwork, and as the room warmed up, finally fell asleep, thinking about how all the movies had lied about what the life of a spy was like.

## 15 HOURS LATER. BLOOMINGTON, INDIANA. 9:35 AM EST. SATURDAY, SEPTEMBER 13, 2025.

Roger put in his next-to-last magazine. Counting the one in the chamber he was down to nine rounds—eight, saving one for himself.

More than twenty tribals on the ground floor below him.

They could come up two staircases, one at each end of the concrete hall-way, but he could cover both of those from his improvised fort at the central desk on the floor. They could set the building on fire and make him come down one staircase, but on his way down he'd have another chance to take one or two with him. *When it comes to getting shot at the end of the game, everybody wants to be in the back row.*

Angry shouting: "All right, follow me!"

Roger set himself. *Just like rifle range.*

The man lunged from the right stairwell. *Point and squeeze.* He fell over. *Another clean head shot. They'd be so proud of me back in Pueblo.*

He got the next one from the right staircase, then another from the left. He was down to one in the chamber, one in the magazine, one magazine to go. He fumbled the last magazine out of his pocket.

It was empty. He must have absentmindedly tucked it back into his pocket sometime in the last three hours of being chased around the U of I campus. It seemed really unfair that he had just lost count.

The two rounds left were what he had. In a few minutes there'd be another rush. He'd take one more with him, and then, remembering Ecco, he'd use the last round to take the fast dark exit.

Since it was almost over, he might as well go comfortably. He stood, stretched his legs, and treated himself to a long, luxurious piss into a drinking fountain drain. He could hear them arguing and squabbling below about who would rush him next.

The big room he'd had his back to was a chem lab; he smashed the window in its door with a chair. Downstairs, they yelped and whined "What's he doing?" at each other. *Wish I had the ammunition to invite them up to find out.*

The supply closet was familiar territory; a year ago he'd been finishing his first year as a ChemE major.

Except for some strong caustics, the dry chemicals had been in plastic jars that had rotted. He swept the heaped-together powders, and the goopy remnants of the jars, into a dustpan, carried the pan down the hall, and emptied it just out of sight of one stairwell entrance. He went back and got more, putting that at the other end of the hall, dragging one body out of the way as if it were furniture. He wiped his hands on his pants, noticing he didn't care that the man was dead but hated how grimy his skin and clothes were. *Funny, before Daybreak the only corpse I'd seen was at Grandpa's funeral.*

Next he took the dry chemicals stored in glass, which were generally the most reactive, and poured them onto the tops of his piles. They were still arguing about whether they should rush him, and what it might mean that he was moving around up there.

Back in the supply closet, he set aside the strong acids. The rest of the liquids in glass were mostly complex organics, which had turned to something like cheese, but a few flammable solvents seemed all right; these he carried, bottles and all, to add to his piles.

Sudden scuffling downstairs. Shouting. Screaming.

Two shots.

RRC agents or maybe TNG troops; Daybreakers had no working guns. Roger froze and listened.

"Hey, don't shoot." A grinning Dan Samson burst from the stairwell. "Roger! I didn't know Heather had sent you too! I surprised'em a little," the big man said. "If we go now, I think we can shoot our way out—"

"Need ammo," Roger whispered. "I have two."

"Seven," Samson said quietly.

"Let's set off the surprise I've been fixing up and see if we can get out with just hatchets. What are they *doing* down there?"

"Trying to figure out what to do because you killed the big boss and two little bosses, and they're afraid to go home and say they didn't get us, and even more afraid to come up the stairs. Let's try your idea. I've always loved surprises."

A few seconds later, they hurled one jug of nitric acid to the far end of the hall; the mess of powder there foamed, fumed, burst into flames, and poured out dense blue smoke. They charged down their own stairwell, staying well separated, and at the first landing, threw the big bottles of hydrochloric and sulfuric acid up behind themselves, through the propped-open doors and into the piles of chemicals. There was a low, pulsing boom and more dark smoke gouted into the stairwell.

Holding their breaths, they plunged down the stairs. At the double doors Samson plowed into a Daybreaker sentry coming in, pinned her to the wall with the door, and chopped her forehead, twisting the blade to wrench it free.

Roger yanked the other door open and charged into the now-terrified group, slashing and thumping with his hatchet, and Samson was on them a moment later.

The surviving Daybreakers fled. "This way," Samson said. They climbed through a broken window onto a low fire escape, dropped to the ground, and ran.

"Those were some pretty shitty soldiers," Roger gasped, as they ducked between two buildings. Behind them, the chemistry building was pouring dense blue smoke from its lower floor.

"Those weren't soldiers. They were slaves. Their leadership was three sorta-soldiers from Castle Earthstone. More afraid of their bosses than they were of us." In the chemistry building, a window belched orange flame. "What did you do back there?"

"I have no idea. Where to from here?"

"Well, not back to *that* building. South, I think. Let's go."


**17 HOURS LATER. PUEBLO, COLORADO. 12:30 AM MST. SUNDAY, SEPTEMBER 14, 2025.**

"This is pretty senseless of me," Allie said. She cupped her wineglass like a baby bird in her hand, looking at the two empty bottles as if they had just appeared from nowhere. "I'm just the tiddliest bit drunk, I'm going to have a hangover tomorrow for the conference when I really need to be patient with Graham, and I'm feeling *so* totally extremely indiscreet." She touched the long red lacquered nail of her index finger to her nose and said, "Numb, numb, numb. Can't feel a thing. Also num, num, num, dinner here was amazing, Arnie. I think in the new post-Daybreak world, if Olympia is the new Washington, it's gotta be that Pueblo is the new New York. Better restaurants, smarter people, I mean what else could it be?"

"Well, Johanna's What There Is is *the* place in Pueblo."

"Yeah, and back in the day you'd have taken me to *the* place in New York, if I'd've even looked at you when you were teaching at that fancy school—"

"Columbia."

"I know, Arn, just having fun with you." She sighed and drank some more.

Watching Allie drink always excited him—many things about her did. She used to tease him that it reminded him of the only way he'd been able to score in college. Actually, he liked the way her deliberate sips always became deep gulps—not so much her lack of control, as her losing it.

He'd been staring. *Cover that.* "Where did you get red nail polish? I thought cosmetics were all gone—"

"The most expensive stuff was all natural ingredients packaged in glass. I just let it be known to some salvage crew heads that good things might happen if anyone brought me unopened nail polish, in glass bottles. One enterprising young man found some. So I have about a fifteen-year supply of nail polish—and he's now a section head with a comfy desk job. *And* my source for a lot of good stuff. At least *some* things still work the way they always have."

When they'd been dating, Arnie had worried that Allie's liking for gifts and favors, normal in a political appointee, might screw him up with Civil Service rules if they got married.

She was smiling in the way that always sent his heart into his throat. "Arnie, babe, honestly, you think some simple favors would matter enough for Chris Manckiewicz to even print it, and risk losing nine states of subscribers?"

Too drunk to argue, Arnie sat back. "I'm just so glad to see you again."

"I'm glad to see you again too. I didn't realize how much I missed you." She started a sip that turned into draining the glass. "Oops. Naughty." She extended her glass to refill; her deep red nails reflected little stars of candle flames until he poured in the red wine, which colored the light around it so that her nails glowed like blood rubies.

**40 MINUTES LATER. PUEBLO, COLORADO. 2:15 AM MST. SUNDAY, SEPTEMBER 14, 2025.**

The watch was on the other side of town and Arnie was exhausted. He could just run, just this once, and it would be okay.

Less than two blocks from his house, Aaron was jogging beside him. "It must be nice to have a chance to visit with an old friend."

Arnie tried to pretend the Daybreaker wasn't there, wasn't close enough for him to smell the man's infrequently-if-ever washed body and clothes, wasn't already causing the sort of fuzziness in his mind that he had now filled two notebooks trying to understand and analyze after the fact.

"Sometimes," Aaron said, as if Arnie had answered him, "there is a harmless pleasure in learning something about a former lover." Arnie picked up the pace but Aaron matched him. "Allie spends many nights sitting up alone, while the president sleeps the sleep of an old, tired man."

Arnie ran faster still; Aaron matched him.

"Doctor Yang, you are thinking, 'How would Aaron know?' and the answer is that we have mutual friends."

Only a block to go. Arnie flung himself toward his front door. Aaron was at his heels. In a final, gasping burst, Arnie leapt and whirled, put his back to his front door, drew his knives.

Dark, empty street.

He waited.

Nothing.

Finally he unlocked his door, went inside, locked it behind him, lit an oil lamp.

"She doesn't sleep with Graham anymore. Not that it's my business, of course, but it's interesting," Aaron said. He was leaning back in Arnie's leather armchair, legs crossed comfortably, bouncing one leg over his other knee. "Doctor, doctor, doctus, docta, doctum, dock ta dock ta dock."

Arnie wanted to speak, to shout, to scream and leap to the attack. Instead he was captivated by the way Aaron's foot moved in the lamplight, up down, up down. . . .

Aaron said, "Been a long time, been a long time, been a long lonely, lonely, lonely, lonely . . . time. So things have been happening. Do you know where Larry, Chris, and Jason are? Are they coming back across the Wabash?"

Arnie felt his head nodding. It was a tiny victory; he knew from having sneaked a look at Heather's notes, on her desk, that Heather had actually instructed them to get out any way that seemed good. It wasn't quite a lie to nod, and it wasn't the truth either, but Arnie hoped, deep inside, it would turn out to be a lie.

More questions, as Arnie cooked a meal for Aaron.

Later, writing in his notepad, Arnie scribbled a whole page of *I must never come home without the watch.*

*I must never come home without the watch.*

*I must never come home without the watch.*

On and on, like Bart Simpson having a bad day, unable to think of another sentence. He took a deep breath and made himself write

*I must remember—*

Something about Allie.

Something hurt; he looked down to see the broken pencil, and some blood where the splinters had gone into his middle finger.

He fell asleep lying across the still-made bed, his notebook dropping to the floor beside him.

## THE NEXT DAY. NEAR HAYSTACK ROCKS, JUST OUTSIDE WILLIAMS, INDIANA. 3 PM EST. MONDAY, SEPTEMBER 15, 2025.

"Hi, boys, what's new?"

Roger sat up from his nap like he'd been electrocuted; Samson, sitting guard, slowly turned his head. "Deb, you could sure scare the shit out of someone that way."

"That's why I did it." Debbie Mensche was grinning. "You guys headed to Bloomington, too?"

"No need," Samson said. "We were there two days ago and nearly got killed."

"And we got our missions done," Roger said. "Or mission, actually. We each had one but it was the same one, and they didn't tell us about each other. When we met up we found out we were compartmentalized, but we'd been sent on the same job, to check out the encrypted radio station in Bloomington."

"Well, we're three for three—that's the mission they sent me on, and I didn't know anything about you all." *That's only a slight modification of the truth,* Debbie thought. "So I guess we're done and we can go home. How did you all do?"

Dan said, "I ran the whole way here, chased and shot at all the time. By the time I shook off my pursuers long enough to go into Bloomington for a look, Roger was already there."

Roger nodded. "Luckily they didn't notice me, so I could take my time picking through what was left of that radio station—troops from Castle Earthstone smashed all the gear with clubs and axes, killed the techs and their slaves, and set the building on fire. So all I learned was that there had been a station here, which we already knew, and we were too late to learn anything more."

"At first I thought none of it made any sense at all," Samson said. "But the thing is, just destroying the radio station—and that's weird enough in its own right, it was their own people, why didn't they just call them back in?—anyway, to shoot everyone and smash it up like that, it wouldn't have taken even a platoon to do it, but they sent a whole battalion. And that reminds me *a lot* of the way they used so many more people than they had to to catch poor old Steve. So I don't think that wrecking the radio station was the main mission; I think they were here to be the trap for us, and for some reason we don't know, capturing our scouts and agents is insanely important to them compared to almost anything else."

"Well, that would explain all the running and shooting I had to do on my way in," Debbie said. "So you had the same experience, Dan, but Roger—"

"Didn't see a single tribal till I saw fifty of them running at me when I came out of the burned-out radio station," Roger said.

Debbie nodded, obviously thinking. "Has either of you reported in yet? Did they issue you a radio?"

Both men shook their heads.

"Do you think the other side has any radio detectors—this side of the moon, I mean?"

"No idea. Why?" Samson asked.

"Because I've got a disassembled radio in my pack and there's a message I need to send to Heather."

"Can it wait till tonight? I'd like to get further away and better hidden from the old trouble before I invite any new."

"Fair enough. I'll transmit tonight, then—but we'll have to stop early enough so I have light to work by. Meanwhile, I'm thinking, the trail and road system in Hoosier National Forest would take us all the way down to the Ohio, and the last tribals I saw were headed back north on the roads. Let's get into some woods where there's plenty of cover and we have way better skills than they do."

For the first hour they were in what had been farm country with many trees along streambanks, orchards in odd corners of land, and fencerows; just one summer without planting or harvest was already making it thick with low brush and tall weeds. Twice, they spotted patrols far off, but evaded them without trouble.

Two miles into the forest, when they stopped for a water break, Roger said, "I don't suppose you can tell me how far we have to go."

Deb looked up in the air while playing with her fingers. "Right around a hundred and five miles walking, and call it two swimming. A hundred seven, give or take." The men were staring at her; she shrugged. "Family knack. I used to use it to keep track of stolen cars in Portland and hidden marijuana patches up in the hills. Dad's the real freak. He'd've told you to the *yard*."

# TWELVE:
# THE CAPTAIN CALLED ME CAIN

Heather ate dinner in the public mess hall because she didn't want to appear elitist, and besides it was fast and she had unlimited meals there. Sometimes it was great—venison stroganoff; usually it was adequate—shepherd's pie; just once, rebellion had threatened when it was rabbit, onion, and cabbage aspic.

With just Leo for company, she was finishing a pile of routine messages, and a plate of fish loaf and field green salad, at her usual table by herself, when Patrick materialized beside her. "Ms. O'Grainne, from crypto, marked OPEN NOW URGENT FAR. You said no matter what—"

"I did." She paid him twice the usual meal coupons. "The second payment is for you to *never admit* you carried a message or found me tonight, *no matter what*. Not even if I ask you in front of others; if I do that it's because I need you to alibi me."

He stood taller. "No messages for Ms. O'Grainne since ten this morning." He was gone.

She grabbed up her things and gathered up Leo. "FAR" meant Field Action Request, i.e. somebody out there had a situation that required immediate action. *Just bad luck that I'm out in public and can't rip it open right now.*

At home, she checked the lock, put Leo in his crib with a gentle settle-down kiss on the forehead, and opened the radiogram.

Debbie Mensche. Good, so she was alive and—
*Oh, Christ.*
The message read:

Arrived Blmgtn, rvz w DA & R **BRK**

Extractn now, expect full success **BRK**

URGENT: De follwd from border & attacked 4x **BRK**

Da follwed from border & attacked 2x **BRK**

R nothing till spotted @ Blmgtn by patrol **BRK**

Full rept from Ft Knx **BRK**

**De** EOM

She knew what it meant but checked anyway. Black envelopes in her safe held materials for her eyes only. Black envelope number 19 held a piece of paper with three simple notes:

*De: A/L*
*Da: J/L*
*R: A/J*

The Daybreakers had been waiting and ready for the two scouts Leslie Antonowicz had known about. The scout Leslie hadn't known about had gone undetected.
*Crap.*
*It's Leslie.*

**25 MINUTES LATER. PUEBLO, COLORADO. 7:55 PM MST.**
**MONDAY, SEPTEMBER 15, 2025.**

"Well," Leslie said, "you can cook, and that's something. Seriously, James, you can't spend the rest of your life being my best buddy and nursing your crush on me. You're way too nice a guy for that." She spooned some of his elk-liver gravy onto the hot cornbread, and joined him at the table. "I can't be your whole social life, dude, it's not natural."

"Who says I'm pining? We like each other's company, right? That's why we keep hanging out together. It was kind of painful, and obviously I wish you'd felt differently. I admit all that, but that was way back before Daybreak. I've been alone most of my life. I just like to have a few good friends, and let it go at that."

"James—really. The city is crawling with widows, nice women your age who would be glad—"

"If *I'd* be glad. Look, Leslie, we're calling each other by name a lot, and that usually means we're pretending we're not fighting. We've been having dinners together most Mondays, pretty much forever. That's not my whole social life. I teach Tuesday, Wednesday, and Thursday, Friday nights I go to martial arts after the school meeting, and Saturday I have the RRC Board meeting. If I like to spend Saturday nights with a book and Sundays loafing around the house, well, that's the only alone time I have for it anymore. I don't spend my whole week pathetically waiting to cook for you on Monday night, and I don't feel like I'm alone too much, in fact—or wait, is it just you want to do something different on Mondays? Without me, I mean?"

"See, James, this is how I can tell you're lying, you should see how afraid you look right now. And the answer is no, I hope we have twenty more years of Monday dinners, especially if you keep making that mixed berry pie, but my point is, the way you reacted to—"

The knock was very loud.

When James opened the door, three big, muscular militiamen came in, without invitation, and a slim young officer came in behind. "Leslie Antonowicz, our orders are to take you with us, and not to let you communicate with other people. We're required to cuff you, and you won't be allowed to bring a purse or personal effects; Sergeant Mason will confiscate any of those and take them with him."

James asked, "Don't you have to read her rights?"

"Not for a national security case."

"When can I say I'm innocent?" Leslie asked.

"As often as you want, but you're not going to be seeing anyone who will do anything about it for a while." The officer added, "We're authorized to use force."

Leslie stood still for a moment, then picked up her purse from the table and said, "Sergeant, this is all I was carrying." James made a noise, but she said, "James, let's not get your house trashed, let alone you arrested. I'll come along. James, please feed Wonder, and get Heather and Arnie—"

"Ms. Antonowicz, we said *no* communication. Is Wonder your dog?"

"Yes."

"Does he have food and water and somewhere out of the weather for tonight?"

"He's in my house, but he'll need to, you know, go, and he'll be hungry—"

"Is he friendly?"

"Too friendly. He'll want to be buddies with everyone."

"Good. I'm supervising the search and seizure on your house. We'll take care of Wonder this evening, and then, Mister Hendrix, if we can set you up—"

"I have a key," he said, flushing furiously. "I'll go over tomorrow morning and move Wonder here, or you can bring him here tonight—"

"We'll bring him here tonight, then. It won't be late."

The care they were taking of Wonder made it all real, somehow. Leslie wiped her face angrily as the tears poured down, but they pushed her hands down to cuff them behind her.

James tried once more. "Can't you say what this is about?"

"Specific orders not to. The order is direct from Heather O'Grainne."

Leslie's blood froze. Her eyes met James's, and he looked as stunned as she felt. Before either of them could speak again, she was dragged out the door, not roughly, but with no possibility of resistance.

The guard held up the lantern just long enough for her to see that her room had a pitcher of water, a cup, a squat toilet, a cot, and a blanket, but no window. He left her in total darkness, sitting on the cot, crying. She had no idea how long it was before she felt for the cup and pitcher and found her way under the blanket, or how long she lay there, willing herself to sleep, and failing.

**ABOUT THE SAME TIME. PUEBLO, COLORADO. 8 PM MST.
MONDAY, SEPTEMBER 15, 2025.**

When Arnie walked into his home, Aaron was apparently asleep in his bed. Arnie grabbed a heavy paperweight, but before he was in reach, Aaron sat up. "Well, you are very fortunate that I am here to save you."

Arnie kept his grip on the paperweight. Aaron rose from the bed, reached out, and took it from him. "Now then. Your information was invaluable. If you hadn't kept digging until the pattern of dummy missions became clear, we might not have realized how important it would be to leave young Roger Jackson entirely alone. But you've done such an excellent job—such a *very* excellent job. Without your having realized that you had been excluded from the dispatching of Mister Samson on that dummy mission, those eager lads from Castle Earthstone might not have known to look for him and intercept him."

*Dan. Steve, and now Dan.* Arnie's knives flew from their sheaths in a cross-draw; Aaron, laughing, fell back on the bed, letting the blades whistle over his head, and kicked Arnie with both feet, full in the chest. He was flung backward, but he braced himself on the wall—

"Knives down. Knives down. Think about your position. You are already in very, very far with me. Think about what you did to Steve Ecco. As far as we know Samson is alive and will come back. Think of what he'll say when he knows that it was you who betrayed your friend . . . think of what Allie will say when you are once again the sort of chump who throws away opportunities . . ."

Arnie thought for a long breath that he might continue the attack, press home his knives, shut Aaron up forever.

Aaron did not move, but he said, "Doctor Yang, you are about to become truly doctus, sir, you are indeed, because one of those questions that you have been trying to ask, and I have always evaded, is about to be answered. You are going to learn how Daybreak migrates from mind to mind, and reinforces itself, without the aid of those little plaztatic computer gizmos that some people seem to miss so very much. All your questions, about to be answered. Now put those silly knives away, you don't want to miss this, it's why you started to talk to me in the first place."

. . .

*I might need to boil the sheets.* They stank, there were stains, and Arnie felt, more than he could see by lamplight, little things jumping from them. He had dragged them off the bed and stuffed them into a canvas duffle, and was trying to think what he'd tell the nice lady that did the wash when she came around. *Could've been worse, he could've taken all his clothes off, his skin has to be even worse than his rags. Jesus, plenty of hot water in the tank from the solar collector; he could have taken a bath, even rinsed out his clothes, he didn't even* want *to be clean.*

*I'm getting a bath as soon as I have clean sheets on the bed to fall into. And I don't know how I'll ever get rid of all the bugs that came off that . . .*

It should have been funny. He'd been about to think *lousy bastard* when he realized how accurate it was.

He felt under his mattress, found his notebooks, heard the little whispers in his mind urge him to tear them up, give them to Aaron, throw them away, and had a thought; he pulled the current one out and scrawled down the page,

*The Deeper It Goes The Less Daybreak Can Do To It.*
*The more it is part of you*
*the more it's who you think you are*
*the more it's you*
*the less Daybreak can change it,*
*the less it bends to follow Daybreak*
*the less Daybreak pwns it*
*I am a scientist, I record things I record things I record things Daybreak can't stop that because it's deep it's deep that I record things I record things I record things There's something Daybreak can't do it can't stop me can't stop me can't stop can't stop I record things I record things. I am I am*
*I am a fucking bag of shit*
*I don't matter*
*we don't matter*
*FUCK PEOPLE*

That last consumed the bottom half of the page in a huge child's scrawl. He forced his hands to close the notebook and rammed it back into its hiding place.

He had just made his last neat hospital corner and was really looking forward to that shower when there was a knock at the door. He froze only for an instant; it wouldn't be Aaron. He wouldn't knock. He set the pen and ink in their standard spot on his desk.

At the door, two militiamen waited for him. *Oh, God, I'm busted. My notebooks—*

"Doctor Yang? Heather O'Grainne asked us to come and bring you. It's urgent. I'm to take you to her right away. She said to bring a blank notepad. Her orders are that I'm not to answer any questions."

He didn't seem to be a prisoner, but then what was he?

In Heather's office, he found her head down on the desk, as if she had been praying or crying. But she sat up, ran a hand across her face, thanked the militiamen, and waited for the door to close and their footsteps to go away.

"Arnie," she said, "in a way, this is good news. We've got a captured Daybreaker who was in deep cover for you to interrogate. You need to start tonight, while the shock of arrest is still fresh." He had a tenth of a second to hope it was Aaron, but Heather went on talking; Arnie missed most of it, in his horror at realizing why Aaron had been so suddenly informative, earlier tonight.

**ABOUT THE SAME TIME. PUEBLO, COLORADO. 10:15 PM MST. MONDAY, SEPTEMBER 15, 2025.**

Leslie was trying to talk to herself. *Got to face things. I don't know why I'm accused, but I'm accused of . . .*

There was a glow on the floor, coming from beneath the door. It opened.

She felt better seeing that it was Arnie Yang—pleasant, sensible, dorkish, slightly sad Arnie, who you could always have a beer with, always so desperate for human company; not exactly her friend, but she trusted his honesty, and she couldn't imagine him treating her, or anyone, harshly.

He squatted down so as not to stand over her. "Are you being well-treated?"

"I guess. It's clean. Nobody hits me or yells at me." Humiliatingly, she began to cry; it was such a relief that someone seemed to care. She wiped at her eyes. "God, I'm sorry. I didn't mean to—"

"You know my job is to hear all about it."

"I didn't do anything, I didn't tell anyone anything, I'm as loyal as you are."

He sighed. "I can't imagine how you could have done it, but the evidence Heather showed me—"

"That's part of it, Doctor Yang, I can't even imagine how there could be any evidence—"

"Were you so careful?"

"No, I mean I didn't do anything, so—"

He raised his hands gently, and spoke quietly and kindly. "Leslie, a moment ago you were talking about the evidence."

"How could it possibly—"

"Leslie, I really want to believe you. But you'll have to put it *all* in my hands. I'm going to ask you about things going back a decade or more, and some of them won't have any apparent connection to this situation. You know that you and I both want to clear you. If there is evidence anywhere that will clear you, if you tell me everything, hold nothing back, I can find my way to that evidence, Leslie. I couldn't tell you why, but I believe somehow you're innocent, and if you'll help me, I can find the path to the truth. But you've got to cooperate; answer my questions, no matter how personal, even if I just ask you to ramble on. Withhold nothing, object to nothing, just give me what I ask for. Will you promise to help me try?"

She wiped her face with the little piece of toweling they'd given him. "With you all the way, Doctor Yang."

"Arnie. If we weren't before, we're going to be friends." He leaned forward and said, "Now, as much as you remember, had you ever heard the word 'Daybreak' in any kind of political or environmental context, any time before October 28th, 2024?"

**THE NEXT MORNING. PUEBLO, COLORADO. 9:04 AM MST.
TUESDAY, SEPTEMBER 16, 2025.**

*This is not going to be easy.* Heather looked down at the notes she had scrawled minutes ago, after her quick conference with Arnie. Leslie Antonowicz had been no more forthcoming this morning, refusing to answer any questions, saying only that she was innocent, *which is kind of what you'd expect, isn't it?*

She looked up; both delegations were silent, either watching her or working over notes. *Probably they both already know. It's not like we're hard to penetrate or anything.* Her own sarcasm was bitter brass in her brain.

She drew a breath and began. "There's something we need to cover before talking about anything else this morning. Last night an ongoing investigation discovered that one of the Reconstruction Research Center's top analysts, Leslie Antonowicz, was working for Daybreak. At this point we don't even know what that really means, whether she was actually in the pay of some Daybreak-related organization or whether she is a believing convert to the Daybreak system of ideas. Ms. Antonowicz is in detention at a secure location.

"My senior researcher, Doctor Arnold Yang, is interrogating her, and I hope within a few days we will know much more about what has been going on, for how long, and how much damage has been done. At this point, however, because she was on our Board, the librarian for our field reporting system, and a senior researcher, and therefore her routine access to information was at such a high level, we have to assume that *no* communications between RRC and anywhere else—including either the Temporary National Government or the Provisional Constitutional Government— have been secure, since the founding of the RRC. The responsibility for this is entirely mine. I urge that you immediately contact your home offices by your own most secure channels and begin appropriate investigations. I ask your patience while we investigate our own very serious situation. Thank you."

General Grayson cleared his throat as if to say something, but Cam froze him with a glance, then pulled a file card from his pocket and read, "'Whereas any agreement on the matters currently in negotiation is absolutely dependent on maintenance of full security, we believe the conference must be canceled for the time being, until RRC is able to show that security is re-established. We expect that this will take a period of weeks or months and therefore will return to the temporary capital at Athens in the TNG District. We regret this necessity and look forward to reconvening at the earliest feasible date.'"

*He had that ready to go on his card; he knew.*

Graham nodded, pulled out three cards (Heather could see they were in Allie's all-caps printed scrawl), and selected the one he wanted; he read, "We will be happy to reconvene as soon as security issues are settled, but we do not believe this can be done at any early date, so we are returning to Olympia, where we will await the successful conclusion of the RRC's investigations."

*And Allie had prepared Graham Weisbrod to go three different ways. Gah. There used to be high school marching bands that had better security than we do.*

That afternoon, walking back with James from seeing off the PCG train to Olympia (just twenty minutes after the TNG train to Athens), Heather spotted a newsboy running up the street toward the riverfront. She flagged him down, paid him, and showed James the extra edition of the *Pueblo Post-Times*. Half the front page was headline:

PEACE TALKS COLLAPSE

SENIOR RRC OFFICIAL IS COVERT DAYBREAKER

PROSPECTS FOR REUNION ELECTION NEXT YEAR DIM

"This might be the first issue, ever, that I don't read," she said. As they walked on they could hear the shouts of "Extra!" in the streets around them.

"I don't suppose many people will be collecting those," James said. "Not the way they did the PEACE headline a few months ago."

After another block, Heather said, "I got all three of your notes about Leslie. James, we all know you're her most loyal friend. There's no reason for us to consider you a suspect, but it's only common sense for us to keep you away from the investigation. And for God's sake, James, it's *Arnie*. Are you expecting him to torture her or something? He's told me already that he really wants to believe she's innocent, but she's not cooperating at all. I know she's important to you, but what else would you have us do? Now, of course you have to worry. She's your friend and you don't think she's guilty. But I know that if she's innocent, Arnie Yang will find that out. And I promise, no matter what, you'll see her again."

James nodded, said, "Thanks for understanding," and walked away, hands in his pockets, head down, kicking at the dirt.

*He's thinking, and that's not as good a thing as it usually is,* Heather thought, turning toward her own office door. *And I hope he doesn't realize how likely it is that when he sees Leslie again, it'll be to sit up with her the night before we hang her.*

## THE NEXT DAY. SAN DIEGO, CALIFORNIA. 8:30 AM PST. WEDNESDAY, SEPTEMBER 17, 2025.

The big thugly types at the main gate of Castle Castro held their black-powder carbines pointed down. Carlucci had left weapons and deputies at home; he carried three letters. The most important one was from Natalie Thanh, a Federal district judge. Finding that Article IV, Section 4, of the Constitution outlawed hereditary monarchy and any form of feudal aristocracy on American territory, she ordered the League of Southern Castles dissolved, voided all oaths of fealty to the League, and demanded the renunciation of all titles.

Carlucci had had to sell that one to Thanh himself, dusting off his law school education, sitting long nights by a flickering oil lamp, reading dusty law books rescued from basements and attics to put together the pieces of *PacTel versus Oregon*, *Gregory versus Ashcroft*, and *Forsyth versus Hammond*, but he'd made Thanh see it his way.

That letter was important, but the other two that Heather had secured for him, flown down to him by Bambi Castro, were what made it matter. Cameron Nguyen-Peters, NCCC of the Temporary National Government in Athens, Georgia, declared that he would use his emergency powers to enforce Judge Thanh's decision "as consistent with constitutional restoration." President Graham Weisbrod of the Provisional Constitutional Government ordered all Federal agents to enforce Judge Thanh's order "without equivocation or delay."

As on every other visit to Castle Castro, Carlucci couldn't help noticing that Castro's brawny, efficient, uniformed guards were much more impressive than anything Carlucci had across the bay, at what was nominally the FBI's California HQ and actually around twenty people in a fortified office building.

Once Carlucci had convinced Judge Thanh that he was right, she had suggested that he arrest Harrison Castro under RICO and the 1903 Militia Act. *And the cat should be ordered to wear a bell under the Cruelty to Mice Act.*

"Okay, they're answering." Castro's guard read the semaphore through his binoculars. "Permit entry, all other checkpoints pre-cleared." He lowered the binoculars. "Well, there you go; do you still remember the way?"

"Yeah, I lived here for a few weeks last fall," Carlucci said.

"Some of us hoped things would work out so that the Feds would work with us, and support what we're trying to do here."

"You never know what may come," Carlucci said.

Between Daybreak and Christmas last year, Harrison Castro had admitted a few thousand selected refugees. About three thousand adults had sworn their allegiance to Castle Castro, and brought along maybe four hundred kids. Since then, Castle Castro had taken over about half the old San Diego waterfront, wrapped in concentric rings of zigzag walls. The walls themselves were mostly the rubble of wrecked and pulled-down buildings between chain link and boards, running across streets between intact buildings; the outer walls were more than a mile inland. *Wonder if Castro got permission from all those property holders? He used to be very insistent that property rights were the whole basis of civilization. . . .*

He hated the feeling of envy that hit him at times like this. Castle Castro had the most reliable food supply in the area, and electricity some of every day. Carlucci had two great teenage kids, Paley and Acey; like others at FBI West, they sometimes went hungry and sometimes were up all night when tribal attacks threatened, and school was a matter of reading when they weren't working, which was rare. Castro had an actual K-12 high school in the main keep there, the only problem being it taught what Castro wanted it to.

Carlucci passed through the second line of walls and buildings; the guards came to attention as he passed. *Probably standard courtesy for a visiting dignitary.* He couldn't help adding, mentally, *From a "foreign power."*

The path wound past greenhouses, fishponds, and animal barns; standing a siege right now might have been awkward, but if the crops in the outside fields came in and filled up their food storage this year, and with the access to the sea and all those sailboats Castro had managed to pull together, Castle Castro would be, for all practical, short-run purposes, impregnable.

The central compound and keep had been built prior to Daybreak, back when Castro had merely been a billionaire nut enacting bizarre power fantasies. Inside its steel fences, a complex maze of roads led anyone who didn't know the system around rather than toward the big house. Wrong routes ended in cul-de-sacs under the guns of blockhouses.

The man at the front door smiled and said, "Nice to see you again, Mister Carlucci."

"How have you been, Donald?"

"Busy, safe, and well-fed," the man said. "The boss is in the main office. I guess you still know your way."

Before Carlucci could knock, Harrison Castro opened the door and said, "Dave. Welcome. Come right this way."

The breakfast table on the balcony was set with fussy precision. "Since this is bound to involve being rude to each other," Castro said, "I thought we might as well start off with something we'd enjoy."

They made small talk while Carlucci let himself get reacquainted with eggs, bacon, and coffee. "One small piece of business I'd like to do before the main business," Castro said. "Tribes are getting bigger and worse everywhere, and the beating we gave them here back in June doesn't seem to have stuck. If you need to shelter at Castle Castro against any tribal attack, the door is open to everyone under your command or protection."

"Of course I accept," Carlucci said. *Jeez, there could be a tribal attack up from Baja any time, and I've got Arlene and the kids, what else can I say but "yes"?* "If you remember my number two guy, Terry Bolton, I was going to have him contact your folks for some liaison. We've got some ops going down in Baja and you're right, something real bad is building up."

"I remember Terry, and if he thinks it's bad down there, he's not the panicking kind; it's bad. All right, well, I'm out of the pleasant stuff." Castro had a sardonic smile. "I suppose you're here to place me under arrest."

Carlucci shrugged. "Not this time, anyway. That isn't how the law works in this case. I'm here to serve a Federal District Court order and to deliver letters from the governments at Athens and Olympia. What you do after receiving those letters is what determines whether we'd ask the court for an arrest warrant. It's one of those things like a restraining order where the activity isn't illegal until you've been told to stop and haven't complied. At least that's what Judge Thanh thinks. Will you accept the papers now?"

"Sure, I'll read anything, unless by accepting them I agree to them."

"All you do is allow me to say you weren't unaware of the order."

"No harm in that I can see." He extended a hand, took the three pieces of paper, and read them. "Shall I make a statement?"

"You could send a letter within a reasonable length of time, decline to respond but send an attorney to Judge Thanh during business hours, or tell me whatever you like. Or I suppose you could declare war and have me thrown out the window."

"Well, definitely not the last alternative. I'll just tell you, Dave, and I trust you to report it accurately enough. The court order and the letters cite the Constitution of the United States. It's no longer in force. The United States of America is over, Carlucci. I wish a brave, decent, honorable man like you could see that. The Constitution was created so that the people who were worth shit could run the country, but it got bent around to all kinds of other shitty, worthless purposes. So now it's gone, and good riddance, and though I wouldn't have asked for Daybreak before it happened, now that it has, well, from now on you can deal with the Earl of San Diego."

"We can't address you by that title," Carlucci said. "Article One, patents of nobility clause. Here's the blunt word from a Federal court: You still live in the United States of America. Our Constitution doesn't permit private armies, hereditary sovereignty, or titles of nobility."

Castro rose. "Can I send you on your way with some food or something?"

**ABOUT THE SAME TIME. PUEBLO, COLORADO. 10:14 AM MST. WEDNESDAY, SEPTEMBER 17, 2025.**

"Can you tell me what time it is?" Leslie asked.

"I *can*," Arnie said, "and I will as soon as I see evidence of cooperation. It's frightening, isn't it, not to know whether it's day or night after a while? But, you know, we need to know what is going on—"

"Doctor Yang—Arnie—I know you don't believe me, but I'm innocent."

"You're right that I don't believe you," he said. He smiled as if it were their private joke. "Yet. But this is only our fifth session, and you are *becoming* more believable. That's at least progress."

"I always feel so safe after you leave but by the time you come back I'm scared out of my mind again." She shifted uneasily in her chair; his gaze stayed on her face, and the corner of his mouth turned up as if something he hadn't quite identified wasn't quite right. He had been sitting and watching her quietly all that time, and she realized that it had been a long time since she'd spoken. "I . . . I should just answer every question, and try not to guess why you ask or what you're looking for?"

"Same rules as every other time," Arnie said, softly. "Are you in good enough shape to do that? Have you been sleeping?"

"Too much," she said. "A chance to run or swim or climb something would be heavenly."

Arnie's mouth twitched, but he said nothing.

"What?" she asked.

"Bad joke. I was thinking if you had a head start, you'd probably get to do plenty of running, climbing, and swimming, at least until they caught you."

She couldn't help it; she laughed. "All right, let's get to work. *I* know I'm innocent, anyway."

He didn't nod or smile, but he didn't scowl either. "All right. Think back to conversations with friends and family *since* Daybreak. Remember times when you've said that Daybreak was sort of a blessing in disguise, or not all bad, or sometimes you were maybe secretly glad it happened. Tell me exactly what you said."

"Do you need to know who I talked to?"

"No, not at all. I'm interested in what *you* said. All right, so when you *have* been thinking about the good things about Daybreak, across these last few months, what do you think of?"

"I'm not sure I remember."

"What do you think you might have said? Just do what you've done before, try not to block anything, blurt out any old thing I ask about, just relax and let your mind open to me. Now what do you say when you're explaining the good parts of Daybreak?"

Part of her wanted to object that she didn't think she ever had, but it seemed that even before she objected, she was already telling him about the positive side of Daybreak, and that she was remembering thinking those things even before Daybreak. It was nice to be sitting here with a guy who understood; Arnie was smiling, listening intently. Just when she realized she was uncomfortable, he poured water for her. "Need a break? Hungry?"

Arnie would get her out of this. She clung to that.

## THE SECOND NIGHT AFTER. PUEBLO, COLORADO. 11:30 PM MST. THURSDAY, SEPTEMBER 18, 2025.

"Leslie." The voice in the darkness was so soft she thought perhaps she was dreaming. She sat up. "Leslie," the voice repeated, "come to the door so you can hear me better. Don't make any noise."

She rolled off her cot and crawled to the door, feeling ahead of her so she wouldn't knock over the pitcher.

"I don't know how long we've got," the voice said. "I've got the guards timed, but if I hear them I'll have to go that second—they vary the timing. If I disappear, don't call out, just get back in your bunk and pretend to be asleep. I'll always be back."

"James?"

"Who else?"

*Reasonable question.* She lay prone to put her mouth and ear by the crack at the bottom of the door. "Can you do anything for me?"

"Working on it. Is Arnie still your interrogator?"

"He's the only person I've seen since I was arrested."

"Jesus, he's got things just the way he planned. Leslie, there were three suspects. You were one; I was another. The third was Arnie."

"Oh, God, James, you're telling me *Arnie Yang is working for Daybreak?* We are so fucked, James, so totally fucked up the *ass*. What can you do? Do you have some evidence to prove I'm not guilty and Arnie is? Are you going to try to break me out?"

"Not right away. If they're going to torture or kill you, or they hold a secret meeting without me, I have a way to know, and I have a way to break you out right then. Otherwise, though, I'm going to keep working on catching Arnie Yang. He says you're refusing to talk."

"I've been totally cooperating! I'm answering every question he asks me! He said it was my best chance!" Her rage shocked her.

"I *bet* he did. Tell me about what he does. He's already got you framed so he doesn't need to create more evidence. He could have had you executed by now. So he can't be after information because he knows you don't have any, and he can't frame you any more than you are already framed. So what's he spend all that time talking about?"

Even there, lying on the dark floor of her cell, and feeling like she owed James her life, Leslie couldn't help noticing that James spoke in the same tone he did on the drunken lonely evenings when she told him too much about her love life. But he was right, he needed to know this, so she said, "Well, he always tells me to put myself into his hands and trust him, and he wants to talk about Daybreak ideas I had before Daybreak day . . ." She told James everything she could remember.

He said, "I think I'm recognizing the basic technique for implanting a false memory, but it's been a long time since I read that circular. FBI thing, I think, about how not to be fooled by things like UFO abduction stories and Satanist conspiracy stories, and how not to lead witnesses into deceiving you. I'll find it and be able to tell you for sure next time. Meanwhile I guess the main trick is to not believe any thought that might have been his suggestion. So if—gotta go."

She rolled onto her cot silently, pulling the blanket over herself. She counted six long, slow breaths before a guard came in with a candle in one hand, and a tray holding a dubious meat patty, fried potatoes, onions, and zucchini in the other; as always, there were no utensils, just one wet and one dry cloth. *Same thing four times in a row; probably another way to break down my time sense.* She ate looking down at her plate, because she never knew when they were watching, or from what angle, and she was afraid they might see her smile. On the last bite, she blew out the candle, wiping her face in the dark.

**3 DAYS LATER. NEAR THE RUINS OF ALTON, INDIANA. 6:45 PM EST. SATURDAY, SEPTEMBER 20, 2025.**

"How deep is that?" Roger asked.

"After it's past your neck, it doesn't make much difference," Debbie pointed out. "Unless you can't swim. Last chance to tell us."

"I can swim. I just hate being wet and cold at the start of a thirty-mile hike in soggy moccasins."

Samson looked up from where he was lashing the last of the 55-gallon drums together. "I agree. We're going to do it, of course, but I agree; I hate it too." Before them, the Ohio River was broad and olive-green.

The flow was faster and deeper than anyone had seen in at least 150 years. Dozens of dams on the Ohio and its tributaries had toppled. A cold early fall was drenching the Appalachians. The Allegheny basin's forests, dying from fallout, were releasing their grip on thousands of mountain slopes, and the water they once slowed and absorbed poured unimpeded over bare earth, freighted with dead black mud.

Lashed together with hemp line, the empty drums made an awkward raft. They tied their packs on top of two closely bound drums, hoping something, somewhere, might stay sort of dry. Not wanting to lose the last of the daylight, they grabbed handholds on the lashing ropes and walked into the river, beginning to kick with their feet, at Samson's direction, when it became too deep to wade.

Roger clamped his jaw and pressed his lips together; he'd drown before he let himself swallow what was in the river. *How many unburied bodies must there be upstream? Pathogen soup, that's what it is.*

Roger kicked when told to, hung on otherwise, and did his best to keep his head out of the filth. Twice something, a tree branch perhaps, bumped at him; once a floating rag, perhaps a diaper or T-shirt, wrapped over his wrist, and he flung it away in a near panic.

After what felt like a century of cold misery, Samson said, "I'm kicking dirt. Don't try to stand yet, but kick harder."

A moment later, Roger felt bottom too, as they passed over a sandbar sheltering the inside of a bend. They entered a slow, steady-flowing channel, kicking the drum raft out of the current upstream of a sloping gravel bank.

When they planted their feet and stood up, the water was only waist deep, and they walked their raft aground easily.

They cut their packs free, held them over their heads, and bore them ashore, mostly dry. Samson waded back in, and pushed the empty raft out past the bar. Holding on with one hand, chest-deep in the filthy water, he slashed the lashings with his knife, detaching the drums and setting them bobbing along in the current. Two minutes later, on a narrow gravel road just above the river, Debbie said, "Shit."

"What?"

"Eaahh, I hate being wrong. Looks like we'll only be traveling 103 miles since you asked me, including the river. Off by four. Damn, damn, damn." She muttered about it off and on, until, an hour later, they made camp for the night, not completely out of danger, but safer than they had been in a long time.

## 2 DAYS LATER. SOUTH OF THE RUINS OF THE FORMER CELINA, OHIO (NEW STATE OF WABASH). 4:30 PM EST. MONDAY, SEPTEMBER 22, 2025.

"The way Earth's curvature works," Larry said, "the horizon on flat ground or water is usually less than five miles off. So all we can say for sure is that it's mud at least that far out." From the burned and crumbled docks at Celina, a plain of drying mud, once Grand Lake St. Marys, stretched to the eastern horizon.

They'd been able to shake the fitful and sporadic pursuit within a mile or two each time. Apparently word was out that three men traveling together were supposed to be caught, but without Castle Earthstone soldiers standing over them, most tribes didn't see it as a high priority, especially not if it involved going into centers of larger towns, where the tribes seemed to fear disease, feral dog packs, or perhaps ghosts.

"So," Chris said, "on the map, anyway, the short way around the lake from here is the north shore. Shall we keep going that way? I'd rather camp here than run into a tribe close to dark."

Larry said, "Let's see if we can break into that lighthouse and get a long view."

The sign in front said ROTARY LIGHT HOUSE. "But I don't see how it could rotate," Jason said.

Larry laughed. "There used to be a service club—sort of like a fraternity for grownups that did good things—called the Rotary Club, and my old man was in it. God, I wish I had him here to hear you say that."

Someone had been there before them; the broken door lay on the pavement. From the top of the tower, about three storeys high, they could see that mud stretched to the eastern horizon, broken up by ponds where the water had been deeper. Grass was coming in around the edge, and big flocks of ducks and geese were on the ponds.

In the open country south of the drained lake, leaves were the thousands of colors of an eastern forest in fall; brush was spreading out of the small woods, fencerows, and creek bottoms into the long grass. Jason said, "This is sort of what we Daybreak people were trying for. The fields are back to meadows, really, already, and there's going to be prairie grass, and bushes, and then the trees will grow tall enough to choke out the undergrowth, and you'll have the old forest back."

"It would look real pretty," Chris observed, "if we didn't know it was a graveyard for tens of millions of people."

They walked around to the southwest side of the tower, and saw a great ravine where the maps had shown none, stretching to the horizon.

"Well," Larry said, "that certainly explains where the water went. I guess we should be good scientistificalable explorers and all, and go take a look."

"Scientistificalable?" Jason asked.

"Add more syllables, gain more authority. First rule of bureaucratic prose."

**ABOUT 20 MINUTES LATER. A MILE SOUTH, NEAR THE FORMER OUTLET TO BEAVER CREEK, ALONG US 127. 5:45 PM EST. MONDAY, SEPTEMBER 22, 2025.**

"You know, they could have done this with one big bomb on Daybreak day," Chris said. "Just loaded it into a pleasure boat, sunk it next to the dam, blown it off. Nobody would have been searching or stopping them."

"This accomplished more of what they were trying to do," Larry said.

"Look how they did it—a tunnel five or ten feet below the lake bottom, so that the water running through would erode the embankment and cut a really deep hole in a hurry. All those graves. Four whipping posts. Shovels and picks just left here when they were done. The *point* of it was to work a few hundred people to death, besides making it much harder to restore that lake, which means nobody can reopen this canal for a long, long time."

"Was the canal open before?" Jason asked.

"No. But we're back to 1800s tech, and that's what this was. Now if we want the canal, we'll have to do all that pick and shovel work all over again." Larry looked over the field where so many bodies had already come to the surface from their shallow graves. "Part of making sure the Lost Quarter stays lost."

"But why?" Jason asked. "I mean, couldn't they do the same thing with half the killing?"

"Once you've beaten starving people to make them dig a tunnel they'll drown in, you're *committed*." Chris looked out to the west, across the field of human bones and the muddy gouge through the flat land, to the setting sun, huge and bloody with the soot of so many burned cities. "It's just the small, personal version of the big picture. Anyway, it'll be dark soon. We'd better camp for the night, and I'd rather not do it here."

"Let's head back to the lighthouse," Larry said. "It has a roof and it's easy to defend. But when you're doing sentry duty and have to look this way, *no brooding*, okay? Keep telling yourself it's just mud in the moonlight, and that's all it is."

## 6 HOURS LATER. OLYMPIA, NEW DISTRICT OF COLUMBIA. 11:30 PM PST. MONDAY, SEPTEMBER 22, 2025.

It was so good to be home and running things again. Allison Sok Banh loved the feel of her familiar desk chair, loved the idea that she was working late at night, loved it all. Tonight it had been easy for her to tuck Graham in and avoid his perpetually attempted conversation about the relationship. He'd passed out at the moment of mattress touchdown.

Allie had Lyle throw an extra bucket of coal into the fire under the hot water tank. From the locked steel box at the back of her bedroom closet, she took pre-Daybreak lavender Castile soap and Wild Turkey, plus Kona that Lisa Fanchion had given her in appreciation of the tax exemption on coffee.

Her scalding shower was at least five times as long as the ration, and in no way "cool and comfortable" as Graham Weisbrod's housekeeping directive had specified, but more along the lines of "sinfully decadent."

*So* bizarre. Before, she'd never really understood that Graham was serious about this good-gov shit. Allie's family had "dove ourselves neck-deep in politics as soon as we ditched the boat and got the vote," she remembered Uncle Sam saying, literally while he was teaching her to work the cash register. "Before you buy a business, buy the cop and the judge so you can keep it, Allie."

Snug in her thick terry bathrobe, she drizzled the scarce and wonderful bourbon into the pot of Kona, poured a cup, and settled in to work. The drink burned down her throat like hot, slick ebony inlaid with gold; she drew the fumes from the cup into her nose, sighed, and reached for the first memo.

"So the summit was aborted," Mr. Darcage said. "And you got to see your ex, and, I should guess, impress him. How fortunate all around."

She put her feet down abruptly, crossing her legs under the desk and tugging at her robe. *Who the fuck lets him in? Lyle? Gotta know!* "Ever think about knocking or maybe showing up in regular hours?"

"My employers would be delighted if you'd meet with me openly and regularly; the tribes *crave* recognition." He stepped out of the dim shadows in the corner of the office; in the flaring lamplight he seemed more gaunt, his face more lined, almost ancient, but his precisely geometric beard and hair were black as pitch. His eyes bulged slightly, his lips were too thick, and there was a patch of old acne scarring along one sideburn.

"That's not what I meant. And you know it." She held her robe closed with one hand, as if afraid it might pop open; her other hand reached under her desk, seeking the pistol—

The space was empty.

Darcage set the pistol down on the desk in front of her. "I don't want you to keep loaded guns around."

"I do many things you don't want me to."

"You *think* you do things I don't want you to. You don't *ask*, often enough, what I want you to do." He gestured toward the gun lying on the desk. "That's why I had to unload the gun for you. I shouldn't have to do that. I shouldn't have to do that for you."

His repetition was annoying her, and she said, "I get it."

"Of course you do."

"Why did you come here and why am I not throwing you out?" she asked, as much to herself as to him. He sat with one leg running along the edge of her desk, curled against the other, a supported flamingo, and leaned slightly forward, but did not speak. *I could suddenly bite his nose and it would serve him right. I wonder if he's trying to see down my robe.* She resisted the urge to look down or yank it closed; *can't let him know he's bothering me. Come on, talk, asshole. This silent act is creeping me out.* "You work hard at telling me what I don't want."

"That's because you're not always clear about what you *do* want. Don't you want to make things run smoothly? Don't you want all the good relations you can possibly get?"

*I know what I* don't *want: to be caught in just my bathrobe, here in the middle of the night, with contraband bribes on my desk and what's obviously a Daybreaker agent alone with me.* "What did you have in mind?"

The silence lay in the room like a dead cow on the floor, too big to go around, impossible to climb over without admitting that there was something in your way. The lamplight from her desk lamp flickered and danced. *Little kid campfire trick,* Allie thought, wishing she could disdain it. *Shine light up on a face from underneath and it looks scary.*

"Don't worry about seeing Doctor Yang again; he is on the right side and more attuned to your needs than you might think. In fact, he'd like to hear from you; why don't you write him a letter?"

The light flickered slightly. She looked up. He wasn't there. Her coffee was now too cool, anyway, the Wild Turkey wasted, the Kona wasted, and she felt sad and lonely. Maybe she'd go down to the main bedroom and curl up with Graham tonight; he always liked it when she did.

She poured her pitcher of Turkey and Kona down the sink, rinsed everything thoroughly, blew out the lamp, and took the back stairs passage down to the main presidential suite.

Darcage had not concealed that Daybreak was more interested in Arnie than they were in her. It bothered her; she didn't like being second to anybody.

**2 DAYS LATER. WAPAKONETA, OHIO. AROUND NOON EST.**
**WEDNESDAY, SEPTEMBER 24, 2025.**

Larry handed Jason a GPO brochure-map from the 1990s, *Scenic Water-ways of Ohio and Indiana.* "Look up Wapakoneta."

"I know that town name for some reason."

"Yeah, you do, but it's not the reason I'm interested in."

"Just look *up*," Chris said, pointing to the landmark sign forty yards down the road. It was like ten thousand other historic-landmark signs that appeared outside almost every small town in the Midwest, except that this one said:

WAPAKONETA, OHIO.
BIRTHPLACE OF NEIL ARMSTRONG,
FIRST MAN ON THE MOON.

"I'd forgotten that, Larry. Probably hadn't thought about it since fifth-grade American history. Crap," Chris said, an odd, desperate strain in his voice. "I remember when the moon was a *good* thing. My dad watched the landing on TV when he was a little kid, I guess along with everybody, and . . . I don't know, I guess you had to be in that generation, but to a lot of people, it meant a lot. Now . . . we look up at the moon, and we're *scared*."

Larry sighed. "Yeah, but what I wanted Jason to read was this." He pointed at the old map-guide.

Jason read aloud. "*The Auglaize River is canoeable from Wapakoneta, a small town pronounced Wop Ock Kuh Net Uh. (Many Ohioans shorten it to Wapak, pronounced Woppock.) The Wapakoneta Canoe Trek Company, just downstream of the Hamilton Street Dam, has canoes and kayaks for rent from mid-June to mid-October. May not be accessible in low-water years.* Shouldn't be a problem, it's rained like a real booger for an hour or two almost every day since we landed. And, okay, Larry, I see where you're going with your idea. It says, *The Auglaize River flows north to the Maumee at Defiance, down which canoes can continue nearly to Toledo.*"

"Unh-hunh, and Toledo's a port on Lake Erie, and there are Provi garrisons on the western side of Lake Erie—Put-in-Bay, Kelleys Island, Port Clinton, and Sandusky."

"You're figuring that if we can get canoes—"

"*Never walk when you can ride*, son, stay in gummint service and you'll learn that's a rule." Larry grinned. "Along with *always patronize anybody with less time-in-grade than you have*. Anyway, that's my thought. And looking up ahead, at least it looks like the town hasn't been burned."

In the warm midday sun, intact roofs peeked through the bright red and orange leaves. Larry said, "This road's as good as any for going into the town, I guess. That little thumbnail map seems to show Hamilton Street, and the Auglaize River, right in the middle of town."

A mile farther on, a sign pointed off to Auglaize Street. "You don't suppose they put Auglaize Street anywhere near the Auglaize River?" Larry said. "It leads into town, anyway."

Half an hour later, after passing a number of intact but empty houses, Jason said, "Weird. The tribals usually burn towns on general principles. But I haven't seen a burned house, or any sign of fighting, or even any human remains."

"But if this place were well-defended," Chris said, "you'd think we'd have met a patrol or run into a sentry by now."

Beyond an overgrown cemetery, a wide, placid stream, perhaps a hundred feet across, appeared below them.

"All right, found the river," Larry said.

In town, most of the big old twentieth-century frame houses and little nondescript brick storefronts still had all their glass; where they did not, they were boarded up. No doors were broken down. Larry said, "This feels like we walked into a Ray Bradbury story."

"Who are you?" a voice asked.

They formed up into a triangle with their backs together.

"I'm waiting," the voice said.

Larry shrugged slightly. "We are Federal agents reconnoitering this area for the Reconstruction Research Center."

"Please wait here and be comfortable. You are among friends. I must alert other people. It may be fifteen minutes before anyone else contacts you."

"We can wait that long," Larry said, slipping his pack off and sitting on it.

There was no answer; apparently the mysterious voice's owner had gone off on his errand—her errand?

"What do you think?" Chris asked, his voice barely a murmur, pointing his face down into the ground between his feet to hide his lips.

Jason muttered, "I think that was a kid's voice, reading from a card."

"I'm trying not to think," Larry said. "Whatever's here, it's not like anything else we've found. Did you both notice, no cars? Not even the muck from the rotted tires?"

"Yeah, and the boarded windows that must have gotten broke," Chris said, "they've swept up the glass around them."

Jason looked around. "They're not tribals. No downed wires, no wrecked refugee carts, so many things that just aren't here."

Larry nodded. "So often what's *not* there is what police work depends on."

"News reporting too," Chris said. "Congratulations, Padwan Jason, you have achieved the level of consciousness in which old poops pat you on the head."

Jason grinned. "My head lives to be patted, oh master. So who *is* here? The tribe of the Extremely Tidy People?"

"Close, but not quite," a deeper voice said, seemingly from nowhere.

Larry said, "You're not as invisible as the first person was. Part of your shadow is visible just beyond the corner of the laundromat. Does that mean we get six more weeks of winter?"

High-pitched laughter broke out all around them.

The deeper voice joined it. "Well, I don't suppose there's much point in keeping this up. Are you guys from Pueblo?"

"That's where we started from but it was a while ago," Larry said. "I'm Federal Agent Larry Mensche, mission commander; we'll be reporting back to RRC eventually. My younger teammate here is Jason Nemarec, and the big bear of a guy is Chris Manckiewicz, who you might remember from when there was net and television—"

"And radio," the voice said. "We heard you on KP-1 and WTRC, Mister Manckiewicz. And if I'm not mistaken you're also the narrator on *Orphans Preferred* and on *A Hundred Circling Camps*. You're a celeb here." A tall, rangy man walked out from the corner of the laundromat. "Although the biggest news this month, if not this year, is going to be that you caught me with my shadow showing, Mister Mensche."

He might have been sixty, or eighty. His face was grooved, more eroded than sagging. His full head of hair was iron-gray flecked with white, he stood straight as any ex-soldier, and his muscles bulged and knotted over thick bones; he looked like the barely covered skeleton of a giant. His khaki pants and faded plaid shirt were neatly pressed. "My name is Scott Niskala. I'm the scoutmaster of Troop 17. Everyone, you can step out of cover."

About twenty kids seemed to appear in a single motion. An instant later one tiny old lady in thick glasses stood beside Niskala. He said, "This, as you can probably guess, is Mrs. Niskala, who is—"

"—quite capable of introducing herself, thank you. Ruth Niskala. Scoutmaster of Troop 541. The outfit that shows the boys how to do things. We were thinking you might like to have a good meal and a good rest, and then maybe we can talk about what we might do for you."

**ABOUT 5 HOURS LATER. WAPAKONETA, OHIO. 6 PM EST. WEDNESDAY, SEPTEMBER 24, 2025.**

The old stone church, headquarters for the Wapak Scouts, had a small library with wooden tables and chairs, where Larry, Chris, and Jason were treated to fresh biscuits and venison gravy. This was followed by hot baths ("There aren't any regular scheduled baths right now so we have plenty of hot water for you"), and a long nap before dinner.

While they were napping, the Wapak Scouts insisted on cleaning and mending their clothing.

"Aw," Larry tried to protest, "you don't have to do this."

Ruth Niskala said, very softly, "Let them do this. This is the day we've promised them for a long time, the proof of their faith, and the reason they've been good all year. Think of it as cookies for Santa. They need to do something for you."

When they awoke an hour later, their freshly cleaned clothing was waiting for them. Scott Niskala guided them up the stairs, away from the main meeting hall. "They're putting something together and they want it to be a surprise. And if you even try to tell the kids that they didn't need to, I'll knock you flat. Let's go to my house across the way here."

Except for the absence of electric lights in the gathering dusk, the room seemed as it might have been before Daybreak. "The first thing I've got to say is that there wasn't any plan. We just made it up as it happened, and it kind of worked out."

Larry Mensche said, "I don't quite see why you weren't just overrun by the nearest tribe; a few hundred crazy tribals could sweep through this town, burn everything, and slaughter everyone. Even if a hundred of them died doing it, Daybreak'd've counted that as a benefit—more burden lifted off Mother Earth. So how are you here?"

"Well," Scott Niskala said, "that's kind of a story, but it's what I wanted to tell you about. Excuse an old man beginning at the very beginning, but it'll be faster if I don't try to edit. So to begin with, my father came from Finnish stock, and learned English mostly in school, from the Iron Country up in Minnesota. The Depression drove him out of his home . . ."

. . .

. . . and he bounced through crap jobs and work camps till 1942; then there was plenty of work for a healthy young man. In 1945 he got a slot in the Regular Army; in 1947, down in Georgia, he found himself a sweet farm girl who wanted to marry anything but a farmer, and in 1948, there I was.

My old man just assumed I'd follow him into the Army, so he trained me up as a good little soldier. I took to the hiking-camping-hunting, Daniel Boone kinda stuff, but *my* war was Vietnam, and when I got home it was the Hollow Army years. Sorta took the fun right out.

I did college, for the money, and majored in forestry, because it was outdoors. I did Forest Service, BLM, all that, but ended up managing state forests for Ohio. Along the way, when I was doing a stint at Ashley National Forest, I ran into Ruth here, who was a Mormon farm girl that went over the fence. Since we couldn't have kids ourselves, it came kind of natural to foster.

We'd usually have four or five kids around the house; we adopted four of them in thirty years or so, when it seemed like the right thing to do, but mostly they just passed through, a year or two at a time, and then kept coming back to visit.

Eventually we retired here in Wapak. Ruth and I'd both been scoutmasters for so long, we just kind of went full-time with it. Our troops were closer to each other than they were to the national organizations, 'cause we agreed with each other more than we did with our nationals.

We were weird scoutmasters, I guess, or if you look at it my way, we were the only scoutmasters who didn't get weird. We skipped out on all the urban crap, excuse the expression, where the kids just went to anti-drug lectures and pep rallies and never out in the woods, because what's the point of being a scout for that? And later on we didn't let the council and the region ram Jesus into everything we did, either. We covered our asses, excuse the expression, with upper leadership, 'cause my troop turned out so many Eagles, and hers turned out so many Gold Awards.

Well, one thing we did, we found local business people to throw in money so all the County Orphanage kids could be scouts. Plenty of the hard-to-adopt kids end up living in those places, with no money for extra-curriculars at school, or anything much else, so getting to be scouts was real big to them, and we had enough donors so our orphans could come on all the trips and camps.

We had our fosters, and most of'em'd keep coming after they moved home or moved on, and later on our old fosters brought *their* kids around. In just a few decades we had a real good bunch of dead-end kids with woods skills. By Daybreak all our assistant scoutmasters'd grown up in our troops, and we even had a few third-generation scouts.

Well, you might remember Ohio tried to evacuate right after the elections last year; this whole area was supposed to try to walk along I-75 down to Dayton to evacuate. Ruth said it sounded like something a couple interns might've thought up, looking at a map and counting beans. There *couldn't* be enough food or shelter at Dayton, and besides the plan bet everything on good weather. Oh, we told them so, but people had been scared out of their minds since Daybreak day. So they didn't listen to us; they bagged up what they could carry and left.

. . .

The room was dark and silent. Chris asked, "Was that the time of that first big storm?"

"Yeah. Three days after they left, freezing rain came down all one night and the morning after, then maybe four inches of snow with high winds the next afternoon. Once the weather cleared, I sent people south to take a look; they found lots of bodies in the highway ditch, especially kids and old people, all within thirty miles, but no survivors. Figure the ones who could kept walking or holed up too far from the road to hear the scouts calling.

"The last we heard of Columbus radio was on the twelfth, when they were begging the counties to send *them* help. Meanwhile the folks in town'd just abandoned the orphanage, so we took those kids in, and our five fosters stayed with us, and some other families just dropped their fosters on us before they walked out. Ruth and I had pritnear all the abandoned kids in Auglaize County, I think, plus around ten families who had stayed. We drew up articles and enrolled 164 Wapak Scouts, which is what we decided *everyone* would be."

Ruth's eyes flashed behind her glasses. "And we had to wreck the whole country to do one simple thing, let everyone be a scout! Look at what it took to get rid of the sexist barrier and the ageist barrier and all the rest! How old do you have to be, after all, before you're too old to be trustworthy, loyal, helpful, friendly, and all the rest of it? Or how does having two X chromosomes let you out of keeping yourself 'mentally awake'? So, anyway, you are now at the home base of the Wapak Scouts, which is still one hundred fifty-seven people, about two-thirds of us under twenty. Our youngest is four, our oldest is Scotty here, and we're still here."

"You still haven't told us *how* you're still here," Larry said. "There're at least three tribes within a day's walk; how come they haven't wiped you out?"

It was too dark now to see Niskala's features, but he sounded smug, or maybe amazed. "That started as an accident, and then just sort of developed."

. . .

By February, we'd dragged all the cars into one common area for salvage, boarded up every broken window, picked up the downed wires, all that stuff you noticed. Originally we did it to keep the kids busy and not to have to look at all that wreckage. By then the big bombs had gone off, and we'd lived through the fires from that big EMP that took KP-1 off the air—that made us feel pretty smart about having picked up all those wires.

Because Ruth's a thinker, the minute she heard about biotes, way back on October 29, she went to the hardware store here in town and made them put all the ammo into mason jars. We lost some ammo to spoilage but not much. There were some older guns, crude enough to be almost all wood and metal: the single-shot bolt-action rifles for the Rifle Shooting merit badge, a bunch of old deer rifles, my personal handguns. We had a couple kids who'd gotten their metalworking badge build replacement parts for the plastic over the winter.

Between some surviving food stocks from grocery stores, and rigging up a grinder for the corn and wheat from elevators nearby, and hunting and fishing, we were feeding everyone. We were pritnear on top of things.

So one day early in March, three guys who looked like a real shitty, pardon my French, imitation of American Indians came walking into town shouting that we all had to obey the high tribe of Booga-Booga. Harry Blenstein, commanding the town watch, sent a runner for me—I was ice fishing.

Meanwhile Harry got *quite* the tribal lecture. Now, he was a pretty serious Christian and I guess they laid on that Mother Gaia horseshit, sorry, French again, real thick, and well, they must've said something to set off his bad temper. He apparently told'em what he thought, and it must've offended'em, because one of them whacked Harry on the forehead with an ax—no warning at all.

Luckily, I'd been paranoid enough to insist there were always snipers covering any visitors coming into town. The two girls on duty for that, Hannah and Meg, did what they were supposed to do—pow-pow, two dead tribals, clean head shots, and the third got two steps before Meg had reloaded and hit him in the spine.

Harry's backup, Jim, tied up that survivor, neat as you please, and started first aid.

The tribals weren't stupid, not even really careless; we just lucked out. They had two men with bows watching from up there on the hillside, with a girl runner ready to go back to a main party a couple miles off. But by pure luck, we had hunters out there that day. Their two bowmen had set up right in front of our deer blind, so my hunters were already watching those creepy guys, and when they heard shooting start, they hit them from behind while they were still reaching for their bows.

More luck was that one of my hunters was a big, strong, fast kid, he'd been a running back for the Wapak Redskins—I mean the Warriors, they had to change that a while back—and he just chased their runner down, knocked her flat, gagged her, and dragged her back. If he hadn't had the presence of mind to do that, I don't know what would've happened.

We lucked out one more way. Trying to get the bullet out of that poor tribal's spine, we made a mess of it—we weren't exactly what you'd call skilled surgeons and we didn't have any anesthesia but whiskey. Between being drunk and in agony, he started crying for his mom, and yelling that he hated Daybreak and wanted his world back. That caused one of those seizures Daybreakers have, and we tried to hold him down but he thrashed so hard he knocked off a hemostat, and bled to death before we could put it back on.

Meanwhile that runner was a thirteen-year-old girl, half out of her head from getting knocked down so hard, being held in the next room. When we went in to talk to her, she was sure we'd tortured that boy to death, and started babbling. We learned how they did their approaches to towns, that those first "representatives" were just there to estimate the population. If any town surrendered to their outrageous demands, great, they'd just take everyone as slaves, but more often they'd all go back to their tribal leaders or council or whatever it was called, and return in a massive surprise assault. The first group was supposed to be just a big enough force to make sure someone always came back.

We also learned that the tribals' main body allowed the "representatives" forty-eight hours to come back, since sometimes a town would extend hospitality and they'd need the time before they could leave without arousing suspicion.

She also told us about what they did when they took over. Some little girls are sensitive about massacres. She was having seizures every few minutes, but she got it all out. Though she still has seizures, she's sworn to the articles now, and one of us.

By that time it was three hours till dawn. She'd told us where their main body was camped.

Ruth had the key idea. We put together a team of our best bow hunters to go in first. The tribals were mostly city people, not many soldiers and probably no hunters, before Daybreak. It was nasty and grim, but their sentries died without making any sound, and then all of us rushed and killed the rest in their beds. Horrible, but better than the other way around.

Ruth's genius idea was that we cleaned up their campsite, carried all those corpses back here, and put the bodies all in one deep basement, and filled in with dry dirt.

We've filled two more basements since. So far they always do things the same way. I'm guessing it's—well, not exactly written out, of course, because they're anti-literate, but it might as well be part of the *Daybreaker Handbook*, if there was one.

So locally, they are too afraid of us to try again—we're the place where everyone disappears without a trace.

. . .

Chris asked, "That's why you keep blackout, and why you don't farm, too, right? You can't let them have a way to count you. But in the long run, how are you going to keep eating?"

Scott seemed very pleased with the question. "We have a plan for that too, and in fact—"

"I wish you hadn't told us so much," Larry said. "What if one of us is captured?"

"One of you won't be captured unless all of us are," the old man said. "Ruth's got a whole worked-out plan."

"My plan," Ruth said, "isn't much more complicated than to get out while the getting is good; I worked out logistics in detail but the strategy is, run fast and be too tough for any tribe to take on. You brought me the last piece of the puzzle, just by telling us where you're headed. Your plans fit beautifully with ours."

"See," Scott said, "the three tribes around us are the Miami Morningstars, which ought to be the name of a football team, over to the east and southeast; the Day's Glorious Dawn People, due south; and the True Gaia People, who are north and west. You went right through the True Gaias and they didn't mess with you because they're pretty weak and disorganized, after taking some poundings from other tribes around them. Now, we've got more than enough canoes—there were three canoe liveries in this town before Daybreak. We just go down the Auglaize to Defiance, and then on down the Maumee. If we go that way we'd only have to run through the True Gaias, and although they'd have the numbers to stop us, they'll probably be too disorganized."

"The Maumee should be fine," Ruth added, "because it's a wide river, hard to blockade, and it has enough current so we'd move faster in canoes than runners could alert the tribes, if any, in front of us. So that was always one of the main ways we were thinking of running, and if you're going that way, we can be ready to go, lock, stock, and Wapak Scouts, at dawn tomorrow. We've furbed up enough canoes and kayaks to haul everybody, and had supplies packed to go for ages. Just tell us where the nearest base is up by the lake, or on the Maumee, and we'll take you there."

"Port Clinton," Larry said.

"Then it's a deal?"

"Definitely. These last few weeks I've walked all I wanted to, and the idea of going the rest of the way by boat—"

"You talked me into it," Jason said, stretching. "I'm looking forward to getting back six inches of height."

"Dinner!" a soft voice said, just outside the door.

"Coming," Niskala said. "You'll hear all about it later. Meanwhile, let's just enjoy the night; it's going to be one of the biggest things in the history of the Wapak Scouts. They were so sure you'd say yes, they've spent the afternoon putting our last council dinner together. Thanks for not disappointing them!"

They followed him across the street; the sanctuary of the old church had been stripped of its pews and filled with big tables.

The Wapak Scouts' last feast before exile was one immense exercise in showing off. The entertainment afterward reminded Jason of his own days in the Boy Scouts—a number of silly skits, some recitations of amateur poetry that made Jason feel considerably better about his Daybreak bard phase, and group singing. He surprised himself by joining in and enjoying it. *I suppose there's a reason why they call it a "kumbaya experience."*

**THE NEXT MORNING. WAPAKONETA, OHIO. 5:30 AM EST. THURSDAY, SEPTEMBER 25, 2025.**

They rose in the dark. In the candlelit main room of the blacked-out church, the morning crew had laid out last night's perishable and heavy leftovers. Everyone was urged to eat as much as they could stand and pack lunches into any spare space in their packs.

"I don't know if this is the most disciplined bunch of enthusiastic people, or the most enthusiastic bunch of disciplined people, I've ever seen," Chris said, tucking in his third sliced venison and fried egg sandwich.

"The real achievement," Ruth Niskala said, beside him, "is that Scott and I and our officers will have enough time to eat. *That* is the proof of organization, discipline, and training. Scott always said *any* scoutmaster who knew his stuff could take ten boys anywhere, but a *real* scoutmaster could take ten boys anywhere and sleep in every morning."

"Everyone is so excited," Chris said. In the last year he'd mastered writing with one hand and eating with the other; he was filling up his fourth pad of this trip with what he thought might become one of the most popular articles in the eventual *Post-Times* series and book.

"Well, it's a big, big event for the adults," Ruth said. "Even more so for the kids—for some of them, Wapak's the only home they've ever really had, and we're as much family as they've got."

Shifts moved through; it took almost an hour to feed everyone. "We thought about leaving at first light," Ruth said, "but it's dark down on the river—it runs between built-up banks and levees for the first twenty miles or so—and the main thing is to just not have any accidents to slow us down, so we can be past the True Gaias before they even know we're moving. If they have to chase us, with them running and us on the river, we've got them beat." She stood. "I'm going to get some of that yellow sheet cake; it won't travel, and it's too good to waste."

Jason said, "Well, then, let me help you out with that." He followed her.

Just as the sun cleared the low line of trees to the west, Scott Niskala walked down the line of canoes and kayaks in a triple file extending from the low concrete dam down Hamilton Street for more than a block, making sure everyone knew the meetpoints for lunch and for putting in for the night, as well as the alternate points if there was trouble.

Larry's decades of outdoor vacations, and fighting experience, qualified him to be a stern man at the head of the main body. Jason's long-ago family vacations and summers at camp qualified him to be a bow man toward the rear of the main body, where his strength might be needed. Chris's total lack of experience qualified him to be a passenger somewhere well up in the middle, "like a sack of beans but less edible," as he put it.

"Don't be so sure," Jason said. "Consider the Donner Party. And these guys can *cook*."

Scott Niskala made a few hand signs over his head; the bank runners took off swiftly, getting a head start. Their job was to run with nothing but their fighting gear, two hundred yards ahead of the flotilla of canoes, on the roads and towpaths, and, as Scott put it, "to get into trouble before we're all in trouble." On each bank there were five runners; if they didn't run into trouble, after an hour they were to switch off with bank runners from the forward canoes of the main body.

The runners were just out of sight when Scott made the next gesture, and the first three kayaks of the avant-garde slipped into the water, struck their paddles as if synchronized, and moved out. Down the long column, everyone in turn picked up their canoe or kayak and advanced one boat-length.

Row of three after row of three moved forward and into the water. The flotilla flowed into the Auglaize, separated enough to not offer easy targets, close enough to cover each other, orderly as ants, in silence except for the occasional soft splash of an awkward launch. When the last kayaks launched, only forty minutes had passed, and if there had been anyone to watch from the dam, the last trees would have closed around the rearguard kayaks as if nothing had ever been there.

## 8 HOURS LATER. PUEBLO, COLORADO. 3:11 PM MST. THURSDAY, SEPTEMBER 25, 2025.

Quattro Larsen looked exhausted. Heather asked, "Long flight?"

"There was a big slow dust devil east of Garden City, and it threw some crap up high and it went right into my intakes. Ten minutes later all the needles for everything electrical are acting like windshield wipers, and that nano-detector gadget that the lab wanted me to try out is wailing like a banshee, and you know, the tradition is that banshees wail for the about-to-be-dead, and I thought this was gonna be one accurate banshee.

"Nanoswarm were *that* close to shutting down the spark. The right side engine was going bang-miss-cough twice a minute. And it was sunny and warm for once, which meant headwinds, turbulence, and general-purpose gnarly air. But the Gooney kept chugging and farting right along. I'll be here at least a week while we tear down, dunk all the parts in lye, and rebuild."

Heather nodded. "Well, I'm sorry for all the trouble, but I was trying to think up a cover for you to be here for a few days. I've got something that will need some discussion. Bambi's due to show up in the Stearman, too, so you might get to see your wife, not to mention we'll have Bambi here to tell us the right thing to do."

"That's what I always do—the right thing, once Bambi tells me what it is." He sat in the guest chair, next to the crib, and set his leather flying helmet on his knee. He pushed his barely controllable surfer's mop of blond hair up and over his forehead, and flashed that big grin. "Hey, the little guy's not so little anymore."

"Yep, growing into a big healthy moose of a kid. All right, now that you're sitting down . . . have you ever thought about being the Earl of the Russian River?"

"No, not for one second, and are you out of your mind?"

"I'm as sane as ever, it's the world that's crazy. Here's the deal. Our sources are showing that Harrison Castro is trying to take as much of southern California as he can out of the United States."

"He is my father-in-law, you know."

"No offense intended."

"None taken. I just meant you don't have to tell me what he's thinking about. He was talking about goofier shit than being an earl clear back when I was trying to lure Bambi into skipping out of high school and shacking up with me in my dorm room for a week."

"I never heard about that."

"Unfortunately, I wasn't much of a lurer when I was twenty-one. My big seductive move was to send her a list of the Xbox games I had. Anyway, look, I know Harrison Castro, and I'm sure you're right about his intentions."

"Unh-hunh. And how do you feel about them?"

"Subthrilled. But you're suggesting I might want to go into the earl business too?"

"I want you to start a League of North Coast Castles. You're in much better shape than any of the other freeholders in your neighborhood. Extend them some aid—or launder aid from us and present it as coming from you. Cut them a much better deal than Harrison Castro gave his poor hapless knucklehead vassals, so that every Castle in trouble will want to sign on with you, and Castro's vassals feel like idiots and resent him."

"But you will be creating another league and I thought you didn't want one."

"Two leagues in a struggle with each other is way better than one league in a struggle against the Federal government. Let alone against both Federal governments. And this is temporary. As soon as you can, you'll sensibly return everything to Federal jurisdiction and put a big hole in the Castle system."

"Couldn't I just do that right now and save everyone the trouble?"

"Unfortunately right now, if the Castles collapsed, California would become a second Lost Quarter. I don't like the Castles, they're about as un-American an institution as there is, but we can't throw them away until we've got a Federal government big and strong enough to do what needs doing. My long-run plan is to just surround the Castles with a free, successful society. Then over time, the dependents and the vassals will walk off, and the freeholders will end up as romantic old poops stumping around in empty fortresses and writing letters to the *Post-Times* about young people with no respect. I'm just asking you to be an earl for a short while, and you and I both know it's a joke; the objective is to make it a joke to everyone."

"Do I get a funny hat?"

She looked pointedly at the antique leather helmet on his knee. "Do you think I can stop you?"

"*This* is practical. If I'm going to be Earl of the Russian River, I definitely want something big, and white, with a plume."

# THIRTEEN:
# NO ISLAND SINGLY LAY

"That's Put-in-Bay," Rosie said. He was a heavy, solidly muscled man with stark white hair and brick-red skin; he and his wife Barbara were the crew of *Kelleys Dancer.* "Sorry this took so long."

Although it was only a few air miles from Catawba Point to South Bass Island, the wind was light and variable that morning, and tacking *Kelleys Dancer* out of Sandusky Bay, around the point, and out to Put-in-Bay harbor itself had consumed the whole morning since dawn.

Jason asked, "Hey, is that a lighthouse or something?"

"Perry's Monument," Barbara said.

"Perry who?"

"Oh, man, you'd have had a hard time when I was teaching American history." She sighed. "Oliver Hazard Perry. War of 1812. 'We have met the enemy and they are ours.'"

"They buried him there or something?"

"No, he won the only naval battle of any size that ever happened on the lake." She sighed. "I wonder if kids will learn more or less history now that history's starting over. Hard to see how they could learn less, actually. There could well be a battle bigger than Perry's next spring—over between Buffalo and Erie there's getting to be a pirate problem, or maybe a tribals-in-boats problem, it's hard to tell. At least *we'll* have work, anyway."

"You'd be in the battle?"

"I hope not, but we'll probably guide them there," Rosie said. "We know that area—actually we know the whole lake pretty well. Barb'n'me spent ten years after retirement as rental crew for old farts that cruised the lake; that's where we got *Kelleys Dancer,* the owner died right after Daybreak once there wasn't no fridge for his insulin."

Closer to Put-in-Bay, there was more and steadier wind. Rosie said, "I'm impressed that you're going to Cooke Castle. Gotta be the last place in North America where they still use the right fork for each course. They might dip you all in bleach before they let you in the front door."

"They're not *that* stuffy." Barbara hugged her husband. "Just because the world has ended doesn't mean people can't wear a clean shirt now and then."

Gibraltar Island sheltered the eastern half of Put-in-Bay; it looked like a nineteenth-century millionaire's estate or a twentieth-century college campus, and had been both. "They have electric power over here!" Chris said, realizing an electric winch was pulling them into their berth.

"Some of the time, yeah, whenever they're not wiping for nanos. Some engineers from OSU built them windmills you see over there south of town, and another guy from Tri-State U's got a wave-power generator running."

They had been told that Dr. Fred Rhodes would meet them at the wharf; the squat, wide-shouldered black man waiting there wore an old Ohio State hoodie, homemade deerhide trousers, wingtips, and a black crusher. His full beard probably hadn't been trimmed for many years before Daybreak, and reached beyond his lower ribs, about as far down as his dreads reached in the back. He pumped Larry's hand eagerly, then Chris's and Jason's, and said, "Everyone is so excited; the first report on an overland traverse of the Lost Quarter."

"I was never any good at oral reports in school," Larry said. "In fact I hated them."

"Too late. Bet you hated field trips, too, and I'll never be forgiven if I don't take you around and show you Stone Lab."

Stone had been OSU's field limnology lab before Daybreak. Just after Daybreak, about a hundred scientists had come to Stone from Ohio State and other universities. They had ridden out the big wave and the fallout from the Chicago superbomb, the fires and the destroyed gear from the Pittsburgh EMP strike, the tribal raids across the ice in the winter and the pirate attacks a few weeks before, and they had rebuilt and gone on.

Now, after the destruction of Mota Elliptica, they were quite possibly the most advanced scientific facility on the continent. Because limnology draws on every other science, Stone Lab could do at least basic work in every field.

Gibraltar, not really much bigger than a couple of city blocks, was threaded all over with blacktop pathways that were breaking down. "We're less than ten miles off shore," Rhodes said. "Biotes blow right on over from all that urban area west and northwest of here."

"What's all that doing to the lake?" Chris asked.

"We've got about twenty scientists with about sixty opinions on exactly what it will mean, but all round the Great Lakes, you have all that plastic, rubber, and gasoline rotting, and the fallout kill zone covered southern Ontario, so you have more decaying biomass and less to keep it out of the water than there's ever been and all that's washing into Lake Erie, and you know, the whole western side of Erie is only about forty feet deep at most, usually less. A decade or two of fast-growing green goo, and maybe we'll be looking at the Great Erie Swamp, or the Erieglades, and this pretty little island might just be a high hill in the middle of it."

Cooke Castle had been a nineteenth-century millionaire's summer house; *a big stone mansion wrapped in faux-medieval frouf,* Chris scribbled in his notebook. With its tessellated tower, it stuck out of the remaining gold, red, and yellow fall foliage like a fantasy Hollywood castle or an imaginary private school.

The auditorium that afternoon was jammed, with the crowd spilling over into the aisles.

"The Wapak Scouts know the local ecology much better than I do," Larry pointed out, "so I'd suggest you see about bringing them over if you want more observations. Plus they're smart, hard workers, and mostly young and until recently you were a university—I think they belong here. And I do think that as long as you didn't run right onto a tribal encampment, one or two of you in the company of five to ten Wapak Scouts could travel pretty safely to anywhere. At least, *I'd* go anywhere with them."

That evening, they rowed across the harbor to South Bass Island, for a feast of roasted perch and new potatoes, with plenty of the island wine to wash it down. In Put-in-Bay Chris found an honest-to-God newsstand, with back issues of the *Post-Times*, *Weekly Insight*, and *Olympia Observer*, plus half a dozen other papers; he could rent a complete set of what he wanted for the rest of the afternoon, and they took Pueblo scrip. Off to paradise by himself, complaining only at the absence of coffee, he vanished into the back reading solarium.

Larry and Jason were trying out fried lake fish (Rhodes had assured them that tritium did not biocentrate) and the local white wine at a dock-side bar, and agreeing that life hadn't been this comfortable in a long time, when Chris burst in, waving the paper and one of his notebooks.

"Did you find a typo or something?" Larry said.

"No, I found the biggest mistake of all time," Chris said. "Look at this."

"Damn. So Leslie was the traitor? I always liked her," Jason said, "even if she was pretty condescending to Beth; I think she just didn't know how to talk to somebody outside her own lifestyle."

Chris said, "Now look here. A couple weeks later. This is the accounts from Deb Mensche, Dan Samson, and Roger Jackson, about their expeditions into the Lost Quarter."

Larry sat back and said, "Shit."

"What?" Jason said.

"We were being followed at least from crossing the Tippecanoe on, right? And how many days' walk from Castle Earthstone is that? So, so far, so good. If Leslie was the traitor, then she found out about our operation, and set us up to be ambushed and fed. But if she knew about that, she'd have known about these three other missions—and those are plain as day Heather using the two-source method for locating a traitor. Leslie would have known that—it had less security than we did, by far—and made it point at someone else. If she was far enough inside *to know about us*, she couldn't possibly have *missed that*."

Jason said, "But the real traitor would not only have put Castle Earthstone on our trail, he'd have made the traitor trap point at someone else—like Leslie. Shit, did they execute her?"

"Not that I've seen, but I think we better radio Heather and everyone else we can think of." Larry's voice was grim. "We just have to take the chance that one of the people we contact will be the traitor, and hope the others catch him or her before any more damage is done."

Larry had a long fight with the local authorities about breaking radio silence—they were terrified of the idea, and kept pointing out that they had nothing like Mota Elliptica's defenses against EMP—but he wore them down, and finally sat down with his one-time pad to send messages to everyone relevant. Extracting the promise that someone would listen all night for a response, he handed over his stack of messages. Then, because there was nothing more to do, the three agents went to the fish-fry, and did their best to enjoy the fish and potatoes, the crowd of healthy, well-fed people, and the lights of a town where they could sleep safe, warm, and bathed tonight. No reply came before bedtime.

## THAT EVENING. PUEBLO, COLORADO. 5:30 PM MST. MONDAY, OCTOBER 6, 2025.

Heather had barely sat down to eat at the communal mess hall when Patrick, out of breath, delivered the urgent eyes-only message from Larry Mensche; it had FAR stamped on it. Grumbling, and hastily dumping her plate of noodles and grouse-nuggets into a go-bag, she headed back for her office, reminding herself over and over that Larry didn't send messages of that kind in any situation except one where most agents would have been screaming for a regiment of infantry.

With Leo settled into his crib, she opened the envelope, read, and sat up as if she'd been shocked. Leo did his nervous cry, the one that meant he felt something wrong, and she went over to comfort him. "Me, too, kid."

Larry had provided her with a cc: list; she could see at once what he was doing, making sure no one could intercept or sweep it under the rug.

She said, "Come in," to the knock at the door before she had time to think.

Debbie Mensche was there, with Beth, Ysabel, Dan Samson, and Roger Jackson. "I kind of thought you'd want to have your team together," she said, "after I got the note from Dad, so I rounded 'em up and brought them here."

It was everyone from the cc: list except for James and Arnie. Heather said, "I think we'd all better sit for a moment, if you can all find somewhere to do it. Deb, brilliant idea, you're right. I take it you didn't bring Arnie or James because—"

"Because they're the only two other guys it can be," Debbie said. "I grabbed Beth first because I wasn't gonna believe Beth would've betrayed Jason; she alibied Izzy. I knew our missions were decoys, but you'd kept that information from Roger and Dan, so they were clean. That leaves James and Arnie. James is probably at home, this time of day; Arnie's teaching a math class over in the literacy program. By now I bet they've both read Dad's note. I don't know how we can—"

James burst in, panting, out of breath. He looked at who else was in the room. His expression of relief was amazing and overwhelming. "All right," he said. "It looks like everyone is here, and I'll be happy to explain why it's Arnie you want, and not me, but you'd better get someone over to the secure holding facility, *now*, to protect Leslie. If they just stand outside and don't let Arnie in, we can probably—"

"Dan—" Heather didn't speak the rest of her sentence because Samson and Jackson were both already gone.


## 5 MINUTES LATER. PUEBLO, COLORADO. 5:15 PM MST. MONDAY, OCTOBER 6, 2025.

James was surprised that he wasn't panting as he squatted next to Debbie. "We'll intercept them about five blocks further on," she breathed, "but we have to wait till Arnie gets turned away, and then see which way he goes. The guy in the blanket over there still hasn't seen us."

"How did you know he'd be there?"

"I didn't know he would. I knew it would be possible."

"And the other guys didn't spot him?"

"He probably got here after they did. Dan's inside, probably with Leslie, which is where you have to be to guard someone that close, so Dan hasn't seen blanket man. Roger's going to be a damned fine agent in about five years, but he's got no instincts right now; he's watching for Arnie because Arnie's the only thing he's been told to watch for." The slim woman squatted beside him. "If I have to move fast, I will. If it comes to a fight, don't get all fussy and worry about catching them alive. It'll be more than enough if we just stop them." She stretched, as if preparing to sprint. "Once I'm in striking range of Arnie I'm going to follow him and his little shadow from a distance, and see how much I can hear and see before I have to move, but when it's time to move, I'll move, and you catch up then. Till then, hang two blocks back, try to stay in the shadows, and make no noise. Now let's—there."

James didn't see what she saw, but he saw where she went, and sprinted after her along the shadowed side of a high wall, through an alley, and through an overgrown public park along the brick pathways. The next ten minutes were an obstacle course of alleys, schoolyards, passages between boarded houses, and underpasses, between rows of abandoned cars and around piles of junk, until, as they squeezed between Dumpsters and garbage piles toward the mouth of an alley, Debbie pointed at the ground. He hoped that meant "wait here" and that her pointing down the street meant "watch me go this way," because that was what he did. He peeked around the corner.

Debbie ran silently, at top speed, seemingly touching nothing. As she passed a point he judged to be two blocks away, James ran after, trying to breathe quietly enough, trying not to think about having old, less-flexible ankles, making occasional scuffing noises but not many and not close together.

At a recessed storefront, Debbie caught him by the shoulder, and told James, "Look ahead. See Arnie? See where his little shadow went into that doorway?"

"The guy that just slipped into the bushes by that house?"

"You got talent. Get ready, any sec now—"

As they watched, Arnie slowed, dragged his feet, as if some invisible cord were pulling him backward. "Okay, James, throw your distraction, and make it loud."

James emerged from the alley, waving his pistol, and yelled "Yang, you son of a bitch, your fucking Daybreak hippie friend killed Leslie!" Keeping his gun leveled (*I hope it's too far away for him to see I haven't cocked it*), he walked slowly toward Arnie, who stood paralyzed in the street, the gun leveled at him. "He killed Leslie!" he repeated. "I'm gonna shoot your worthless ass!" He kept walking toward the slender figure of Arnie Yang.

*Oh, man, let him just have those knives he carries, this would be totally the worst time* ever *to get shot,* he thought, and tried not to smile at his mental imitation of Leslie.

Debbie said, "It's done," firmly and loudly.

The corpse of Arnie's watcher plunged out from the bushes and lay still. Arnie made a strange noise and pelted away as if his feet had a will of their own; Debbie shouted "Shit!" and ran after.

Not sure what to do, and having run about as much as he could already, James walked after. He paused to look at the corpse. Debbie's wire garrote was sunk deep into the flesh of the thin young man's neck, and his eyes bulged and tongue protruded. His hands were at his throat, where he'd made a futile try, probably, to dig the wire out. He wore several layers of shabby old clothing, a full beard, and long curly hair.

James looked up to see Deb returning, with Arnie in a hammerlock-and-nelson, bent backward brutally.

"Well," James said, "I guess one of us needs to go get Heather, and she'll want to bring along—"

"One meal ticket," a voice said, behind him. He turned and saw Patrick, who was grinning. "For one meal ticket I will go find anybody you like and send them here."

"How the hell—"

"Hey, Mister Hendrix, it is not my fault if you're *way* more interesting when you're not teaching us to read *Great Expectations*." Patrick was bursting with pride. "I saw you guys following Doctor Yang and followed you here, 'cause I knew you'd both got those special messages."

Debbie winked at James, and said, "See what happens when you don't look for things? How's this guy doing with Dickens?"

"Top of the class."

"I'm glad to hear it," she said. "Any agent I'm going to train can't have enough Dickens."

Between them, James and Debbie figured out who Patrick needed to bring, and he went on his way with "a slightly swollen wallet and a slightly swollen head," James said. "And hey, why does a spy need Dickens?"

"Because you're making me read it in the adult class, and if I have to, so does any poor bastard I train. Same principle as fraternity hazing, if I went through it, so does everyone."

The sun descended slowly, the shadows lengthened, and it was the better part of two hours before everything was sorted out, but at the end of it, people were where they belonged: Aaron was on his way to the morgue, Arnie was in Leslie's cell (and the guards had been carefully coached by James about the four different ways someone could get in, and fixed them), and everyone else, including Leo, was at James's house. "Even Wonder," Leslie said, her face buried in the big dog's fur.

"Well, he's been living here."

"I can tell," she said, thumping the big dog's sides. "Too much good food and not enough exercise, you lazy old goof, you're gonna be running your ass off for a couple months. And you too, Wonder."

"That was an evening," Heather said. "I guess I've never been happier to miss out on meat lumps and noodles."

Leslie looked up from Wonder, and said, "James, it's Monday night, still," and pausing only to consider that he had enough in the larder, James said, "There're three big jugs of wine in the lower drawer in the living room hutch, and glasses on the top two shelves. Everybody grab a glass and fill it, and then sit down and stay out of the way—I'm about to cook."


**THE NEXT DAY. PUEBLO, COLORADO. 9:30 AM MST. TUESDAY, OCTOBER 7, 2025.**

"I'm really not totally cool with this," Izzy said. "He might be able to send me into a seizure, and even though Beth has never had one, she's pregnant. I don't like doing this at all."

"Me either," James said, "but it's all I can come up with."

Since five o'clock that morning, James, Izzy, and Beth had been practicing the "mutual correction" protocol that he had evolved to keep Leslie from slipping into Daybreak. It had begun as a pure desperation measure, with James adapting tricks from a twenty-year-old pamphlet, *Interrogation Tips: Avoiding Implanting False Memories*. But it seemed to have kept Leslie out of Daybreak, and even to help her develop some immunity—whatever it was that immunity might mean in this case. It was as good a protection as they knew how to do against the version of Daybreak in Arnie.

According to the guards, Arnie had been sitting upright on the bench-bed ever since his arrest. He had risen to stretch twice, and to use the chamber pot once. Mostly he sat and stared into space.

Arnie looked up and said, "Hello," tonelessly, when they came in.

James said, "Sit up and look at me." It wasn't a sharp command, or a harsh order, but it was clear he expected to be obeyed.

Arnie sat up, and by visible effort, made himself look at James.

"Now." James held his voice flat and neutral. "Tell me about what you think happened. Start with the first time you thought about Daybreak as anything other than a problem to be solved."

Arnie stared off into space. "I am visualizing reading a paper in a journal and the title is, 'On the identification of Daybreak in the Psyche of Test Subject AY.' The abstract says, 'Keller's Conjecture [2003]'—"

James found it impossible not to laugh.

"Yes," Arnie said, "I really am seeing it in my head, brackets and all, and if I read from that imaginary journal article, I can speak. So the abstract says,

'Keller's Conjecture [2003] postulated that for every activity found in logical/memetic systems, an equivalent can be postulated in biological/genetic systems, and vice versa, in every case with a very high probability of real-world occurrence. Terms like virus, infectious, resistant, and worm have been freely used in information science for decades, and biologists just as easily speak of transcription, expression, and reception. Before Daybreak we simply failed to see the analogy to the exceptionally dangerous diseases that attack through the immune system.

'Specifically, just as dengue, HIV/AIDS, and BSE turn the identification system for pathogens to their own purposes, the capacities needed to understand, rebut, refute, and reject an idea, such as empathy, subjunctivity, hypothesis, and theory of mind, become the pathway by which the susceptible mind acquires Daybreak.'"

"'Theory of mind'?" Beth asked.

"The mental model each of us has of other people's mental processes," Arnie explained. "The thing in your mind that you use to guess what the other person is thinking. What you need to run con games, get jokes, and understand what your mom is mad about. The thing that doesn't work right in Asperger's syndrome and maybe isn't there at all in autism."

Ysabel asked, "So what you're saying is, Daybreak gets to you through your process of rejecting it, because to reject it you have to understand it first?"

"It takes over minds that try to understand it; it doesn't matter *why* they try to understand it. Most Daybreakers wanted to understand it because some part of it was attractive to them. Some found it so repellent that they studied it to fight it, like St. Paul studying Christians, or witchfinders studying witchcraft, or the way spy-agency analysts in the Cold War sometimes quietly converted to the other side. As for me . . . God, it was the most fascinating thing a guy in my field could have hoped for, and I wanted to plant my name on the first real study of it."

James asked, "So who's immune?"

"Stupid people, because they never try to understand anything. Bigots, ditto. Anybody with a strong enough belief system who becomes aware, before Daybreak takes over, that it contradicts what they believe—doesn't matter much what it is if they really believe it."

"But most people believe something, so how could so many people catch Daybreak? Even if it was only a few million people worldwide, that's still a lot."

"Well, Daybreak is pretty good at mimicking beliefs, so people who are shaky about what they believe, or used to giving lip service to some vague version, can be vulnerable. Compulsively fair-minded people are toast. And most of all, if there's a basic contradiction—if the basic belief is that you need to believe because you're bad or evil—it double binds you and you're either bad for not believing or bad because you believe. Unfortunately that's basic to all the monotheistic religions, many other religions, and some of the biggest secular political movements. I wrote a lot more about it in all in the notebooks you found under my mattress tress *tress*—" Arnie Yang screamed. His hands flew wildly around and his legs thrashed; they backed out and let the guards handle him.

"That looked like it hurt," Beth said.

"It did, I guarantee it," Izzy replied. "We'd better run the mutual confirmation protocol, James; I don't *think* he tried anything but that's kind of like *thinking* your sex partner was *probably* okay."

"If Arnie's telling the truth, it's exactly like it," James said. "All right, remember he only talked about Daybreak because we asked. What did he say and was it true?"

There didn't seem to be much to correct this time, but they still checked to make sure he hadn't referred to anything that hadn't happened. "Just the notebooks under the mattress," Izzy said. "Dude, we are such a bunch of amateurs. Wouldn't a professional operation have torn his place apart two minutes after he was arrested?"

Beth nodded. "Prolly right, but we are *all* amateurs here. The pros are mostly dead, and the ones we have like Heather and Larry can't be everywhere. If we're gonna win the amateurs'll have to win it."

The door opened. A guard said, "He wants to talk to you again."

Arnie looked pale and sick but determined. "Read those notebooks, but make sure people read them together and keep stopping and questioning each other, exactly like what you're doing right now. If you can find a few rock-hard believers in anything—I don't care if it's a Republican or a Communist, a Catholic or an atheist, just so they're dead certain they're right—who have the rhetorical chops to approach it in a completely detached way, that would be best, but they still need to check with each other *constantly*." His grin was ragged but real. "I finally beat it, just then. I made myself assume you'd found the notebooks, and that tricked it into letting me give the information. I don't know why but it couldn't seem to stop me from writing those, after everything it could make me do or keep me from doing, that was one thing that was outside its power. Maybe because keeping good records of research is the only thing I really believe in."

"Maybe," James said. "Arnie, you know that everything you tell us is making it crystal clear we can't keep you as a research subject. The people interrogating you would be in danger."

"Yeah, I know," he said, quietly. "And I don't think Daybreak will let go of me . . . let go of me . . ." and he began to scream. He was still shrieking *Let go of me!* when they decided he wouldn't be coming back for a while, and left the building. They could still hear him a block away.

**THAT EVENING. PUEBLO, COLORADO. 5:45 PM MST.
TUESDAY, OCTOBER 7, 2025.**

Heather would rather have been alone with Arnie, but everyone, including Arnie, had agreed that it would be just too dangerous. So MaryBeth
Abrams and James Hendrix sat with her and Arnie while they waited for
the time. They had found a secure-enough room with windows; it was too
cold to have them open.

He'd had his requests: a pitcher of Dell's beer, a fresh steamed trout and
fried potatoes, and a can of pineapple for dessert. Every now and then, a
tear ran down his face, but otherwise he didn't talk much.

Finally Heather said, "Arnie, it's getting to be time. I didn't mention
it before now because I didn't want to trigger a seizure, but we found the
notebooks. Nobody will ever be alone with them, and we'll watch everyone
who reads any part of them like a cat at a mouse hole. I wish we could keep
you; your ability to analyze—"

"Would only make me brilliant at devising traps, sending you down
wrong alleys, and hiding the truth," Arnie said. "And eventually I'd find a
way to plant Daybreak in some of you. I'm a smart guy and I spent my life
studying how ideas move, Heather. In the long run you can't safely talk to
me with Daybreak in me, and you have no way to be sure Daybreak isn't
in me.

"Besides, having me pay for it, in public, will do you a thousand times
more good as an example than I would as a research subject. Just hit the
obvious themes about it: nobody's above the law, nobody's too big to be
seized by Daybreak, be alert, never never never talk to it, fight it. Don't
save my reputation; you can't afford to have anyone find anything attractive
about this."

The sun descended; it was inadvisable to let Arnie talk without interruption, but what he seemed to want to do most was just share memories with
Heather, about the time before Daybreak, so they took turns interrupting
him, encouraging him to skip from one memory to another.

When the time came, as Arnie rose to take the final walk, James said,
"Arnie, I know you've been touching a piece of paper in your pocket. I have
to ask to see it."

Arnie reached for his pocket and collapsed in a howling seizure. Heather and MaryBeth pinned him down; James picked that pocket. The guards rushed in.

When Arnie was tied to a stretcher, Heather said, "We knew this might happen. We'll proceed with the plan for the seizure; frankly I hope he doesn't come out."

James showed Heather and MaryBeth the note:

**I WILL ALWAYS LOVE YOU**
**AND WE WILL ALWAYS**
**LOVE THE EARTH TOGETHER.**

Arnie woke up as the stretcher neared the scaffold, but he was too weak to walk, and too disoriented to maintain any dignity. The militiamen lifted him from the stretcher, bound his hands behind him, strapped the sandbag to his feet, hooded him, and fitted the greased aircraft-cable noose to his neck ("uglier but faster than rope," MaryBeth had promised). In the little square of the trap door, he was weeping, and struggling for his balance, and when he asked Heather for a last hug, his own whining tone must have humiliated him.

She held him tight and close, and said, "Over quick, now. All be over quick. Just stay quiet, now, Arnie. I'm so sorry."

The muffled sound might have been "Thank you" or "Fuck you." His breathing was harsh and irregular; MaryBeth said, softly, "He's close to another seizure."

"Go in peace, Arn." Heather hugged him hard, one more time, and stepped back. Arnie had requested no chaplain, and he couldn't be allowed to say anything to the crowd, so the executioner simply checked to make sure the trap was clear, and pulled the lever. The gallows worked perfectly; afraid of making a mess of things, the engineers had overdone everything, and Dr. Arnold Yang plummeted into a broken neck and pinched carotids.

The vast crowd made no sound until the massed low moan as Arnie dropped; they walked away as if they had all been part of some secret shame.

As soon as they lowered him and wheeled his body into the examining room, MaryBeth swiftly checked for a heartbeat, poured the ice water into the ear, focused a bright light on the pupils of each hideously protruding red eyeball. "All right. This man is dead." She felt around the cable and added, "And unofficially, you're lucky you didn't decapitate him with this rig."

In Heather's office, after each of them had had a shot of whiskey, James said, "About that note," and Heather said, "Yes, of course, you're right. I'd know that messy block printing anywhere. It's Allie."


**THE NEXT MORNING. PUEBLO, COLORADO. 8:30 AM MST. WEDNESDAY, OCTOBER 8, 2025.**

It was a fine clear October morning, the Indian summer kind that occasionally blesses the Arkansas Valley with clear amber light, a promise of a warm afternoon, and just enough tang in the chill morning air to make everything seem extra-alive, the last brief warmth before the plunge into icy winter. The sooty skies had brought the day about six weeks early, but early or not, the day still tasted clean and fine.

Recent trains had brought sharp cheese from Green Bay, canned spinach from Castle San Jose, and molasses from Morgan City. James had made cheese, elk sausage, and spinach turnovers and molasses and chokecherry muffins, and warmed up some elk sausage for Wonder, who ate with his flank pressed against Leslie.

"Funny how eating breakfast at your place feels like home," Leslie said. "Got time before you go to work to take a walk down along the river?"

"I'm not going in to the GPO today. Heather's going to be talking to me about a change of job over lunch. Okay for Wonder to finish off my scraps?"

"No problem, he can wait a day to start his diet."

On their way down to the river, they barely spoke, not because they didn't have things to say, but because it was all so overwhelming. Wonder showed no interest in chasing sticks, staying so close to Leslie that she occasionally tripped on him.

Finally, walking by the Arkansas, where ice rafts already floated by, James thought to ask, "So, did you find your place to be too much of a mess?"

"They'd tossed it but they weren't too rough, I guess 'cause they were trying for thorough; all my underwear disappeared. When you see Heather, tell her she's got a perv in the staff." She knelt to scratch Wonder under his collar. "James, how the hell do I say 'Thank you'?"

"You already did."

"How about coming to Monday dinners forever? I mean, I know letting you cook for me is a pretty lame way to thank you—"

"It worked just fine this morning, I don't know why it wouldn't work forever."

She reached out and lightly pushed his shoulder, palm flat against it, her little gesture for *I like you, I want you to know I appreciate you, but never think it's any more than that*, and as he always did, for a split second he rested his hand on hers.

"Same old deal as before?"

"Always."

"I'm so glad. So do you have to do anything before you meet with Heather? And when is that?"

"I need to be at Johanna's at noon. Subject to that constraint, I'm all yours, as always."

"You're one of the sweetest deluded old farts I've ever allowed to feed me." She socked him on the arm.

"Ow. Don't abuse your elders. Isn't it time for your nap?"

They walked as far as the last guard post along the Arkansas, catching up on gossip, criticizing the technique of the fishermen, and relishing the freedom and safety.

**1 HOUR LATER. PUEBLO, COLORADO. 12:30 PM MST. WEDNESDAY, OCTOBER 8, 2025.**

James was one of the higher-paid people in Pueblo, with a triple salary: he sat on the RRC Council, was a senior librarian at the GPO, and received a covert stipend from Heather's black budget. So Heather was surprised that this was his first time at Johanna's What There Is. "You can afford it," she pointed out.

He shrugged. "Before Daybreak, I was a civil servant with more than twenty years in, no debt, even a paid-for house. I could have afforded Cuban cigars and high-end French wines, but I don't smoke and I prefer beer. Besides, Johanna and I are old buds from the local cooking club, and I happen to know I'm a better cook than she is."

Heather laughed. "Well, let's give Johanna a shot at beating you today. She was able to get fresh beef tongue, and she's braised it in wine and onions."

"That deserves reverence," James agreed. "So no business till after."

When they had finished, Heather said, "Here's what I'm thinking. The position of chief research director is vacant. I want you."

James gaped at her. "You've got to be kidding. I've never done anything remotely like—"

"None of us is in a job remotely like what we did before Daybreak."

"I've never done research or managed more than two people—"

"Arnie only directed research when it had to do with crypto or semiotics, and didn't supervise most of what we do. What he was, was my consigliere. And even before he took up treason, not a very good one, I'm afraid; bouncing ideas off him was sort of like hitting tennis balls against a wall of Jell-O, they always came back messy and often not recognizable. I need a person who wants to improve my thoughts, not make them more creative and subtle. Also somebody who can make it up as they go."

"Make what up? I don't think—"

"Make up whatever needs making up, right away, make the people to do it, make it happen. Like how you caught Arnie."

"Debbie was the one who caught—"

"Debbie *tackled*. *You* caught. Without your work I'd have had no idea what to do except arrest you both. You had all the evidence, you just didn't have any reason to think I'd believe you. Besides, you can't mean I should hire Debbie. Should I put her behind a desk and start parachuting you into the boondocks?"

James leaned back, looking at the ceiling. "All right. I have to admit I'm already starting to think about how to make it all work. I just want to state for the record that you're hiring me with no experience—"

She leaned forward and pinned James with her gaze into his eyes. "James, my other possible candidates don't have nearly the relevant skills you do, and have never done it at all. Whereas you do have the skills and have done it right once."

"Yeah, but then you'll expect me to do it right again."

"Unh-hunh. And over and over. And hold you accountable each time."

James shrugged. "It's the kind of deal I've been looking for all my life.

Okay. I'm in." He nodded at the handwritten blackboard. "Do you have time for dessert?"

"For raspberry fool? Absolutely!"

"Good, because I'm feeling very much like a fool, myself."

## ABOUT THE SAME TIME. ATHENS, TNG DISTRICT. 4:30 PM EST. WEDNESDAY, OCTOBER 8, 2025.

Cameron Nguyen-Peters walked to the Council meeting with a light step for the first time he could remember. *So odd, I even liked Arnie Yang, and I'm sorry for what happened to him. And he did so many good things for me, before Daybreak and after. But he never did a better thing for me than he just did by getting caught.*

Whilmire led the prayer, thanking God for making the United States a Christian nation, veering close to thanking him for Daybreak. *Hmm. The Board demanded that I start jailing people for false preaching. Wonder how they'd react if I started by arresting Whilmire?*

Cam looked around the room after the prayer. He had no expression as he said, "Late yesterday, Doctor Arnold Yang, the former chief director of research at the RRC, was executed for treason in Pueblo; he had been taken over by Daybreak. His Daybreak contact or controller, code-named Aaron, who planned and carried out several of the most damaging attacks on Daybreak day, was killed in the process of capturing Yang. Heather O'Grainne, the director of the RRC, has presented me with convincing evidence that they have completely rolled up the espionage network in Pueblo. Incidentally, Leslie Antonowicz, who was initially arrested, has been exonerated. I thought you might like to know that particularly because several of us worked with Ms. Antonowicz during the recent, aborted summit in Pueblo. Also, James Hendrix has been appointed to take Doctor Yang's place."

"''Scuze me while I kiss the sky,'" the oldest reverend said. This was the first time the old man had spoken and he was making no sense. "James Hendrix," he said. "Jimi . . . oh, never mind."

Grayson, who had been pre-informed, nodded approval. "Good job at Pueblo. Pity they didn't catch him sooner."

Cam made himself smile; it didn't come naturally, though he felt like singing. "Luckily it was soon enough. You will all recall that talks with Olympia in preparation for the restart election broke off just a few weeks ago when it was discovered that Daybreak had penetrated the Pueblo staff. That impediment is now removed. We've lost a month, but there's no reason we can't make it back in the next thirteen months. Gentlemen, we're going to put our nation back together under the Constitution." He waited a moment to see that the reporter from the *Weekly Insight* was scrawling frantically and looking up with light dawning in his eyes. Now was the moment. "I am therefore contacting Olympia immediately to determine the earliest possible date at which we can meet to resume the process, and I have already received the following message from Ms. O'Grainne in Pueblo, and I quote, 'For peace and the Constitution, our door is always open. Tell everyone they can have their old room back.' End quote. I therefore ask the Board to endorse the resumption of this effort to restore our nation, and gentlemen, I'd appreciate it even more if you can make it unanimous."

It was the least enthusiastic chorus of *aye* that Cam had ever heard, and at least a third of them did not participate. But the dead silence when he called for the *nays* allowed him to declare the vote closed and unanimous. When he asked Whilmire, "Reverend, could you lead us in a closing prayer now, so I can send our reply as soon as possible?" he had a clear, confident undertone of threat.

He and Grayson, as usual, were the last ones out. "General, thank you for making this possible."

"You appealed to my oath. It's hard to resist that."

"Of course." They walked to the end of the corridor in silence, and Cam added, "You're entitled to be along for the historic moment. Please come along while I do the radio conference. How are the plans going for an expedition against Castle Earthstone?"

"I think we've settled on the route north of Terre Haute. The forces will be adequate for the job, and if I have anything to do with it, we'll be ready as soon as we have dry ground in the spring."

Cam smiled slightly. "Are you a history buff, at all, General?"

"Most career officers tend to be."

"Yes. I was just wondering . . . you know, winning the *first* battle fought along the Tippecanoe made someone president."

Grayson laughed. "I assure you, that's not any part of the reason for the plan, but now that you've mentioned it, I'll always suspect myself. Well, I'll supply a victory on the Tippecanoe—you supply an election—and perhaps we'll see. You wouldn't know any politicians named Tyler, would you?"

Cam laughed as much as he could manage, given that he almost never did, and the two men walked in what was almost companionable silence. *Now I've got you,* he thought, *and if that didn't feed your ego, God alone knows what will.*

## THE NEXT DAY. PUT-IN-BAY, SOUTH BASS ISLAND, OHIO (OR NEW STATE OF SUPERIOR). 4:30 PM EST. THURSDAY, OCTOBER 9, 2025.

"When I was little," Chris said, "I remember there was some show in reruns, where a midget would yell, 'The plane! The plane!' at the beginning of every episode. I just thought the midget was interesting, when I was a kid, but now I realize how interesting a plane is. Especially compared to waiting for fish." The airplane engine, and the glimpses of a biplane moving in the sky to the south, had just given them an excuse to fold up for the afternoon and head for the airport.

Jason lifted out a stringer holding two decent-sized walleyes, a steelhead, and four perch. "Jeez, I hope Doctor Rhodes doesn't turn out to be right. The fishing's so good, I hate to think of all this turning into green goop and then a swamp."

"Yeah. You know, we thought Daybreakers were environmentalists."

Jason shrugged. "*We* thought we were. We worked hard at not being human-centric, but it was just another way of acting out the basic Daybreak idea: humans suck and ought to die. We just wanted to kill people, for being mean and inconsiderate, for being too numerous, mostly for just existing at all." A cold breeze blew into their faces; Jason's gaze shifted to the gray sky over the trees, not watching the plane anymore. "If destroying the Great Lakes meant killing more people, Daybreak would do it. Daybreak isn't right or left, or Green or racist, or anything. It's just Daybreak—people suck and ought to die."

They walked the mile of winding, crumbling road in dead silence. At the end of the runway, they found a short-winged little biplane, an Acro Sport, painted in red and yellow stripes, marred by the black and gray smears where the biofuel engine and its lye spray had stained it with burnt-soap exhaust.

Since they couldn't open the package marked EYES ONLY till they were back in their rooms at the Edgewater Hotel, waiting for the wagon and riding back gave them time to catch up on gossip. Nancy Teirson, the pilot, mostly flew from Green Bay, the capital of the New State of Superior, alternating between the northern mail route to Olympia and a circuit of the Castles and walled towns in Michigan. "And out to here maybe once a month," she said. "This time I had orders to swing further south and east, overfly the Lost Quarter more than usual."

"Tell'em," Larry said.

She lowered her voice, plainly not wanting to be overheard by the wagon driver. "Tribals on the march on the old roads. Bands of hundreds of them, maybe one band more than a thousand."

Back at the hotel, the instant the door was closed, Larry ripped open the envelope. "Mail for all three of us." He tossed Beth's letter to Jason, who went into the other room to read in privacy.

Chris dove into the notes from Cassie and Abel, chuckling and tsking in the corner.

Larry read Heather's orders—just a few sentences—several times, keeping his eyes on the page to look like he was concentrating intently, or like they were lengthy. He wanted Chris and Jason to have time with their mail before he shared the part he was supposed to share:

URGENT TO DO OVERLAND TRAVERSE, BUFFALO NY TO ALBANY & DOWN HUDSON; SHIPS AVAILABLE IN NYC HARBOR, RETURN VIA TNG TERRITORY. GO AT ONCE

When both of them had savored their mail, and asked what the orders were, he showed them.

"Overland in the Lost Quarter, with winter coming?" Chris asked. "Is she nuts or does she hate us?"

"Not mutually exclusive," Larry pointed out. *And if you knew what was in the message that was just for me, you'd be pretty sure the real answer is "Both."*

Chris rose and stretched. "Larry, if you could give me an hour or two to write something for Nancy to take back—"

"You have the night. I'll need to arrange a ship, and I'm guessing we won't be able to sail before tomorrow morning, maybe longer. You guys just write what you need to write, so it's ready to go out, and it's all right if you sleep all day after we're on the boat, okay?"

Jason looked almost pathetically grateful. "Yeah, thanks."

Larry shrugged. "If I just send Debbie a note that she's a great human being, and to try to only kill people that deserve it, it'll make both of us happier than we've been in years—and won't take me five. Plan to be packed at dawn tomorrow, and I'll fill you in sometime before I go to bed. I'd better get down to the docks before everyone buttons up for the night." He was out the door almost instantly.

Chris and Jason exchanged glances; there was obviously something the senior agent wasn't telling them, and just as obviously if Larry didn't want to talk about it, they shouldn't. As they both sat down to write, Chris said, "Funny thing, I wish I had time to go fishing."

Jason stared. "You complained about fishing all afternoon."

"And rightly so. And if I had the time, I'd do something better than go fishing. I just wish I had the time."

## THE NEXT DAY. ATHENS, TNG DISTRICT. 4:15 AM EST. FRIDAY, OCTOBER 10, 2025.

The dank cold of predawn early winter mornings in Athens smells like a soggy snowball shoved up your nose. Cam's warm coat and watch cap felt good as he hurried along the path. No point in varying his route; his awkward shadow, who occasionally crashed around in the bushes behind him, knew perfectly well that he was going to the crypto radio facility. *And he knows I'm going there to call Pueblo or Olympia, because I need enemies and neutrals to keep my "friends" from taking over. Must be how the last few Bourbons, Romanovs, and Tokugawas felt.*

While Athens techs talked to Pueblo techs, he savored the big mug of coffee that the night tech had waiting for him, concentrating on each sip, drinking it all before it could cool, finishing it before Heather came on the line.

They talked at this hour because it was Cam's getting-up time, Leo's middle-of-the-night feeding, and the best time in the ionosphere for long-range radio. But since it looked sneaky, they needed the appearance of a possibly innocent reason for sneaking. So this morning, like every other, they began with the usual array of flirty double-entendres, wasting ten minutes or so out of the half hour in pretending to be on the brink of phone sex.

Next Cam rattled off a list of sentences about colors, animals, and a not-impossible-to-break code for dates and times that coincided with meeting various officials in the TNG government, none of which was at all important, except that since he knew Grayson's people would be trying to match up codes to people and actions, looking for RRC agents, he sowed suspicion onto some of Grayson's loyalists.

Today he began with "Brown Hen polishes silverware with Green Dog" and read on down through "Gray Weasel is cooking macaroni for Red Squirrel's barbecue." As always, purposely he used Red Dog to refer to a passionately Post Raptural lieutenant he saw for a few minutes every week, implying that he was betraying Grayson's secrets to Peet.

In fact, all the apparent messages either referred to random events of no real importance, minor matters it didn't hurt for the opposition to learn, and things it was useful to tell them (whether true or disinformational). If the other side read them, they would gain nothing other than another layer of deception. The real message was in a positional code, one of the World War One era pencil and paper expedients that the absence of computers had forced on them. The first eight and last three sentences were nulls. The number of messages between the first eight and last three was an hour between one and twelve, the first letter of the last word in the eighth sentence indicating a.m. or p.m., and the last letters of the last three null sentences coding urgency, possible topic, and level of danger.

Together, they told Heather what to relay to Red Dog: a safe meeting time and the relative urgency of meeting. Today Cam was sending VERY HIGH URGENCY, POLITICAL MATTER, HIGHER THAN AVERAGE DANGER, TEN THIRTY A.M.

After the cryptic sentences they traded gossip about mutual friends for a few minutes, and Heather gave him a quick summary of what the Lost Quarter expedition had reported. She read him a nonsense text; he memorized every fourth word, after the first number in the text was "seven," because he added seven to the first number and dropped the high digits. This was a longer message than usual; twenty pairs of words.

They finished by talking longingly about how lonely they were. Cam found that much too easy.

Back at his office, Cam riffled through his dictionary as he did so often; lately he'd made a habit of complaining to his assistants about their limited vocabularies and improper use of words, and leafed through the dictionary often. This time, though, as he waited for his breakfast, he took the first word pair: *tear clearance. Tear* was the eleventh word on page 648, *clearance* the third on page 98; reversing pages and positions gave the eleventh word on page 98 (*clean*) and the third word on 648 (*team*).

Writing nothing down, he lost his place and had to start over a couple of times, but finally he knew

*Clean team available november two zero early est smash stall if can or bail and defect if must halt messy extraction possible on one week notice fractionate but even after success civil war certain and failure risk astronomical replete whoa*

Heather's coding always amused him; she was always careful to use synonyms for *stop* and *break* so as not to create a pattern that might identify the dictionary to the opposition, but there was something inspired, he felt, about *fractionate* for *break* and *replete whoa* for *full stop*. Also, he liked *astronomical* and *horrendous*; in a dictionary code it is not only as easy to send a big word as a small one, but more secure because it varies the vocabulary.

*November 20th at earliest,* he thought, pulling his attention away from the interesting coding to the frustrating message. *Forty days from today. The time it rained on Noah, or the time Jesus spent in the wilderness. Of course, they had a hell of a lot more and better backup on tap than I have.*

## 4 DAYS LATER. CASTLE LARSEN (NEAR THE FORMER JENNER, CALIFORNIA). 2 AM PST. TUESDAY, OCTOBER 14, 2025.

*I'm glad the weather held,* Bambi Castro thought. She sat on the big chair next to Quattro's, on the platform at the south end of the hastily hand-mown soccer field. Before them, at least a thousand people were scattered in a gradient of seriousness—the rows up close to the platform were filled with freeholders and their families, all sitting very straight and serious for the investiture and pledging ceremonies that would create the League of Northern Castles. Behind them were prominent locals, trying to look as serious as the freeholders. The less interested and the less serious had arrived later, till the back area faded into Standard California Outdoor Festival, with guys playing hacky sack, mothers chasing babies around and playing silly games with them, friends picnicking on blankets and loudly critiquing everything they saw, hairy shirtless guys playing guitars, and girls in long skirts twirling rhythmlessly wherever there was music.

The one problem with the best seat in the house, Bambi realized, was that she could see everything except what she wanted to see—Quattro in his finery: a splendid combination of French diplomatic corps formal attire, the Marine dress uniform, and German petty king, with tall black boots and a magnificent plumed hat that looked like something between a European doctoral cap and one of the five hundred hats of Bartholomew Cubbins, as re-envisioned by D'Artagnan and modified by a feather salesman. He said Heather had insisted, which didn't sound anything like her, so Bambi figured it must be some obscure joke.

Anyway, there was no question about it, Quattro was gorgeous, and this was a show all about him—all that Bambi had to do was look nice in her long dress. So it seemed as if, being his wife, she should be allowed a good view of the beautiful front, rather than stuck here watching his back as he accepted the allegiance of seventeen other freeholders and the shouted acclamation of the assembled crowd. *Four times the vassals Daddy's got, representing probably ten times the economic strength and population; no wonder Daddy has that funny expression. He's got peons envy.*

Harrison Castro was seated at the extreme left—the right side of the audience—in the highest spot for visiting dignitaries. Next to him, two chairs stood conspicuously empty: the seats reserved for the PCG and the

TNG representatives. They had been invited and had sent the curtest possible snubs. *Wonder who Heather had write those notes for them, now that she doesn't have Arnie?*

This just meant more attention for Harrison Castro. *Daddy looks like an Imperial bureaucrat from* Star Wars *or the Postmaster General of San Banana. But all the same, he definitely adds something. Too bad we couldn't get a bishop.*

After the ceremony, they posed for pictures, hoping that state-of-the-art redeveloped photography would produce some acceptable result. Standing between her father and Quattro, Bambi turned on the beauty contestant smile.

Castro said, "Hey, you realize your firstborn child can inherit the Duchy of California?"

Squeezing Bambi's hand, Quattro said, "Just so you don't mind my family tradition of naming kids after cars. I kind of like the sound of Duke Lexus of La La Land."

## 3 DAYS LATER. SAN DIEGO, CALIFORNIA. 10:30 PM PST. FRIDAY, OCTOBER 17, 2025.

Harrison Castro's first awareness that anything was wrong, as he entered his bedroom, was when a strong man yanked a bag full of feathers over his head, pinned him to the wall, cuffed him behind his back, and bound his feet. Unable to remove the bag, unable to breathe through the dense feathers, Castro was reeling, red flashes in the blackness of the bag, sucking desperately at the little bit of air that penetrated.

"You can have air and you won't be further harmed," a voice said, seemingly from a million miles away. "If you give your word of honor not to shout or try to attract attention, then tap my hand, here, twice."

Terrified, suffocating, Castro tapped. At once the bag was ripped from his head, and a great mass of dense feathers knocked from his face. He gasped; the air pouring in made him dizzy all over again.

The man in front of him wore black shoes, pants, gloves, and hoodie, with the drawstring hood pulled tight around his face, and a black ski mask. He said, very softly, "Should you break your word I am quite capable of cutting your throat, ethically, and equally capable of escaping, practically. Keep your voice down, Mister Castro, I would dislike cutting your throat over the semantic difference between speaking loudly and shouting. There are so many better differences."

Still gasping, Castro nodded, and let himself sink backward to sit on his bed. The man moved forward to stand in striking distance, blocking Castro from rising again from his seat. "Here is what you will do. We would like to see your League of South Coast Castles succeed, and we want you to be the sole sovereign in this part of the world. You will stand back and close your doors when the Bright Venus Tribe and its allies strike at the FBI Headquarters, the naval command, and the other Federal offices around the bay. You may accept refugees but only on the condition that they leave the area by the first available ship; there are to be no Federal offices, either Temper or Provi, anywhere south of Los Angeles or west of the mountains, ever again. The authority of the Constitution is ended.

"Once that is accomplished, the tribes will want to discuss alliance—which you and we will both need, to keep the Federals from returning. We will be more than willing to ally with you, and even to swear limited fealty, as long as it is understood that most of this area must become wilderness again; San Diego can be a trading post where we obtain some of the things we'll need, but it must not grow into a city again. That is what we propose in broad outline; we will tell you details once you agree."

Castro said, "You're talking about the future of my land, my family—you have to give me time to think. I don't need much, but I'd rather die than make a decision of so much importance in two minutes with a knife at my throat."

"We thought you might feel that way. We will strike in about two weeks against the Federals. You may have ten days, though it would be better to say 'yes' sooner."

"And if my answer is no?"

The man shrugged. "We can get to you. If your answer is no, someone else's won't be. After I free you, you will remain quietly in this room for at least half an hour. It would be very inadvisable to shout for help or bring guards in any sooner; I might not be alone and I might not be gone, and we have already established that I am not afraid to die, and you are."

He hauled Castro painfully to his feet by the hair, turned him, and flung him facedown on the bed. The cuffs fell away. "You may untie your feet."

Castro rolled over, brought his ankles up, and grasped the rope; the knots came apart in his hands and he kicked them from his feet. When he looked, just a moment later, no one was there, just black rope beside the bed and great wads of feathers scattered everywhere.

# FOURTEEN:
# NOW ONE BY ONE THE TREES

*Kelleys Dancer* crept through the dark; even under black sails, with the moon not yet up, and no lights on shore as they approached, they couldn't be sure they weren't being watched.

*And then once we're on the canal, it will be worse,* Larry thought. *Painting the canoes black won't help much there.*

They sat murmuring together in the bow, while Rosie took the helm.

"I'm thinking your problem won't be rapids, but mud," Barbara said. "The water from all those broken dams is long gone. But Stone sent us to investigate the Canadian shore, 'cause they wanted us to find out if pure-fusion fallout behaved like they thought it would. Well, it did—the Geiger counter hardly made a noise, so there wasn't much lasting contamination, but practically everything was dead except grass and bugs. No plants or trees to hold the soil; upstate New York was on that same wind path, so lots of streams and small lakes will be silted up."

*Kelleys Dancer* crept slowly south and east, aided by the slow current in eastern Lake Erie that pulled toward Niagara. After a while Barbara took the helm and Rosie went forward and began sounding with a bob on a line. Whenever they tacked, he'd scramble to adjust the triangular foresail.

At quarter of four, off to starboard, a dim, low urban skyline appeared, with a small knob that had to be the lighthouse, their landmark. The sun would follow less than an hour behind the moon; they needed to move.

The last they heard of Rosie and Barbara was a whispered "Good luck" as Chris and Jason climbed into their black canoe and followed Larry, paddling slowly across the dark harbor. Behind them, they could hear the creak and thump of *Kelleys Dancer* tacking to head back to the western end of the lake.

The canal entrance loomed in front of them like a concrete-scabbed wound. Paddles came up dripping scum, black at first, but as the sun came up the color of a bloody bruise, climbed, and turned the gold color of old chicken fat, the slime was a deep blue-green, in long yarns and strands.

Two hours later the land they paddled through was still urban, though empty and dead. The green scum smelled like fresh horse manure when the paddles turned it over. Chris, in the bow of the lead canoe, saw a headless corpse still wearing a bra and panties; a swollen hair-covered lump that must have been a dead horse or cow; and scattered human bones, including two small skulls, around the black smear where a rubber raft had rotted.

"Kids trying to get out of the city that way?" Jason asked.

"Or kids looting somebody's abandoned raft, killed by something bigger and meaner than them," Chris said. "Or maybe feral dogs got them and it just happened to be near a raft. The amount of really sad shit that happened is just plain impossible to imagine."

Apart from the green slime, nothing lived; the trees that leaned over the canal had no leaves, the clay and stone banks eroded without plants growing on them, no fish jumped in the water, no bird flew overhead, nothing scuttled in the dead brush. Skeletons of humans and dogs lay on the banks; probably for a while the bodies had swarmed with beetles and worms, but now those were gone.

By noon they were well into suburban areas. Jogging trails and little decorative shopping malls bordered the canal at intervals between long stretches of factory yards and common dumps. Hearing booming and thundering ahead around a bend, Larry had them pull over and tie up; Jason drew the short straw. He came back to report an old landfill seething with fires and explosions. "Probably the biotes that infected it are methanogenic," Jason said. "And lightning or something started the rising gas burning."

Not wanting to give up the canoes, they walked along the bank opposite the landfill, towing the canoes on long ropes. "'I got a mule, her name is Sal,'" Jason said. "Except I don't. I got me."

"But we can probably do better than fifteen miles today," Larry said, "and right now, every mile is looking like a blessing."

After relaunching the canoes, they paddled till twilight. The sun crawled down behind them, turning from mucus-yellow to gory red again; they slept under the beached, overturned canoes that night, taking turns sitting watches.

## ABOUT THE SAME TIME. PUEBLO, COLORADO. 9:30 AM MST. SATURDAY, OCTOBER 18, 2025.

"Yes, even in Pueblo," James said, looking at the crowd of excited people jumping and waving as the Gooney Express came in low to verify the FUEL CLEAN, NO NANOSWARM white flag with the blue slash. One bunch of young, clean-scrubbed kids of both genders had been singing praise songs while waiting to see Reverend Whilmire, but much the larger component of the crowd was young women in their best clothes, and old men in veterans' organization caps, clutching small Cross and Eagle flags and whooping it up for General Grayson. Nobody was cheering for Cameron. "Maybe one in ten of our people are Post Raptural. What's it like up in Olympia?"

"About the same," Allie Sok Banh said. "But we've been putting some more pressure on the Pus Rupturals, telling them to be less overtly political or they can kiss the tax exemptions and parade permits good-bye."

Norm McIntyre added, "Plus twice we've raided the Piss Wrapper Church of Olympia for arms caches."

"Did you find any?"

"Yes and no. So many of those assholes pack all the time that if you raid their services you'll always find personal weapons. But we didn't find any arsenals under the altar. Yet."

"We're a little more laissez-faire here," James said, noncommittally.

Allie shrugged. "Typical Heather. More important to follow the rules than to win, and even after Daybreak she won't admit an idea can be dangerous."

"Oh, I'll admit an idea can be dangerous," James said. "Though having spent a good part of this summer teaching in our night school here, I've also noticed that ideas aren't terribly dangerous to very many people."

The Gooney rumbled to a stop. Reverend Whilmire emerged first, waving as the crowd cheered; the cheering became overwhelming when Grayson came down the stairs, holding hands with his wife, Jenny. "You know," Allie said, "if I were a spiteful, jealous person I might be annoyed that you and I didn't make anything like that kind of splash when we arrived."

"It's not obvious yet that we're going to run for president," Graham Weisbrod said. "Perhaps we should put out word?"

Allie gave her husband a broad grin. "On five minutes' notice the whole country can know."

"Let's talk soon."

As Allie resumed watching the Athens team coming out, she was leaning back against Graham with a happy little smile. James thought he was probably meant to see that.

Whilmire and Grayson each gave a short speech to their cheering crowd. Meanwhile, Quattro shut down the Gooney, and came down the steps with Cam and a couple of aides. The party headed over to join the Olympia delegation and James. "Leo was fussing, so Heather deputized me. I'm supposed to deliver you—"

Cheering from the runway, heavily laced with "Praise the Lord!" drowned out James for a moment. It didn't last long, but immediately after, even louder whooping covered Grayson's short speech.

When they could hear again, Cameron said, apologetically, "This might take some time. Were they like this when you came in last night?"

Graham raised an eyebrow, and smirked. "It was terrifying, Cam. There were thousands of them out there chanting for 'a precisely calculated, carefully designed, culturally nuanced mixture of incremental reform and necessary innovation.' Must've taken them ages to learn to chant that whole phrase in unison."

Cam's small, wincing smile was about as close to an outright guffaw as he would ever manage. "Trust a bureaucrat to ask a dumb question, and get a flip answer from a professor."

"Touché. It's going to be a different world, isn't it? Look at the way Grayson speaks, all that arm pumping and flying hands, like an old-time whistle-stop orator." His hand closed around Allie's. "I guess I'll have to learn to do that too."

When the reverend and the general had been torn from their adoring publics, James directed the TNG and PCG delegations to the row of carriages and buggies to be taken to Johanna's What There Is, which Heather had reserved for a special breakfast. Once there, James moved quietly to a corner and concentrated on his plate, which might be the last chance to get food in for the rest of the day, given how busy life was about to become. Johanna paused beside him with a tray of eggs and trout, murmuring, "All clear upstairs as vetted by Heather."

James finished the last bite just as Cameron announced, "You know, I don't really feel the need to go to our rooms first. I slept like a brick on the plane and I feel pretty fresh. We had discussed holding the opening meeting this afternoon, if everyone was feeling up to it, but I was just thinking, why don't we do it now and have time for some real work this afternoon?"

"Well," Heather said, "it would take some time to move you all over there in buggies and carriages—"

"Isn't there a meeting room here? I thought there was, the last time I was here."

"This seems like a great idea to me," Graham said. "I was wondering what I would be doing with myself till this afternoon." He appeared to be completely unaware of Allie trying to hit his instep with her heel, except that his foot kept dodging just enough so that if she were going to hit her target, she would have to make it clearly deliberate.

In less than five minutes Heather had reached a deal to keep Johanna's What There Is through the lunch hour if necessary, and they were all trooping upstairs to the meeting room that she, Johanna, and a couple of trusted agents had spent the morning creating. Last in the procession came Johanna and two slightly awkward waiters—Roger Jackson and Debbie Mensche—carrying coffee and water urns.

As soon as everyone was seated, and the transcriptionist signaled *ready*, Heather said, "All right, here we go. For the record: I am Heather O'Grainne and I am convening the Third Intergovernmental Summit of 2025, with Graham Weisbrod, President of the Provisional Constitutional Government, and Cameron Nguyen-Peters, National Constitutional Continuity Coordinator of the Temporary National Government, and—"

She rattled through the list, alternating between the governments and laddering down in order of rank, finishing with ". . . invited guest Jenny Whilmire Grayson. We will commence with opening statements. Call it, Mister President." The coin was in the air.

"Heads."

"Heads. Graham, when you're ready."

*Wonder if she bothered with a two-headed coin or just figured no one else would get a look?* James thought, idly.

Graham Weisbrod pulled out a short, typed document and spread it before him, adjusting his reading glasses. *Okay, definitely, he cut Allie out of the game to do this,* James thought, *because she looks like she's trying not to let anyone know she just felt a snake go up her pant leg.*

Weisbrod's grandfatherly smile had been famous in the media for more than a decade before Daybreak; somehow, seeing it now, James had a flash of the old sense of security. Weisbrod said, "Please keep in mind that this is preliminary and that large parts of it are intended to start discussion about details and implementation; this is merely the beginning of overworking our staffs." He raised the paper and said, "The Provisional Constitutional Government proposes to issue an overall order stipulating that all Federal employees are to accept, support, and obey the government to be elected in 2026. By all, I mean all. All the military forces down to privates, every postal carrier and every clerk filling out forms. Accept means if you believe the restored Constitutional government's not legitimate, you quit your job before you say so. Support means you do everything in your power to make the restored Constitutional government succeed even if its policies are exactly what you don't want. Obey means just that." He looked around the room. "Of course, the truth is, we're just telling people to do what they're supposed to do anyway: obey the 2026 restoration government. Fundamentally what it says is that whether either side likes the election results in 2026 or not, what's elected is what there is. No option for either of us to stay in business and try to negotiate a deal we like better. Vote the new government in, hand off to it, and be done with it."

Cameron Nguyen-Peters nodded. "I believe I understand your proposal in broad outline, and of course we'll want to go over the text of your order. May I ask what you're hoping we'll do in return?"

"Nothing," Weisbrod said. "This isn't a negotiating position. It's the right thing to do, so I'm doing it unilaterally."

"Oh." Cam was genuinely smiling. "I thought that might be the case. In that case, we'll need to issue a similar order, also unilaterally, so that we're *all* in good faith here. If you don't mind I'd like to look over the exact text of your order; perhaps we could order exactly the same one."

Grayson sat bolt upright. "Sir, this really requires discussion."

Allison Sok Banh's expression was very like the general's, but prettier. "Shouldn't the staff explore some proposals—"

"Oh, exactly," Cam said. "If you've got copies of your text, Graham, maybe we should adjourn for twenty minutes or so to read it?"

"Right here," Graham said. "And I have copies for my side as well. Heather, do we have any kind of separate conference rooms available?"

James, from his corner, thought that the biggest problem in moving to separate caucuses might be maneuvering everyone around all the dropped jaws on the floor.


**IMMEDIATELY AFTER. PUEBLO, COLORADO. 11 AM MST. SATURDAY, OCTOBER 18, 2025.**

The door had barely closed before Whilmire asked, "Did you even *intend* to consult with us?" in a tone suitable for asking a waiter what's in the food while hoping not to learn anything.

"We agreed," Cam said, "that you would always be *informed*. And so you are. You know what's being said as soon as it's said. As for the policy Graham Weisbrod announced, if it's as advertised, it simply declares that we are going to do our duty, as bound by our oaths—that is my oath and the general's, Reverend. As a gesture to allay some very legitimate public concerns about whether the Constitution is going to stand, considering the recent unrest about that very issue, it seems wise. Now let's use our time and make sure it says what Graham Weisbrod says it says."

"Just when what's always been the best part of the country has the free-dom to be the way it should be, you go running to bring these people back." Whilmire stared at Cameron Nguyen-Peters as if he were a specimen in a pathology lab.

"Those people are as American as you or I," Cam said, "and the Consti-tution says what it says. We work for the American people, not the church-approved people, and we took our oath to the Constitution, not to Jesus. Or to Reverend Peet—since some people confuse the two. For example, the Constitution allows me to say things that piss you off, such as, for example, that there has not been any Rapture, there never was going to be, there never will be, and that what you're running is an exceedingly cruel con game on people who have lost loved ones."

There was a stunned silence.

"Well," Cam said, "I don't know about anyone else, but I found that rather refreshing. Reverend, if your Post Raptural Church intends to gerrymander the nation so that your followers are a majority in the rump that's left, you will not only have a fight from those of us loyal to the nation as a whole, you will have an even bigger fight from those of us who might be trapped in the rump. The United States is going back together, without provisos or take-backs. The president elected in 2026 will be the president of the whole thing. Now let's look and make sure that Graham Weisbrod is committed to that too, and that he's not pulling a fast one."

The silence dragged on until Whilmire said, "I'll pray for you."

"Let me know how that works out." Cameron sat still for a long moment. "And the document?"

Grayson took his copy, put it on the table in front of him, and adjusted his reading glasses. "I'm no lawyer but I'll do my best." He pointedly did *not* look up at his father-in-law.

Whilmire pretended that the paper was not there, and said, "I need to pray—"

"Daddy," Jenny said, "maybe you and I should have a little talk outside. While the Natcon and the general see what they can figure out about that document, I mean. Why don't you and I have a chat?"

She led her father out by the arm. As soon as the door closed, Grayson, not looking up, murmured, "She'll get us the time to work but we better use it."

Cam nodded, and brought his concentration to the pages before him. A few minutes later, he said, "I see nothing wrong on the first reading."

"If I were teaching a class on writing orders," Grayson said, "I'd use this as a model, and it says exactly what he said it does."

"One more time through?"

"We should."

At the third time through, they agreed that there was no question: it unambiguously ordered every Federal office and officer to accept, support, and obey the government elected in 2026. "And actually," Grayson said, "those last three paragraphs boil down to *No barracks lawyering, no attempts at barracks lawyering, and you know damn well what I mean by 'barracks lawyering' so don't even think about it.* They make it *better.*"

"Yeah. Unofficially, just between us—will this set up a country you want to run for president of?"

"Unofficially, hell yes."

"And have I completely messed up your relationship with your father-in-law? I got pretty carried away there."

"Jenny has always been able to handle him. Doubt my qualifications for the presidency all you want, but never doubt she'll make a hell of a first lady."

"Wouldn't dream of doubting it. I guess we're ready, then, so we'll go in and agree to—"

The door opened. Whilmire came in, looking tired and old, with Jenny holding his arm in a grip midway between support and arrest. "We don't live in the same universe, Mister Nguyen-Peters, but I am serious when I say I shall pray for you. And for myself. And I think even for the general here. I don't believe I will have anything of value to add for the rest of the conference; I'll talk with you sometime after I consult with the Church leadership." He pressed his daughter's hand down off his arm, and closed the door with no noise, but firmly enough to send a shudder through the floor.

"You have a free hand," Jenny said. "He won't like whatever you do but he can't stand to be left out of a deal. And you're welcome."

## ABOUT THE SAME TIME. PUEBLO, COLORADO. 11 AM MST. SATURDAY, OCTOBER 18, 2025.

"No you are not! You are not restoring the United States! You are giving everything away to a usurper!" Now that only McIntyre was present, Allie was screaming at Graham. *I guess Norm must be used to this by now.*

Graham was wondering if she'd slap him this time. *If she does I'll make*

*Norm testify and leave her here, in jail. Let Allie* try *to work one of her deals with Heather.* The thought strengthened him, and she seemed to feel that. She sat back in her chair, rubbing her face. "This is so *wrong.*"

McIntyre, as he usually did, appeared to be checking the paint for spots.

Graham said, "The Tempers need our legitimacy. We need their effectiveness. The restoration government will need both. First we put the United States back together so it won't come apart again; then whoever—"

"You aren't listening to me at all, are you?" Allie stared as if she had never seen him before. "For whole *lifetimes* everyone who was serious about really doing public policy well in this country has had a never-shrinking heartbreak list: all the things we couldn't do because of the anti-intellectual, anti-government, anti-competence forces that came out of the churches, and business, and the army, the people who insisted we had to have a backward, non-functioning, nineteenth-century government. So they finally threw their big hissy fit and went off to Delusion City to play soldiers of God, we finally put together an expert, policy-oriented, smart government, with the full blessing of the Constitution. We totally shut down those people, the ones who think because they take an oath to the Constitution, they own it, and it says what they want it to. We have a complete set of social programs, Graham—"

"On paper," he said. "They only start once there's money—"

"But we *have* them. And a national civil discourse law, and real environmental planning, and conduct of private business regulations—"

"All of that," he said, "is a provisional Congress and Cabinet giving shadow orders to phantom agencies. Mostly about ghost problems, things that mattered before Daybreak. What the Provisional Constitutional Government has been doing, I am ashamed to say, is not just all about the words, it's *only* about the words."

"We got everything passed that Roger Pendano ever wanted to do, in three months."

"But Roger wanted to *do it.* No one is *actually doing* any of the things the Congress keeps voting in; for some of the new agencies, we haven't even provided for office staff. Meanwhile we have famines, troops going home on their own because they haven't been paid, nutball Daybreakers smashing in from all sides—"

"So why aren't we controlling some of those war expenses, by making an alliance with tribes that have the power to do us some good, instead of with the Jesusoids and the Army people instead?"

Graham blinked. "Allie, are you seriously proposing allying with the tribes? After all they've done, after what happened to Arnie, after what the RRC has established—"

"It's politics, Graham, you make alliances where you can find allies. We share so many values with the tribes—"

"Name one."

"A concern for the Earth—"

"Have you looked at the sky lately? Where do you think all the soot came from? The tribes are Daybreakers, Allie, they're how Daybreak continued itself. It means to kill us. Bless his heart and rest his soul, Arnie Yang went too far and fell into it, but he warned us while he was falling and he was right. There are things you can't cut a deal with and problems that aren't matters of policy."

"You are throwing away everything we have worked for," she said, now very quietly, rose to her feet, and opened the door. "You won't need me this afternoon. I am going to take a nap."

In the silence after she left, Norman McIntyre said, "Mister President, I think you'd better get the deal nailed down while she's still gone and sulking. And it's none of my business but I don't think you should take her back."

"I have to take her back to Olympia," Graham said. "I can't very well just abandon her here—"

"Not what I meant."

"I know, but it was what I was ready to answer."


**IMMEDIATELY AFTER. PUEBLO, COLORADO. 11:30 AM MST. SATURDAY, OCTOBER 18, 2025.**

As soon as they were seated, Cameron Nguyen-Peters said, "We found that your text was fine as is. I'll send it out at the same time you send your version out. I suggest as a general principle that the restoration government should not have its hands tied. It's going to be the legitimate Constitutional government. We've just been caretakers. The caretaker should not bind the real government."

"I absolutely agree with that principle," Graham said.

"Good," Cameron said. "I'll ask my staff to prepare a list of all the decisions we've made since the TNG was formed; we'll send the list to the restoration governments so they can ratify, nullify, or whatever."

"I'll do the same for the PCG's actions. What's that leave from *your* list?" Cameron looked down at his notepad and read aloud.

"Mechanics for the election
What to do about the New States—which overlaps
the election issue
merging the armed forces
hard line against the Castles, no recognition and no special position.

"Also we wanted to propose a joint military expedition into the Lost Quarter, which might overlap most of the other issues. We want to at least take down Castle Earthstone, and General Grayson has suggested that if the TNG and PCG cooperate fully, we could do a great deal more."

Graham grinned. "Almost exactly my list, except for that last bit—which I like a lot."

In the next few minutes, they delegated every complex issue to joint committees and resolved every simple one. Election procedure and military merger went to joint committees to be set up in Pueblo in the next month. The New States of New England, Chesapeake, and Allegheny, never having assembled governments, were void; the PCG would cease trying to organize them. The New States of Superior and Wabash, having now functioned for some time, would exist until the restoration government took power, would have electoral votes based on their seats in the Provi legislature, and would then be admitted, or not, at the discretion of the restoration government. Any former state could secede by majority vote from a New State until the restoration Congress provided otherwise. Regular, pre-Daybreak Army units, which mostly answered to Temper civilian control, would cooperate with New State governments in exactly the way they cooperated with older, pre-existing state governments.

Both governments agreed to accord no special legal status to any Castle, and that no government communications were to refer to any of the titles the freeholders gave themselves, "except internal reports for law enforcement," Weisbrod added. "General Grayson, if I may suggest, why don't you draft a list of options for dealing with Castle Earthstone, and with the Lost Quarter in general, and forward it to General McIntyre for comments? Assume you've got any resources we are not obviously using for immediate defense. Give Cameron and me some cheap options in case we have to be misers, but also give us a couple of Cadillac plans, the biggest and best things you think are within our grasp."

"I'll do that immediately, sir," Grayson said.

Weisbrod smiled. "Now, if there's nothing left on either list, should we, maybe, think about a declaration of principles at the end of the joint communiqué? Something to guide any future courts or our successors in what our thinking was?"

"The principle we're after," Cameron Nguyen-Peters said, "is to trust to the common sense of the people who are going to be elected, which also means to the common sense of the people electing them."

McIntyre sighed. "I'd like that principle better if it didn't sound like a complete abdication of responsibility."

Graham Weisbrod peered at the general over his glasses; of the people in the room, only Heather knew he couldn't see a thing that way, that it was purely an intimidation trick Graham had picked up decades ago. Graham waited two beats. "Well, General McIntyre, it's appropriate to abdicate responsibility when you've made a mess and there's someone else around who can clean it up better than you. As for the mess, look at my government, or at Cam's. As for cleaning up, there are thousands of small towns, dozens of military units, tens of thousands of small businesses, community organizations, you name it, that are doing the cleanup right now. I assume we've both read the news from Wapakoneta in the *Post-Times*?"

Fussing with exact words took a couple of hours, but the president and the NCCC seemed to enjoy it, and insisted on continuing over a late lunch. Long before dark, they were shaking hands for the camera. *Sure hope we've got film that lasts now,* Heather thought, *because whoever publishes the history books is going to want that picture.*

**THAT EVENING. PUEBLO, COLORADO. 7:30 PM MST.
SATURDAY, OCTOBER 18, 2025.**

Allie had always wondered how she'd handle a serious defeat, because she'd never had one. *Uncle Sam used to say I was his trifecta niece because even if I didn't win, I always finished in the money. Wonder what he'd say now?*

Sam and a big part of the family had chartered a wooden sailboat just after Daybreak and set off to the south, heading for "somewhere warm where the food won't run out." They had not been heard from since. Perhaps they'd been caught by the fringes of the big storm (but they should have been well south by then); perhaps they'd had a fire at sea from the EMP of the superbomb (but they should have found landfall by then); maybe they'd run into those first-wave pirates, the ones out of Florida and Bermuda, who had badly disrupted the southward exodus? (But they'd been well-enough armed and they should have been a match for anything roaming around.) In any case, she hadn't heard from them since waving good-bye from the dock, and since her name was on the radio and in the *Post-Times* often enough, they should have been able to find her. Maybe they didn't want to. *You are a big success girl but you are not a wise girl or a patient girl and people do not like you,* Papa had said.

Her thoughts went round and round; if she just had a friend to talk to, a friend who would have her back no matter what.

Sitting on the bed and looking out the window, she was amazed at how dark it was outside. She'd eaten nothing since breakfast, had moved only from armchair to bed to desk within her small room since she'd stormed out on Graham. *That dickless sycophant McIntyre stayed. Why didn't I—*

There was a soft knock at the door. "Come in," she said, expecting Graham Weisbrod, expecting a fight—

Not expecting that pudgy, balding little man who had taken over Arnie Yang's job. His name was—some piece of obscure oldies trivia, they used to play trivia in the bars in college—"Mister Hendrix," she said.

"Yes. May I come in and close the door? This room is secure, and there's something vital we need to discuss."

"Oh, sure," she said. "Sit down. I'm amazed that anyone discusses anything with me."

"Don't be." He turned up the oil lamp on the side table. The orange light bathed both their faces and etched the shadows into high contrast. "You're still one of the most powerful and important people on the continent. We would have to talk to you even if Heather didn't like you and worry about you."

"You're blunt. Is that why Heather sent you instead of coming herself?"

"She said it would get too personal if she did."

"Close enough. All right, obviously you have a message to deliver and you're supposed to take back an answer. I'd better hear the message."

Hendrix nodded, and said, "We found a note from you in Arnie Yang's pocket. It was, um, intimate, though not explicit. Now, we have no great concern with whether it was a love affair or just the two of you sharing loneliness, but there seemed to be a strong Daybreaker element in the note—"

"Why do you think it was from me? I don't remember ever writing him a note—"

"Your personal stationery and handwriting—"

"Do you have it with you?"

"I do. We have a copy, by the way—"

"I'm not going to destroy evidence in front of you. Give me some credit." She held out her hand, looked at the note, and felt as if she'd been kicked in the belly. *Darcage. During one of those blackouts he induces, he must have told me to write this.*

Allie had read the RRC's top-secret, unredacted report on Arnie. She knew Hendrix would believe her if she—

The whole universe rolled down a stony slope, bouncing and spinning from stone to stone, and she fell onto her side on the bed. Hendrix was bellowing for a doctor, and then she felt strong hands pushing her out of the fetal position, soothing her, a warm voice. "Mom?"

"Wish I was, I could help you better."

Allie looked up; it was Heather's doctor, maybe the RRC's doctor or Pueblo's, they were pretty scarce and the world was pretty small. She was sitting next to Allie on the bed, smoothing her hair and face; it felt good. "Was that a Daybreaker seizure?"

"If it wasn't, you're a hell of an actor. You'll want to sleep for a while, maybe, unless there's something you want to say while you can."

"Doctor—"

"Abrams. You can call me MaryBeth as long as you remember I'm the doctor, not your mom."

"No problem remembering that, Doctor, I *need* a doctor. Can I sit up and have some water?"

Hendrix fetched her a glass. After drinking it all, Allie took a deep breath, and another. "Do I remember right, if I don't sleep, I get about an hour where it's easier to talk about Daybreak without having a seizure?"

"It seems to work that way," MaryBeth said. "We don't know why. But it might still hit you again. It's not a guaranteed immunity."

"All right," Allie said. "Let's try. I want to finish this. Got a pencil, Mister Hendrix?"

"Ready when you are."

"My contact calls himself Mister—Mister—Mister Darcage, I have to not say Mister, say Darcage, just this skinny good-looking guy in dreads, and . . ."

She blurted the whole story into Hendrix's notepad, weeping and sometimes feeling another seizure creeping toward her. *So now I know what Ysabel Roth went through. And why.* "Can I have something to eat? Uh, maybe a lot?"

As she finished eating, Heather turned up with a hug, and said she didn't want to lose Allie, too. It was a while before Graham came in; her husband had insisted on being alone with her, and she hadn't let the rest of them go until they promised to do things the way she wanted to.

When she was finally alone with him, Graham just held her; she felt like he might do this forever, and that would be okay with her. "I was so worried," he whispered.

*My husband loves me, my friends love me, thousands of good people depend on me, and I am going to hurt Daybreak so—*

*Not again.*

The seizure was fully as bad as the first. As she came out of it, Graham and Dr. Abrams and Heather all looked worried sick, but Allie said, "Let me just sleep and heal," enjoying the post-seizure luxury of thinking, *Daybreak, you have no idea what a big fight you picked*, and of looking up at people she could trust, till she drifted off.

**2 DAYS LATER. REPTON, ALABAMA. MONDAY, OCTOBER 20. ABOUT 1 PM CST.**

Before Daybreak, Repton, Alabama, had been a cluster of houses in the woods where a few hundred working people could afford land to build on. Since then the town had prospered due to the accidents of a hobby printer, who had established a small local paper; three fast-thinking local farmers, who had used refugee labor to put in vine cuttings of sweet potatoes over as much land as they could reach; and an alert local militia commander, who had been able to control and channel the refugee stream on US 84. Now it was almost three thousand people, mostly still in tent-roofed cabins, but eating, building, and gradually becoming a community.

On Monday afternoon, the old church bell rang, the signal for news to be announced at the old gas station that served as a makeshift newspaper office. The *Repton Vindicator*'s editor stood up on a crate to read the announcement that the government in Athens and the one in Olympia had both declared that whatever was elected in 2026 would be the real government, and enjoining everyone to accept it. She had wondered how people would react to it; the wild cheering answered that, and supplied her with a local angle for her Wednesday headline—

CITIZENS GREET "SATURDAY SUMMIT" ACCORD WITH JOY!

She used her ham set to relay the story to the *Athens Weekly Insight*. An hour later they called back to tell her that the story would be used and that she would be mailed fifty dollars of TNG scrip. *At least I can use that to pay taxes. If they ever get their act together enough to collect them, out here.*

**THE NEXT DAY. ON THE TRAIN TO ATHENS. 10:30 AM CST. TUESDAY, OCTOBER 21, 2025.**

Across the hill and prairie country of eastern Nebraska, the train sometimes sped up to fifty miles an hour, when the tracks were clear and in good shape, but it spent much of its time standing still since coal and water were still mostly loaded in by awkward jury-rigs. *In 1880, anybody with money and reason could cross the country in about a week,* Cam thought. *I guess we're at about 1870, when in a really urgent case we could get a train across the country, now and then, as a stunt.* In the still, frosty hour after dawn, plumes of smoke rose everywhere, from thousands of stoves and fireplaces. With the big machines and the banks gone, refugees coached by Amish extension agents were reopening small farms.

*Grayson's drive up the Yough Valley was about our finest hour,* Cam thought. *I won't even complain if it makes the son-of-a-bitch president. I've worked for worse presidents.*

A thin blanket of snow covered the land in front of him; good for the winter wheat, and thank all the gods that WTRC and the *Post-Times* had screamed since May that winter would start early, go deep, and leave late, so that the winter wheat was already planted. This next year would still be tight, but by next fall they should be past the risk of famine. *Jeez, a year ago the Ag Department guy had to explain winter wheat to me; I just knew I liked Wheat Thins with smoked gouda while I watched the Series.*

At the knock on the compartment door, Cameron rose from his desk to shake Whilmire's hand and join him at the table. A staffer carrying breakfast had followed the reverend in. While the two men ate silently, the sun pierced the overcast, sharpening the colors of the rolling brown land with its smears of snow and a few leaves still clinging to the trees.

"It might have looked this way a hundred fifty years ago," Whilmire said, "with a big slow steam train crossing it. And on Sunday you hear church bells everywhere; we've got missions all over. Daybreak was hard, and we'll miss all the good people that left in the Rapture, but it's good to see a cleaner, more traditional world coming back."

"With, I hope, a traditional United States re-established next year," Cam said. "You said you wanted to talk about that at breakfast."

"Last night I received a long message from Reverend Peet. We know you won't come along with us on Biblical prophecy, of course, and you know, to the Church, that is very nearly as serious as that old Jewish professor not thinking we were in a war. So, frankly, Cameron, much as I like you personally, you and your administration will have to go in 2026. As far as we can tell you're backing General Grayson, is that correct?"

"Just now he's the most credible conservative candidate—"

"And my most credible son-in-law. I don't know if he's told you the offer we made him: we'll back him if he promises you won't be any part of his government."

*Poor Grayson. He was so embarrassed when he made himself sit down and tell me.* "I was going to retire and start a second career anyway. I already have applications in to either pitch for the Angels or fly for NASA."

"That's funny." Whilmire's voice and expression were flat. "We need a government to fit our Bible-based culture, a strong military ready for Armageddon—which will be very soon—and because one big part of the country will be ex-Provi, we have to have someone who's not afraid to say what Weisbrod really is."

"Oh, is it official that Graham Weisbrod is the Antichrist?"

Whilmire shook his head. "Absolutely not. The preachers who have been pushing that are Bible-ignorant and don't know crap about prophecy. Weisbrod doesn't meet most of the criteria in Revelations. I meant we need to call him out as a secular humanist, socialist, anti-Christian—"

"He's Jewish, for God's—"

"Exactly. And he has an outspoken atheist in his cabinet. And General McIntyre."

"Norman McIntyre is the highest-ranking surviving American officer and a decorated combat vet, and—"

"And he should never have been allowed to be either. The only reason he was allowed to defile an American uniform is that Obama allowed perverts—"

"Defile? So now the uniform is like the cross or the flag?" Cam's tone apparently froze Whilmire. "This doesn't sound conciliatory; it's more like your manifesto before another armed uprising."

"Armed uprising? Those were merely vigorous demonstrations. When there's an armed uprising, you'll know the difference." Whilmire let that hang in the air before ostentatiously switching to a smooth, flattering tone. "You know why you can never be a real ally to us. But it doesn't matter what you call the people's protests, really it doesn't, because Reverend Peet prayed on it, and we're committed to a peaceful election—which we will win, no matter what it takes. Reverend Peet believes a peaceful, uncorrupt, trouble-free election is the only way to guarantee the special position for the Post Raptural Church. We have to have a legitimate Constitutional government in place to amend the Constitution."

"So, you'll back Grayson because you think he'll play ball with you," Cameron said. "I'll back him because he's conservative and after working with him I know he'll do a decent job, maybe out of pure ambition, but he won't let himself be a bad president. But what really matters is what the people think, and to give them their chance to think, and make this a real election with real debate, next week I'm going to void all orders against blasphemy, obscenity, sedition, and disrespect for the armed forces and the flag."

"We want you to go ahead with that." Whilmire leaned forward, his red scalp showing through his iron-gray curly hair. His finger stabbed at Cam like a feinting copperhead. "Of course we'll protest, we can't be seen endorsing it, but it's what we want. Let Weisbrod run against God, and the flag, and the Bible, and the Army—and remind people about how things were before Daybreak and the Rapture. It will pull them together for the Tribulation, and clobber Weisbrod at the polls." He grinned at Cam's discomfiture. "Besides, Weisbrod has already given us the presidency, and you've ratified it. Before Daybreak, the United States had about twenty-five conservative states, about fifteen liberal states, and about ten toss-ups. Now out of thirty-two states that are still calling in, twenty-three are conservative. And Graham Weisbrod has combined three liberal states into the New State of Superior, and three toss-up states into the New State of Wabash." He leaned forward, his face almost in Cam's, relishing the moment. "So here's the précis: You, out. Grayson, in. Reunification, on. New States, definitely. Your opinions, irrelevant."

After the door closed behind Whilmire, Cam reached into his bag and dug out the paperback Thucydides that he'd started reading at Lyndon Phat's suggestion, but he found he had no better ideas than Pericles had. After a while a soldier came in to tell him that they had received a report of tribal activity in the area, so they were shuttering the windows and manning the turrets.

**3 DAYS LATER. ATHENS, TNG DISTRICT. 2 PM EST. FRIDAY, OCTOBER 24, 2025.**

Lyndon Phat's face was bent down into the chessboard to make it hard to read his lips, and he barely murmured, "So no more than a month at most. I'll miss these chess games."

"I'm hoping to come with you."

"If we both make it out, we'll both be busy. Neither history nor Heather will let us sit on the sidelines." Phat sighed. "Yes, the answer to your question is yes. Find a way, and I'll go along, and I'll run for the office. I don't see how I can possibly be the popular guy that you say I am, out there. Not considering how I screwed the pooch when I had the chance. But if I am, I'll run, and if I win, I'll do my damnedest." He finally moved his rook, still staring down at the board. "The minute you said Graham wasn't fit to be president because he didn't agree with us, I should have stuck to my oath like glue and said, like hell, he's the only lawful successor."

"That was *my* mistake. You just went along with it."

"And Norm's mistake too—he should've kept his job and made you do the right thing, not gone off to jail with Weisbrod. The only person whose mistake it *wasn't* was Grayson. He doesn't have either the brains or the balls to make a real mistake."

"He did all right up in the Yough."

"Grayson'll do all right most of the time. Hell, nearly every time, he'll do fine. He's got talent, charisma, energy, and medium-good humility about his own limitations. Ninety-nine times out of a hundred, he'll do a good-to-exceptional job. He knows that the best way to succeed is to help others succeed and he has the smarts to see how to help them. Many people who have served with him adore the man."

"I hear a big hanging *but* waiting to crash down."

"Phat shrugged. "It's the thing that there's bad blood about, between us. It was a long time ago. I found out, back when we were both absolute nobodies, that Grayson's only got two problems. One, his definition of 'success' is much too close to his definition of 'what Grayson wants,' regardless of whether it's what it would be good for him to have. Two, although he knows what the *best* way to succeed is, and usually does it that way—which is why there are so many people who've had a good experience with him—well, he *knows* what the best way to succeed is, but if he can't succeed the best way, he's willing to succeed in ways that are . . . not the best. Which is why there's also some human wreckage, here and there, near his trail."

"You don't want to tell me what it was, I guess."

"I promised people I respected that I would not talk about it. I shouldn't have. But not talking about it got to be a habit. I guess if I start to think he might make it to president, I'll *have* to talk about it, because there's a level where you can't have a man with a . . ." His hand waved as if seeking the word in the air in front of his face. "Moral crack? Defect of the soul? Can you call it a character flaw if it only comes out a few times in decades, under the worst kind of pressure?" Giving up on the question, he said, "Well, whatever you call it, an officer shouldn't have it and a president can't. There's a Buddhist proverb I like—or at least the guy I heard it from, when I was little, was Buddhist. 'If you want something bad for you in the worst way, that's exactly how you'll get it.'"

"So . . . uh, if we're talking flaws here, why should two guys like us, who already made huge mistakes—"

"A mistake is not what I'm talking about. Mistakes happen to everybody. And there's no reason it shouldn't be us; Graham has made about as many mistakes, about as big. The voters can decide which mistakes they like better. But Grayson has a rotten core to him, and the one thing a big job always finds is the core. And what he does when that happens won't be a mistake; he'll mean to do it, no matter what it does to everyone else, or even to himself. So here's to honest blundering." He raised his wineglass; Cam tapped his against it. "By the way, you're in check."

**1 HOUR LATER. ATHENS, TNG DISTRICT. 4:30 PM EST. FRIDAY, OCTOBER 24, 2025.**

Crossing the lawn to Terrell Hall, Cam saw Billy Ray Salazar, and waved; the colonel waved back and came over, loudly saying, "Sir, just wanted to thank you for the weekend, I think it's the best thing you've reinvented."

Cameron said, "You're welcome. Headed up to the lake for some fishing?"

By now his hand was in Salazar's hand, and as they shook, without moving his lips, Salazar asked, "Anything to tell our mutual friend?" In a normal conversational tone he said, "Yeah, well, it's protein. They're biting. I have a smokehouse by the fishing cabin, too, so I'm laying in tons for the winter. You wait till January and you'll wish you'd gone with me."

"I already do," Cameron said, adding softly, "the Red Queen is in," before letting his volume come up for, "and I don't even fish, but it must be great to be out in the quiet."

"It is, and you don't have to fish, sir. I've got a spare bed and you're welcome anytime." And softly, "I'll communicate that. Are you taking advice?"

Murmuring at his shoes, as if too socially awkward to accept a friendly invitation (not a hard thing for him to fake), Cam said, "I already know it's dangerous, if it fails *everything* will unravel, and the longer I delay the worse it'll get."

"That's all the advice I had. I'll be on the line to our friend early tomorrow," Salazar said quietly. "Really. I wish you'd reconsider, and I'm inviting you because I like your company. Though if it means you'll come, I promise to do some career-booster upsuckage too."

Cam shook his head. "Not this time."

"Well, have a good weekend in town then, sir."

Walking away, Salazar noted that they'd managed to hit the center of a big open space, more than enough protection because the other side didn't have any surviving long-range directional mikes.

As he saddled up, he thought, *I could set up and transmit tonight, then sleep in tomorrow. I haven't seen any reports that anyone has even noticed a sporadic beep-radio transmission from outside town yet, let alone put direction finding on it. But this would be a hell of a time for a first. Stay on the path, even when no one is watching.*


**5 DAYS LATER. SYLVAN BEACH, ON ONEIDA LAKE, NEW YORK.**
**10 AM EST. WEDNESDAY, OCTOBER 29, 2025.**

The big cache of canned goods came to them at the end of a real run of good luck. They had paddled and poled for a few days, then spent three tiring days walking along the bank, two men each towing a canoe, the third man keeping the lines clear, pushing the canoes out from the bank with a pole, doing much of the observing, and staying alert against attack. They had not expected to be able to keep the canoes all the way to Oneida Lake; once they reached the western lake port of Brewerton, though, a makeshift sail on each canoe had been enough to carry them all the way across the lake to Sylvan Beach before 3 p.m., traveling farther in half a day than they had just done in three.

A big cache of canned goods in an empty, clean house with a woodstove was an opportunity to enjoy warmth and food, and a chance to mend, clean, and thoroughly dry everything; they decided to lay over for at least a day.

When they rose, at least half a foot of fresh snow covered the ground. More was still coming down—big, wet, soft flakes that stuck to everything and turned to slush at a breath. They had stashed the canoes under a pier and carried everything up into the house, and the previous occupants had left behind a large pile of firewood, some oil candles, and three big cans of olive oil that burned in a smudgy and dirty way in oil candles with cloth wicks.

Everything was clean and fixed up by early afternoon. They decided to eat another couple of big meals here and sleep warm for one more night, especially since the coming descent of the Mohawk was likely to be rough.

Larry had reports to write, Chris had his diary and his articles, but for Jason, the shelves held no paper books or magazines, no musical instruments, not even a Parcheesi set. One large cabinet drooled a brown jelly that had probably once contained millions of songs, movies, books, games, and so forth, but now it was too gooey even to make decent modeling clay.

Jason pulled on his coat and went to look for a bookstore or library somewhere. Snow was falling thick and fast; the gray half-light swallowed up the house behind him in less than two blocks. He turned right as he came into the business district, five blocks from the house by his careful count. Four blocks later, he found a senior center, and broke in at the back door.

The building was lighted only by high windows, but he could make out the mummified remains in chairs around the big tables, on cots along the walls, or on rotted blankets. Massive-dose radiation sickness is horrible but quick. Lumpy fans of crusted gunk lay by the mouths and anuses of most of the mummies. No animals had survived to come in here, and the windows were unbroken, so the dead lay where they had died; only the first few had been lined up in a storage room, covered with sheets.

Two mummies in a corner were holding hands with a cup beside them; the sitting one must have been bringing water for the lying one. He hoped they'd both lost consciousness at the same time.

A back room with immense windows and the remains of several couches and armchairs contained shelves of military history; the old-fashioned kind of chick books, where it was always just the turn of the century, everybody hooked up constantly, and everyone was always about to have a great career;

bios of forgotten actors, singers, and athletes; and some of the classics. Jason pocketed half a dozen paperbacks, figuring Chris and Larry might want to read and the added weight wouldn't be much if they did manage to keep the canoes all the way down the Mohawk.

Shadows passed by the window. Silently Jason took one long step backwards into the arched doorway of an open bathroom, letting the darkness hide him. Huddled human forms, hugging themselves and stumbling, wrapped in blankets over multiple sweaters and hoodies, passed by the window in rows six abreast, with an armed guard every eighth row; the guards wore heavy red wool coats and earflap hats, and carried steel yardsticks, which they sometimes swung full force against the backs of the stumbling slaves. For more than twenty minutes, he watched an army of wraiths in rags go by, herded by these frightening parodies of hunters.

*You come to me as hunters, but I will make you hunters of men,* he misquoted to himself. It did not seem funny.

Counting rows, Jason guessed that about three thousand blanket-wrapped slaves and just over a hundred guards passed by, southward, along the edge of the lake, with no sound except when a guard cursed or hit a slave. After the slaves, a loose formation of about three hundred tribal soldiers passed by, followed by twenty rulers or chiefs or whatever they called themselves, another group of a hundred soldiers, and ten minutes later, a rearguard of about fifty soldiers, weapons at ready, moving as if they expected trouble.

Jason timed off an hour by his watch before emerging to look at their tracks.

Their trail bent around the lake, away from the house where Chris and Larry were; no one had turned off where Jason's faint tracks came in. *Didn't see them or didn't care, I guess, and the fire probably wasn't putting out any smoke you could see through the falling snow.* Taking a roundabout way, wading briefly along the icy canal, he finally reached the little house just as the sun was setting. The snow was still falling.

They banked the fire and spread his clothes and moccasins before it. When Larry awakened Jason for his watch, his clothes were dry but no longer warm.

**THE NEXT DAY. SYLVAN BEACH, ON ONEIDA LAKE, NEW YORK.**
**7 AM EST. THURSDAY, OCTOBER 30, 2025.**

It was still snowing heavily. They'd found kids' sleds hanging in the attic space, and each of them pulled a sled-load of canned goods. Their muscles were already aching by the time they had tossed the sleds in and loaded and launched the canoes, paddling along the lakeshore to the canal entrance; slush an inch thick floated on the lake's surface, and on the canal.

All that day, they paddled to each successive lock dam, unloaded and portaged the canoes, sledded their packs and supplies down to the canoes, and resumed paddling; Jason guessed they were spending twice as much time portaging as paddling, but in the empty, dead country around them, they didn't want to abandon the supplies that only the canoes could carry.

It was still snowing as it began to get dark, less than twenty miles beyond Oneida Lake. At the public access where they stopped, Larry said, "Now that we know whole armies of Daybreakers might come by, I don't think we can risk a fire tonight."

They pulled the two canoes almost face-to-face on a ground cloth, threw a camo tarp and some loose brush over the top, and crawled under to wolf down a can of beans and a can of salmon each; huddled as closely as they could, they went to sleep.

**THE NEXT DAY. A LITTLE WEST OF DEERFIELD, NEW YORK.**
**6:50 AM EST. FRIDAY, OCTOBER 31, 2025.**

Dawn crept under the canoes, and the men fidgeted, waking each other. The sun was an orange disk through the morning fog. They knocked snow off a picnic table, and risking a small fire in a grill, they fried Spam, heated canned potatoes and green beans, and warmed water from the hand pump to mix with condensed tomato soup.

"I hate to admit how good this is," Jason said.

Larry rose from the table. "That well water is probably cleaner than anything we've seen in a while, and this fire will last a while; let's dump our old containers, and boil enough water to refill them with clean, hot water, and then, unless you all want to do a little yoga or maybe linger over the sports page, I think there's not much to do but get going."

When they pushed off and paddled eastward the fog on the canal was so thick that they could not see the banks twenty feet away. Later that morning, the fog turned suddenly golden as the sun broke through. Not long after they slipped out of the rapidly dispersing fog. In front of them, dead trees clawed at the sky beyond the crooked silhouettes of burned buildings, and three naked bodies dangled by their necks from a pedestrian bridge, on which someone had painted

PLAZTATIC = DEATH

## ABOUT AN HOUR LATER. ATHENS, TNG DISTRICT. 8:45 AM EST. FRIDAY, OCTOBER 31, 2025.

When Jeffrey Grayson stepped out onto his porch to inspect the day, it was a fine Georgia autumn, fit to make a man glad he lived here. Now if the Friday meeting of the Council were canceled, he could walk in the gardens with Jenny, take a long lunch outside, and spend the afternoon in bed. So when he had bathed, shaved, and put on his uniform, he still hung around for an extra moment, talking to Jenny, giving a cancellation one last chance to reach him, and just enjoying being with her. And maybe Reverend Whilmire had a point about the power of prayer, because just as Grayson put some extra time and effort into kissing Jenny at the door, a loud knock made them both jump.

Grayson tugged his uniform straight, and Jenny brushed his hair tenderly with her hand. When he opened the door, the messenger saluted and held out a note.

Grayson returned the salute, watched the man go, and tore open and read the note while standing in the open doorway. "Your father needs to confer with Reverend Peet, and Cameron Nguyen-Peters wants to get some more reports in before the Council meeting. Postponed till Monday!" He closed the door softly behind him and whooped like a loon.

Jenny winked, said, "Find something to kill five minutes," and darted into their bedroom.

She emerged in a tight white dress with pink pumps. "Baby, I'm ready to take a walk in the gardens," she said. "Harness up the trap."

Grayson was proud that he'd learned to drive a one-horse trap just for fun, well before Daybreak, and Ironside had been his harness-horse for a couple of years before. It had always seemed so satisfying, more so once Jenny had entered his life. As they rolled through the brilliant green of the fields with Ironside's hooves clopping away, Grayson thought any man who saw him with this carriage and this girl must be dying of envy.

They had gone more than a mile, about halfway to the former State Botanical Garden of Georgia, when he thought to ask, "Jenny-baby, how did you know this was what I most wanted to do in the whole world?"

"You were hanging around the house instead of charging off to your meeting, honey, it's a beautiful day, and mornings like this are your favorite lead-in to afternoons in bed."

"Anyone ever tell you you're perfect, Jenny?"

"You, almost every day. Keep it that way, 'kay, baby?" She moved to put her leg against his. "Well, I'm glad everyone is busy figuring things out among themselves, so you don't have to be caught in the middle."

"You mean between your father and Cam? They don't like each other but they'll both keep their bargains."

"Daddy has been known to re-interpret what the original bargain was, and that weird little man has too. I wish you were a teensy bit more suspicious of him."

"I don't like him much either," Grayson said, "but at the moment, he's a stepping stone to the presidency, and I don't see any reason to stomp on him."

"Just watch that that stone doesn't turn under you." Workers on the roadside waved and yelled; Jenny turned to return the wave in a big, enthusiastic, cheerleader style. She sat back down and said, "Baby, you have to learn that you always at least give them a nod and a wave."

"You were saying, about Cam—"

"I just can't see what that weird little man really wants."

"He's probably the most honorable, principled guy I know," Grayson said. "If he's sure he's right, you can't change him or buy him or scare him, all you can do is kill him."

"Are you afraid you might have to kill him?"

"I won't want to. He's been pretty straight with me even though we don't agree. And our interests overlap. He wants there to be a president again—and a Congress and a Supreme Court and I suppose a Department of Transportation—and I want to be that president."

"So as long as you're his best candidate for president, you're on the same side. What if he found a better one?"

"He's got a lot of personal loyalty," Grayson said.

"Aww, baby, didn't mean to upset you." She snaked a hand up his back, under his collar, rubbing his neck. "But you know, you do always tell me you don't have a personal relationship with him, not really. Respect and cooperation is great, but he's not, you know, family, or your BFF, or anything like that. I just think maybe you should watch him, a little. Now—let's enjoy the day. Happy Halloween!"

*Another great thing about life after Daybreak,* Grayson thought, *is that you can accept a long tender kiss while driving, because the horse knows enough to keep you on the road.* They walked in the Botanical Garden like the first people on Earth, and if thoughts about Cam sometimes crept in among the shadows, they slipped away whenever he paid attention to anything else. With Jenny around, that was nearly always.


## ABOUT THE SAME TIME. ATHENS, TNG DISTRICT. 10 AM EST. FRIDAY, OCTOBER 31, 2025.

Whilmire said, "No, at this point my sense of the public is that we cannot step up and guide the nation directly. The non-Christians, and even the well-meaning Christians in the other churches, won't be ready for that till after the big war. We're still early in Tribulation—it's only the first year of the seven. So far neither the Whore of Babylon nor the Antichrist has clearly emerged, and that would be the earliest time we could make a really bold move. So we're stuck with what we're stuck with."

The Reverend Arthur Peet nodded somberly. He had known Whilmire for most of both of their lives, and he knew the way the man's mind diced and dissected the world into manageable slices. "So where should we throw our weight?"

"We're just waiting for the right time, allies, and pretext to give Nguyen-

Peters the boot. He counts for nothing. Weisbrod has zero following in TNG territory—Democrat-liberal-Jew professor? Forget him and his Dragon Lady wife. The fringy types in the little splinter churches are nuts and they scare people, which helps us look moderate to people who think moderation is a virtue. The Army has no leader except Grayson or Phat, and we've got Phat locked up physically and Grayson politically. So I say, for the moment, don't do something. Stand there. But be ready to jump when the time comes."

Peet nodded. "Very much my own thinking. Tribes? Castles?"

"We need the Castles economically, but they're no big problem; we just gradually convert freeholders; ramp up some of that kingship and lordship material if you want to play for them. As for the tribes, the big drive that the Natcon and the general want to do up in the Lost Quarter will take them off the table next spring. Preach so you tie them to the Canaanites, that's our promised land, that kind of thing."

"What's your assessment of your son-in-law?"

"He'll be ready to step in as soon as it's time, if Jenny has anything to do with it. I have much more faith in her than in him. He'll come along as long as we feed his ambition and vanity."

Peet shrugged. "Human tools are imperfect. The Lord Himself only hired twelve guys and one was a dud. So no real change?"

"Everything's the same as last week but more so," Whilmire said. "But it was pretty good last week."

"Indeed." Peet rose and stretched. "I think I'll take a walk."

As Whilmire descended the steps of the former UGA chapel, the sunshine was pure gold, and it hadn't been windy or stormy enough down here yet to take the fall colors from the trees. Real time off was impossible, but at least he could work at a table outside at some café or tea house. So many people were waving, smiling, and calling out "Praise the Lord" to him that he thought he was maybe catching one tiny little glimpse of what heaven might be like.

## ABOUT THE SAME TIME. ATHENS, TNG DISTRICT. 10 AM EST. FRIDAY, OCTOBER 31, 2025.

"Happy Halloween, General Phat."

"Sorry, I'm not stocked up with candy, and I haven't had the time to get into costume. How's it going, Cameron?"

"Meh. Right now the Church and the Army are each hoping the other one will get sick of me first, eliminate me, and leave the more patient one with clean hands. Wish we were—" He saw Phat's hard headshake, and the long piece of toilet paper he held up, scrawled with pencil:

*Guards all changed yesterday, some too friendly, some too quiet, think someone is watching much more closely, assume we are overheard*

"—ah, excuse me," Cam said, coughing loudly. He took a strip of the toilet paper to eat. Phat followed suit. "Let's start on the wine, it's the best thing in my trick-or-treat basket." He washed down the blob of paper with a swallow of wine, watching as Phat did the same. "God, the wine tastes good. And I brought bread and other stuff. I was going to say, wish we were free of all this politics crap, it's a nice day and it would be great to parole you, go hang in the sunlight, and just cry into my beer, or my wine, for a while. It's going to be a relief when they retire me."

"Planning to go peaceably?"

"How else? It's still America. But I'm still the only legitimate authority, and it's my duty to hand off to the Constitutional government, *not* just whatever people in my neighborhood have the most guns, the biggest crowd in the street, or the Holy Zap from Reverend Peet. After I say no, whether it's peaceable or not depends on them, I guess."

They ate the rest of the toilet paper with the bread, thickly spread with butter. When they had finished, and enjoyed some wine-without-paper, Cameron thought, *Well, they already know we talk politics. And we're not going to fool them about what we think. But let's encourage them to think we're all talk and no action.* "I wish I could tell you that you're safe, but if they come for me, I suppose they might come for you."

Phat leaned back and looked at the ceiling. "Look, the bravest American of his generation said, 'A man who won't die for something is not fit to live.'

But down through history, smart soldiers have refused to be the last casualty on the losing side. And you and I are the last of our breed. Whatever the people to come are like, they won't be us. It's not the country, or the army, that we grew up to run. Have you noticed most of them call it *the forces*? when I was a kid, adults called it *the service*. You see? Different world, Cam, just plain different, and our world is fading away."

"You think I should just step down and let whatever happen?"

"I'd never tell a man to run out on what he believed in. What I'm saying is all we can do is give the next version of our country the best start we can, then get out of their way, and try not to let whatever they make of it break our hearts."

**30 MINUTES LATER. ATHENS, TNG DISTRICT. 11:45 AM EST. FRIDAY, OCTOBER 31, 2025.**

Reverend Arthur Peet liked to walk the path in Dudley Park along the North Oconee alone. Most days, he was completely alone on the trail.

Though the paving on the path was slowly coming apart as biotes ate the binding tars. It felt like gummy gravel under his feet. The river was ceaselessly changing and always the same; the fall colors gorgeous; before Daybreak he hadn't realized how much mental energy went into shutting out other people's engines, motors, yakking, and music.

On these walks, whenever he thought of something positive and uplifting, Naomi seemed to appear. Here she was again. Sometimes she would just walk with him for half a mile or more before speaking, or not speak at all, but today the scrawny girl with ash-blonde dreadlocks spoke almost at once. "Do you really think you should call it Tribulation?"

Peet shrugged. "It's the English word for it, and everyone in any Bible-believing church knows what it means."

"I suppose so. But how can you feel Tribulated on such a nice fall day? The colors so bright, the smells and sounds so sharp, and all you have to do is just walk along and listen to your feet swish, swish, swish in the leaves, swish swish swish . . ." She whirled, holding up her ankle-length hippie-girl skirt, dancing up and down the path in front of him. "You know I love our conversations. It's so interesting to meet someone with a different take on Daybreak."

"I'm glad I can help," Peet said.

"I'm glad you can help too." Naomi was back at his side. "And I hope I help you."

"Certainly you help clarify my thoughts."

"Here's a thought I've been working with," she said. "Just a thought. I know that traditionally the idea is that during the Rapture, people vanished because they were good."

"Not necessarily good, as the world knows it, but Christian and believing and trying to be good," Peet said, gently. "Real saints are always messier and always falling out of their sanctity, unlike plaster ones."

"Organic all-natural free-range saints instead of plaztatic saints?"

He laughed. "I would use that in a sermon if 'plaztatic' didn't have such a Daybreak connotation."

"Oh, honestly—you! Should've been an English professor!" She had a provoking half-grin.

He clapped his hand to his chest. "Stabbed through the heart."

She put her hand gently on his arm. "Anyway, my point was, what if the idea is backwards? It's not that the people were good and therefore they were taken away; having been taken away, they became good."

The idea made him feel strangely queasy, as if he'd just swallowed something he shouldn't. "How so? I'm not following."

"Notice how quiet and lovely it is here? Notice how soft both our voices can be and yet we understand each other perfectly? Notice how much of the natural music there is in the air, and how much the world is better since Daybreak?"

"Except," he said, "almost everyone is dead."

"Except or because?"

Before he could ask what she meant, she had disappeared.

Three small boys came around a bend in the trail. They carried cane poles, slingshots, and sharpened sticks; probably they'd be contributing to their families' dinners tonight. Swift and silent, they darted around him and were gone into the brush on the other side.

*Good or dead,* Peet mused. *Or good and dead. Or the only good one's a dead one.* He was sorry Naomi had left so quickly. He'd have liked to talk more. He sat down on a rock and watched the river roll by. When a bird's cry startled him, he sat up with a sense of well-rested contentment. According to his watch, it was past time for lunch.

**1 HOUR LATER. ATHENS, TNG DISTRICT. 1:50 PM EST. FRIDAY, OCTOBER 31, 2025.**

Whilmire recognized that his chief was not going to be swayed from this. A lifetime as an executive assistant and leader's gofer had trained him to surrender gracefully. "Does this change imply any new course, politically?"

Peet looked up across his spectacles. "It's not a change, just a re-emphasis. I don't believe politics has anything to do with it. We need to say publicly that the new world of the Tribulation is a better place to raise and instruct Christians, and thus by their departure, the Christian loved ones who have gone to heaven before us have paved our way to a planet that will become more and more beautiful during Christ's thousand-year reign, which we agree will start in six years. Yes, the idea partakes a little of Stewardship Christianity, but honestly, Reverend Whilmire, did you never go walking in the woods yourself? And let's be honest here too; the tribals have souls as much as we do, and the tribes have been sliding into a weird, crude paganism. We can leave their souls to perish—or we can meet them on common ground, about mutually important concerns, and perhaps get the access to win them for Christ. I have not seen an asterisk next to any of Christ's promises, with a note at the bottom of the page saying *except former Daybreakers*. So we will shape our message to the situation; so did Saint Paul and for that matter so did Jesus."

*This one's going to be a tough sell to Grayson,* Whilmire thought, walking back to his quarters. *But the old man is right. Grayson may thrash around some, but he'll slither over to our side soon enough.*

# F I F T E E N :
# PINK BOYS IN BIRTHDAY SHROUDS

"I wish to God that Terry Bolton would knock off the jokes about trick-or-treaters," Dave Carlucci said to Arlene. "I also wish you'd take a less dangerous position."

When Arlene had married him, he had already been with the FBI for two years; now, nineteen years later, she knew more than he did about how his mind worked. "Hon," she said, "do you want to review everything we decided in the last week, or do you want to get ready?"

"You know I—"

"Terry cracks bad jokes, repetitively, when he's waiting to go into action. You second-guess every previous decision. As for where I'm going to be, I'll be as far inside the building as is possible, so my chances of getting hit by stray fire are zip, especially since the tribals have spears, slings, and bows and all the gunfire will be going out, not in. If they manage to get into the building it will only be because all of you are dead. I'm a lousy shot but I'll shoot at them to keep them off my patients, who I wouldn't leave behind anyway, because I'm a nurse, dammit, and you Feds are not the only people in the world who take your jobs seriously. If I end up dying, I'll be one of the last to go, and everyone else will be gone too."

"Annie and Paley—"

"She wants to be called Acey, remember? She's been telling you for more than a year. They're good shots, they'll be high up, they're smart enough to make something up if something goes wrong, they'll be fine. Now, go worry about something else, or recheck everything one more time, or make up some new material for Terry."

"Everything's ready for our little trick-or-treaters," Terry said. "Gosh, I hope we get lots of the little rascals."

"Please," Arlene added, quietly, to Carlucci, and despite himself, he smiled.

. . .

Shadows were short in the bright, overhead moonlight. Acey Carlucci retied her do-rag more tightly, to keep her black curly hair from escaping, and rechecked everything on her Newberry Standard by feel. She lay on a thick old truck cargo pad, under a heavy wool blanket against the chill, and waited, watching the alley directly across the street; the concrete facing, all the way up the first storey, made it a perfect sniper's backdrop. When the dark silhouette moved across it, her hands found the right places on her rifle as her hands, eye, sight, and target aligned; her breath stopped, the rifle was perfectly still, she squeezed the trigger, and as the smoke cleared, she saw the man lying on the pavement. The next one rushed, low, but she didn't hurry her shot, and he fell over at a broken angle, dragging himself by his hands.

Really, it wasn't much different from deer or wild cattle; you pulled a trigger, they went over.

She focused on the alley. Off to the side she could hear Paley's first shot, and then another. She glanced toward the street he was covering; just one down, crawling toward the shadows. *Poor Paley,* she thought, *he's an okay shot but it kills him that I'm better.* She watched her assigned alley and waited for another target.

. . .

Paley thought, *If I puke, I will never hear the end of it. Keep watching. Another one will pop out any second now.* He breathed deep; the tribal he'd shot—twice because he didn't go down the first time—was crawling toward the shadow, maybe for cover, maybe because he was hurt so bad that even the moonlight was too much for him?

Paley wished he could shoot again to put the man out of his misery, but the rules Dad had laid down were firm: no shooting the wounded who weren't fighting and couldn't escape—they were all wanted for interrogation.

Another figure in the moonlit street.

He didn't let himself hesitate; if he did, he might never shoot again. He solved the abstract problem and pulled the trigger. The figure lay as if sprawled out to look at the stars.

He could feel his face was wet. *I am so not the right guy for this.*

. . .

Harrison Castro waited with three hundred of his best guard, weapons already drawn and ready, half a mile from the FBI "compound," if you could dignify a decaying office building that way. They were formed up in long rows; he'd spent a while explaining that to the tribal war leaders. He had said that in this formation, they'd be able to keep up with the tribals and lay down covering fire during the final assault on FBI headquarters. Castro's men, and a few women, handpicked and utterly loyal to him, waited in perfect stillness; he knew they would do exactly what he had ordered, when it was time. The waxing moon crept from the zenith toward the sea, silhouetting the strange mixture of hats and robes in the tribal crowd downhill from Castro's men.

The plan was that a runner from the tribal war leaders was to bring the starting message to Castro. Two minutes after the messenger signaled that Castro had been alerted, and was ready, the massed tribals below would hit the FBI headquarters in a human wave with Castro's men trotting at their heels. His guards would pick off defending snipers, overwhelm the doors with concentrated fire to clear the way for the final assault on the building, and then follow them in to help in mopping up.

Harrison Castro had formulated the plan, but that had not stopped the war leaders from each taking a turn explaining it to him at great length, again and again, while he held his tongue; he knew that explaining it to him was important to their self-esteem or some such woo-woo crap.

There was a small scattering of shots; the "handpicked elite" from the Awakening Dolphin Children must not have been as invisible in their rush as they'd thought they'd be. Castro waited, and sure enough, in a couple of minutes a message-runner appeared in the bright moonlight, headed for him.

"Get ready," he said to his troops. "This is going to be it."

They had been ready anyway; in the long breath as the runner approached, they became poised, taut with eagerness. Below, the tribals milled about with unfocused energy and nervous excitement, and the war leaders shoved and kicked at them, keeping them in place.

The runner approached. "Earl Castro, sir, our scouts report that our advance attackers have been intercepted, and we—"

The boom was terrifyingly loud as Castro shot the man in the chest at point-blank range. On that cue, the guards, already formed into rows for volley fire, fired their first volley; the second followed within a long breath, and the third. Backlit in the bright moonlight, with nowhere to go, the tribals were hit with a dozen volleys in less than a minute. At Castro's command, his troops advanced down the hill, killing the seriously wounded, handcuffing or hog-tying everyone else, and marking those with treatable wounds so the medics could find them.

. . .

When Dave Carlucci heard the volleys roaring out up above, he blew his whistle; his small force moved to its second set of firing positions, and in less than a minute he began to hear the occasional claps of his snipers picking off fleeing tribals, ensuring that the few who ran away successfully would keep running for a long time, panicking many back into the arms of Castro's troops, and leaving some dead or dying in the street.

At the sound of the bugle from Castro's force, he blew his own whistle three times, and heard the calls back from everyone; they had ceased firing, they knew the forces now approaching were friendly. *And there were twenty-two of them; everyone checked in. No losses on our side.*

It was the first time Carlucci enjoyed shaking Castro's hand; they agreed to talk the next day, and Castro made it a lunch invitation.

As Carlucci walked around his now-much-more-secure HQ, he looked in at the infirmary; Arlene had seventy tribals in there, mostly being tended and guarded by forces Castro had left behind. Carlucci waved at Arlene and was about to get out of the way when he realized who was working right next to him, applying pressure to stop a girl from bleeding to death through her shattered arm. "Paley!"

"Hey, Dad. Mom said I could help here, and I couldn't sleep anyway, so here I am. Just trying to keep Avril alive. Least I could do, I guess, since I shot her."

Carlucci paused and peered at his son; underneath his deep outdoor tan, the young man was pale, as if he'd been wounded himself. "That sounds like her real name, not her tribal one. Did you know her?"

"She was in my high school. I guess I'm glad I didn't kill her." He looked at his father, shyly, obviously trying not to sound defiant. "Dad, I think I want to be a doctor or a nurse or something in medicine. I feel like I could work here for a week without sleep if it would save Avril, or anyone else, but . . . when I was shooting—"

With his thumb, Carlucci smoothed the tears down his son's cheeks. "You know, it's a *good* thing we're not all born killers, Paley. If it's what you want to do with your life, we'll find some way for you to do it. And to tell you the truth, I'll be pretty happy if you're always busier than me." He wiped Paley's tears again, and blotted with his handkerchief. "Now do what your mother tells you, because she's the best and you'll want to learn it right."

### THE NEXT DAY. CASTLE CASTRO (SAN DIEGO, CALIFORNIA). 12:15 PM PST. SATURDAY, NOVEMBER 1, 2025.

When they had finished the meal, Carlucci asked, "Aren't you afraid of being killed?"

"Sure, isn't everyone?" Castro looked surprised at the question. "But I'm in about as safe a place as I could be—after that guy sneaked in we did some serious purging, and I not only know how he got in, I know a few other ways he could have. Those are all plugged now, and my best people are going to be looking, all the time, for people who are trying to find new ones. Meanwhile, the tribes in the area just took another ass-kicking, and the Tempers and Provis are both promising to reinforce you. For the moment, we have them on the run."

"And about the Constitutional issues?"

"You're not going to disarm me, or even try, because you're not crazy. And if you think I'm hard to deal with, wait'll you try Bambi."

"Actually, your daughter and I have always gotten along."

Castro shrugged. "Ever tried to tell her no?"

"Uh, no, she's always been right."

"As long as you keep believing that, you'll be fine." He stood. "Dave, I really did just want to have lunch with you and work on developing a friendship. I know there wasn't much business to do today, except to agree to be civil about whatever either of us has to do later on. You're welcome for the help in smashing the tribes and, while I'm not going to comply with your court order, I will try not to rub your nose in my defiance any more than necessary. I need to run to another meeting, which I will not enjoy nearly as much as this, so before you go, I have to hurry up and cover just one more thing on my agenda." He handed him a thick manila envelope. "This is everything, absolutely everything, from our investigation of that Daybreaker that broke in and threatened me. I'll send you updates regularly. Keep it on file."

"Life insurance?"

"Sort of. More like revenge insurance. I don't think anyone will fuck with me successfully, but if they do, I want something or someone to be on their tail. You strike me as the type that doesn't give up a pursuit, Mister Carlucci."

Returning to his suite, Harrison Castro reflected that if Carlucci had asked, he'd probably have admitted the surprising truth: aside from his rage at having a bunch of mind-controlled bush hippies trying to order him around, aside from finally grasping that the tribes would always be more dangerous to him than the Federal government, aside from his unwillingness to see people he despised slaughter people he respected, there was an overriding consideration: he had discovered that he *didn't* want to overthrow the Constitution, or put the Feds out of business, or anything else he'd been saying he wanted since . . . *jeez, since the Clinton Administration. Pure case of being careful what you wish for.*

He just needed to change his shirt before his meeting with his tech advisors; he knew his perfect valet would have everything laid out on the bed.

Inside his suite, he opened the bedroom door and found his valet lying on his back, blood pooling around him, his throat slashed open. He had half a moment to think *not again* and *it can't be* as the bag of feathers went over his head, and he did manage to kick his opponent in the shin this time, and shoulder him against the wall, but neither made the man—*the same one?* Castro wondered, through the rising panic of not being able to get enough air—neither made him—let go.

*Let go.* Castro fought the man, his grip, the bag, everything, with all he had, but the man was forcing Castro's hands behind his back. Castro twisted and turned, jumped and jerked, but nothing freed him. It was even more impossible to breathe in here than it had been last time, and he was swiftly running out of air. Tasting bitter shame, he tapped the man, signaling that he would talk.

The man grabbed his little fingers and pressed them the wrong way. Castro tried to gasp for air, involuntarily, and only pulled in a few feathers that set him trying to cough with air that he didn't have. The terrible pressure on his wrists drove him forward, and then to the side, stumbling on something slick.

His bound hands were forced upward behind him, and the cuffs were tied to something.

He knew where he was, now, but it did him no good.

His bound hands were tied to the showerhead behind him. The man turned the shower on, all the way hot. Scalding water poured over and through the cloth bag, into the feathers, blocking his last fresh air; smothering, drowning, and cooking him in the water, steam, and feathers; turning his cough into wracking spasms. The feathers held the hot water against his scalp and face, burning the soft flesh deep red. After far too long the darkness of the bag merged into the darkness of his mind.

**THE NEXT DAY. HERKIMER, NEW YORK. 4:30 PM EST. SUNDAY, NOVEMBER 2, 2025.**

The little park where the Mohawk split off from the Erie Canal had a nice old log building. A small sign told them where to call to rent it; a bronze plaque said

VETERANS LODGE
CONSTRUCTED IN MEMORY OF THE 1,131 VICTIMS
OF THE ATTACK ON USS *FRANKLIN ROOSEVELT*, CVN-81
ON 4 MAY 2022
HERKIMER VETERANS LEAGUE REMEMBERS.

Below that, in smaller letters, there was a list of wars, beginning with Vietnam and running up through Iran II. "Folks were patriotic out here," Chris observed. "Looks like they didn't get anyone from Grenada, Bosnia, or Guyana, though."

"Maybe those were the vets that just weren't joiners," Larry said. "Wonder if the chimney's clean enough to chance a fire?" He went to the fireplace and peered upward. "Fresh swept. Figures. Every vet's group I was ever in, some super-responsible volunteer would do something or other perfectly. I don't know his name but I can picture some quiet guy who just decided the vet's lodge chimney would get swept every fall." A shadow crossed his face. "We lost a few of those in every little town."

Jason nodded. "Along with great scoutmasters and first-rate piano teachers and people who repainted their city halls or changed the flowers in the public gardens. And we also lost whole cities full of them. But if I let my Daybreak mind slip back into my head, I see them as fat self-satisfied slobs who needed to die for thinking that all that stuff they tried to do was important, when only our duty to the Earth really matters. In one of my poems I wrote

'No one has the right to read Auden out loud while
there is one car running anywhere
Do not fool people into thinking that anyone
can put goodness into the air.'

"For all I know they're still quoting it, and the goal is to be quoting it when no one knows who Auden was, or what a car was."

Chris shrugged. "You never know what words will live, if any. More than one writer has written the war cry of his deadliest enemy."

"Was that a poem? Are you quoting something?"

"No, I'm just tired, which makes me melodramatic. Part of why I'd rather work on paper—later, when I'm not tired, I take squishy crap like that out and replace it with rock-hard bare-boned facts. Anyway, let's start that fire and block off the windows while we still have light to do it."

"Volunteering for fire duty: Chris Manckiewicz," Larry said. "Jason, let's find towels or something around to cover those windows with. Once Chris has his fire going, we'll need to see how much smoke it sends up, but right now there's enough wind to shred it before it goes too high."

The sun had not quite set when they were snug inside. Hot Spam and beans, eaten at a table, tasted much better than the cold version under a canoe. Sweet potatoes cooked in the opened can was very nearly a real dessert. After dinner, Larry spread out the maps to show them the path. "From here on out it's down the Mohawk, and the descent is steep. Busted dams, washed out levees, fallen bridges, God knows what. It won't be rafting the Colorado, exactly, but it's going to be a rougher ride than anything we've done so far."

They all had another round of warm food, taking turns reading aloud from the copy of *Nostromo* that Jason had brought from the senior center. Jason and Larry sacked out close to the fire, and Chris took the first watch, scribbling in his pad, trying to explain just how dead and empty it was up here, wondering how many synonyms for "nothing," "lost," and "gone" there were, and if they'd be enough.

# SIXTEEN:
# TURNING THE NAVIES UPWARD
# ON THEIR HEELS

There was no hope of keeping it secret in the relaxed discipline of an extremely prolonged voyage. CVN-77, *George HW Bush*, the last remaining nuclear carrier in the Navy and on Earth, had always been like a floating small town, and now it was a floating small town with nanoswarm. Everyone knew that at least a day before it was official.

Yet until the captain made the announcement, in the crew's hearts the great ship was not really walking dead, even though everyone knew that all the carriers which had come down with nanoswarm, no matter how hard their crews had worked to save them, had been dead in less than a month.

When he emerged and stood on the dais before the assembled crew, many were already crying. He braced himself and said the key word first, afraid he might not be able to say any more before breaking down himself: "Savannah. We're going home to Savannah."

But then his heart returned enough to say, "Most of you are from the continental USA, so at least we'll be getting you where you can walk home. Savannah has decent rail service to Athens, which is connected to all the TNG-controlled part of the country, with links to the central states, the PCG area, and California.

"With less need to conserve our remaining fuel and aircraft parts, as we pass within range of Africa, South America, and eventually our homes, we'll be flying off reconnaissance missions, preserving as much data as we can about the changing world. So we'll be busy with an important scientific and geographic mission right to the end, and I want to remind you all that until we put you ashore at Savannah, you're still in the Navy or the Marines, and I—and the people of the United States—expect you to do your duty to the utmost."

Minutes later, her great turbines thundering, *Bush* pointed her prow west, toward the Cape of Good Hope, and drove across the placid Indian Sea. In the next few days, everyone seemed to spend as much time as they could on deck, enjoying the spring weather, and just saying good-bye.

## 2 DAYS LATER. RUINS OF WATERFORD, NEW YORK. 12:15 PM EST. FRIDAY, NOVEMBER 7, 2025.

The passage down the Mohawk had been no worse than unpleasant and tiring, with some long portages around wrecked locks and dams, and a couple of fireless nights, but they had only seen three signs of Daybreak since the hanged bodies on the bridge: two bridges surrounded by trampled mud and snow where large bands must have passed, and one fortified farmhouse where the condition of the bodies piled outside suggested it had been sacked just before the big snowstorm.

From Buffalo, past Oneida, and for most of the way down the Mohawk, the biggest living animals had been spiders, and grass and moss were the only green; the radiation-killed trees and bushes had put out no leaves last spring.

But the previous day, they had seen traces of living things reclaiming the empty, dead land. The Chicago superbomb had been pure fusion, so the radioactive isotopes in the fallout were nearly all light-metal salts produced by neutron irradiation of the vaporized city. The ferocious, life-erasing energy of those isotopes also gave them short half-lives; the fallout had been far more deadly in the short run than the fission-fragment fallout from an "old school" atom bomb, but there had been less of it and it had decayed to harmlessness much faster.

Today, nearing Albany, the river contained more junk, but it had also broken through flood control in so many places that even its central channel was broad and comparatively sluggish; they found the Lock 6 dams still standing.

"We could walk to the Hudson in less than an hour from where we are," Chris pointed out.

Larry shrugged. "But then we'd have to keep walking. There's a perfectly good river over that way, and perfectly good canoes here, so I figure we'll paddle up to Lock 6, portage around that chain of locks, and canoe down to Peebles Island. We've been seeing living trees all morning, and that squirrel came from somewhere and has been eating something. So we're out of the worst of the fallout belt. If there are non-tribal people up here, they're trading, because that's what civilized people do, and if they're trading anywhere it'll be at Peebles Island, because it sits between the Mohawk, the Erie Canal, and the Hudson." Larry shrugged and stretched. "And whether we make contact with anyone there or not, I'd rather ride than walk for the rest of the trip."

Chris stood, rotated his trunk, and swung his arms in circles. "Well, I guess it won't get any easier for waiting."

A canal-side exercise trail with long flights of stairs made it easy to descend the four locks by lowering first the canoes, then their packs, on ropes alongside the closed lock gate.

They paddled past the empty warehouses and little houses, with yards full of junk, that had been run down long before Daybreak, and on across the slow-moving outlet of the Erie Canal, catching their first sight of the broad Hudson beyond the tip of Peebles Island.

Down here, many trees had some leaves clinging to them, which probably meant they had been green in the summer and were not dead, and as the early fall evening crept over the Hudson, they saw splashes of fish jumping.

On Peebles Island, they beached just upstream of a trestle bridge and carried the canoes up the bank. Rabbits broke from the snow-patched, thick brown grass. After weeks of seeing so little life, the long back legs kicking away, and the bouncing powder-puff tails were more miraculous than unicorns.

"I still wouldn't eat one," Jason said, "but at least they're here and alive."

Chris said, "It looks like the grass was growing all summer; I don't think your trade fair has—"

"Sail!"

They looked where Jason was pointing.

The boat coming round the point of Peebles Island was about three times the size of *Kelleys Dancer*, with a much taller mast. Jason ran forward onto the beach, waving and yelling; someone in the crow's nest waved back, and presently the boat took down its sails, dropped anchor, and lowered a small rowboat.

They walked down to meet it. The man who sat in the bow, hollering at the imperturbable rowers, had deep brown skin, close-cropped white hair, and a little white goatee hanging from his upper lip like a cocoon. He wore big wire-rimmed glasses, a billed cap tied closed with twine to replace its lost plastic strap, several layers of sweaters, and bell-bottomed canvas pants; he seemed to be on the brink of laughing out loud.

The rowboat drew near. The big man threw Jason a painter; he tied it off to a small tree, and in the gathering dusk, they all shook hands. "Jamayu Rollings," the big man said. "Captain and owner of the schooner *Ferengi*, and these are my sons, Geordie Rollings and Whorf Rollings. We've been on a trading and salvage expedition up to Troy, and we were going to put in for the night here."

"Larry Mensche, Chris Manckiewicz, and Jason Nemarec, Reconstruction Research Center. We're a scientific expedition, overland traverse of the Erie Canal route."

"Hunh. Well, that'll cause some conversation in Manbrookstat. You guys wouldn't be looking for anything to trade, or maybe for a ride, would you?"

Larry nodded. "We could be. We're right where we were ordered to be; from here on, how we get home is up to us. You mean you have room somewhere for three passengers?"

"Room and then some for three *paying* passengers."

"Is the credit of the U.S. government good enough for you?"

"Can you prove you have it?"

"I have letters from the RRC in Pueblo, the TNG at Athens, and the PCG in Olympia."

"Hunh. I don't have any way to confirm any of those, do I?"

"You could trust our honest demeanor and smiling faces."

"I've been trading for a while now. I wouldn't trust my mother if she offered me a free Thanksgiving dinner."

Larry noted that both boys were rolling their eyes.

"Well, then, perhaps we're stuck."

"Maybe, maybe not. You wouldn't happen to have any trade goods?"

"How do you define those? All we've got is our gear, which we need to keep if we're going to travel, plus our two canoes and a couple big bags of canned goods." Larry saw the flicker of attention from the two boys, and said, "How about passage for the three of us if we let you have the canoes? We won't need them any longer, and good aluminum canoes can't be all that common in New York Harbor just yet."

"What's in the cans?"

"We've got baked beans, sweet potatoes, peas, salmon—"

Both the boys looked like they'd been poisoned.

"You won't be able to give the salmon away. Manbrookstat eats fish three meals a day. But how many of those beans and yams you got?"

They settled on both canoes, and five cans each of baked beans, peas, and sweet potatoes. For his part, Jamayu threw in full meals while on board, and oil for a stove and a lamp in their cabin. "You'll probably only be on board two nights, anyway," he assured them. "Tonight, and then one farther downstream somewhere."

An hour after coming ashore to contemplate a cold, uncomfortable camp, they found themselves sitting down to fresh grilled fish at the captain's table of the *Ferengi*, and in celebration of having someone to drink with, he even gave everyone a small, free shot of pre-Daybreak brandy.

After dinner, that night, Jason went up on deck for some air; he could tell that the closet-sized cabin was going to be stuffy, *not to mention that I'm in there with two old guys who've been eating a couple cans of baked beans a day for more than a week; I don't think I ever really grasped the expression "old fart" before now.*

As he sat in the bow, Whorf Rollings joined him; the two sat together quietly for a while. Finally Whorf said, "You're from Pueblo? Where they broadcast from? The people that ran WTRC?"

"Yep. I've got a wife there with a kid on the way."

"Suppose a guy was pretty smart and wanted to work hard, but kind of showed up with nothing. Would there be a place for him there?"

"Yeah, I'm pretty sure there would."

"Just thinking." Whorf leaned back and sighed. "Here I am crew on

Pop's big stupid boat that he worked all his life to buy and that we all made fun of."

"Yeah, what is it about old poops and boats? My family sailed all the freakin' time. Snob appeal, you know? I mean, we were from Connecticut—oh, God, were we *ever* from Connecticut—and my dad was just a sales manager for a medium-sized electronics firm, but he wanted me and my brother to be full-bore—and I do mean *bore*—preppies."

Whorf was laughing. "Tell me about it. Pop was a dentist. Our older sister Deanna wanted him to call this boat either the *Root Canal* or the *Gold Crown*." They sat silently for a long while; then Whorf asked, "You okay?"

"Just remembering I used to avoid trips to New York because the folks were always reminding me they could take the train down from Connecticut and meet me. And now . . . well, they're probably not even alive. And they've got a grandchild on the way, and I'd give anything to see them and talk to them."

"Hunh. In two days I'm going to be in Mom's kitchen, listening to Pop tell lies about this trip and . . . well. Some of us don't know when we're lucky."

"If you come on out, ever, it's lucky to be in Pueblo too. There's always a spare bed for anyone who will work. And there's definitely always work. Just don't come the way I did; there's got to be an easier path, even if you have to take the boat to Morgan City."

They chatted idly till the night river chill set in. Jason went below. The tiny cabin was dry and warm from the oil stove, and his two companions were stretched out on their bunks, reading by the overhead oil lamp. Chris said, "We eat breakfast with the second shift, so we're getting at least ten hours of uninterrupted sleep. Soapy water bucket on the left side of the oil stove, and warm rinse water in the other one, and we left you a clean dry towel."

As Jason cleaned up, trying, in the narrow space, not to cast shadows on their reading or burn his buttocks on the stove, he thought to ask Larry, "How did you know to do all that bargaining with Captain Rollings to get a good deal?"

"Because his sloop is named *Ferengi*, his sons have the names they do, and . . ." He sighed. "One of those things where you had to be there. Went off the air when I was ten."

Jason was too sleepy, and not curious enough, to pursue the question further. As soon as he was dry, he snuffed the oil lamp, climbed into his bunk, and was barely conscious long enough to relish the feel of clean sheets on bare skin.

## DURING THE SAME DAY. CASTLE CASTRO (SAN DIEGO, CALIFORNIA). 10 AM PST. FRIDAY, NOVEMBER 7, 2025.

The waste of it all seemed obscene to Bambi; they had used precious electricity in one of the few places that had it reliably to run an even more precious freezer, just to keep her father's body in condition for this memorial. Then Bambi and Quattro had taken one of the few precious airplanes the United States had to fly here for this memorial, in part so that she could claim her father's inheritance and declare herself Freeholder of Castle Castro, Earl of San Diego, and Leader of the League of South Coast Castles. *And Daddy was right, damn him, there is now every likelihood that Quattro and I will be having the future Duke of California. Or Duchess. Have to tell Quattro that there's not going to be any stupid rules about boys first in* my *absolute monarchy.*

More waste as she threw the big feast to feed all of Daddy's vassals and their households (at least there weren't quite so many of those, since everyone left big forces back at their Castles, with so much recent tribal activity). Even more in the salutes and flourishes, speeches and pomp, as a few thousand people didn't do any useful work for a couple of days. *Daddy, if you had to set up your own little world to run, why couldn't you have been a Stalinist? We'd've been done in ten minutes and everybody'd be happy with their black bread and potato soup.*

Then the long meetings with the vassals, being applauded for changing their conditions of fealty to the same generous ones that Quattro used for the North Coast Castles. Then the endless meetings with stewards in which she told them to keep things running well and she'd be back as often as she could, and that she was sure that anyone who had her father's confidence would do a fine job. *And have the patience of a saint, and be somewhere near perfect, because you were pretty damned hard on help that wasn't, eh, Daddy? But at least I'm safe assuming these people know their jobs and will do them.*

And after that, the long meeting with Carlucci and Bolton in which her old, trusted friends apologized over and over for not preventing what no one could have foreseen, and discussed their efforts to find the holes in Castle Castro's security and the confederates in her father's murder. *Any other time it would be so soothing to just talk cop talk with these guys; now I have to put all this energy into assuring them I trust them to do the right thing and don't blame them for what happened, and make myself pay attention because later on I'll want to remember all this. And not keep thinking* Daddy *when they say* the victim. *I wonder how long there is to go?*

It was past midnight when Bambi Castro could finally curl up next to her husband, put her face on his chest, and just let herself cry because Daddy was dead, and she was going to miss him forever, and she hadn't been ready to say good-bye. It was much later than that when she finally fell asleep.

## 2 DAYS LATER. MANBROOKSTAT HEADQUARTERS (IN THE FORMER BATTERY GARDENS, NEW YORK CITY). 12:20 PM EST. SUNDAY, NOVEMBER 9, 2025.

"If there'd been any natives here to bargain with," the Commandant was saying, "I probably could have gotten it for twenty-four dollars, though not in beads. Canned hams, that would've been a deal in a second. But almost everyone was dead by the time we got here; we have six thousand people now, but only maybe four hundred were from Brooklyn before Daybreak, five hundred from Staten Island, and less than fifty from Manhattan. And the ones we have didn't ride it out here in the city. Most of them sheltered over on Long Island or New Jersey someplace, but they were just such compulsive New Yorkers that they came back as soon as the city stopped burning and the Hudson stopped running radioactive. I'm real glad to have them, though—they had to be tough and clever to do what they did, and what would New York be without New Yorkers?"

"Aren't you calling it Manbrookstat now?" Jason asked.

"It'll be New York ten generations after I'm dead. And the inhabitants will still be known for talking too fast, hustling too hard, and telling everyone else what to do in an accent that sounds like a duck using nasal floss." The Commandant himself had a soft Maryland accent; he was younger than Jason, with movie-actor good looks, and dressed beautifully in what Jason thought of as Latin American Fascist Rococo.

He seemed immensely proud of the settlement surrounding the Upper Bay. *But then ensuring food and shelter for everyone in Manbrookstat is bragging material,* Jason reminded himself. And by all accounts it was the Commandant's iron determination that had put everyone who could do it last spring to fishing; to digging up golf courses to plant potatoes; to going overland to the west to trade for living pigs, sheep, and goats and turning them loose in Central Park; and to building greenhouses and coldframes in every open space.

*Manbrookstat* was a composite of Manhattan, Brooklyn, and Staten Island; the name was already unfair, because the settled area was really a sliver of Bayonne, extreme lower Manhattan, Brooklyn facing the bay, and the shore side of Staten Island.

"I know Pueblo had no idea you had anything like this here, and I'm sure Olympia didn't either."

The Commandant didn't so much shrug as twitch a shoulder impatiently. "The TNG knows we exist because we trade loot south to them, but I doubt they know much about us. Right now, most ships come in from Argentina."

"What do they trade?"

"They bring in canned beef, and you can't imagine how much people here want that. In their spare time, our people dig out copper pipe, aluminum siding, and heavy-gauge wire from all those empty buildings, and mostly it goes for canned beef. The Argies cheat us but nobody cares. At Savannah or Charleston, they offload all the junk we sell them, because the factories around Castle Newberry are screaming for raw materials, and will pay for metal with corn whiskey and tobacco. Liquor and tobacco trade for coffee in Colombia, and the Argies go back rich as kings."

"They're canning beef in Kansas right now," Jason pointed out.

"Find a way to get it to us. Long before the Dead Belt runs out of minable junk, we'll be making stuff good enough to sell—a bunch of the artisans have already got some good-sized looms running, and we have a couple old chem professors, a sculptor, and two blacksmiths working on making iron and steel."

The Commandant had been a senior at West Point; after the Chicago and Washington superbombs, he had led the cadets who chose to stay at the Academy through that terrible winter, with nearly half of them surviving. In early April they had come downstream to claim the best harbor in the world.

When Captain Rollings had introduced them, the Commandant and Jason had hit it off, and since Larry had some particular business with the TNG trading agent in town, as well as arranging passage, and Chris wanted to put together a long piece for the *Post-Times*, that left Jason to socialize with the Commandant, who seemed to be eager to show off his city.

"One reason you didn't know we were here," he said, "is that we're going very, very slowly with radio—we have so many wires and pipes still out there, an EMP would still cause fires everywhere, which would burn inward from the abandoned part of the city and get us here. That's why I limited your boss Larry to sending 150 words, and to one acknowledgment for one message back. Besides, even if the moon gun doesn't take an interest in us, it's better not to have any extra attention from the rival governments. We don't want to become a prize for the Provis and the Tempers to fight over." He gestured north toward the fire-gutted skyscrapers, then around them to the shantytown in what had been Battery Park. "If we're lucky, by 2050, we'll have grown back to Canal Street, maybe even to Houston. The last thing we want to do is get into a war between Georgia and Washington State, about anything, on either side. Right now, whether or not the quarrel between Olympia and Athens is America's business, it's just *not* Manbrookstat's."

Larry booked passage on an Argentine trader, the *Martin Fierro*, sailing the next morning. If there was anything suspicious about the quickness of the arrangement, or the early sailing time, Jason figured that the Commandant was entitled to his paranoia.

*Martin Fierro* was a rusty old bucket whose engineer had installed a restored coal-fired steam engine from a museum; to save coal, she traveled under sail whenever possible.

Dawn the next morning found them passing Miss Liberty, webbed with scars from the EMPs that had caused currents in her copper skin; some streaks had re-smelted in place, creating new-penny copper bands on her; some had blackened as the old corrosion oxidized. "Something between camo and a leopard print," Chris said. "The white trash version of Miss Liberty—"

"You can shut up now," Larry said, walking away.

Jason, sensing that it would be a great time to be invisible, went up near the bow to read *Nostromo* and watch for dolphins; the Commandant had said the harbor was full of them.

The sun was full up as they passed through the Narrows. The crew banked the fires and hoisted the sails, and *Martin Fierro* made a wide, slow turn, heading south.

*Chris is irritating sometimes,* Jason thought, *but Larry's usually easygoing. And this was the first chance he got to communicate with the RRC since Put-in-Bay. I wonder if I want to know what's eating him.*

Then he looked up to see dolphins playing in front of the ship, pulled out pen and paper, and added another couple paragraphs to his long letter to Beth. He'd mail it in Savannah, and he might get home before it did, but so what? The half dozen leaping, splashing dolphins were the kind of thing a man shares with his wife and his kid, and this was the only way to do it right now.

# SEVENTEEN: WHAT NONE COULD HEAR

Jeffrey Grayson was not a man to feel normal sneaking around. When he was out in public, he liked to be seen, and he seldom did anything he didn't want people to see.

But this was important, and he had no other choice. His office was one door from Cameron Nguyen-Peters's office, so he couldn't very well have one of Phat's guards reporting to him there. He couldn't plausibly slip over to the guards' break room for a conversation while visiting Phat in prison, because he couldn't plausibly visit Phat: the two had openly loathed each other for more than a decade before Daybreak. Besides, Grayson saw no reason to provoke Phat into repeating that story that he'd always feared.

So Jeffrey Grayson had cultivated a habit of going for a run in mid-afternoon, occasionally mentioning that that was when solar-heated water for a shower was apt to be at its most available, and letting people figure that an older man with a hot young wife is motivated to stay in shape. On his off days, Porter Perkins, the guard, would sometimes be fishing off a bridge in Dudley Park, along Grayson's usual route. Whether Perkins was at the bridge or not, Grayson always stopped to bend over, hands on his knees, and breathe hard.

Today, Perkins, without moving his eyes from the North Oconee below, said, "They talk sometimes while they play chess. Low voices and heads down so you can't read their lips or hear them too good. But they forget that the table's by the wall, and the wall is thin. So I've been hearing some back and forth, and it sounds like that Phat one might be catching a flight, late November."

"Where to?"

"The place where the other one has a long-distance affair going. And it sounds like there's a price; if he rides now, he's gotta run later."

Grayson stood, braced his hands on the stone railing, and pushed down into a hamstring stretch he didn't need any more than he needed breathing time. Face toward the stones, he asked, "So any idea what the one that isn't Phat is getting out of all this?"

"Probably he just thinks it's a Nguyen-win situation," Perkins said.

Grayson never timed himself, but he suspected that the anger pushing him through the remaining hills probably fueled a personal best. There had not been enough sun that morning, either, so the shower was first luke-warm, then suddenly cold, excusing his furious scream.


**THE NEXT DAY. ATHENS, TNG DISTRICT. 10:45 AM EST.
THURSDAY, NOVEMBER 13, 2025.**

Cam and Grayson always forced themselves to finish their Thursday morning meeting by looking through the graphs in the last folder, "ongoing statistics." The intel clerks added new data points as they came in and drew connecting lines on the master graphs; the analysts traced them, worked out a fitted curve with adding machines and slide rules, and drew the curve on their tracings. Cam and Grayson turned to the graphs for a sobering dose of reality.

This week, only three bad things were decreasing: uncontrolled wide-area fires, dam bursts, and bridge collapses. Cam grimaced. "Even that's not good news—we're just running out of unburned urban areas, standing dams, and functioning bridges."

"I'm afraid so. The only upward trend in a good category is that the food-supply-to-demand ratio is trending up—because dead people don't eat." General Grayson tapped the last graph. "*That's* the hard one to face."

The graph showed the size, frequency, and damage from tribal raids; the size of the military response; and the estimated damage to the tribes. For the eighth week in a row, the tribes had raided more, with bigger forces, and done more damage. Responding armed forces were bigger but winning less. "If the RRC has the tribes figured out, their goal is a high death toll on both sides—and how do you beat that? By the time our troops get there, the tribals have already gotten most of what they want, and nothing in the world can deter them, if Pueblo is right."

Grayson forced himself to say, "There's a Pueblo issue we should consider."

"Yes?"

"It's my belief . . . sir. Um. I have ample evidence that you are planning to assist General Phat in escaping to Pueblo, and you're working with the top leadership at the RRC to do that."

Cam had no expression. "Obviously there would be no point in my lying to you about it now. Would you like to know why I am doing it?"

Grayson's lips compressed and he looked down. "I *do* know why you're doing it. I *understand* that you are trying to get the United States back together, Cameron, one nation indivisible, all of that. I understand that I'm not the ideal candidate."

"That was a pretty good rally when you came into Pueblo, and not a bad one when you left, the last time."

Grayson shrugged uncomfortably. "I'm sure you know the welcome rally at the airport was orchestrated by the Post Raptural Church. They even cheered for Reverend Whilmire, and he's *painfully* dull."

"I suppose a son-in-law would know. But the send-off at the train station was real enough."

"Oh, it was real. Just most of them were there to cheer for you and Graham Weisbrod, for promising to bring their country back. They were cheering for me too, but mainly because I wasn't being in the way." He gripped his own elbows, like a small boy stubbornly insisting on his feelings when the whole adult world is telling him he feels something else. "I understand why Phat is better for your purposes than I am. You need a president who isn't a regional candidate, someone who gets votes all over. And . . . well, it's childish, but I feel like you promised me, and on that basis I helped you . . ." After a moment, he said, "I really do feel screwed."

Cameron said, "I probably did screw you—for the good of the country, but I'm sure that doesn't make it feel better. Technically I never promised you anything, but of course I let you feel that you had a deal, and that wasn't fair or honest. So you may not trust me for this, but I do have an offer I hope you'll take, all the cards on the table this time."

"Let's hear it."

"You're already going to command the first real offensive against the tribals in the spring. Graham Weisbrod and I have discussed the list of options you gave him. Your biggest 'Cadillac plan' is doable, but rather than a punitive expedition to trash Castle Earthstone and a march out to the south, ripping up the tribes as you go, what if you just roll right on in that area, reconquering and occupying it?"

"How big an area? And you mean you'll give me everything in the high-end plan?"

"I would like you to smash the tribes so hard that by autumn our new frontier with them is at the Miami—or at the Scioto, if you get enough breaks. For the summer of the election year, you'd be in the news constantly, and if you succeed, you'll reduce the Lost Quarter tribes from urgent menace to persistent nuisance."

"Well." Grayson was taken aback, startled by the scale of the offer. "You're offering me the best command a man running for president could have. Do we even have the resources to do all that in one fighting season?"

"If you think we can do it, and you need more than was in your original plan to march from the Tippecanoe to the Ohio, I'll get you the men and guns and money, from our forces, from twisting Graham Weisbrod's arm, from the state armies and the Castles if we have to. Put all your planning staff on the problem. Figure out whether it's doable by October 1st, 2026. Plan on a short, wet fighting season, because all the soot in the air is predicted to make next winter even colder, damper, and earlier than this coming one. Remember spring will be late too. If it can't be done in one fighting season, take two—but one is better."

"And you're willing to take the chance I might be elected president? You know if I am, your career here is over."

"Ending my career is my *job*. We've already had a Natcon for about ten times as long as we ever should. Yes, I'm giving you a big, important chance—if you smash the tribes, you are going to be a hero in Superior and Wabash. For that matter *all* the Provi states have had major tribal raids."

Cameron Nguyen-Peters moved his hands across the table, palms down, as if laying out cards. "Don't misunderstand me, I'll personally vote for Phat—I'd like a secular, moderate conservative with good national security credentials. But a conservative Christian is acceptable too, and so for that matter would be a foaming liberal, just as long as our first restoration president will follow the Constitution—all of it—*and* get substantial support from every region. We can't afford anyone who creates even the appearance of shutting out a side or a region."

"So you're offering me a great chance to win the presidency, but you want me to win it across the whole country, and you are not offering me an in-the-bag deal."

"That's right, General. But I was never offering an in-the-bag deal anyway—it wasn't mine to offer. I am sorry that it sounded like I was, and I admit I should have made sure you understood that I can position you but you have to win the election yourself."

"Why do you care, if you're voting for Phat?"

"He might not win. General Grayson, I know you, I've seen you, I know your abilities, if you're the president the country can survive and thrive. I'm worried about who or what else might be a candidate with the backing of the churches. I'd rather you had that Christian-right slot, because I can live with you winning—but not with most of the other likely Christian-right candidates."

"What do you get out of offering me this big chance, other than buying me off again?"

Cam shrugged. "I didn't think I bought you before; you're not for sale. Look, the military and political advantage is that retaking those areas would give the Temper Army a short, fast overland connection to the Provi bases and fleets on Lake Erie. That way, the next year, in the spring of 2027, the new president will be poised to take back the Lost Quarter. You know how serious I am about reuniting the country."

"But you think Phat's a better candidate than I am."

"To unify the country, sure. I want him to do that, and you to win the war. As for who would be a better president, let the voters figure it out. They may well come your way if you put an end to the tribal problem. Can you see yourself in that role?"

"I can, of course. You know me well enough." Grayson stood. "It's a pretty handsome offer—if I can trust you after the last time. I'm going to have to go home, talk to Jenny, maybe pray; I'll let you know whether I'm in or out. If I'm out—"

"You'll move fast, and probably do something big. It's the way you are, and that's why I'm offering you this campaign command if you want it." Cameron stuck his hand out and Grayson shook it, more in respect than in contract. Cam's faint smile twitched momentarily into being. "General, you will not be the only man praying tonight."

**IMMEDIATELY AFTERWARD. ATHENS, TNG DISTRICT. 12:15 PM EST. THURSDAY, NOVEMBER 13, 2025.**

*I really should not be trying to make up excuses as if I'd disappointed Mama, when the person I'm worried about is young enough to be my daughter.* Grayson was frequently subject to little, odd thoughts about how weird life was; the only times they didn't show up were during sex, combat, or sleep. *My three favorite things,* he thought, *which is another weird little observation in its own right.*

At the front door, he paused a moment to straighten his tunic and finger-comb his hair before going in decisively. "I've got time for a long lunch, and we should talk."

Jenny came out of the back room smiling. "Baby, how'd the conference go?"

"Well, I either won more than I thought I could, or gave away the store, or nothing's settled yet. I don't know quite what I feel."

She held him by both elbows and beamed her most hypnotic, dazzling smile at him. "Suppose I tell you right away that no matter what happened or what you said, you're still my guy, one hundred percent and no take-backs. Then after that come in to lunch—Luther outdid himself—tell me all about it while we eat, and we'll figure out the next move together." She turned and led him into the dining room, her hips swaying just a little more—or was that just his imagination? Definitely, the tight short white dress was his favorite and she knew that.

Over the soup, which was as good as promised, he told her what had happened. "I guess I was so ready for him to deny everything, or confront me or be defensive, that I just stood there and listened while he explained his offer. On the other hand . . ."

She was half-smirking, but it seemed like it was a joke to share, not a joke on him. "Baby," she said, "on the other hand, you are a smart man and you realized at once that he was offering you an awesome, amazing deal which you might have to be crazy to turn down. I mean, it's true, right, that you can reconquer Indiana and part of Ohio? And make a good show of it?"

"Well—"

"I'm not modest about who I am, don't you be modest about who you are. Modesty should be reserved for when there are people to see it." Her eyes twinkled but he could feel how strongly she meant it.

"All right," he said. "Straight truth, I want to do the numbers, but I'm quite sure that if we grab an intact bridge somewhere near Terre Haute on, say, April first, and if Cam can spare me the right brigades, add in the Provi rangers and scouts, who are excellent, and some of their regular infantry, who are tolerable, with some Texas and New Mexico cavalry, and a few of the RRC's planes . . . then, yeah. Drive to the Miami/Maumee line for sure, probably all the way to the Scioto/Cuyahoga. Big smashing victories every week, or even more often, all summer long. If a ghost writer comes along—"

"Of course I will, darling, and no, I don't mind camping out all summer." Her smile had something sharklike about it. "Two years ago I was editor of the *Phoenix*, at Sarah Lawrence. Now, I want you to imagine just how good you have to be to get that job when you're the conservative Southern daughter of a fundamentalist minister and everybody you're competing with keeps calling you 'Barbie,' sometimes to your face. I am *that* good, baby. Haven't you noticed those speeches go over pretty well?"

"Why can't you do something about your father's sermons?"

The big whoop was not her usual polite lady-laugh at all. "Oh, baby, I have asked him that question *plenty* of times, and he still won't let me help. Now, let's get back to our problem here. You do want what Cam has to give you. You know he has shaded the truth and cheated you in the past, but then, you know you're not really friends either."

"He's not a bad man."

"He's not. He's a confused man pursuing an outdated ideal that nobody else even thinks about. But for the moment, he's going the same direction you are. So go with him. Help him, even, if he asks you to. Let him feel how smart and right he was to give you that command. And then one day, he'll want to go one direction, and you'll want to go the other." Her deep blue eyes leveled into his, open and staring like a fish's, but her mouth smiled like she tasted something good. "That's when he goes his way, and you go straight ahead as hard as you can and run the fucking weird little gook over and leave him dead in the road." Her smile softened. "You'll know when the time comes. And speaking of the time—"

"I've got about an hour—"

"That's plenty, baby. I love that little twinge I see in you whenever I talk a teensy bit vulgar or act a little psychobitchy. Want to teach me who's boss, before I get too big for my tight little silk pants?"

Afterward, lying beside him, she ran her smooth thigh over his muscular, hairy one. "Now let's talk it through; you have twenty minutes before you have to dress."

So as they stroked and kissed, they plotted out their lives, and how they would sell the whole thing to her father, and to Cameron Nguyen-Peters, and to the country. Just before he reluctantly got up and dressed, he had another of his weird little thoughts: *I am going to be far more successful but there is no way I can ever be happier than I am right now.*

## 40 MINUTES LATER. ATHENS, TNG DISTRICT. 2:30 PM EST. THURSDAY, NOVEMBER 13, 2025.

"Cam, can we do five very private minutes?" Grayson said, leaning into his office.

"Always." The Natcon got up and closed the door, and they sat in the chairs in the corner that faced into the soundproofing. "I take it you have a decision?"

"I'm in. Even as far as letting Shorty Phat out to run loose, though we sure can't have that known to anyone in the Post Raptural Church, and I really can't have it known to Reverend Whilmire."

"Understood. Drive the frontier to the Miami/Maumee. Whatever you say you need, I'll find it for you. Wreck the tribes for good. Take all the credit. Run for president, and may the best man win—or rather, may the people have the vision to see the best man, and the will to support him. And I won't be sad if it's you."

Grayson rose, they shook hands, and the deal was done.

Ten minutes later, as Cam went out for a stroll and a stretch to clear his head, Colonel Billy Ray Salazar happened to be crossing the quadrangle in front of the First Church of the United Christian States. Cam asked him politely how the fishing had been lately, Salazar stopped to tell him, and in the middle of a long story about a monster catfish that had broken the line at the last minute, Cam was able to say, very quickly and softly, "We're blown, and we're going to have to go ahead anyway. Usual protocol for emergency conference. Let our absent friends know."

Salazar went right on talking about fish; only the slightest twitch, once, of his cheek indicated to Cam that he had heard.

## 2 DAYS LATER. MOUTH OF CHESAPEAKE BAY. 2 PM EST. SATURDAY, NOVEMBER 15, 2025.

As *Martin Fierro* made its way south, the weather continued fair but cold. The three passengers had an after-lunch habit of bundling up in borrowed sweaters and having a last cup of hot tea in a sunny spot out of the wind; it was as secure a place as they could find for private discussions.

Today, without preamble, Chris said, "Since morning we've been headed northwest."

Larry nodded. "I woke up when I heard them bringing the ship about, looked out the porthole. We were passing Sea Gull Island as we turned north into Chesapeake Bay."

Jason stared at him. "How did you—"

Larry grinned. "When I was assigned to Bureau headquarters and still married, my wife and I, every chance we got, used to love to spend the weekend driving around the bay in a big circle. So this morning, well, you really can't mistake the Chesapeake Bay Bridge-Tunnel for anything else. After the turn this morning, *Martin Fierro* ran parallel to it for several miles before it found an open channel. I was surprised at how much was still standing after the DC bomb, but the Bridge-Tunnel was made to stand hurricanes, and even something as huge as the Washington nuke, at this distance, was just a big wave, a strong wind, a small earthquake, and I guess some fires if there was anything to burn. Probably the tunnels flooded when the ground shock wave cracked them, and I saw some trestles that had fallen over, so you couldn't cross the bay on it, but most of it is still there, and not hard to recognize."

Chris looked around for Argentine crew again, before asking, "So what do you suppose they are doing? There's no resettlement, nothing to trade with, probably not even a surviving dock."

"Well," Larry said, "since early morning, Roberto's been hauling up water samples and logging them every half hour. I'm guessing that's meant to look like he's just taking soundings. And a couple of times they've sent a dinghy out, which came back with a wet bag of something—bottom samples, or maybe they're going out to a shore just over the horizon. And fish coming up off the trawling lines are going into jars of alcohol, not to the kitchen as they usually would. So my guess is that they're doing a biological survey for someone back in Argentina, along with maybe a certain amount of mapping."

"Why would they do that?" Jason asked, quietly.

Larry shrugged. "I'm the president of Argentina, okay? Now, here I am, the head of one of less than a dozen nations that came through Daybreak sort of functional. Not only am I located on a whole collapsed, disorganized continent I can overrun in the next generation or two, there's an even bigger continent to the north with huge depopulated areas and the rest in political chaos. Not that I wish them ill, but you know . . . maybe if I knew more about the devastation, I could help them better. Plus I should be keeping an eye on what kind of craziness they might do after what's happened. So why not know something about one of the biggest and best bays in the world for harbors and fishing, since the *yanquis* aren't using it right now? Especially since who knows what things might be like in ten years, or a generation?

"In fact, speaking as El Presidente, despite the Commandant's sharp little eyes, I'd be looking over New York Harbor too. In fact it's just possible the Commandant pulled a dirty trick on me and found a way to force one of my ships to carry American spies.

"Am I planning an invasion? No. Right now I couldn't invade Uruguay. Am I thinking of seizing parts of the old United States? Not anytime soon. Do I think I'll have to fight the *norteamericanos*? I hope not; peaceful trade would do us all so much more good. But do I need to know everything I can? Oh, yes. Very much yes." Larry shrugged. "We'd be doing similar stuff if the situations were reversed."

"If you're right," Chris added, "they're also checking out Cape Cod and the Long Island Sound. Not that they are extra-special wicked or anything but just in case, you know? That's how this stuff has been done since Sumer."

They stayed out in the sun on the deck as long as they comfortably could. Their cabin door had barely closed before they heard quiet orders and scrambling feet, and felt the ship swing round to another tack.

### THE NEXT DAY. NEAR FORT STEWART, GEORGIA. 1 AM EST. SUNDAY, NOVEMBER 16, 2025.

These streets were abandoned but far from empty. To the north, Fort Stewart had shrunken away, retreating into a real fort. To the south, the Hinesville city government had given up any enforcement or patrols. What flourished between was everything authority disapproved and people wanted.

Grayson felt ridiculous in his Hawaiian shirt, blue jeans, broad-brimmed hat, and Castle Newberry sunglasses. Jenny had carefully picked out an outfit to conceal his identity while signaling *rich*. Apparently it had worked; on his way to the bar, half a dozen hookers and a dozen moonshine and pot touts tried to entice him, but none had begun with, "Hey, General Grayson."

This swath of unauthorized bars, drug houses, and brothels was strictly off-limits to soldiers. *I wish the MPs* would *grab me, because I hate this.* It had to be done for his career, for the Army he loved, for the country. It had the approval of the one living person he really loved, and for that matter it even had the blessing of clergy. Nonetheless, he felt vaguely sick.

He found the Bug Out Tavern, went in the front door, and gave a pass-word to the man at the improvised bar. The man gestured toward the back; in the dark hallway Grayson saw candlelight playing from under the crack of one door. He knocked, repeated the password, and was admitted.

As he moved to the front of the table, he thought, *Nazis in Toyland*. They were men who loved to strike the pose and wear the clothes, but couldn't or wouldn't do the job. They were dressed in scraps of camo, almost all with bare chests impractical for combat, and looked like some comic-book designer's concept of a postapocalyptic bad-ass gang. But Grayson saw the bad balance on the standing ones, the unfocused gazes, the flab and blood-shot eyes and shallow breathing, the way their weight was back as if they were already half out the door; these were not men to have at your back, or anywhere upwind.

Yet their eyes shone with hunger to hear what he had to say; *before Day-break, they'd've been mom's-basement right wingers and 7-Eleven clerk sol-diers of fortune. Still hanging around the Army, still no use—till now.*

He cleared his throat, and began. He laid it on thick; he'd never have been so prolix with an actual elite unit, let alone with the sort of dirty-dozen-fighting-for-honor-and-redemption that these poor posers wanted to be. Three of them were fresh out of the stockade, on paroles he had arranged. Two were deserters. Two needed their paper records destroyed. Parker, the closest thing to a leader they had, had been on his way to a gen-eral discharge for the good of the service when Daybreak had rendered men with training too valuable to let go; he'd rewarded the decision to keep him by making corporal—twice, so far, tied with the number times he'd lost it.

But at least Parker's eyes focused on Grayson, and not on his shoes or on some hazy movie in his forehead, and he asked some questions that indi-cated he'd been listening. *I guess every outfit has a top guy,* Grayson thought.

Walking back, he walked fast; people in his path stepped aside. *I know thousands of real soldiers, but I don't know one I could look in the eye and ask for what I'm asking for.*

A voice in the shadowy street, close to him, asked him for something—money, probably, or a drink—and he lashed out, but his fist found only air and darkness.

**8 DAYS LATER. SAVANNAH, GEORGIA. 9 AM EST. MONDAY, NOVEMBER 24, 2025.**

The captain of *Martin Fierro,* a quiet Norwegian with excellent English, was sometimes talkative. Gradually they had learned that he had been try-ing to find some ship going to Norway to search for his family. They had heard the story of his jury-rigging sails when the engines died on his Polish freighter, and how he had limped into Buenos Aires just a week before the failed nuclear attack. Almost every conversation with him ended with his saying that he took ships where they were supposed to go, trained his officers, and hoped for some strong reason to live.

"The thing I always liked about Savannah," he said, "was the no-nonsense. They were a great port city but not just because they were sitting in the right place like Buenos Aires or New York. The most modern freight-handling system on this continent and always upgrading, eh?"

"Used to move a lot of freight real fast," the pilot said, never taking his eyes from the channel.

"But you see they built it all downriver from the city, because it's faster to unload to rail as soon as you can, so the piers and the docks up in the city, they were for smaller ships and museum pieces and pleasure boats, you see? They kept those in good shape too. And when Daybreak came and everything stopped and rotted where it was, the big modern ships at the big modern facilities just stayed there along the south bank—but they had an open channel up to decent docks in the old city. This will be a big city before Manbrookstat is one again. This and Morgan City, they're your new America, you know."

"If the country even looks outward at all," Larry said.

"I'm a seaman; a country is its ports."

"How was Daybreak down here?" Jason asked.

The pilot shrugged. "Bad—but we lived. Things were a lot worse, other places. Down here, people coped. 'f they'ad friends or relatives to walk to, they did. Some rioting and shooting from people who I guess didn'ave nothin' better to do. Lotta rationing, people boarding up their houses and moving to shelters, the Army and Guard ran the place till'bout July. Lost a lotta old people and everyone who depended on modern medicine, and there's people calling this the Year of No Babies, so many things carried off the little ones. But between us and the military and the Lord, we got through and it's looking better. Maybe three-quarters of the people that were here on Daybreak day ain't back yet, 'cause they need hands out on the farms."

Around the bend, the old city spread out before them. The pilot asked if they'd ever been to Savannah before; only Chris had. "But only as a camera-man for the news, so I never saw anything."

"Well, people from elsewhere tell me it's real pretty," the pilot said. "I've never been anywhere else, really, so to me it all looks kind of regular."

The walk through a functioning city made them all feel like hapless hicks. Savannah had been a rich and beautiful town for 150 years and more before Daybreak, and it had reverted, painfully but effectively, to a real human place. "Like Put-in-Bay," Jason said, after a while.

"Yeah," Chris said. "Or Pale Bluff, or Grant's Pass. One of those places that's just managed to hang on as a good place. I guess that's what it's all about."

Larry nodded. "Good, then it's worth it." He seemed distant; when he spotted the telegraph office, he all but ran to it. Shrugging, Chris and Jason sat down on a park bench to wait for him.

Twice in the half hour while they waited, men in a tan uniform asked them what they were doing, and having established that they weren't local, took down their names and the fact that they would be leaving town soon. The second time, the man said, apropos of nothing, "You're not in Olympia, here, you know."

When he was completely out of earshot, Jason said, "I don't think I like local law enforcement."

"I'm not even sure those are cops," Chris said. "But I'm pretty sure they're not the Welcome Wagon."

Larry came back looking grim. "I'm sure you both guessed," he said, looking down at the ground and speaking very softly, "that there was a secret part of this mission that might or might not be activated?"

They nodded slightly, in unison.

"It's activated. I've been advised to tell you nothing more than to follow me if things suddenly go off plan. They don't want you to know too much. Your lives could depend on that, if things go wrong. Just stay loose and ready to jump."

"Right on," Jason said.

"You bet," Chris added.

"Okay, now the public, non-coded telegram I have here apparently is our pass onto the train, if we just present it to the FedRail desk in the railroad station. Let's see how that part goes."

Finding it was easy. Just south of downtown, Savannah had had a railroad museum before Daybreak, and like the one in Golden, Colorado, having so much old steam-train gear in one place had made this area a center of development. "You must rate," the clerk said, smiling at them. "First class all the way with all the extras. The train leaves at 3 p.m., none too sharp, but it'll help us if you're here waiting, and when it goes it goes, so be here at three unless you want your packs to go to Athens without you. Got your ration cards and chapel passes?"

"A ration card sounds like a good idea," Larry said, "if we can write you a purchase order on the RRC's account. How's the food in the mess halls?"

The clerk had obviously heard that question before. "We don't have public mess halls here anymore. We got over socialism quick. The thing is if you don't have a ration card, no one can sell you any food in any form, restaurant or grocery or anything. You don't legally *need* a chapel pass if you stay less than twenty-four hours, but it helps to have one if a militiaman stops you on the street, and you have to have one to buy printed matter like newspapers or books. And yeah, I'll take a draft on Pueblo; it's easier to process than the farmers that come in and give me okra."

"Well, then, whatever number of ration coupons we need for our meals today, and three chapel passes."

"You going to eat on the train? Honestly it's better'n anything local, so you should make that your supper."

"Thanks, yes, we'll do that."

The clerk scribbled on a carbon pad, speaking quickly and without expression, going through a well-rehearsed routine. "Ration coupons coming up. You show it to the waiter or clerk going in, and then they take it from you at the end. Don't let them grab it before you've got your food and paid for it. A lot of them lie and threaten to turn you in for not giving them one. If they do trick you that way, the going price to let you go is four times the price of a ration coupon.

"Now about those chapel passes, you can buy one, good for three days, from the reverend, every time you attend a service, as long as they have the LICENSED NON CULT plate up on the pulpit.

"Don't pay a door cover, ever, that's how the cults trick people into coming to service and not getting a chapel pass for it—the Jews and those little African churches are famous for that, everyone says, but in my experience it's the Mormons who pull that trick every time.

"The Steam Train Chapel, down to the other end of the station there on the right, has a service every half hour, and it's quick. The reverend there'll give you a pass that's as good as any, and his prices aren't bad." The clerk winked. "He's also my brother-in-law."

The service was a sung doxology, a reading of three Bible verses, a recitation of the Lord's Prayer, singing one verse of "God Bless America," and a two-minute message in which the preacher urged them all to realize that all the missing good people, especially their friends and relatives, were Raptured, this was the Tribulation, and therefore they needed to get to a "real Christian" church, by which he apparently meant a Post Raptural Church, to be fully slain in the spirit and rebaptized. Then they sang one verse of "Stand Up for Jesus" and the reverend pronounced them blessed.

They purposely maneuvered to be last in line for their coupons, hoping to get a chance to talk alone with the reverend.

"We're out of Pueblo and just back from a scientific expedition to the Lost Quarter," Larry explained, "so we don't really know how things work down here."

"Well, we know that a terrorist, a Satanist, a Muslim, or a possessed man is not going to be able to bear to hear the word of the Lord," the man said, pleasantly, as if explaining how an athlete's foot cream worked. "That's plain as day in Matthew 18:18, Hebrews 13:15, and Psalm 22. So we bring them in here and I give'em some Bible and hymns and see if they can say the Lord's Prayer. Like screening them for evil, like they used to screen for metal and stuff at airports. But all that does is make sure you ain't consciously with Satan right this second. If you're going to come out of the Tribulation on the right side—and there's only six years left—you really need to go to a real church."

"And the people who live here, they go to chapel twice a week, to have the passes?

"Lots go daily. And it's not just for the passes. With Tribulation on, a man just can't be too careful."

They met friendly people everywhere, happy to talk about life in Savannah. The restaurant meals were good but almost identical: fried or grilled fish, cornbread, and greens. One place had a side of two eggs available at an outrageous price, and the other didn't but expected to the next day.

Polite militiamen stopped them on the street three times, and each time the chapel pass extracted them instantly—though the last of the militiamen, who didn't look a day over sixteen, with red hair and more freckles than it should be possible to grow on one person, shook his head when he saw where the chapel pass came from. "Next time you hit town," he said, "go over to the Lord's Table Chapel—it used to be a house, they just converted it—by Forsyth Park. Your pass'll cost you half what this one did, and you'll get a real whole hour service with serious spirit-infused, Bible-based preaching, and you get communion at no extra charge."

"We'll keep that in mind," Larry said. "You wouldn't happen to be related to that preacher, would you?"

"You mean the way Ed at the railway station is brothers with that clerk Steve? No, sir. But Reverend Earl at the Lord's Table Chapel is my girlfriend's dad, and I have seen him at work, and I believe in my heart that you'll get a better deal there."

After looking all day, Chris finally found a newspaper just as they were returning to the railroad station; an elderly African-American lady, who had three chapel passes, all from today, pinned on the front of her dress, was selling papers from a crate on the sidewalk. After carefully inspecting his chapel pass, she sold Chris a current *Athens Weekly Insight* and a three-week-old *Pueblo Post-Times*. She gave them to him wrapped in a paper bag, the way he remembered his father buying pornography.

On the train, opening the papers, he found that a third of the material in the *Post-Times*'s back page, and half a dozen stories in the *Weekly Insight*, had been painted over with black ink. Jason and Larry had a fine old time teasing him about not having seen that coming.

The conductor came by to announce dinner in the dining car; they pulled out their ration cards, and he laughed. "Steve pulled that one on you, too, didn't he? The ration cards are a local Savannah thing. You don't need 'em to eat here."

Chris thought he might burst with smugness as Jason and Larry took turns grumbling all through dinner. It wasn't bad, for the third helping of fried fish, cornbread, and greens in a day. The few lights of Savannah had vanished behind them, and the old steam train was chugging along, zigzagging from one still-usable track to another. He settled back to read the parts of his paper that he was allowed to see. *At least for breakfast in Athens, there probably won't be fish, and if their paper is censored* here, *it's got to be freer* there.

# E I G H T E E N :
# WHISPERED TO THE BRAID

"I think some people are starting to wonder if we're dating," Cameron said, setting down the picnic basket.

"Well, if we are, then I'm mad because you never take me anywhere." Lyndon Phat looked down at the pieces of tissue paper that Cam dropped into his lap as he began to unpack the basket. "By the way, I appreciate the chance to eat something good, and your friendship flatters the hell out of me."

"Glad to hear it, because you're about the only friend I've got locally."

Phat nodded, looking down. The first tissue contained the simplest message:

*Extraction party arrived Savannah 1 hr ago*
*Will be here tonight*

The second tissue spelled out the planned extraction, told him to memorize it, and stressed that he might be the only member of the group who knew the plan.

The third was a set of directions for—"And this is for later," Cam said, handing him a paper bag; in it there was a baguette, and a glass jar of jam (or at least the thin outer layer next to the glass was jam; the instructions told Phat what to do with the thing in the inner jar).

Their eyes met; the two men sighed silently, because they genuinely had enjoyed the conversations, and no matter what, this would be the last.

## THAT NIGHT. ATHENS, TNG DISTRICT. 11 PM EST. MONDAY, NOVEMBER 24, 2025.

They had pretended to sleep on the train, sharing a big couch in a private compartment, while Larry briefed them via squeeze code. The essential information boiled down to expect trouble; don't resist the fake arrest; expect to get the rest of the script from Cameron Nguyen-Peters; and if anything went wrong, make as much noise as possible, improvise, free General Phat, and run.

"That's a lot of light up ahead for nowadays," Jason said, quietly, as they neared the Athens station.

Larry and Chris leaned across him to look where he pointed. "Orangey and flickering, so it's torchlight," Chris said. "Not good. I don't think they're holding a parade for us."

As the train neared the station, silhouettes swept by on both sides of the tracks, and the train whistle blasted over and over. The dark human shapes, backlit by torches, thickened into a wall of heads above bodies, faces flaring out of it in the flickering, uncertain light, like snapshots of angry ghosts.

At the platform, backs covered with Rorschach camo blocked the view through the windows. "Soldiers standing three deep," Jason said. "And the crowd sounds like bears."

Their conductor leaned in. "They said to ask you not to sit too close to the windows, and wait for someone to come to you."

Outside the praying and singing was growing louder, and some objects thudded against the side of the train car. "Is there a next station we could maybe go on to?" Chris asked.

"It's a spur line," Larry said. "To get off it we would have to back up. Which can be pretty easily blocked."

So far, no gunfire had punctured the angry rumble of the mob outside, and what was hitting the train sounded like rocks or bottles, not shots. "I like the singing better than the shouting," Chris said. "They don't throw stuff when they sing."

Cameron Nguyen-Peters came in. "This is going to be a nuisance. We need to make a public display of arresting you all as spies. You will be going to a discreet high-security facility and the man you came to meet will be there. My assistants will bring along your bags separately."

He paused for a moment as the shouting and screaming outside rose to a crescendo and then quieted. "That's our cue. General Grayson is speaking to the crowd. He can usually persuade the Post Raptural crowds to behave, at least for short periods of time. He's defusing the situation for public peace, and he'll do what it takes to protect you. He knows what your mission is and supposedly he's down with it—but if he's going to stab us in the back, it'll be tonight, so stay alert and trust him only as much as you have to. For this ceremonial arrest, just try to look like the general has overwhelmed you by his sheer force of personality."

As they waited in the shadow to go onto the platform, while General Grayson prayed at length, Larry muttered, "Who's the low-rent Madonna clone beside him?"

"His wife," Cam said. "Ten times smarter and fifty times more dangerous than he is, and don't forget it."

The prayer finished with the Post Raptural coda—*help us during this Tribulation to make Your chosen nation fully fit for Your return.* There was wild cheering, but Grayson held his hands up for silence. "Now we are about to proceed with a difficult moment, my friends, and I am depending on each of you to be calm, reasonable, and fair. These men believe they are carrying out their duties in accord with their oaths, just as sincerely as I believe I am keeping my oath. I, and the other competent authorities, must have the freedom and time to investigate and reach an impartial conclusion that will stand the scrutiny of God and man. To do that, we *must* have quiet and order. So I'm going to ask you to return to your homes after you see these men taken into custody. Rest assured we are dealing with any danger they may pose to God and country—but we are doing so fairly and dispassionately. Now, will you please all join me in the Pledge of Allegiance?"

It was no mere recital; the crowd seemed to speak in one passionate voice:

*I pledge allegiance to the Lord*
*Of the United and Christian States of America,*
*And to the Cross and Eagle which stands for His Presence,*
*One nation under God, faithful to Christ,*
*With liberty, justice, grace, and love for all.*

"I am going to find a way to crucify that son of a bitch," Chris whispered.

"Gotta let me help," Larry whispered back.

"He doesn't believe it himself," Cam pointed out.

"I don't care whether you're a bear yourself, don't feed the bears," Jason said.

When the three men moved forward into the light, the crowd fell into a deep silence. Grayson publicly ordered Cam to take them into custody for questioning. Cam declared he would hold them according to Grayson's orders, and came forward to take Larry by the elbow.

As they passed out of the light, Grayson was urging the crowd to go home. A few little bunches of them were striking up hymns or chants, but it didn't seem to be contagious. A long flight of steps led down along the solid brick wall of the power plant, plunging into deeper darkness.

"Why was he willing to do that?" Larry asked quietly.

"Because it means I've been publicly seen taking orders from him, now," Cam explained. "That's worth a great deal to him. Look, time's short, here goes. Two blocks from here, I am going to lead you into a dark area behind an old classroom building. I will appear to just be taking a shortcut across a lawn. You will *silently* turn away from me and follow the row of magnolias to the north; at the edge of campus there's a dark patch where you can run across to a warehouse. North and west of the warehouse there's an old bike trail. Follow it about half a mile to a frame house by the east bank of a creek—if you cross a bridge you've gone too far. In that house are men I've assigned to the job, loyal to me and the United States. Give them the password 'Four larks and a wren.'

"If by any chance you are arrested that's the place you will be taken anyway, and the guards will free you as soon as the arresting party leaves and you can give them the password. They will release General Phat to you. He knows the extraction procedure, which is—"

"Stop were you are," a voice said from the shadows. Cameron walked on and was gone. Chris felt his arms pinned; beside him Larry and Jason struggled. Pistols cocked, and Chris felt the press of the muzzle at the back of his neck, pointed a little upward in the executioner's angle.

"Prisoners, hold still while we secure you."

Bags went over their heads instantly, bars slipped between their backs and elbows as neat as knitting, and choke ropes slipped over their necks like a period onto the end of a sentence. Chris recognized Grayson's voice when he said, "Follow me to the secure facility. They'll be held there till morning. No noise and forget this the moment we're back." Hands turned him around a few times and then guided him into a new direction; he sensed the others beside him. "Prisoners," Grayson said, "if you pick up your feet and obey your handlers, you won't get hurt on your way there."

Chris noticed that nothing had been said about after they were there.

**THAT NIGHT. ATHENS, TNG DISTRICT. 12:20 AM EST. TUESDAY, NOVEMBER 25, 2025.**

Mama had taught Jeffrey Grayson to "get good stuff that'll last." He'd had his first pair of good Italian shoes at the age of twelve. His first car had been a mechanic-approved used BMW. Mama's first personal assistant had still been with her on the day she retired, they had had two cooks—mother and daughter—in all their time in the big old stone house, and the gardener's grandfather had worked at that house. You knew you could count on quality shoes, cars, and people.

Unfortunately, what he was doing right now required low-quality disposable people, and they were behaving just like it. A squad of first rate MPs at the facility, and maybe a half dozen Rangers with him, and Grayson would have no worries.

These dopey misfits were obviously enjoying the feeling of being Big Tough Bad Guys. Parker, the closest thing Grayson had to a reliable subordinate, had to remind Ethan twice to keep his finger out of the trigger guard; probably it scared the shit out of the prisoners to hear that.

At the secure facility, it was worse. They didn't even know how to straighten up and behave right—instead of saluting, standing at attention, and carrying out the orders quickly and crisply, they sort of waved their hands at their heads, looked around the room, and hunched and slumped as they put the prisoners into the rooms. They drawled like clerks at a 7-Eleven.

As soon as the prisoners were shoved into their cells and locked in, Grayson pulled off his ski mask and said, "There is one more empty cell and we're going to have one more prisoner. You all on guard, stay on guard. Arresting party, go get the last one and bring him in—as gently as possible, give him the chance to come with you voluntarily, and you are by no means to use violence; if he just walks past you, let him."

*God I hope they remember what they are really supposed to do.* But at least they took off quickly, ski masks pulled down, running in the right direction, and beyond that he'd just have to hope.

"For the record," he said, loudly, so that the men in the cells could hear him, "it was necessary to arrest this party because the Reconstruction Research Center at Pueblo has been penetrated by Daybreaker and other subversive elements, and we became aware that this purported scouting expedition was actually an attempted prison break by Lyndon Phat . . ."

The speech went on, sounding more and more lengthy, flat, and phony to Grayson himself. He wanted to just cut it entirely and tell everyone he'd be back later, but he had to drive on through the excruciating, repetitive speech, because he had to be seen here, after giving orders for which he would have independent and even hostile witnesses. There must be no question of either what his orders had been, or that he had been here, when—

Distant gunfire. It began as a few shots, then erupted into what sounded like a brief firefight that trailed off in ones and twos within a minute.

"What is *that*?" Grayson demanded. Not staying for an answer, he ran into the night as the last shots punctuated his exit.

**ABOUT THE SAME TIME. ATHENS, TNG DISTRICT. 12:40 AM EST. TUESDAY, NOVEMBER 25, 2025.**

*If I'm not being stabbed in the back,* Cameron Nguyen-Peters thought, *then Grayson did that perfectly; we told them just enough to make sure they'll accomplish the mission, and to cover Grayson and me if things go to shit. And the only catch is that if Grayson is backstabbing me, I've just given away every advantage I had. Well, they always say that if you want someone to be trustworthy, you have to start off trusting—*

An explosion tore through the downstairs, shaking the building, throwing him to his hands and knees; the coffee in its fine cup flew across his immaculate desk. Plaster spattered on the back of his suitcoat.

Gunshots downstairs, and shouting. He didn't recognize any of the voices. Probably the intruders were killing any of his surviving, wounded loyalists.

The shaking of the building frame must have jammed the window, because it wouldn't budge when he yanked at it. He kicked it in the center as hard as he could—it was bulletproof but secured with just a few screws in case of something like this—and it fell away. He stepped over the window-sill, out on the fire escape.

A man had been waiting for him by the window, and as Grayson turned, he was facing into the muzzle of a Newberry Standard carbine.

"You don't want to do this," Cam said, softly.

"Shut up."

"Grayson can't afford any connection to killing me; do you want to be one of the few living witnesses? Do you think he won't dispose of you, like he's disposing of me?"

"He said not to talk to you because you're a slick liar."

"Well, he *would* say that, wouldn't he?" Careful not to move his head, with only the light from the oil lamps in the office behind him, Cam studied every detail of the man, trying to make his gaze friendly and sympathetic. *No anger. No pity. He'll pull the trigger if he sees either.*

Pudgy, out of shape, lines too deep in his face, slumping like he wanted his ass out of here, the man wore a long untucked homespun shirt; his belly bulged over too-small Levi's. *Of course. Grayson couldn't have gotten a regular soldier for this job.*

"Do you love your country?" Cameron asked him.

"What kind of a question is that? Would I be here doing this if I didn't?"

"I was appointed by the last serving president of the United States," Cameron said quietly, "and I appointed Grayson to his present job."

"Who says he has anything to do with this?" Something defensive in the man's tone.

This was going the wrong way. *Try something else.* "If he didn't, I'm very glad to hear it. Someone sent you. Loyal American citizens don't come armed to attack their government unless someone has been telling them stories."

"What makes you think Grayson . . . I mean—"

"He was usually honest with me up till now. But if you're going to kill me, can't you tell me what it's about?"

The man's eyes rolled up and away, slightly, toward his low, broad-brimmed hat. *He's thinking about that, he's thinking—*

"Hold it!" the man shouted, not at Cam. Cam did not turn around, but felt another man behind him on the fire escape.

*All my life I've depended on finding the smart one and talking to him, but sometimes the smart one can't—*

"We ain't spoza talk to'im." The voice behind him was expressionless. "He said he'd get us talkin' and we wouldn't do it."

"Maybe—"

"Aw, bullshit, Parker. Think think think, talk talk talk, all the time and you never wanna do nothing."

On the last syllable, the world roared, and Cam felt an immense shove high on his back. Falling forward, trying to catch the fire escape's railing, he barely formed the thought *Don't.*

As he clung for a moment to the railing, a fragmentary image of the ground below was the last thing that ever crossed from Cam's optic nerve into his brain. Then Parker shot him in the head. The world disappeared into an unbearable bright light and roaring sound.

Denny kicked the reeling body hard, and it tumbled over the railing, off the fire escape, thudding to the pavement below. "Hey Parker, hey motherfucker, we got the fucking Natcon! We're fucking *famous.* See, when it's time to do it, you gotta do it. Mother*fuck*er! Famous!"

Parker looked down at the gun in his hand as if it had just appeared there. He wanted to say something, or have a thought, but nothing came. He descended the fire escape slowly, as if in a drunken stagger, with Denny beside him, slapping his back, slugging his shoulder. "Got him, hey, we got him. Motherfucking *famous,* Parker, we're motherfucking *famous.*"

General Grayson was waiting for them at the bottom, with three regular soldiers that Parker hadn't seen before now. Grayson had been crouched by the Natcon's body; now he stood up, an expression of horror on his face.

*Now is when we're supposed to point our weapons at him and he'll back away, and then—but he didn't say there'd be other soldiers.* Parker felt more than thought, *So this is what it felt like for the Natcon,* and tried to make his mouth open to say, *Please! I'll never tell anybody!* and tried to frame the thought that they had to talk, that Denny must not point that gun.

But beside him, he felt Denny's gun swinging up, just like in practice. Then the general's pistol was up, and firing.

## ABOUT THE SAME TIME. ATHENS, TNG DISTRICT. 12:40 AM EST. TUESDAY, NOVEMBER 25, 2025.

"Four larks and a wren," Larry Mensche said, loudly—but not nearly as loudly as the wild laughter from the guards. "Fuck you," one of the guards said. "We even knew that would be your fucking password, but we ain't none of *those* guards. You got the *wrong* guards. You stayin' where you stayin'."

On the surface of his mind, Chris thought, *I am deranged by this. I am mad. I cannot comprehend the failure of the plot. What do I do?*

Deeper down, he thought, *Thank God you couldn't be in broadcast news without getting some actor training.*

Chris drew a deep breath and tightened his vocal cords. Make 'em jump. Sound like a gut-shot cougar. He screamed, "Four larks and a wren, four larks and a wren, four larks and a wren."

The guards roared with laughter. So far so good. He wailed it, sobbed it, chanted it, and kept it coming. "Four larks and a wren, four larks and a wren."

"All fucking right," one of them yelled, "that's enough, you know it ain't gonna work, you poor stupid bastard, cut it out."

He stepped up his volume and energy, driving his voice till his throat was raw and his ears rang from his own volume. "Four larks and a wren, four larks and a wren, four larks and—"

The guard burst in, shouting, "Shut up!" and reached for Chris's collar.

Chris reached over the man's arm, gripped the little finger, and yanked back, turning the arm over and extending it. His left hand, fingers compressed into a spear-hand, jabbed along the man's extended arm and over the shoulder to strike his throat with crushing force. Chris grabbed an ear, pivoted forward so that he went up the man's still-extended arm like a swing dancer coming back in, and slammed his right fist into the man's already-crushed larynx.

He felt his opponent's body go limp. *Ecco, Samson, thanks.* Chris pulled the pistol from the guard's holster.

This wasn't any weapon he knew, but it didn't matter; the next guard through the door was still unsnapping his holster when Chris swung the gun by its barrel backhanded into the man's chin. He followed him down as he fell over, and used the gun like a hammer on the man's forehead, twice.

Chris backed away on the opening side of the door, and lunged forward when it opened and the third and final man came through. With the gun jabbed against the man's temple, Chris screamed "Open all the doors now!" like a movie psycho.

The man raised his hands above his head. "The keys are in my pocket, you'll have to—"

The man was staring at the gun and never saw Chris's foot sweep; with a startled cry, he fell backward, and Chris raised the gun high and brought it down with all his force on the top of his head, and then on the face.

With the keys from the guard's pocket, Chris unlocked Larry's cell, and Jason's. Behind them, a door clicked open; General Phat came in with his hands up. "Don't shoot, the irony would be too much for anyone. I thought with all the action going on, it was time to use the screwdriver Cam had smuggled to me last week as a just-in-case," he said. "I need to grab something and then we need to be on the road west, now."

Outside, torches and lanterns, whooping and shouting, filled the campus a few hundred yards away. "Wish we knew if that was a good thing or a bad thing," Larry said.

"If it were a good thing, Cam would already be with us," Phat said. "That's either his failed diversion, or he lost his gamble. We'll have to say our prayers for him while we run."

"One more thing to check," Larry said. "Chris, hand me that gun you took off the guard."

Gingerly, Chris did. "I didn't feel any safety and I wasn't sure I could figure out—"

"Yeah. It's a Newberry .65, bastard child of a horse pistol and a modern automatic." Larry pointed it into the air and pulled the trigger; it dry-fired. He pulled out the magazine. "Not loaded. So they weren't supposed to kill us, so Grayson doesn't expect to hear gunshots." He darted into the main guard room, rifled the desk, found eight full magazines. "Works just like the Newberry Standard rifle," he said. "Bigger slug because it's a smoothbore. Accurate to about arm's-length compared to anything you're used to. Massive stopping power if you do manage to hit anything. Let's go."

As they hastened along the dark road, Larry said, "Cam said you had the plan."

"Such as it is," Phat said. "We're going to cross this bridge and follow the maintenance road onto the abandoned golf course, out onto a big flat stretch of fairway. Once we are there, I'll use this gadget in the jar to call in help. Meanwhile, for a bigger challenge, you will be laying but not lighting a triangle of three fires, about a hundred yards apart."

"Has it been cold enough to send all the snakes to ground?" Chris asked.

"Not being a snake, I wouldn't know. I'd avoid sticking your hands down holes or under bushes."

"Also," Larry said, "our gear is gone; I don't suppose you have anything we can light a fire with, assuming you do want them lit eventually?"

General Phat chuckled. "This is the first time since I was twenty-one that I've been glad I smoke."

**ABOUT 3 HOURS LATER. ATHENS, TNG DISTRICT. 1:15 AM EST. TUESDAY, NOVEMBER 25, 2025.**

Jenny had never looked more beautiful than she did in candlelight; she had been waiting in his favorite nightie to give him a hero's welcome, and he'd accepted enthusiastically.

Now he sat cross-legged and upright on the bed, catching his breath. Jenny lay gasping like a trophy marlin. *Pity that the only men I actually killed were those pathetic stooges*, he thought. *I would have liked to see old stone-faced Cam-boy beg for his life. . . .*

The thought of Cam screaming, the real memory of his slack dead face, Jenny's spill of blonde curls across the pillow, and the sheen of sweat on her big breasts, started him again. He sprang onto Jenny, pinned her, pushed her legs apart.

She squirmed and cried out; this was past the point of her pleasure. He knew she was sore, and he knew too that she would not only forgive him but come to treasure the memory, as she had their wedding night and the other triumphant nights when he had been like this. Teenage-boy bragging resounded in his mind: *she'll walk funny for a week, she won't be able to sit down—*

Her cries of pain and fear brought him to another climax. She curled away from him. "No more, please, baby. I *hurt.*"

Instantly remorseful, he brought her ointment, stroked her hair, soothed her while she cried about how *scary* he was. She clung to him; he rubbed her back. If ever he had really made anything his own—

Pounding, then shouting, at the door.

He rolled from the bed, yanked on sweater and pants, put his boots over his trousers, and threw the door open. Reverend Whilmire and Reverend Peet stood there, escorted by four soldiers with rifles.

Whilmire said, "We have an emergency. The Pueblo spies and General Phat are gone, two of their guards are dead, and the medic doesn't think the third one will regain consciousness. Did you know anything about their escape plan?"

"Only that Shorty Phat was supposed to be the guy that knew it, and if we kept them all locked up it wasn't going to matter." Grayson grabbed his coat from the rack; it was freezing outside. "Are any troops in motion yet?"

"We told the sergeant that brought us the news to alert the officer of the watch. He sent back that he's bringing Second Battalion to Terrell Hall, and he's also activated the lockdown plan, so there will be troops at the airport and railway station—and on every bridge, ford, and road—in a few minutes."

"How long ago?" Grayson was solving the problem already; airport locked up, trains locked up, guarding the roads would slow them down, moonless night so horses couldn't move much faster than a healthy man could walk. "How long ago?" he demanded, again.

"Sir, the message from the officer of the watch came back eighteen minutes ago, sir," the sergeant of the escorting soldiers said. "And the situation at the facility was discovered about ten minutes before that."

Grayson nodded. *They have at least forty minutes' head start, but not an hour.* The Pueblo spies and Phat had to be within a couple of miles; call it three by the time he had his troops—a long head start, but if they were hiding somewhere to await pickup, *maybe.*

"Two of you men come with me," he said. "I've got to go to Terrell Hall and take command. Reverend Whilmire, go wake up the Board, drag them into a meeting, no matter what the actual numbers are it's a quorum, and vote in a temporary declaration of martial law. To expire in two weeks—if we haven't salvaged things by then we've lost anyway."

"I'd only slow everyone down," the Reverend Peet said. "I'm going home to bed to let younger people cope with this. Reverend Whilmire, you have my proxy."

*Most useful thing I've ever heard Peet say,* Grayson thought. "Mine too," he said. "Good luck."

As he ran, the sergeant and one soldier at his heels, he thought, *Ask me for anything but time. Supposedly Napoleon said that. For the first time, I really understand him.* He ran down the road, faster and faster as his eyes adjusted to the starlight, everything forgotten but the need to be there now, now, now.


## IMMEDIATELY AFTERWARD. ATHENS, TNG DISTRICT. 1:35 AM EST. TUESDAY, NOVEMBER 25, 2025.

Abner Peet had waved off the offer of a soldier to see him home safely. Whilmire and Grayson, he thought, without real disapproval, had certainly fallen for their own act. It was true, of course, that there were dangerous, violent people afoot in the capital tonight, but it seemed to have slipped the general's mind, and Whilmire's, that *they* were the dangerous, violent people, and the enemy were hunted fugitives.

There might be material for a sermon in that idea, though of course he could not use that particular example. The tendency to become obsessed with . . . well, of course, it was all in the Bible, just as everything else was, motes and beams, and—

"I came as soon as I knew you needed me," Naomi said, falling into step beside him.

*And* that *was why I sent the soldiers with Whilmire,* Peet thought, things making sense at last. "It's a frightening night," Peet agreed.

"What are you afraid of, Abner?"

He was startled that she called him by his first name, but it seemed more comforting and familiar than presumptuous. She asked again what he was afraid of.

After a moment he said, "That it will all come back. That I'll wake up and the Rapture won't have happened, the cities will be full of crime and evil, all the good work we've done will be undone."

"Is there someone out there trying to do that tonight, Abner? Our scouts heard shooting and explosions and saw fires, and we didn't know what it was, so I came in to find you and see if we could help."

"We thought we had caught some of the worst of them, we thought . . . we thought we had them locked up—"

Her breath hissed in. "What were they doing? What has happened?"

As he explained it to her, he had the strangest sensation that he was surrounded by a crowd of warm, dirty bodies, all listening intently, but when he finished telling her everything (*should I really have told them about who killed the Natcon and why?*) they didn't seem to be there anymore. There was only Naomi, resting her hand on his arm and saying, very gently, "You have done the right thing, you're helping to bring about the final triumph, you have served your Lord well."

He felt lost but happy; bewildered but safe. He drank in the frosty air that reminded him that Thanksgiving was only two days away, and Christmas just around the corner after that, and in the glow, something made him ask, "Are you an angel?"

But there was no answer. He opened his eyes fully; he was standing in a windswept deserted street, and except for the stars and a few flickers of distant flames, in the deepest darkness. The shouts far away had nothing to do with him, he knew, so he went home to sleep.

**3 HOURS LATER. ATHENS, TNG DISTRICT. 4:45 AM EST. TUESDAY, NOVEMBER 25, 2025.**

General Phat took the radio from his ear and sat up straight. "Jason, is your stick still burning?"

"Yes, sir."

"Time to light the fires; they'll be here in about twenty minutes."

Jason pulled the smoldering stick from the little heel-dug trench where he'd kept it under wet leaves, leapt to his feet, and waved it overhead, shaking off the ash, bringing the embers to a bright red glow. On his third swing, flames showed again; a few more swings and it was blazing. By then Larry and Chris, at the two other fire points, were showing bright flames too.

Jason slid the burning stick under the little teepee of kindling. For tinder, he'd come up with a dried-out bird's nest and pine twigs fuzzed with a steak knife from the guards' kitchen, to eke out the crumpled pages of Thucydides. The blazing stick set it all off in a yard-high eruption of flames, engulfing the small teepee of deadwood sticks within the larger teepee of broken pine branches.

Jason looked up to see that Chris's fire was jumping up even higher; Larry's was ignited, but burning low and smoky.

"That'll be enough fire to bring 'em in," Phat said.

In a few minutes, Larry and Chris joined them; this was the upwind fire, the easiest one for the helicopter to pick up from.

. . .

The war leaders of six tribes squatted on the hillside. Every few minutes, a scout came back from crawling down to where the four men built had three fires and now waited to light them. All night they had been telling their followers, *wait, wait, of course we will kill the men, but we can also destroy whatever is coming for them, have a last glorious chance to smash some of the old plaztatic technology.* Grumbling, the soldiers listened, obeyed, and continued to prepare for the attack.

One torch blazed up; two more answered; the fires themselves were lit. "This is it," the senior war leader said, and they all stood up to give their war cries.

Before the last whoops and shrieks from the leaders were over, the hillside was dense with the silhouettes of fighters rising from their hiding places, and the cat-screams and bear-roars of a human wave gathering to pour down the hill toward the three fires.

. . .

Grayson looked out from the roof of Terrell Hall with some satisfaction; he didn't know if they'd succeeded yet but he'd done all he could. At least now he had competent troops. He saw the three fires blaze up, marked their place on the map, and by the time that he reached the bottom of the stairs, he could hear the distant helicopter. In the quad, he shouted, "Major!"

"Sir!"

"Form up! We're going to the old golf course north of campus, we're running, and we might have to fight when we get there."

"Right, sir. Bravo Company, up in the van; Delta Company, rearguard; Alpha, Charlie, and Echo, in that order, main body. We move in *one*, weapons ready."

It was much less than one minute. With Alpha Company, in the lead of the main body, Grayson raced north along the old brick walkways, across the street, and into the abandoned part of town.

"What are we going to find, and what are we going to do, when we get there?" the major running beside him asked.

"We'll get there about the same time as a helicopter from the *Bush* lands—I hope. There are some dangerous people, menaces to national security, who are there. I'm not sure what side the helicopter is on; the plot reaches very high up into our military. We don't want to fight our own men—we've had enough of that already—but we can't let the men on the ground get away, either."

"Are they the spies from Pueblo, sir, the ones we busted last night?"

"Some of them." Inspiration struck Grayson. "One of the reasons I want them is to question them about the Natcon's murder. I don't think they did it but I think they witnessed things that might give us a clue. So we can't let them leave for Pueblo even if they're innocent."

"I'll pass the word along, sir."

Grayson continued at a swift jog; the cold bit at his toes and seared his lungs. *Don't slip and bust a leg on the bridge,* he thought, *that would be one irony too many.*

. . .

"What the fuck is *that?*" General Phat blurted.

"Tribals, close, coming this way," Larry said. "We can't stay by the fires, we'll be silhouetted."

"The helicopter—"

"Talk to them if that gadget still works, but come *on.*"

Chris and Larry dragged Phat, almost by main force; Jason backed a few steps away from the fire, trying to put it between himself and the oncoming wave. "I'll be along in a minute," he yelled.

*I think I owe this to the cause,* he thought. *Could have been me out there howling like a nut and dying just to kill other people; as Daybreaker poet I was all set up for it. Instead I got a nice clean comfy world, if you don't mind the company of so many billion corpses.* He hoped he was far enough back not to be readily visible; black-powder pistols made nearly as much light at night as they did smoke in the day, but he wanted to get off at least one shot before they knew where he was. *Besides, I want to try something.*

Dark shapes swarmed on the far side of the fire. "Mister Gun!" Jason shouted at the top of his lungs. "Mister Gun lives! Mother Gaia is a lie, Mister Gun lives!" Chanting, the tribals had entered the firelight in a solid wave. Jason pointed into the thickest part of the crowd and pulled the trigger.

In the split second of silence, he let the Daybreak poet he had once been merge with what Larry and Debbie had brought back about *The Play of Daybreak,* and shouted, "Mister Gun rises from the dead! Slay them all, slaughter them, Mister Gun is mightier than Mother Gaia!" He fired again, then bellowed, "Mister Gun!" as he fired again.

The crowd faltered, whimpered, tried to raise its chant, and that gave him a moment to swap out magazines. "Mister Gun!" a voice cried behind him—*Larry, of course, he saw what I was doing!*—and another shot lashed into the milling Daybreakers. One with a spirit stick stumbled and fell.

"Mister Gun slays your spirit stick!" *Blam.* "Mister Gun shits on your spirit stick and breaks it!" *Blam.* "Your spirit stick is dead!" *Blam.* Jason fired at the end of each scream.

Now Chris was shouting about Mister Gun, too. *I swear,* Jason thought, reloading with his last magazine, *if I somehow get home alive, I am organizing the First Church of Mister Gun.*

It had delayed the human wave, made it falter when it might have swept across and killed them all, but they had only had forty rounds to begin with, and those were almost gone. "Jason," Larry said, quietly. "Back up with us. Phat's got the chopper coming into the center of the triangle. It'll be here soon. We just have to hope—*Mister Gun! Mister Gun, feed on the tribes, rape Mother Gaia, Mister Gun!*" He shot into the crowd; Jason used up his last magazine doing the same, and then fell back with Larry and Chris. Chris was almost shaking with laughter. "I didn't think humor was called for here, but my dear sweet *God* I wanted to shout that Mother Gaia swims out to meet troopships."

"Not long now," Phat murmured, as they joined him. "The chopper—Right!" he held the little radio to his ear. "Yes, in the center, that's us!"

Chris listened hard. "An H-92. It's a distinct sound. Jocking a camera in Eritrea, you couldn't mistake them for anything else. I always followed that sound, it meant Navy, and that far inland, Navy meant Marines—"

Phat was shouting instructions into the radio; they heard "Mister Gun" a few times before the helicopter roared over them. Its searchlights swept outward, revealing hundreds of tribals milling in confusion.

"They're not afraid of guns," Jason said. "Not out in the real world. They're afraid of Mister Gun. Mister Gun lives in the part of them where Daybreak lives." Phat repeated that into the radio, loudly. The searchlights swept a second time.

"The light hasn't touched us," Jason pointed out.

"No need," Phat said, "they have us on IR, and why show anyone where we are? They just have to look around for a second first."

"What are they looking for?"

"Trees, bad ground, bad guys," Phat said. "If I was flying what's probably the last working chopper in the world on what's probably its last mission ever, I sure as hell wouldn't want to get ambushed—let alone run into a tree, or sink in a swamp."

The helicopter crept forward toward the milling tribals. Its loudspeaker thundered, "You have not respected Mister Gun! Mother Gaia cannot save you! Mister Gun must punish you!"

The machine guns blasted into the tribals, who had been staring into the searchlights. Some fell; the rest fled. The searchlight winked out.

The helicopter descended to ground height, and the four men ran to it, diving forward, letting the crew drag them in by the arms. "That everyone?" the crewman shouted, as he pulled Jason aboard. "How many of you?"

"Four."

"Got the last one, sir."

The door slid shut behind him, the crewman pushed him into a seat, and the helicopter went up the way Jason had imagined a rocket might. "The skipper isn't about to lose this thing to ground fire at this point," the crewman said, apologetically. "We have every luxury we could snag from the *Bush* that wasn't too big and heavy. How about coffee and ice cream cones?"

. . .

So the rendezvous had been the old golf course; Grayson had been able to put watchers on every road, on the railroad tracks, and at the airport, but there had simply been too many open, grassy areas to cover on foot, and he hadn't been willing to risk the few trained cavalry ponies trying to cover the territory. And honestly, he couldn't have imagined that *Bush* would be in league with Pueblo; just one more proof that you could never trust those Navy bastards. *Rum, sodomy, and the lash,* he quoted to himself. *Especially sodomy. Which is what they're doing to me and the whole TNG.*

He heard gunfire ahead, and shouting. Ahead of them, above the low rise, he saw the helicopter against the stars, descending beyond the hill. Then brilliant electric light, unintelligible shouting and loudspeakers, and machine guns—real ones, firing fast and without the slow hollow claps of hand-turned black-powder guns.

"Pick up the pace and expect a fight," he told the major.

They had covered only about two hundred yards more when Grayson saw the helicopter rise vertically and fly away to the northwest.

"Did they get away, sir?"

"I don't know, Major. I think we've got to go take a look. But—"

Gunfire from the van.

The main body plunged into the ditches on either side, all in the dark shadows of the trees in starlight.

A messenger was at Grayson's side. "General, Bravo captain says we plowed into the flank of a big party of tribals, and Second Platoon, out front, is fighting them; First and Third are moving to flank. He thinks they were going somewhere else and we just ran into them—"

Grayson was shouting again, sending forces around on each of his flanks, firming up his center with his rearguard, and driving them forward to find and massacre the tribals. Frustrated by failure and betrayal, he exulted in the volleys and single shots and the screams in the dark. *And either these tribal fuckers stopped Phat or they didn't, but I was too late and too slow, and that makes me mad, and by Christ I'm going to make them pay for making me mad.*

. . .

When Athens was tiny, winking red fires far behind, Chris asked, "I don't suppose anyone would care to tell us where we're going?" He had consumed his ice cream cone with more reverence than he had ever shown the Host as an altar boy.

The Marine captain said, "Well, they told me to get you to anywhere with a runway, and take all the fuel I wanted because *Bush* was dying of nanoswarm, and didn't have biotes yet, so we've got an extended-range Superhawk II here. Theoretically I could run all the way to Columbia, Missouri or so, but to be safe, we're just going to Pale Bluff, Illinois, which should be friendly and has an airfield."

"My ex-wife and my son Sam still live there," the pilot added, "which is why I volunteered for this mission, it's my chance to get back there. You might have heard about it if you ever read that Pueblo paper, or listen to the radio stations that read it on the air."

"I might at that," Chris said.

"So poor old *Bush* is gone, and that's the last carrier, isn't it?" Phat said.

"Yes, sir," the Marine captain said. "More coffee all around for the guests, please, Chief? And for everyone? And there's more ice cream, guests go first but I don't want one drop of that wasted. We've got a while ahead of us, these things are fast but not that fast. Randy, let me know when you want me to take over and fly for a while."

As they flew on to the northwest, the pilot revealed himself as a man who liked to talk. Jason decided that in light of his second bowl of ice cream, he could listen for a week if he had to. The pilot said, "Funny that the old Nimitz-class carriers outlasted all the new Ford-class ones, but those Fords were bad-luck ships from the beginning—the *Ford* herself set a record for going aground that I don't suppose any carrier could possibly match, the terrorists sank poor old *Franklin Roosevelt* the year she was launched, *W* was zapped in the South China Sea EMP and then eaten by nanos, and, well, who the hell decided to name a ship after Jimmy Carter? It was like they were asking for what happened to it. But the Nimitzes kept right on ticking for most of this past year. *Bush* was the last, though, and in twenty years no one will remember there ever were aircraft carriers at all. I guess if Sam dreams about the sea, he'll dream about commanding a ship-of-the-line."

Phat cleared his throat. Very softly, he said, "Do you know who I am? Because you came here to rescue me."

"Uh, no, sir, I don't, and I didn't mean any offense—"

"And none was taken. Lyndon Phat, known to those who do not wish to live much longer as 'Shorty,' general, U.S. Army, at one time the commander of military forces for the TNG, and as soon as I get to Pueblo and announce it—candidate for president of the United States in 2026. Which I will win, if for no other reason than that I will be damned if I'll lose to that slimeball Grayson. And as for that ship-of-the-line, by the time Sam is your age, he'll be bucking for a berth on the expedition to the moon, to shut that Daybreak gun down. Depend on it."

"We all like to fly, sir." They flew on through the silent dark. Hours later, dawn raced out from behind them and illuminated the mountains. Recent snow, and wood smoke rising from hundreds of chimneys, made it all look like a Christmas card from a hundred years ago.


**THAT AFTERNOON. ATHENS, TNG DISTRICT. 3 PM EST. TUESDAY, NOVEMBER 25, 2025.**

Grayson had slept until almost two; Whilmire, sitting across the table from him while he ate an enormous mid-day breakfast, said, "Well, it's not any surprise to *me* that you have excellent taste in wives. Jenny issued a number of remarkably brutal threats about what would happen if you were not allowed your sleep, and having known her since her birth, I knew enough to take them seriously."

"Daddy," Jenny said, "I've got a husband to take care of." She squeezed Grayson's biceps. "And the next president of the United States."

"I was going to ask if that was still on," Grayson said, "because it seemed to me, after last night—"

Whilmire smiled. "Actually, things are *better*. First of all, as far as anyone in Pueblo can prove, you and Cameron Nguyen-Peters were trying to free Lyndon Phat, and the Natcon was killed by people blocking your plan. I'm sure the public will have their suspicions, but for public consumption, you come out looking like a fair man so devoted to the Constitution that you'll risk your own life to restore it. Second, the actual interference with the escape came from a surprise assault by tribals that you defeated in battle. Of course, again, that O'Grainne woman won't believe us, she's not stupid, but our friends have every reason to keep believing us, our enemies were not going to anyway, and the people who just can't make up their minds have an excellent reason to lean our way, because we've got the more appealing story. And to top it all off, problems between the Post Raptural Church and the government will be diminishing very shortly."

Grayson said, "I realize I'm less doctrinaire about the Constitution than Cam—"

"Oh, I know there will be less truculence from the government side, but there will be *far* less pressure and hassle from the Church side." Whilmire looked professionally sad. "I am afraid that Reverend Abner Peet has found it necessary to step down." At Grayson's startled expression, he added, "We've put together a story about the stress of the job. Confidentially, what happened is that the militia, pursuing tribals who were trying to flee through town after your battle, discovered he was harboring a wounded tribal girl in his house, and when they tried to arrest her, Reverend Peet assaulted them. It emerged that she was hiding in his house because she knew he would hide her, and that the relationship had been a close one for some months. It would appear that poor old Doctor Arnold Yang was not the only person Daybreak had found a way to."

Grayson peered at Whilmire, looking for any reaction or feeling, and saw none. "You know, I never really liked either man, and I tried to tell myself that the reason Arnie Yang could be sucked into Daybreak was that he was too interested in it, and besides he was a liberal elitist who thought he was smarter than all of us, and since I didn't like him anyway . . . well. I didn't like Peet, either, but you sure can't say he was vulnerable because he was too smart. Or too impressed with his own cleverness. And looking back, I wasn't being fair to Yang, just being scared about what it meant. Daybreak is going to try to take over all of us, at least if we're potentially useful, I mean, and it doesn't just want to kill us. And Daybreak could probably succeed with any of us; nobody's immune or secure against it." He shook his head, looking down into his coffee cup, not wanting either his political partner or his wife to see how shaken he was by the thought.

"It's a lesson in caution for us all. So Reverend Peet will be staying at a secure facility while we try to understand what happened to him; we can't let Pueblo be the only outfit that understands how Daybreak works in the individual mind. Unfortunately the girl went into a seizure, lost consciousness, and died, to some extent of her wounds."

"So with Reverend Peet out of the game, the new head of the Post Raptural Church is, uh, *you*, sir?"

Whilmire spread his hands. "There was really no one else with my knowledge or experience, and at a difficult time like this, we need a steady, skilled hand on the job. Not to mention a prepared mind." He leaned forward. "And your life is going to become easier because I believe the Church *needs* to liberalize on several issues, and I'll be pursuing that both within the Church and on the Board of the Temporary National Government. It is my belief that we have to respect the fact that our people are independent and diverse, which are my polite words for cranky and mixed-up, and therefore the Church cannot expect full obedience yet, which is my very discreet way of saying that even down here, we are overrun with unbelievers and secularists and nutcases from the cults, and they will go off like a bomb if we try to exert our authority too quickly, so we have got to lay low till we have the strength to make them do the right thing.

"For the time being, my church and your government will be tolerated as long as we don't impose much on our people, especially as long as we don't call attention to the fact that Mister Nguyen-Peters was our last link to legitimacy. We cannot even think of reversing anything he agreed to. So since we cannot beat them, I suggest we join them. Ease up our grip, you know? Let people have one old-fashioned roistering anarchic election, let our supporters see the leftists run loose, to remind the Christian Americans how furious it makes them to have God and the flag disrespected. For every recruit the other side gains by being able to say and print whatever they want, they will lose five people into our column, from people hearing socialist anti-God crap they never wanted to hear again. Look at the map—a religious conservative candidate, especially if he can become popular in Wabash and Superior, can win in a landslide, with long coattails. The losses of last night are truly nothing compared with the chance to put in a legitimate, Constitutional government of principled religious conservatives to lead us for the remainder of Tribulation.

"So, General Son-in-Law, there is nothing to worry about, which is the real reason why I didn't object to letting you sleep. Things are better than could be hoped for. You'll still have your expedition, your victories, your fame, and your campaign; we'll still defeat the Provi liberals and socialists, whether they run Weisbrod or Phat, and especially if they run both. You're still going to be president. And that's why I came here to tell you personally. We all have our duties, and some are pleasant."

**THAT NIGHT. OLYMPIA, NEW DISTRICT OF COLUMBIA. 10:30 PM PST. TUESDAY, NOVEMBER 25, 2025.**

"You do realize you are taking a huge risk by being here," Allie said, coolly opening the closet door in her bedroom to reveal Darcage.

It was the first time she'd ever seen him at a loss for words.

"Did Daybreak tell you to try again even though you hadn't been able to get in the last four times?" she asked. "Didn't that make you worry that Daybreak might be sacrificing you?"

"It would be an honor to be sacrificed for Daybreak." He stood, a little dignity returning. "I am deep-trained," he added. "You know what a seizure is like in someone who is only partly recruited. You know how much worse it is in someone like Ysabel Roth. You cannot take me prisoner without sending me into a seizure that will be fatal."

"That's what Daybreak finds it useful for you to believe. Stop being melodramatic; if I wanted to catch you, it would have been guards, not me, that opened the closet door." She perched on the edge of her desk, crossing her legs and letting her skirt ride up. *Hunh. I'd get more reaction out of a gay zombie. Interesting.*

"Your husband the president, and all his security people, must surely know that you are meeting me and what we are talking about," Darcage said. "Perhaps I should just allow myself to think that I am hopelessly caught and my death would be best for Daybreak."

"You could do that and you might die before our people sedated you," Allie agreed. "Why don't you?"

"It would be better to hear your offer first."

"Come back through the rear entrance at 10 a.m. sharp tomorrow morning. Don't dress tribal. No tricks. If they find a weapon on you they'll kill you right there. You have an appointment with me. I will tell you how Daybreak can be useful to me, and you will carry the message back to Daybreak, which will then either decide to be useful, or not."

"And if I refuse?"

"Daybreak won't. Now go. Guards will take you out by a secret route." The door opened and two of the President's Own Rangers, their ears swathed in gauze, came in, nodded, and grabbed Darcage, pushing and shoving him along, none too gently.

Graham came in and said, "Well, we listened. I suppose I should be alarmed at how convincing you sounded."

"Just part of the job," she said. "Tomorrow morning will tell the tale, and as you heard, there's not much to analyze about the conversation. Early bed tonight?"

"I'd like that."

As she brushed her long, thick black hair, Allie watched herself in the mirror and thought, *Everyone keeps me in the game because they think I might work for them. But who do I think I'm working for?* She saw only her own smile in the mirror.

# N I N E T E E N:
# WAR BEGAN NEXT WEDNESDAY

Heather thought about telling them all, since there was no one there to remember, that it was the anniversary of Lenny's death, that Leo was too young to understand words about his father, that in a world where the great majority were dead, and her old friends from that time all lost to her, she ached to talk about Lenny and could not. She had wanted to put together some kind of celebration with her friends, not to be alone that night.

Reading her mind, as he often seemed to these days, James had claimed he felt like cooking a big meal, gathered everyone to his house so that Heather had nothing to do but be there, and told her to talk about whatever she wanted, to whomever she wanted, and just do whatever felt right.

James himself was over in the corner, laughing and happy because Leslie was there, hanging with Larry and Debbie Mensche and with Jason and Beth. *There's a group of people that appreciates civilization,* she thought.

She looked around to see if Chris was still telling stories—"some true" as he liked to put it—to Cassie, Patrick, and the other younger people; Patrick had been all but struck mute with awe that he and Ntale had been invited, but good food and attention from friendly adults had thawed him out. Chris had moved on, and the kids were laughing and whispering like any teenagers trapped at a grown-up party and entertaining each other.

Heather went into the main room. She missed Quattro and Bambi, still stuck in California straightening out the mess of merging the Leagues, and the presence of so many friends seemed only to remind her of the ones who were not there.

When she saw Chris talking with Phat—and taking notes as he did—she came over and said, "Hey, this is a party. No working at the party."

"Okay," Chris said, slamming his notepad shut and mock-whining like a small boy, "but I want to get started turning the general into a hero. Remember, when Leo over here is an old fart like us, he'll tell stories, and the more heroes and the less truth they contain, the better everyone will like them. Right, Leo?"

Leo made a sleepy, whining noise.

"I think that means 'leave me out of this,'" Heather said. "And it's probably time for me to call it an evening."

With no moon out, the clear sky was smeared with stars, twinkling fiercely through the still-sooty upper air. Leo was pressed in tight against her, under her cloak, and she hurried toward home in the cold.

Ahead of her, lights were disappearing as candles and lanterns were blown out; nowadays, Pueblo, the liveliest city in America, went to bed early. *The day you died, Lenny, we were a united country, but in the deepest shit we'd ever been in. And here we are again, except less united and in deeper shit. But overall, it feels like a victory, which makes no sense.*

She stood a moment in the street, as if listening to his voice, and then turned to look back at James's house, still crowded with light and people— *her* people—and saw, as plainly as all the lines and charts, tables and notes that occupied her working hours, that it did make sense, after all.

# ACKNOWLEDGMENTS AND A THIRD-HAND STATEMENT

Among people who were very useful in formulating this second install-ment of the story were Ashley Grayson, Soren Roberts, Diane Talbot, James Fallows, Trent Telenko, S. M. Stirling, John Ringo, Tom Holsinger, John E. Johnston III, Mike Robell, Jack Greene, and the utterly invaluable Howard Davidson. Special thanks are due to Susan Allison for immense patience and for a number of absolutely necessary commandments; to Michelle Kasper, the production editor, who took the immense, sprawling mess I had made and my notes about what I wanted it to become and fought with the mess and the notes until they worked together, making it look as if I'd known what I was doing all along; and to Deanna Hoak, who achieved the miraculous: a copy edit which was a positive pleasure for me to review. Because of all those good people, this is a much better book than it might otherwise have been, and I'm deeply grateful.

Len Deighton attributed to James Jones the statement that "Readers should remember that the opinions expressed by the characters are not nec-essarily those of the author." I would go farther and say that if the author is keeping faith with characters and readers, it is essential that any opin-ion expressed by a character be *the opinion the character would have in the imagined world*, rather than anything the author might have in the real one. That is, characters should—artistically, *must*—hold the ideas and say the words that fit with who, what, and where they are imagined to be, taking the actions they take, and *not* the ideas and sayings that the author might have included in a letter to the editor or a blog post. (Unless the unfortunate character has been created to always agree with the author, a situation which I think is best avoided, however difficult it may be to avoid.) Within the imagined world, the author, of course, has full responsibility to the readers for whatever *happens*, which necessarily reflects the author's sense of what is possible in the universe of human thought, feeling, and behavior. Any responsibility of the author to the characters for what happens in their universe must be answered as Jehovah answered Job, except without giving them all their stuff back.